JEWS
QUEERS
GERMANS

JEWS
QUEERS
GERMANS

a novel/history

MARTIN
DUBERMAN

Seven Stories Press
New York • Oakland • London

Seven Stories Press
140 Watts Street
New York, NY 10013
www.sevenstories.com

College professors and high school and middle school teachers may order free examination copies of Seven Stories Press titles. To order, visit www.sevenstories.com/textbook or send a fax on school letterhead to (212) 226-1411.

Book design by Jon Gilbert

Library of Congress Cataloging-in-Publication Data

Names: Duberman, Martin B., author.
Title: Jews, Queers, Germans / Martin Duberman.
Description: Seven Stories Press first edition. | New York ; Oakland : Seven Stories Press, 2017.
Identifiers: LCCN 2016048510 (print) | LCCN 2016056395 (ebook) |
ISBN 9781609807382 (softcover) | ISBN 9781609807399 (E-book)
Subjects: LCSH: William II, German Emperor, 1859-1941--Fiction. | Kessler,
  Harry, Graf, 1868-1937--Fiction. | Hirschfeld, Magnus, 1868-1935--Fiction.
  | Germany--Politics and government--20th century--Fiction. |
  Germany--Social life and customs--20th century--Fiction. | Upper
  class--Germany--Fiction. | Intellectuals--Germany--Fiction. |
  Homosexuality--Germany--Fiction. | Trials--Germany--Fiction. | BISAC:
  FICTION / Historical. | GSAFD: Biographical fiction. | Historical fiction.
  | Legal stories.
Classification: LCC PS3554.U25 J49 2017 (print) | LCC PS3554.U25 (ebook) |
  DDC 813/.54--dc23
LC record available at https://lccn.loc.gov/2016048510

Printed in the USA.

9 8 7 6 5 4 3 2 1

~

FOR BETH BLUMENTHAL AND RON CORWIN

much more than cousins

PROLOGUE

The strong-willed Margarethe Krupp has decided to take her complaint directly to the Kaiser. She's aware that Wilhelm dislikes outspoken women, but in the face of the calamitous charges against her husband Fritz, who's been declared incapacitated, she's placed the family's huge steelworks at Essen in the hands of a management team, and she needs the Kaiser's approval. Marga intends to tell Wilhelm that she has made those decisions in order to avoid catastrophe for Germany itself. Given the central importance of the Krupp works to the Reich's growing power, she feels confident the Kaiser will grant her an audience. After all, she tells herself huffily, we've spent a fortune hosting his damn hunting parties at Villa Hügel, not to mention the preposterous preparations when His Highness attends the Meppen weaponry site.

Still, Marga feels uneasy. In the past the Kaiser has treated her with civility, but never warmth. Nor does she much care for him. She finds him bombastic and self-absorbed, and has laughed with friends about his preening wardrobe of 200 uniforms—and the 12 valets needed to ensure that his ermine cape is fluffed to perfection and his chestful of medals properly aligned. Wilhelm's love of ceremonial display has led one indiscreet friend to claim that the Kaiser prefers unveiling a monument to reading a book. Their merriment, Marga remembers, had alarmed her husband Fritz, and she'd made fun of his anxiety: "The Kaiser should be afraid of *you*!" she'd nearly shouted at him. "Let *him* turn out steel-armored battleships, if he's so clever and powerful!"

Wilhelm does grant Marga an interview, but when she refers to His

Highness "doubtless" having heard the rumors regarding Fritz's "predilections," the Kaiser bellows, "What rumors? What are you talking about, woman?!" (He has in fact not only heard the rumors, but personally counseled Krupp not to return to Capri—none of which is he about to acknowledge to Marga).

"Capri?" Marga tentatively offers. "The Italian newspapers and ... Capri?"

"Yes, yes ... Fritz's amateur archeology ... I know all about that ... That yacht of his, the, the ... what's it called?"

"The *Maya*. He's refitted it for expeditions to collect aquatic specimens."

"Damned nonsense ... dilettantism ... shirking his duties to Kaiser and country."

Contrary to her intentions, Marga reflexively defends her husband. "He enjoys it ... it's harmless enough." Then she adds with a smirk, "He *has* discovered five new species of worms." Despite herself, Marga laughs.

"What's worms got to do with weaponry?"

"I don't begrudge him his hobby, your Highness. It's the other, er, hobby, that concerns me—concerns me for Germany."

"Stop talking in riddles, Marga! My patience is limited."

"Very well, Majesty. Someone clipped an article from the Neapolitan scandal sheet, *Mattino*, and sent it to me anonymously."

"Yes, yes—so?"

"It describes what it calls the 'immoral' festivities that have been taking place on Capri. Other Italian newspapers have picked up the *Mattino* story. Those clippings as well were sent to me."

"Immoral? What does any of this have to do with *me*?!"

"It has to do with Fritz and ... and teenage boys ... Not that the news surprised me."

"What news?! Damn it, woman, I have three ministers waiting outside! Did you expect to spend the day?!"

"My apologies, Majesty. To come directly to the point: Fritz's beautiful home on Capri ... the renowned gardens ... In recognition, the governing council of Capri has made him an honorary citizen and—"

"—damn it, Marga! You've got two minutes!"

She swallows hard: "Fritz is accused of impropriety with teenage boys. His special favorite is an eighteen-year-old barber named Adolfo Schiano. Should I go on?"

Wilhelm stops pacing. "Who accuses him?" His expression is solemn.

"Last week it was the Social Democratic Party paper, *Vorwärts*. It accuses Fritz of 'corrupting youth.' He's said to exemplify capitalist culture at its grossest. The SPD calls for his arrest and trial under Paragraph 175 of the German penal code."

"—the *what*?" Wilhelm loudly interrupts.

"Paragraph 175, Majesty . . . it criminalizes sexual intercourse between men. Fritz has initiated libel proceedings against the paper."

The Kaiser scowls. "Socialist scum . . . Who gives a damn what *Vorwärts* thinks?!"

"I do, your Majesty. Fritz and I have not shared a bed for years." She's frightened at her own boldness.

"You think such matters interest me?! Have you lost your senses, madame?"

Marga is cowed but defiant. "There have been *orgies*, Your Highness. Fritz invited the Grand Duke of Hesse and Prince Aribert of Anhalt as his guests to—"

"—stop it! Stop it this minute!" Wilhelm thunders. "You're a hysterical woman! Leave me at once!" He turns and marches off to an adjoining room.

That same day Kaiser Wilhelm orders the Berlin police to ransack the offices of *Vorwärts*, to break into the private lockers of Social Democratic members of the Reichstag, and to enter the homes of subscribers to seize copies of the issue containing the accusations against Fritz Krupp. He fails to intimidate the socialist editors of Vorwärts. They denounce the Kaiser in print for passing sentence before a pending trial has even commenced, thus placing the court in the invidious position either of contradicting the Kaiser or of creating the dreadful impression that his opinion has influenced its judgment. Soon after, to the Kaiser's embarrassment, chief prosecutor Hugo Isenbiel announces that he's dropping the libel case against the editors of Vorwärts—the implication is that Krupp is guilty as charged.

Undaunted, the Kaiser has Marga Krupp arrested on charges of maligning her blameless husband and soiling the good name of the house of Krupp. He further declares that she's unbalanced—the result of meddling in political affairs and overtaxing her brain with too much reading—a conclusion the Kaiser reaches based on Krupp's insistence that his wife's "symptoms of illness" have been increasing of late. Wilhelm orders Marga carried by force to the lunatic asylum at Jena for "an extended rest." Krupp assures the Kaiser that Marga "has agreed to submit herself willingly to a thorough treatment" for an undefined period of time, and he thanks Wilhelm "for the kind and gentle way in which Your Majesty has intervened on behalf of my person and my interests."

But the intervention backfires. Krupp, it turns out, has made little effort to conceal his activities on Capri—or, for that matter, in Berlin. Commissioner Hans von Tresckow, head of the police unit that reports on the city's homosexual scene, has learned, among much else, that Fritz Krupp regularly watches near-nude wrestling matches in one of Berlin's theaters, and that he's seen to it that the city's fashionable Hotel Bristol, where he often stays, employs as waiters a number of young men he's imported from Capri. Von Tresckow also discovers that from 1898 on, Krupp has spent several months a year in the Hotel Quisisana on Capri, spending lavishly on his favorites and holding "boisterous" parties.

After the *Vorwärts* article appears, the local authorities on the island appoint a commission of inquiry to investigate further; it has no trouble locating witnesses to confirm the industrialist's "unclean" activities. King Victor Emmanuel III promptly orders Krupp banished from Italy, never to return. On November 22, 1902, the German News Agency announces—to widespread incredulity—that Fritz Krupp has unexpectedly died of a stroke. He has in fact taken the course followed by many homosexuals of the time when threatened with exposure or blackmail—he takes his own life.

The rightwing press immediately blames the SPD and *Vorwärts* for "hounding" the great industrialist to his death. Marga is abruptly declared entirely well and released from the Jena asylum. She refuses to attend her husband's funeral at Essen. Given that the rumors about Krupp's proclivities have not been disproved, the Kaiser's entourage urges him not to attend either, but he does so nonetheless—bedecked in full battle gear. Arriving at Essen, he seeks assurances from several of Krupp's associates that the munitions king was *not* homosexual. Anything to please the monarch: "Of course not, your Majesty! He had an exceptionally soft, gentle, sensitive nature—which is sometimes confused with homosexuality." "Just as I thought!" the Kaiser thunders. "*Vorwärts* has hounded my exemplary friend to a needless death."

Appeased, Wilhelm marches behind the closed casket to the cemetery and delivers the funeral oration, telling the assembled crowd that the Socialists—"men unworthy of the name of German"—have "murdered" Krupp, and he dismisses as groundless (though he knows better) the "false and ignominious" attacks that have been made on "this great German's" honor. Have no fear, the Kaiser concludes—henceforth, *he* will "raise the shield of the German Emperor over the house and memory of Krupp."

And he does, though the house of Krupp comes to regret his protection. Fritz Krupp's teenage daughter Bertha inherits the company, but the Kaiser declares it unthinkable for a woman to be in charge of a firm so vital to the interests of the Reich. He personally chooses Gustav von Bohlen, a Prussian nobleman, as her husband and at their wedding awards him, by imperial proclamation, the surname Krupp. Marga is allowed to return to Villa Hügel, the family estate, but on condition she remain out of sight.

PART I

~

THE BELLE ÉPOQUE
1890–1910

IT'S AS IF NAMING it brought it into being. During the uproar over the Krupp scandal, Wilhelm is startled to learn that the Berlin police have for several years been compiling extensive files, the so-called Criminal Album, listing those who flaunt Paragraph 175 of the German penal code by engaging in homosexual acts (whether proven or rumored). The Album cites many who hold high office: the King of Württemberg is said to be in love with a mechanic, the King of Bavaria with a coachman, and Archduke Ludwig Viktor, brother of the Austro-Hungarian Emperor Franz Joseph, with a masseur.

The incriminating Album is sent under seal to the head of the Kaiser's Civil Cabinet, with the implication that the material will be shown to the Kaiser. The mere suggestion that such "filth" could possibly interest him, outrages Wilhelm. He refuses to break the seal, announcing that it is "all lies" anyway, and orders the Album returned to the Police Commissioner. But Wilhelm knows more than he's publicly admitting. He's already been informed that the marriage of his cousin, the Grand Duke Ernst Ludwig of Hesse-Darmstadt, has been "a failure from the beginning" and he is divorcing his young wife. Why? Because, the Kaiser is told, the Grand Duke has "homosexual tendencies."

Wilhelm, just past 40, is somewhat older than the Grand Duke, but both were grandchildren of the recently deceased Queen Victoria and often played together when young. Those memories soften him; he writes his cousin a long letter that expresses some empathy—but embedded in the moralistic posturing more typical of him. Avoiding any mention of the Grand Duke's "tendencies," Wilhelm focuses instead on the need for the Duke to come to an "understanding" with his wife that will allow their marriage to continue. "That will mean," Wilhelm writes, "sacrifices, perhaps very difficult ones ... I know many a marriage in which things are just the same as with you, but which have not ended in divorce." Whether Wilhelm is advocating celibacy *outside* the marriage bond as well as within, the Grand Duke declines the "sacrifice."

Matters go no better when the next scandal hits the Hohenzollern drawing rooms. This time it's Prince Friedrich Heinrich of Prussia, eldest son of Wilhelm's uncle, Prince Albrecht. Rumors about Friedrich have been circulating for years; at one point the President of the Berlin police even feels the need to warn Friedrich to rein in his indiscretions—not the sort of advice Princes of the Realm welcome or take to heart, sexual indiscretion being something of an assumed prerogative. Prince Friedrich is fond of his prerogatives—and the result is that his imprudent behavior becomes a matter for open discussion in the Reichstag; but given the reluctance of all but the Socialist deputies to bring "discredit" on the Hohenzollern dynasty, the debate is stillborn.

Maximilian Harden, the most famous journalist in Germany, is far less respectful of the Imperial family. In his weekly paper, *Die Zukunft*, Harden, characteristically, minces no words. Prince Friedrich Heinrich, Harden bluntly writes, suffers from "hereditary perversion of the sexual drive." He further reveals that the Kaiser has pressured Prince Friedrich to renounce his election as Grand Master of the august Order of St. John of Jerusalem. The Kaiser—having regained his reflexive rectitude—proceeds to banish the Prince from court. Since no one in Berlin will receive him, the Prince is advised to live abroad. Any number of Berlin's luminaries scatter to the underbrush.

But the elephant is now decidedly in the room. Within a mere two to three years, a far greater scandal bursts over the head of Prince Philipp of Eulenburg—the man who'd been closest to the Kaiser throughout the 1890s. For some time, the Prince's "moral conduct" has been tut-tutted over in the drawing rooms. Eager to discredit the regime, Max Harden prepares to fan the flames still higher. Catching wind of Harden's intentions, Eulenburg abruptly resigns his post as ambassador to Vienna and retreats to his estate at Liebenberg. "Grief over my mother's recent death," he explains in a letter to the Kaiser, "has affected my already frail health and I have become a burden to Your Majesty."

"You must receive trustworthy care," the Kaiser loftily responds. "Such episodes don't mean much."

The words alarm rather than comfort Philipp. Is the Kaiser slyly suggesting that he, Philipp, is exaggerating his symptoms, feigning incapacity in order to keep hidden a quite different source of anguish?

"I am bed-ridden with fever," Philipp hastily replies. "For the time being I'm only a ghastly parcel. There is absolutely nothing more to be expected from my wretched body. But I don't complain."

If Philipp is magnifying his symptoms, the grief he feels over the death of his mother, Alexandrine Hertefeld, is very real. From early childhood she's been his sympathetic confidant, his model of true womanhood—selfless in her devotion to her emotionally extravagant, artistically inclined son. She'd steadfastly mediated between him and his militaristic father, Philipp Konrad, who's disparaged his son's interest in music and literature, scowled at his charm and sense of humor—so unsuitable in a truly manly person—and denounced his professional ambivalence.

"You wish to do—what?!" Philipp Konrad had thundered when Philipp suggested, after graduating from the War Academy at Kassel, that he wished to abandon a military career and enter the civil service.

"Why work at all?!" his father shouts. "Why not loll about in the garden reciting verse?!"

Alexandrine softly interjects her view that a person of many gifts might do well to sample them.

"By all means! Why not try needlework? Or perhaps become a fisherman?!" Philipp Konrad storms from the room.

Half fearful that his father's view of him is accurate, Philipp had gone on to earn a doctorate in law from the University of Giessen in 1875—

the same year he married Augusta Sandels, daughter of the last Swedish Count Sandels. In the first 10 years of their marriage, she gave birth to eight children, the last born in 1886, the year Philipp meets Crown Prince Wilhelm, the future Kaiser. Most observers believe that from the beginning of his marriage Philipp has treated Augusta indifferently, though he's a loving father toward his children and suffers greatly when two die in infancy.

After their first meeting, Philipp and Wilhelm quickly become good friends. By 1888, when the Crown Prince ascends to the throne at age 29 as Wilhelm II, he's already describing Philipp, a dozen years his senior, as "my bosom friend, the only one I have." Philipp introduces the youthful Kaiser to his own small group of intimates—the so-called "Liebenberg Circle," a reference to his country estate in Brandenburg not far from Berlin. Philipp accompanies the youthful Kaiser on exclusive hunts at a succession of noble estates, and in the evenings he often entertains the other guests by singing his own ballads while accompanying himself on the piano.

By the 1890s Wilhelm has installed Philipp in the cabin adjoining his on the royal yacht, *Hohenzollern*, and Philipp has become a regular participant in the all-male, month-long summer cruises to Scandinavia. When Philipp's ballads are published as a book—*Rosenlieder*, a popular success—Wilhelm prominently displays it, alongside a picture of Philipp, on his desk.

The two men are in many ways dissimilar. Philipp, warm, tactful, and somewhat shy, has nothing of Wilhelm's grandiosity, nor his restless, volatile, hyperactive temperament (Philipp describes his friend at one point as "highly charged with electricity"). Nor does Philipp require, as does Wilhelm, constant praise and admiration; as Philipp privately puts it, the Kaiser "is grateful for it like a good, clever child." What the two men do share is a strenuous belief in the monarch's personal rule, based on divine right and free of dictation from a fledgling, politically fractious Reichstag. Wilhelm's entourage commonly refers to him as the "All-High," and Philipp eagerly escalates the fawning praise by sometimes referring to his friend as "Wilhelm Proteus"—the ancient prophet able to assume whatever shape he chooses.

By the 1890s it's widely acknowledged that Philipp has become the most powerful member of the Kaiser's civil entourage, uniquely positioned to influence his policies and appointments. It's Philipp who first suggests in 1897 that Bernhard von Bülow be made head of the foreign office; knowing exactly which string to pluck, Philipp emphasizes von Bülow's "true, deep personal love for Yr. Majesty." Wilhelm not only accepts Philipp's ardent recommendation but subsequently promotes von Bülow to Reich Chancellor, a post he will hold from 1900 to 1909. During his tenure von Bülow will outdo Eulenburg in sycophancy and in carrying out the Kaiser's every autocratic wish; he will also return Philipp's favor by cunningly maneuvering against him behind his back. Philipp himself at the turn of the century is named ambassador to the Kingdom of Württemberg, then to the more prestigious post at the Kingdom of Bavaria, and finally as the Reich's representative in Vienna, capitol of Germany's foremost ally, the Austro-Hungarian Empire.

Like everyone around the Kaiser, Eulenburg often has to lavish ingratiating praise on His Majesty, yet he's able to see clearly many of Wilhelm's unappealing qualities. They're legion—his adolescent humor; his harshness; his inability to listen; his pretension to knowledge and wisdom he doesn't possess; his assumption of infallibility in all matters, including the artistic and the spiritual; his limited attention span—and even more limited compassion (it's "as if," Philipp writes a friend, "certain feelings which we take for granted in others are suddenly simply not there"). "He wants to instruct," Philipp admits, "but does not take to being instructed himself."

Wilhelm often visits pranks and practical jokes on his guests. His sadistic notion of "fun" is to turn inward the many rings on his right hand (his left arm is withered, having been severely damaged at birth) and then squeeze a visiting dignitary's hand as hard he can, relishing the anguished reaction. He thinks it the height of hilarity to come up behind an old general and cut his suspenders, and to have another jump over a stick in imitation of a dog. Alternately, Wilhelm enjoys suddenly pinching someone or hitting him hard on the behind with a baton.

The sensitive, gentle Eulenburg is shocked during one Nordic cruise at what he calls "the quite disgusting spectacle" of the Kaiser assembling the older members of his entourage on deck for morning gymnastics—their groans and the Kaiser's gleeful shouts producing an unsettling medley. Sometimes Wilhelm will baptize a newcomer to the yacht by pouring champagne on his head—or have him carried around on a block of ice. On a visit to Eulenburg's Liebenberg estate Wilhelm has another guest parade about as a circus poodle, sporting long bangs made out of black wool and a tail appended at the back, performing "tricks" like howling at the moon in response to music cues or a pistol shot. Occasionally His Majesty orders a member of his entourage to cross-dress in a feathery hat and tutu, and dance—as Wilhelm roars with laughter. Eulenburg firmly refuses to participate in any of the Kaiser's capers.

Serious people bore Wilhelm, yet he requires their unqualified assent to his authoritative pronouncements on a host of weighty matters. Along with dabbling in painting seascapes, he spends millions of marks furnishing multiple royal residences, and confidently compares his garish taste with the Medicis. Eulenburg encourages his interest in art, but not the superficiality of his pronouncements about it. Wilhelm's artistic preferences are entirely conventional (as are Eulenburg's for that matter, but unlike the Kaiser, he makes no effort to inflict his opinions on others).

Wilhelm despises anything that smacks of the avant-garde; when a group of Berlin artists withdraws (the so-called "Secession") from the annual exhibition patronized by the Kaiser, and form their own show, Wilhelm vetoes awarding the gold medal to Käthe Kollwitz because her etchings depicting the plight of impoverished cottagers lack, Wilhelm announces, "patriotic" content and stray from "the feelings in mankind for beauty and harmony." The Kaiser's idea of a great painter is Anton von Werner, director of the Institute of Fine Arts in Berlin, whose most famous canvas is *The Proclamation of the German Empire*, depicting the coronation of Wilhelm I—a picture the discriminating modernist Count Harry Kessler dismisses as "a fashion illustration for military tailors."

Kessler, approaching 30 at the time of the "Berlin Secession" in 1898, has been edging his way into prominence as an ardent advocate of "modernism," a posture neither predictable nor "fitting" for someone of his social standing. Harry's father Adolf comes from a banking family prominent in the world of international finance. His mother, Alice— whom Harry adores—is a renowned, high-spirited beauty whose salon in Paris (where the couple mostly resides, and where Harry and his sister Wilma were born) attracts the likes of Ibsen, de Maupassant, and Sarah Bernhardt. The old emperor, Wilhelm I, not only ennobled the Kesslers but skipped over the traditional stepping stone of "baron" to go straightaway to "count"—as much in tribute, it's widely believed, to Alice's extraordinary good looks as to Adolf's exemplary good deeds.

As a young man, Harry's life has followed the traditional pathways of a privileged patrician. He's enrolled in the fashionable St. George's school in Ascot, where he becomes fluent in both Greek and Latin—and where his classmates include Roger Fry, later a renowned art critic, as well as a handsome boy named Maat with whom Harry becomes romantically infatuated. Harry then returns to Germany to enter the university in Bonn, where his already-impeccable credentials are further burnished through election to the aristocratic Borussia fraternity—which boasts Wilhelm II among its alumni.

Harry is particularly drawn to a fellow member of the Borussia corps, Eberhard von Bodenhausen, whom he describes in the diary he started keeping at age 12 as an "almost ideal beauty, tall, blond, with a slender, nimble, perfectly proportioned body . . . a Greek statue, come to life through some inward fire." A future industrialist and art patron, von Bodenhausen will become allies with Kessler in the struggle to advance Impressionist and post-Impressionist art against the "dead weight" of the academic establishment.

But first comes a stint at the University of Leipzig, where Harry becomes friendly with another fellow student, Gustav Richter, whose grandfather is the composer Giacomo Meyerbeer and whose mother, Cornelia Richter, holds a famed salon in her home on the Bellevues- trasse. Harry attends with some regularity, as do any number of promi- nent figures of the day, some of whom will loom large in his immediate future—the poet and playwright Hugo von Hofmannsthal, the industrialist and writer Walther Rathenau, and, now and then, the Kaiser's close confidant Prince Eulenburg, occasionally accompanied by his own dear friend, Count Kuno von Moltke. Harry's already impressive network of contacts expands exponentially.

His studies, simultaneously, are broadening his critical faculties. Lujo Brentano's Leipzig lectures advocating trade unionism as a necessary tool for improving working-class conditions lead Harry to personally explore slum conditions; the deplorable plight of laborers and their families further sensitizes him to the need for reform—yet does not convert him to socialism; in 1888 he still defines himself in his diary as "a conservative at heart." Yet he's already abandoned a number of orthodoxies: he deplores the upper class treatment of women in Germany as "decorative dolls"—as well as the middle and working class vision of them as "exalted housekeepers and perfect cooks."

In a similar way, the lectures of Anton Springer—the first professor of art history in Germany—in defense of contemporary art, confirm Harry's aesthetic taste even as they move him to unconventional speculations about the nature of "beauty" that will resonate far into the future. "The beauty of a thing," he writes in one diary entry, "lies much more in our imagination than in the thing itself ... it corresponds to something inside of the person who cherishes it. The truth of an ideal is always, even if it were held by all of mankind at the same time, a subjective one." In short, so-called "timeless, universal" truths—the "natural laws" shibboleth of an earlier age—are a chimera, a hunger for certainty which is unobtainable. "You cannot answer," Kessler concludes in his diary, "the fundamental question of aesthetics, 'What is an artwork?' ... You must put the question this way: What processes must a work evoke in the psyche of the observer in order for it to count as a work of art? Then you would discover that something can be a work of art for someone and not for others."

Such views, when Harry takes up residence to Berlin late in 1893, are the currency of a new generation of artists in rebellion against the hyper-realism of the art academies, artists who—going back at least to the 1870s—concern themselves with the transient play of light, contemporary (rather than historical) imagery, and the quick-change instability of modern life. It is in France that the "Secessionists"—among them Monet, Sisley, Degas, and Pissarro—first make their influence known. And it is in Paris that an independently wealthy young Harry—having tried his hand as an apprentice law court official and quickly realized that it was "a mistaken vocation"—begins to haunt the galleries and studios.

From an early age, he'd always visited the Louvre when in Paris, initially with his mother, then on his own. When 19 he'd taken himself to the exhibition, the Artistes Indépendants, of those Impressionist painters denied access to the official art salons—but this initial exposure had repelled him: "orgies of hideousness and nerve-shaking combinations of colors I thought impossible outside a madhouse," he wrote contemptuously in his diary.

Over the next five years, Harry began increasingly to question his previous allegiance to traditional culture. It's "striking," he confided to his diary in 1894, "that an age that has been more creative than any other in producing original and important forms for machines, railroads, warships, and weapons still has not exploited these forms artistically." It had, but at the time Harry's vision had been myopic. Once he dropped the lorgnette, his eyes quickly came into focus. By the time of the "Berlin Secession" in 1898, Harry had become an ardent champion, though never "vulgarly" passionate in his admiration—hot-blooded fervor is foreign to his well-mannered temperament.

He goes now far less to the Louvre than to the avant-garde galleries that have sprung to life on the rue Laffitte—the elegant Durand-Ruel establishment; the daring—he's among the first to buy and display van Gogh and to give Cézanne his first show in 1895—Ambroise Vollard's smaller, less luxurious space; and the Bernheim-Jeune gallery, which specializes in the so-called "Nabi" (the Hebrew word for "prophet") artists, most prominently Bonnard and Vuillard. Paris will for some time remain the center for contemporary art, but one important gallery does open in Berlin— Paul Cassirer's establishment on Viktoriastrasse, designed by Kessler's recent acquaintance, the Belgian architect Henry van de Velde (whom he hires to design his own audaciously elegant apartment).

Harry also joins a group of young artists and writers who decide to inaugurate a new illustrated journal, *PAN*, with the intention of giving voice to insurgent movements in the arts. A noisy, contentious bunch, mostly still in their twenties, they meet haphazardly at a rundown tavern, Turkes Wine and Beer Cellar, at the corner of Unter den Linden and the Wilhelmstrasse. The Swedish exile August Strindberg, who lives in the neighborhood and first discovers the tavern, rechristens it the Black Piglet during one of his alcoholic stupors, a hallucinatory reference to the Armenian wine sack that sways over the entranceway.

The *PAN* contingent gathers in one of the tavern's two rooms, just big enough for a solid wood table to hold pitchers of beer and wine, loaves of round black bread, sausage and cheese—and an upright piano, on which one of the group's central figures, the Polish writer Stanisław Przybyszewski ("Staczu" to everyone), is given, especially when drunk, to pounding away on his own version of "Chopin." Staczu is married to the beautiful, enigmatic Dagny ("Ducha", Polish for "soul") Juel; Ducha is promiscuous as a matter of principal, and several of the other young men, in particular the painter Edvard Munch (for whom she models), find her erotically irresistible.

The slender, impeccably groomed Harry Kessler, his penetrating eyes alert with intelligence even as his courtly bearing hints at the need for emotional distance, is on the surface something of a fish out of water when compared to the unbridled bohemianism of Staczu's circle. But various other young people move in and out of the *PAN* group, including several of Harry's more disciplined classmates and friends: Eberhard von Bodenhausen (his Borussia fraternity brother), the poet Richard Dehmel, and Julius Meier-Graefe (whose forthcoming book, *The Impressionists*, will win a mixed review from Harry).

Besides, Harry can more than hold his own when Staczu and his acolytes—all of whom find Nietzsche a source of profound inspiration— heatedly debate the merits of Huysmans, Baudelaire, and Mallarmé, or Staczu's mystical views on the value of hypnosis and alchemy, or his theory (pre-Jung) of a collective memory and the importance of the unconscious forces (what he calls "psychic naturalism") underlying our surface behavior. Staczu's mesmerizing voice and biting sarcasm are potent persuaders, yet Harry meets them not with a competing brand of uninhibited clamor, but with the more disarming style of graceful urbanity. (Once again, as with his sexual encounters, Harry deliberately omits from his diary any details of the turbulent combat that characterizes *PAN*'s meetings. He keeps his worlds distinct). Staczu and the others in *PAN*'s more profligate contingency recognize in Kessler not only a first-class intelligence, but also a genuine desire to foster the journal's fortunes. They're in agreement that Harry would be the best choice to visit the poet Paul Verlaine in Paris with an invitation to contribute to the new journal.

Kessler first calls on the poet on July 10, 1895. More than 20 years have passed since Verlaine fell obstinately in love with Arthur Rimbaud, abandoned his wife and infant son (after an abusive, alcoholic scene), later shot and wounded Rimbaud in a fit of jealousy, and went to prison for the crime, where he converted to Roman Catholicism. When Harry enters Verlaine's decrepit building on the rue St. Victor, the place smells to him "of cats, coal, and the drying diapers of the proletariat." Feeling his way through a dark antechamber to the designated door, Harry opens it to a melancholy scene: a sparsely furnished room, with a few straw chairs, a white wooden table, and a large double bed. In it lies Verlaine—to Harry, "the greatest lyrical poet of France"—amidst a disordered array of pillows, fully dressed and with slippers on his feet.

The poet explains that rheumatism and the heat have forced him to take to his bed. But he does rouse himself, brings Harry over to the flat's sole window to show off the flowerpots and birdcages that surround it, and explains that the "little, old, fat" woman (as Harry describes her in his diary) making currant wine in a corner of the room "takes cares of me very well"; in Harry's view she seems more "a governess than a mistress." He tells Verlaine about *PAN*, describing it as "an important journal with money to offer" in return for some of his poems. The poet lethargically mumbles something indistinct in response, and then lapses into silence.

Thinking to rouse him, Harry deliberately makes reference to Rimbaud and notices at once "a nervous flame darting" in Verlaine's eyes. When he speaks, it's with quiet simplicity: "He had a great influence on me. He was the cause of a great deal of pleasure and pain for me. We left together in pursuit of adventure. A lot of absurd things, à la Wilde, were said about us. The publication of his poems is encountering difficulty because his sister, an old spinster, wants to censor everything that, in her opinion, portrays her brother in a satanic light. She wants to make of him an angel, which he wasn't at all, but rather a man, or rather a child, of genius." Verlaine stops abruptly and Harry's highly developed sense of discretion prevents him from pressing the poet to continue. Seeing Verlaine's face cloud over with a heavy veil of melancholy, Harry suggests that he return some other time, and diplomatically takes his leave.

He does visit Verlaine several more times, and each time finds the poet spruced up a bit more in clean white pants, a black coat, and a brown velvet hat (and even the "fat *grisette*," as Harry refers to her, has on a pink blouse "in which she almost looks smart"). With each visit Harry finds Verlaine "more sympathetic"; he begins to understand "how this man can exert an irresistible charm." Verlaine speaks no German, but there's no need—Harry is fluent in English (and in French as well), which Verlaine does speak. Without prodding, the poet returns again and again in their conversations to Rimbaud, describing "his Herculean figure, his deep blue eyes with their somewhat fixed stare, the striking mobility of his face, his little turned-up nose, which had, like his character, something mocking and pert about it, and his great, fantastic genius standing in almost uncanny contrast to his childlike exterior and his youth."

Reflecting back on the experience years later—Verlaine never does contribute to *PAN* and dies in 1896, within a year of Harry's last visit—Kessler concludes that despite the poet's "great sexual passion" for Rimbaud and his incessant pressure on the younger man to yield, Rimbaud had the stronger will—"exceptionally strong"—and managed to hold Verlaine at bay. "Unhinged" by his unconsummated passion, Verlaine, in Harry's view, shot Rimbaud "in complete desperation." Even then, Rimbaud refused sex, and the relationship—"very much against Verlaine's will"—remained chaste.

The details will never be known, but many—at the time and since—draw a conclusion opposite to Kessler's, thus raising the question of why he chooses to believe the theory of unrequited love. His verdict of chastity is likely the result of superimposing his own recent and exceedingly painful experience onto Verlaine's. Just two years prior, during his prescribed year of military service (in his case with the aristocratic Third Guard Lancers), Harry roomed with another cadet, the handsome 19-year-old Bavarian nobleman Otto von Dungern—and fell intractably in love with him. They rode together, swam naked in the Karthane River, spent hours exchanging stories and experiences—and never touched, other than glancingly. When they parted, Harry wrote in his diary that he was "right lonely without Dungern." And that is all he wrote.

Harry is fully aware that his sexual attraction is solely to other men, but just as his diary says almost nothing about the boisterous side of his evenings at the Piglet, so it's scrubbed clean of all but the most oblique references to his homosexuality. Like every diarist, Harry knows (or hopes) that he's writing for posterity as much as for himself—after all, he *saves* his voluminous journals. Yet his avoidance of certain topics isn't solely due to conscious dissembling. Social discretion has been bred into Harry's bones. Much like his contemporary Edward Carpenter in England, who *does* openly acknowledge—and publicly champion—his homosexuality, Kessler carries what one of Carpenter's friends calls ineradicable "tattoo-marks of gentility" (the comment made in regard to Carpenter burning his dress clothes and leaving his house barely furnished in a futile effort to divest himself of all outer marks of class privilege—gestures which Harry would have found grotesque).

The closest Harry ever comes to a frank declaration of his sexual attraction to men is a diary entry he makes in 1888, when 20: "I have flirted more or less seriously with over half a dozen young girls within the last two years, but love I have never felt for any of them and I am sure I do not wish to break anybody's heart. I know by experience"—that is, with Otto von Dungern, unnamed—"what it is to love passionately and hopelessly, and that fearful misery I would not bring on anybody for the world."

When it comes to evaluating others, Harry often ignores what some see as homoerotic—even transparently carnal—behavior; the verdict of "chastity" that he passes on the Verlaine/Rimbaud relationship carries over onto his judgment of a variety of other relationships. He blankets with the discreet gloss of "social rituals" the common practice in the military of officers and cadets dancing together, tossing bouquets to one another, and forcing drunken younger men to strip naked. And in the next few years, as the so-called "Eulenburg Affair" begins to heat up, Kessler will deplore what he views as the confounding of conventional rites of male friendship with homosexuality, deploring the "sea of dirt and contempt" unleashed on Eulenburg and Count Kuno von Moltke—both of whom he's gotten to know and like at Cornelia Richter's salon.

That storm is still a few years down the road. Eulenburg, for now, remains sequestered at his Liebenberg estate and the journalistic muck-raker Max Harden, temporarily appeased by the Prince's retirement—yet still rabidly opposed to the regime—bides his time. As for Harry Kessler, he remains happily preoccupied with developments in the arts, involving himself in a host of projects beyond *PAN* that encompass painting and sculpture, dance, theater, and design. For roughly the next five years, Kessler puts his energy, contacts, and wealth centrally at the disposal of those individuals and organizations increasingly determined to "secede" from the acceptable forms of expression dictated by the academies and controlled by the central government.

Despite the enormous growth of Germany over recent decades—the population nearly doubles between 1870 and 1900—Berlin, its capital and financial center, remains something of a backwater in regard to the arts. In those same decades, as the dynamic revolutions of Impressionism and post-Impressionism sweep France (and in its wake, most of the cultural capitals of northern Europe), Berlin, in the mid-1890s, still has a grand total of two art galleries. Even within Germany itself, the cities of Munich and Dresden are far in advance of Berlin in accepting the new art.

All of which is about to change—and Harry Kessler, along with his newfound friend, the art dealer Paul Cassirer, are in the vanguard of the transformation. When Cassirer decides in 1898 to open a new gallery on Viktoriastrasse, a fashionable street filled with large homes that abuts the famed Tiergarten park, Harry persuades him to hire Henry van de Velde to design the space. Van de Velde creates a spare, sleek interior, its light gray linen walls decorated with discreet oak paneling running along the top. The gallery's mission, Cassirer announces, will be "the promotion of a number of great artists who are virtually unknown in Germany."

True to his word, Cassirer, within three years, fills his gallery with the first full-scale exhibition of the works of Vincent van Gogh. By then, Harry Kessler, through his writings, organizational efforts, and patronage, is also emerging as a key figure in transforming Germany from a timid straggler in the current aesthetic revolution to a serious contender for front-rank status—though never able to overtake France, its historic enemy, as the paramount center for artistic innovation.

The pace of change within Germany resembles a tortoise more than a steamroller. From the start, the new art runs into fierce opposition. Its critics are a resourceful, powerful, and unrelenting lot, and at certain points the secessionists suffer a string of reverses that at times resemble a total rout. More is involved than aesthetics; inherent in the sustained debate over art are contending political assumptions that centrally involve the Kaiser and his court. It's recognized on all sides that what is at stake is not only the kind of art Germany will endorse, but the kind of political rule it will sanction.

The fine arts in Germany have long been dependent on the Kaiser's favor. It is he who dispenses state patronage, controls exhibition space, and decides whose work will be exhibited. Wilhelm II takes his role as art patron seriously; he has decided tastes and doesn't hesitate to intervene directly to reward favorites and blacklist dissenters. Aesthetic "truth," he declares, lies in the "eternal laws that the creator himself observes, and which can never be transgressed or broken without threatening the development of the universe." The Kaiser refrains from revealing the precise content of those eternal laws (or when and how the creator transmitted them)—but he knows aesthetic truth when he sees it. After all, he rules by "divine right," which mandates automatic respect and legitimacy for his pronouncements. Kessler puts it succinctly: "the state spends money for hot air, but not for art."

Much of the German establishment, and the middle class as well, strongly agrees with the Kaiser's tastes and actions. The powerful conservative and anti-Semitic elements that dominate German life equate innovation with degeneracy, and any challenge to tradition is seen as a cosmopolitan plot to destroy German folkways. The Kaiser's favorite painter, Anton von Werner, specializes in depicting scenes from Germany's "glorious" past and, like the Kaiser, believes that historical verisimilitude is *the* marker of artistic merit. Werner detests modern art, yet is not, like most of those who side with him, a kneejerk conservative: when presented with an anti-Semitic petition from students and faculty of the *Verein Berliner Künstler*—the association of artists that Werner heads—he not only rejects it but forbids any circulation of comparable material.

The city of Weimar, capital of the small Grand Duchy of Saxe-Weimar, boasts a glorious past. In the early 19th century it had been home both to Goethe and Schiller, the storied eminences of German letters. Yet in the middle of the century, Franz Liszt had abandoned Weimar in disgust over its retrograde values, and the town sank into mossbacked oblivion. The first intimation that it might emerge from its smug slumber and again become an important cultural center is the interest Elisabeth Förster-Nietzsche shows in moving her brother Friedrich's archives there. The philosopher is still alive at the end of the 19th century, but in a ruinous state of health, wholly dependent on his sister's care. Nietzsche's doctors diagnose his disorder variously, as mercury poisoning, debilitating strokes, brain cancer, psychotic dementia, and tertiary syphilis (now thought to have resulted from visiting a male brothel in Genoa).

Harry Kessler first meets Elisabeth Förster-Nietzsche when he travels to her home in Naumburg in the fall of 1895 to negotiate for the publication in *PAN* of some of her brother's speculative works on music. Förster-Nietzsche has a reputation for being exceedingly difficult—

malicious, spiteful, obstinate—but she's much taken with Kessler's debonair manner and lucid intelligence, invites him to stay for dinner, and gives her assent to publication in *PAN*. When Kessler tells her that he's an enormous admirer of her brother and a staunch supporter of his work, Elisabeth allows him a rare glimpse of the great man. Nietzsche sits immobile in a chair—and according to Elisabeth will do so for hours on end—in a kind of stupor. He recognizes only acquaintances from childhood, and even that connection is soon lost.

Kessler's visits to Förster-Nietzsche not only continue but gradually increase; he becomes something of a confidant and advisor. Elisabeth shares with him details of her many quarrels, especially with Wagner's widow, Cosima, and with Lou Andreas-Salomé, the gifted writer (and later psychoanalyst) who is the only woman—so Nietzsche once declared when proposing marriage—that he'd ever found attractive. Harry is an attentive listener and discreet counselor, though he often finds Elisabeth's conversation "silly" and "self-pitying." But it gradually dawns on him that if he succeeds in persuading her to move her brother's archives to Weimar, the coup would instantly boost the city's profile and open the way for its return to prominence—and could even, conceivably, turn it into a dynamic center for fostering avant-garde art.

By the time of Nietzsche's death in the summer of 1900 Elisabeth, under Harry's guidance, has made Weimar the permanent home for her brother's archives. Kessler has even persuaded her to hire his friend Henry van de Velde to design a building to house the material. Through Elisabeth's introductions over the next few years, and then through the grace and subtlety of his own personality, Kessler moves with consummate ease in Weimar society, which he mostly finds comically parochial. The exception is the young grand duchess Caroline, who is genuinely attuned to artistic innovation and becomes his particular champion. Among his other new acquaintances is the Polonius-like figure of the court chamberlain Aimé de Palézieux, who also serves as director of the Weimar Museum; for a time Palézieux expresses enthusiasm for the idea of returning Weimar to its former glory—yet only for a time.

Förster-Nietzsche, pleased with van de Velde's architectural plans, successfully lobbies for his appointment as director of the Weimar art school. From there, in what seems like a natural progression, Kessler is himself in 1902 given a curatorial post in the Museum of Arts and Crafts and then, the following year, accepts the offer to become its official director. He buys a house in Weimar, and begins to travel frequently between London, Paris, and Berlin to attend exhibitions, personally meet with many of the most innovative artists and gallery owners of the day, and make plans for some of them to take up short-term residence in Weimar.

Kessler assumes his new post at the Museum with eyes wide open to the petty quarrelling and entrenched conservatism of the local populace. He's aware early on that court chancellor de Palézieux, on the surface friendly and enthusiastic, is intriguing behind his back, filling the fairly empty head of the Grand Duke with accusations of Kessler's "immoral" preferences in art. Kessler characteristically retains his poise, rarely allowing any extreme emotion to show. Initially he's too involved in the work at hand, too excited at finally having an official platform from which to foster contemporary art, to heed the steadily mounting drumbeat of opposition. "We will build what we have in mind," he writes van de Velde, "a clear, clean, healthy, invigorating apprenticeship. Let the others follow with sour expressions. It won't change anything."

The plan he comes up with is for van de Velde's school to serve as a design center for local industries and for his own museum to transform itself into a center that, through exhibitions and lectures, will convert the public to the cause of aesthetic modernism. The culminating moment of several years of effort on Kessler's part is the foundational gathering he organizes late in 1903 of scattered groups of secessionists from various parts of Germany to form a new body—the *Deutsche Künstlerbund* (the German Artists League)—designed to counteract the influence of Anton von Werner's own union of German artists, the *Allgemeine Deutsche Kunstgenossenschaft*. Kessler's aim, as he describes it in his diary, is "to eliminate the historical point of view insofar that history does not provide an *aesthetic* insight." To that same end he succeeds in bypassing the Museum of Arts and Crafts and creating the "Grand Ducal Museum for Craftsmen"—after all, he writes, "painters are, or should be, principally craftsmen."

In a pamphlet, Kessler spells out his vision for the new German Artists League: it must be tolerant of a great variety of styles, and *not*—unlike the von Werner coalition of artists—seek to "eliminate individualism." "We must create," he writes, a counter-force "which will enable talent to follow its artistic conscience in safety . . . For there can be no doubt, in art only the exceptional has value . . . Everything else is not only worth less; it is worth nothing." Kessler explicitly draws the political parallel: the protection and fostering of individualism, he argues, should "be accepted as well in the political life of the nation."

Though Kessler believes that the central purpose of the Artists League is to maximize the individual's free expression, he doesn't extend the democratic principle to organizing the affairs of the League itself. He argues against the proposition that the opinion of every member should have equal weight in deciding every issue that arises; that sort of mistaken egalitarianism, he insists, would invite chaos and paralyze the decision-making process. Kessler proposes instead that an executive committee of 30 members, elected for five-year terms, be empowered to make all decisions regarding such matters as membership applications and appointing juries. "You may call this framework elitist if you like," Kessler boldly asserts, "but I call it representative—*functioning*—democracy." His proposals easily carry the day and he, along with such friends and allies as Henry van de Velde, Max Liebermann, Max Klinger, and Eberhard von Bodenhausen, are chosen to serve on the executive committee.

During these same few years at the turn of the century, as Kessler invests enormous time and energy into creating an institutional structure to support contemporary art, he's simultaneously augmenting his own private collection. Sometimes he buys through the galleries—two Cézanne pictures and a drawing from Vollard; Bonnard and Renoir from Durand-Ruel; Maurice Denis from Paul Cassirer, and then, also from Cassirer, he purchases in July 1904 for 1,689 marks—the equivalent then of $399, and today roughly $10,000—van Gogh's masterful *Portrait of Dr. Gachet*; in 1990, *before* the recent art boom, it will re-sell for nearly a hundred million.

As Kessler meets and forms friendships with many of the leading artists themselves, he often visits their studios and buys directly from them—Signac's *Brume du Matin*, two of Vuillard's paintings, a bust by Rodin, several of Aristide Maillol's sculptures, Odilon Redon's lithographs, Max Liebermann's drawings, Monet's views of London, and so on—filling his Weimar home, amassing one of the critically important modernist collections of the time.

It's a heady period for Kessler, yet his triumphs are shadowed by growing antagonism in Weimar to his "scandalous" attempt to corrupt the citizenry. As one local artist writes in the provincial newspaper, "in the new museum we encounter paintings and drawings that deeply offend our feelings. What is displayed is so revolting that we must warn our wives and daughters not to visit the museum." The smear campaign against him reaches a climax in 1905 when Kessler mounts an exhibit of Rodin's watercolors of female nudes, and the Grand Duke joins in denouncing it. Appalled at such crude philistinism, Kessler submits his resignation. The Grand Duke ignores it, informing Kessler instead that he has been *dismissed.*

When Prince Eulenburg retires to his estate in 1902, his intention, of necessity, is to keep a low profile. He does remain in touch, however, with close friends in Berlin and, to a diminished degree, with the Kaiser himself. Family life proves no substitute for the excitement of being at the center of the Emperor's entourage and his chief confidant. "I enjoy the family little," Eulenburg writes to Axel Varnbüler, one of his closest friends in the Liebenberg Circle. "I gladly go my way, like a peculiar sheep, who avoids the herd with a scowl. The dog ceaselessly and pitilessly drives him back to an acquired sense of duty. Heaven knows it's not innate."

Varnbüler is a suave, somewhat irreverent voluptuary whose diplomatic career Eulenburg has in the past advanced, and who sees Harry Kessler occasionally on the upper-crust social circuit. Kessler finds Varnbüler's wife Natasha, with her flare for the dramatic—"all artifice and Slavic cleverness" (her father was a Russian sea captain)—more consistently entertaining than her husband, and Kessler and Natasha Varnbüler occasionally go together to the theater. Both are particular fans of Ibsen and George Bernard Shaw, and Kessler deeply admires and forms close friendships with the contemporary theater luminaries Max Reinhardt and the designer Gordon Craig. Harry thinks his theater outings with Natasha are making her husband jealous—"laughable, if it's true," Harry writes in his diary.

Eulenburg is still closer to his other dear friend, Count Kuno von Moltke, his ghostly doppelgänger. Both men are gentle, musically inclined, ill-suited to military rigor—and problematically attached to family life. Kuno does marry, but he and his wife Lily are constantly at odds, sometimes arguing in public; the marriage quickly dissolves, and Philipp plays a role in its failure. He opposed the union from the first, having described the prospect as "extremely *gruesome* to me" and having claimed that Kuno was in a state of "despair" over the pending alliance.

Philipp does his best to advance Kuno's career, though the task isn't easy. Kuno's sensitive, passive temperament, even his posture, bears so little resemblance to the ramrod model of Prussian manhood that few take him seriously. Though he manages to botch every political appointment Philipp gets for him, Eulenburg's influence is such that Kuno, with each failure, somehow continues to move up a notch until his starting point as a mere military attaché culminates in 1905 with Wilhelm appointing him Commandant of the city of Berlin.

Many upper-class 19th-century men, especially in Germany, share the view that male friendship stands at the apex of human relationships, but Kuno's version is so mawkishly sentimental that "friendship" with him takes on intractably erotic overtones. In letters between Kuno and Axel Varnbüler, they refer often to Philipp as "Philine"—the feminized version of his name—and Kuno, in describing his feelings during a temporary separation from Philipp, writes "I long for the old Philine ... [I] must see her out of the feeling that we must hold each other doubly tightly after this tear in our intimate circle." If this is "friendship," it's of a declared profundity that neither Kuno nor Philipp has ever made to their wives.

Harry Kessler knows both men from their occasional appearance at Cornelia Richter's salon, and he finds both likeable enough, though in their linked sentimentality and deference to authority, foreign to his own sensibilities. Kessler's capacity for friendship is profound, but he recoils from bonds he finds artificially cloying. He equates sentimentality with "phony feelings"—its presence is to him a sure sign that no genuine emotions are at hand; sentimentality in his view equates not with strength of feeling, but with its absence.

Kessler also feels at odds with von Moltke and Eulenburg's adoring attitude towards the Kaiser, exemplified by their conviction that he rules by "divine right." Absolutism of any kind raises Kessler's hackles. In his view there are no preordained masters and no absolute truth, there are only ideas that are "absolutely compelling" because they meet felt needs at a particular point in time—and those ideas lose their validity with the passage of time and the rise of different needs. So it is, he feels, with the idea of God: "You can *no longer* argue," he insists, "about whether the idea of God is true or untrue. It has been shown to be untrue"—shown by Nietzsche, among others. In all these ways Harry Kessler is a renegade, a traitor to his class.

Kessler is startled, in the summer of 1906, to get an invitation from Maximilian Harden, the hard-hitting editor of *Die Zukunft*, to lunch with him at the posh Palasthotel. It happens to be one of Kessler's favorite restaurants in Berlin, but given his hectic social schedule he accepts reluctantly. He hardly knows the man, though they've been introduced here and there. Everyone, of course, *hears* about Harden; given his penchant for provocation he's become the most feared—and widely read—journalist in Berlin.

Kessler shares many of Harden's views, and in particular his fierce criticism of the person and policies of Wilhelm II. But Kessler's interests are at this point in his life centered on culture, not political polemics. Increasingly connected to artistic circles throughout the continent, he spends nearly as much time in France and England as he does in Germany, and he tends to think of himself more as an urbane cosmopolitan than a German nationalist.

Could it be, he wonders, as he works his way across the Tiergarten to the hotel, that Harden wants to write a piece about the avant-garde German Artists League that he's done so much to form? No, that seems unlikely; the League is nearly two years old and art has never fallen within Harden's purview. What then? Some controversial aspect he's dug up regarding the removal of the Nietzsche Archive to Weimar? Possibly, since Harden manages to find controversy wherever he looks and since Kessler did play an active role in the transfer of the archives from Naumburg. Still, Harden isn't known for his interest in matters of philosophy or literature either.

Perhaps he's caught wind of the splash Kessler made as director of the Weimar Museum and the whispering campaign that the town's conservative burgher class designed to get him removed from his post. Yes, that's probably it, Kessler decides, as he moves through the crowded Berlin streets (its population has nearly tripled in the years since it became the capital of a unified Reich following the successful 1870–71 war with France); Harden is thinking of writing about the Weimar controversy. Well, Kessler tells himself as he pushes through the fortress-like doors to the hotel, whatever it is, I'll know soon enough.

On entering the restaurant, Kessler immediately spots Harden's distinctive face—he's still ruggedly handsome, Kessler thinks, though older than me, probably in his early forties; a pity he compromises his good looks with a permanently-creased brow of suspicion, his thin lips tightly drawn, his eyes beadily intent.

Harden is already seated at a quiet table toward the back of the crowded restaurant and, as Kessler approaches, rises quickly to greet him.

"So sorry to be late," Kessler says, as they crisply shake hands.

"I'm grateful to you for coming at all," Harden replies. "Most grateful."

"When was it we last met? At the Richters'?" Harden looks puzzled. "Or perhaps it was at Walther Rathenau's?"

"No, I think this is the first time. I should certainly have remembered."

"Oh? My mistake. I thought we'd crossed paths earlier." Curious, Kessler thinks, as he sits down opposite Harden: does he have a bad memory or a bad conscience?

"Perhaps I'm mistaking you for someone else," Kessler mischievously adds.

The two are now seated facing each other. "I've taken the liberty of ordering lobster and wine," Harden says. "I hope that meets with your approval."

"Indeed yes. Very extravagant of you." They smile warily at each other.

At that very moment a waiter in white tie arrives at the table and, after serving the food, pours a small amount of white wine in Harden's glass. He tastes it and smiles with pleasure. "Superb!" he tells the waiter, who, with a flourish, pours wine in both their glasses, then bows and departs.

Kessler glances at the bottle. "Château d'Yquem!" He exclaims. "You *are* being extravagant!"

"My pleasure . . . And the Ducal Museum, is it still making the locals rabid?" Harden asks.

"I've ended my role there. Too much else to do. My friend and ally Henry van de Velde will carry on the good fight."

"I've seen a few of his buildings and admire them."

"Did you know he designs furniture as well? My own house in Weimar—which I'm keeping—is filled with it. It's wonderfully comfortable, elegant yet unpretentious."

On they wander for a time, at one point segueing somehow into Pre-Raphaelite painting, with Harden expressing special enthusiasm for the work of Burne-Jones.

Kessler politely dissents. "Burne-Jones," he says, "dreams of women he's seen in photographs, not of real women in flesh and blood. But I do credit the Pre-Raphaelites with agitating for something new. Millais, I believe, is the only one of them to hint at a glimpse of the unforeseen. At best, he's a continuation of Constable."

"I'm clearly out of my depth here," Harden responds, aiming for a graciousness that doesn't come naturally.

"Augustus John," Kessler continues, "is the real comer, though still in his twenties. He's an uncombed bohemian, with more passion and fire than anything I saw in the Pre-Raphaelite exhibit recently in London."

At the mention of London, Harden perks up. "And how do you find the English these days?"

Ah, Kessler thinks, so politics is to be our topic—what else would it be with Harden? "If you mean working-class Englishmen, their plight is lamentable. Everywhere I go, on the streets, in the shops, I see the same exhausted, pale faces, or rather clueless remnants of faces, that make you despair of democracy, if that's what the English system is."

"Surely more so than Germany," Harden offers.

"I find, strangely, that autocracy and religious intolerance *can* go hand in hand with absolute freedom in moral, artistic, and economic matters—in Turkey, for example."

Harden noticeably perks up. "Surely the democracies of England and America are in advance of our own autocracy."

"I can only say that in both countries I saw a public of mute, tired workers too worn out from their daily labor to engage with political matters. When you see the people, you despair of democracy. When you see the nobility in Germany you despair of the aristocracy."

"Yet Germany, thanks to Bismarck, is unrivaled in passing legislation to provide health insurance, pensions too, to factory workers."

"Yet the average work day is still twelve hours long, six days a week— hardly conducive to health, not to mention participation in public affairs."

"Forgive me, my dear Kessler, but nothing seems to please you."

"Not in politics, you're quite right. I don't think the form of government most conducive to individual freedom has yet been invented. Which is why I devote myself to promoting contemporary art."

"But there, too, our dear sovereign runs the show. Is that not true?"

"To a great extent, yes. And his taste is abysmal."

"Did he interfere with your work in Weimar?"

"No, no. That would have been beneath him. But two years ago, he interfered with the committee appointed to choose art pieces for the St. Louis World's Fair."

"In what way 'interfered?'"

Kessler laughs. "He disbanded it!"

"Really? I hadn't heard a word . . ."

"It seems the committee dared to select a few—a very few—modernists. The Kaiser promptly turned over the choice of paintings entirely to—Anton von Werner!"

"Of course!—The Kaiser's favorite."

Kessler thought they were moving from art to politics, but as Harden's guest he lets him have the reins.

"Several of us from the Artists League started a petition," Kessler continues. "The Kaiser, you know, views the League as an alliance for the advancement of the Jews—as he so delicately puts it."

"The Kaiser isn't fond of Jews. I am one, you know."

"I do."

"That is, I was born one." Harden stares fixedly at his guest, as if daring him to pursue the subject.

Kessler decides to oblige, annoyed at his host's transparent eagerness for combat. "I see. You converted."

"I'm a Lutheran now," Harden says evenly, his tone some unpleasant amalgam of sarcasm and melancholy.

"Would it be rude of me to ask why?" Kessler asks blandly.

"Yes, it would!" Harden cheerfully responds. "But rudeness is my middle name. Haven't you heard?"

"I ask because my good friend Walther Rathenau, also a Jew, regards conversion—though he's in no formal sense religious—as futile. In two senses. Christians will still regard you as a Jew: superficially acceptable—unless you're a Jew from Poland or Russia—yet fundamentally alien. And futile, too, because you cannot disinherit, will away, what is indelibly ingrained—like the Jew's profound sense of apartness."

"Your friend Rathenau is wrong. Judaism in Germany has become no more than an empty shell. It has outer form, but no content. A hereditary relic."

"An empty shell? I myself am not Jewish, but—"

"—you're a Count—of course you're not Jewish!" Harden can't help but chuckle.

"Yes, of course. I see your point." Kessler looks uncomfortable.

"Come, come—I didn't mean to interrupt you."

"I have no religion of any sort myself, you understand, but it does seem to me that Jews are culturally distinctive in a number of ways. Their intense respect for the intellect, for one. And—at least so their detractors claim—an aggressive desire to achieve, a will to power, if you like. Both traits, as you surely know, have often been ascribed to *you*."

Harden can feel his temper flare, but manages to control it. "It's possible to be culturally distinctive within the context of absolute patriotism."

"*If* public opinion will permit. Jews, as you have been quick to remind me, are barred from the higher ranks of the civil service, the nobility, and the officer corps."

"And are disproportionately represented in the medical and legal professions, and in science—for heaven's sakes, my dear Kessler, men like Einstein and Paul Ehrlich stand at the very pinnacle of the scientific world!"

"And silently endure the intense resentment of their colleagues."

Harden shakes his head in dismay. "I can see there's no persuading you." Harden is ready to abandon the topic, but Kessler feels the need for a final statement.

"I cannot help but think it a fantasy, a fiction, to insist that the Jewish people are fully assimilated into German life. Such assimilation as exists seems to me partial, superficial, and hollow. I plainly see anti-Semitism in myself. Yes, I admit it. At lunch yesterday at the Natansons' I thought to myself, 'There's an awful lot of talk going on here about how much something costs or is worth.' What nonsense! There was a great deal *more* talk—excited talk—about the Nabis school and Vuillard and Bonnard's new paintings. At the Richter salon, I daresay, there's at least as much talk of how much something costs, yet I pass right over it. I tell you anti-Semitism is ingrained in all of us. And not just in Germany, though it surely flourishes here."

"And I can only respond by telling you that as a dissimilated—converted—Jew, I find no doors closed to me that I would care to open in any case. Nor any venue for expressing any views I might wish to offer."

Topic closed—though Kessler cannot resist a final thrust: "I've been told the Kaiser is furious that 'a Jew'—which is how he refers to you—"should be able to make money by insulting him."

"When I attack the Kaiser," Harden icily replies, "it's because he's done or said something stupid. He provides abundant copy." Harden pushes away his plate and signals the waiter to bring coffee. "Come now, Kessler—this petition you mentioned earlier . . . tell me more about that . . ."

"I doubt it will interest you . . . The petition's in support of the modern movement in art. Max Reinhardt, Hugo von Hofmannsthal, Max Liebermann, Gordon Craig—a number of luminaries have signed it. Though not—predictably, I suppose—Stefan George. He objects to something he calls 'interference with the transcendental importance of individual sovereignty.'"

Harden laughs. "Such rubbish. Affectation only suits genius; everyone else is ruined by it."

"Exactly! It was in order to *foster* 'individual sovereignty'—in opposition to lockstep academic conventions—that we formed the Artists League!"

"Has your friend Rathenau signed the petition?"

Kessler picks up Harden's arch tone, but chooses to ignore it. "He has. Though not before lecturing me about the need to call more attention to the aesthetics of the machine—to 'suggest to the workers,' as he put it, 'the freedom to be found in technology.'"

"I'm afraid you've lost me."

"Never mind. Rathenau's a brilliant man, but I fear his longing to combine Prussian order with utopian socialism will never bear fruit."

"Yes." Harden has the uneasy feeling that Kessler's range of interests and suavity will keep them moving further and further away from his agenda.

"Allow me, if I may, to return for a moment to the Kaiser. You see, aside from the sheer pleasure of your company, I did hope to seek your advice today about a certain matter that directly involves his Majesty."

So here we are at last then, Kessler thinks. The topic *is* the Kaiser. Why beat around the bush so? "I consider his meddling with French influence in Morocco foolish," Kessler offers. "It will bring Britain to France's defense and further cement the Entente."

This is not the topic Harden has in mind. Better to play along a bit, he decides, rather than risk another abrupt divergence. Harden shakes his head in mock sadness. "First the Kaiser provokes a crisis by visiting Tangiers, then when a conference is called at Algeciras to deal with the crisis, he impedes every effort at compromise—all the while announcing his 'cherished hope' for a 'unified Europe.'"

"Meaning a Europe *he* controls. About as likely as Victoria returning from the grave—which I don't doubt she *could*." The two men chuckle. "Is it any wonder," Kessler continues, "that our only remaining friend in Europe is Austria—so feeble it hardly counts as an ally."

Harden lowers his voice: "I'm glad to hear we're of one mind about this ... this situation. But ... but I ... I in fact invited you to dine to ask for your counsel on quite another matter."

Kessler inadvertently sighs. Another shift in topic? Oh well. "What then?" he mildly asks. "Do speak freely. I'm not as reserved as most people think, though I am discreet."

"Precisely why I've come to you ... the matter at issue is ... is delicate ... Prince Eulenburg, you see. Do you know him?"

"Our paths occasionally cross. Mostly at the Richters' salon. But I barely know him. We move in quite different circles."

"Gossip has a way of traversing them all."

"Gossip about Eulenburg?"

"It relates to Kuno von Moltke."

"The Commandant. We've met. He's close to the Kaiser, is he not?"

"Not as close as Eulenburg. No, not nearly."

"No one is. Have we arrived at the gossip?" Kessler smiles at his own bravado.

Harden pauses. He thinks one more circumvention may be needed. "Can I pour you more wine?" he solicitously asks. "Or perhaps a *blanc-mange*—a lovely sweet."

"No thank you, I'm fine." Whatever is coming, Kessler muses, I do wish it would hurry.

"Is ... is Count von Lynar ... Johannes ... familiar to you?" Harden asks tentatively.

"Of the Potsdam Guards?" Kessler doesn't wait for an answer. "I know *that* gossip, if that's what you're asking . . . about getting too close to his orderlies . . ."

Harden's taken aback at Kessler's frankness—as is Kessler. "Well, yes . . . after all, a commander in the Gardes du Corps, right-hand to the Crown Prince . . ." A pause ensues. Kessler is determined not to rescue Harden, but then his own civility takes over.

"My dear Harden," he finally says, "in regard to such personal matters I prefer to speak in generalities only. Perhaps if we begin on the plane of philosophy . . ."

Harden looks perplexed, as if unable to make out a foreign tongue. The pause lengthens, then Kessler speaks again.

"I regard 'sexual morality,'" he says, as if pronouncing the words from a great height, "as the artificial rules currently dominant in a given society . . . Such rules should never be confused with ethical behavior. You see my point?"

Harden manages an unconvincing murmur: "I . . . I believe so."

"Take the case of Oscar Wilde. Surely a superior soul, a man richly gifted. Following his trial, the same people who once brazenly fawned over him, now insolently shun him. For what? There was nothing unethical in his behavior. But he'd broken the rules. My question to you is: Has Prince Eulenburg been unethical or, like Wilde, merely reckless?"

Harden runs through several possible replies in his own head, then settles for an unresponsive, "Both."

"The same answer, I suspect, that the Kaiser would give." Kessler is enjoying being more candid—enigmatically candid—than the man notorious for frankness; the competitive game has pierced Kessler's natural reserve. "Which leads me to the next question: What purpose will you serve, in whatever it is that you're proposing to do?"

"I haven't determined on a specific course of action. Yet something must be done."

"About?"

"About the Kaiser's entourage."

Kessler feigns astonishment. "The entire entourage?! That takes in rather a large group."

"The Kaiser ignores and belittles most of them. Eulenburg and the Liebenberg Circle are among the few who actually have the Kaiser's ear."

"But my understanding is that Eulenburg has retired from court circles. Rheumatism and gout, I believe."

"Retired until recently. It seems he's written the Kaiser expressing a longing to see him again. His Majesty has promptly responded with a visit to Eulenburg at his Liebenberg estate. The two have subsequently hunted together in Silesia. At this point Eulenburg has not only rejoined the entourage, but the Kaiser has invested him with the Order of the Black Eagle. As you know, the highest Prussian order."

"Should I be surprised? Offended? I don't understand."

"During the Kaiser's visit to Liebenberg"—Harden lowers his voice to an ominous whisper—"only half a dozen other guests were present."

"That strikes me as too large a number for intimate conversation. Don't you agree?" Kessler is having a wonderful time. Harden looks dumbstruck. "I find that with six or more people," Kessler continues, "the conversation splits off into two groups, each vying for triviality."

Recovering his voice, Harden's tone remains grave: "Among the few guests were Jan Freiherr von Wendelstadt, Raymond Lecomte, and—"

"—do you mean the secretary of the French legation?"

"One and the same." Harden's eyes are now alight with suppressed glee.

"Oh I see," Kessler quietly responds.

"I'm sure you do." There's just a hint of accusation—or is it threat?—in Harden's voice. "Lecomte—the most notorious homosexual on the continent. With von Wendelstadt a close second. It's outrageous of Eulenburg to have surrounded the Kaiser with so rakish a group. Think of the possible scandal!"

"My dear Harden"—Kessler can't conceal a smile—"just a minute ago you were deploring Wilhelm's autocratic hold on power. I should think you of all people would *welcome* catching the Kaiser with a group of—what shall we say?—'reprobates.'"

Even when trapped, Harden is quick with a comeback: "Did I mention that 'Herr Tutu' was also present?"

Kessler laughs—both at the nickname and at Harden's agility. "I fear I'm not enough 'in the know,'" Kessler replies, "to know who 'Herr Tutu' is."

"'The Sweetie'—why Kuno Moltke, of course!"

Kessler tries not to smile, but fails. "Moltke seems a perfectly decent fellow. Where's the harm?"

Harden sighs deeply, suppressing the strong desire to blurt out "Don't play Mother Superior with me, you sodomite!" Instead he blandly says, "I'm not alone in thinking that Moltke—and even more, Eulenburg—encourage the Kaiser to overestimate his abilities."

"I doubt the Kaiser needs encouragement."

"Look here Kessler!"—Harden's exasperation suddenly boils over, though he quickly reins it in.

Aware that Harden is notoriously volatile, Kessler retreats to the innocuous. "Perhaps you overstate the danger of Eulenburg's influence," he calmly replies. "As I hear it—and to be sure, I hear little about politics—he's using his influence with the Kaiser to ease our antagonistic stance towards the French. All to the good, in my view. But I take it that you disagree, you find his influence baneful."

"I do ... but not because of his peacemaking efforts."

"Would you think better of him if he was a warmonger?"

Harden's face flushes, but he manages once more to control his temper. "You confuse me with the Kaiser," he says, his tone indignant despite himself. "Are you aware, my dear Count, that the Kaiser has declared that until the leaders of the Social Democratic Party are dragged out of the Reichstag and shot, Germany will never achieve its place in the sun?"

"Good heavens." Kessler is genuinely surprised. "I count myself a loyal member of the SPD."

"Prince Eulenburg recently wrote to a friend that he felt—"

"—excuse me, my dear Harden, but you seem to have access to Eulenburg's entire correspondence! How can that be?"

Flaring at the implied accusation, Harden's tone is more curt than he intends: "A portion of it only. As I've explained, I have some well-placed sources."

Kessler discards indirection: "Wouldn't 'spies' be the more accurate term?"

Kessler's insistent parrying leads Harden to try on the alien role of supplicant: "Would you rather I not continue?"

The strategy works: Kessler abandons the game. "See here, Harden," he says directly, "I *am* having trouble understanding where all this is leading."

"If you'll indulge me just a bit longer . . ."

"Very well . . . a *bit* longer . . ."

"As I was saying . . . Prince Eulenburg writes in one letter that he feels he's 'sitting on a powder-keg.' He reports hushed talk of the Kaiser being on the brink of a nervous breakdown, perhaps even insanity."

"I've heard such talk myself."

"We all know that the Kaiser's traumatic birth made his left arm useless, but who can say what other, unseen damage may have occurred? Damage perhaps to the brain."

Harden lowers his voice to a conspiratorial whisper. "I tell you the man must go. Yes, I say it openly—at least to you. The Kaiser must be forced to abdicate before he drags the country into some monstrous adventure that engulfs the entire continent in war."

Kessler's eyes narrow, as if squinting to see clearly. "I think I begin to understand what you . . . you plan to force an abdication by discrediting Eulenburg, the Kaiser's closest friend. Guilt by association, as it were."

Harden finds himself yearning for a return to indirection: "I should have known. You're way ahead of me," he says placidly.

Kessler smiles grimly: "I'm barely keeping pace."

"The era of personal rule *must* come to an end," Harden spits out. A pause follows while both men take in the implications. "I assume," Harden adds warily, "that such a view is congenial to you."

"Are you inviting me to join a *coup d'état*?" Kessler smiles at what he knows is an absurdity.

"No one is planning a *coup d'état*—as you put it."

"But you do have some plan of action. That much is apparent. Shall I guess?"

"If you like." It's no longer clear who is the cat and who the mouse.

"Let me be forthright, your preferred style: On what grounds do you plan to attack Eulenburg? What specifically has the man done? I've barely met him, but he seems charming and genial, if too conservative for my taste. Hardly the conspiratorial type."

"Friedrich von Holstein disagrees. He blames Eulenburg for ousting him from the Foreign Office. He despises Eulenburg—and von Holstein can be a fierce enemy."

"Holstein has many more enemies than Eulenburg. He's played the intriguer for years."

"But unlike Eulenburg, Holstein has a low opinion of His Majesty's abilities and works to limit his personal rule. Here, let me show you something."

Harden reaches into his breast pocket and extracts what appears to be a letter. "This is the copy of a recent letter Holstein wrote Eulenburg after resigning from the Foreign Office."

Kessler holds up his hand in protest. "I don't think so, Harden, I really don't wish to—"

Harden interrupts him, his voice authoritative: "—this you *must* hear! No one will ever learn that you've heard it." Without waiting for Kessler's reply, Harden starts to read from the letter: "'Your aim of many years, my removal,' Holstein writes Eulenburg, 'has now at last been achieved . . . I am now free, I need exercise no restraint, and can treat you as one treats a contemptible person with your characteristics. I do so herewith and expect to do more—"

"—'your characteristics,' indeed!" Kessler scoffs. "Should I assume the reference is to Eulenburg's penchant for writing poems? Really!—what vileness . . ."

"Eulenburg has challenged Holstein to a duel."

"A *duel*!—in this day and age! The whole thing's preposterous."

"Light comedy, I'd call it. It's all been settled. In return for Holstein withdrawing his letter, Eulenburg has solemnly sworn that he had nothing to do with Holstein's dismissal as Foreign Secretary. Both, of course, are lying through their teeth. And both will continue to intrigue against the other. Holstein at seventy has more taste for battle than Eulenburg at sixty."

"How did you ever get hold of Holstein's letter? Haven't you had your fill of being charged with *lèse-majesté*?"

Harden smiles broadly. "I've been fined and jailed four times," he says insouciantly. "Only a bit more than other journalists worth their salt. But it won't come to that this time."

"How can you be sure?"

"The dossier I've gathered is very full. Holstein himself has been most cooperative. And, I might add, Chancellor von Bülow as well. They believe more is at stake here, that the Liebenberg Circle is aiming at a full-scale seizure of power."

"What nonsense! Eulenburg's a poet, a spiritualist. His aim has never been anything more than becoming the Kaiser's devoted friend. He wouldn't know what to do with power if it was handed to him."

"Perhaps you're confusing your own distaste for intrigue with Eulenburg's? As the dossier I mentioned proves, poetry and power can coexist very comfortably."

"Dossier? You make it sound like a criminal trial." Kessler uncharacteristically raises his voice: "How do you know what is slander and what is truth, especially when it comes from sources as self-interested as Holstein and von Bülow? What precisely are the charges contained in this so-called 'dossier?'"

"To give you but one example: the Baden envoy, von Berckheim, has written in a letter that—I believe this is verbatim—Prince Eulenburg 'harbors passions allowed in the Orient and tolerated in Russia, but punished as a criminal offence in this country.' Von Berckheim cites various letters in his possession in support of his claim—including the Bavarian Prime Minister's reference to Eulenburg's 'moral defects.'"

"I must say, Harden, I don't wish to hear any further confidences. Nor am I prepared to provide any."

Harden's ears perk up. "Which suggests that you could if you chose . . ."

"I lead a private and circumspect life," Kessler replies enigmatically but firmly. "Whatever it is that you plan to accuse Eulenburg of, I don't wish to be implicated on any level."

Harden decides he might as well go for the jugular: "As an 'insider' you must have heard talk of Eulenburg's 'activities'—some information that could—"

Kessler stands up abruptly. "An 'insider'? That's quite enough, Harden! I've heard all I intend to . . ."

"I can assure you of absolute anonymity," Harden replies suavely. "You are not, after all, a political person."

"Your suspicions are exorbitant, Harden. Like your reputation." Kessler is angry, a state he rarely allows himself.

"Yes, I'm known for that," Harden counters. He gestures invitingly to Kessler to sit back down. "Why don't we shift the subject entirely . . . Do stay for a cognac. I understand you're off to the continent for the summer . . ."

Kessler remains standing. "Should I act surprised that you know my plans?"

"Come now, Kessler . . . I am capable of congenial conversation, you know—"

"—regretfully, I have another engagement."

Harden also stands up. "Very well. I can see you're adamant. I do thank you for your time . . . it's very good of you," he rather formally adds.

Kessler nods stiffly. "This is a nasty business, Harden. You would do well to back off."

"It's not in my nature." Harden's voice somehow has a teasing edge, or so Kessler believes.

"More's the pity." Kessler turns unceremoniously and walks away. Harden smiles at his disappearing back.

~

Soon after, the scandal breaks. On November 17, 1906, Harden begins publishing in *Die Zukunft* an extended series of open attacks, culminating in two articles in the spring of 1907 that strongly imply the secret homosexual nature of the Liebenberg Circle. Harden places the revelations within a "disinterested" framework that expresses concern for the baneful political influence that Prince Eulenburg—"an unhealthy late Romantic and spiritualist"—exerts above all others over the Kaiser.

Eulenburg, Harden charges, has strongly endorsed Wilhelm's view "that he is called to rule alone and that, as an incomparably blessed being, he may expect and beseech light and support only from the seat among the clouds, from the heights of which the Crown was bestowed on him; and to feel responsible only to that place." Eulenburg's "calamitous influence," Harden writes, "should at least not be allowed to continue in the dark" and "the vermin surrounding the Kaiser must be cleared out." Chancellor Bernhard von Bülow contributes his own bit: from the Berlin police he extracts the information that Prince Eulenburg has recently "slept with a rent boy in a hotel in Berlin."

Shards of the Harden bombshell land everywhere, setting Berlin aflame. His focus in the articles is on Eulenburg and Kuno von Moltke, but Harden mentions by name a number of others, including the French diplomat Raymond Lecomte ("who as we know does not have to rely on the front entrance"). The gossip mill proceeds to grind out still other names—Eulenburg's close friend Axel Varnbüler, and the general-intendant of the royal theater, Count von Hülsen-Haeseler. Some of the whispered gossip even has it that Eulenburg and the Kaiser have long been lovers.

Only Wilhelm himself seems disengaged from the enormity of the sensation Harden's articles produce. The Kaiser has earlier denounced Harden as an "insolent Jew," a "poisonous monster from some bottomless pit," and he's refused to allow *Die Zukunft* within sight. Yet his advisors realize that someone has to tell him about the articles, and some response must be made. Chancellor von Bülow is for a time considered the appropriate messenger, but his influence with the Kaiser has of late declined. Besides, von Bülow's manipulative personality makes for uncertainty; will he attempt to defend Eulenburg, his benefactor? And if he does, will the Kaiser listen to him?

Someone suggests as a possible go-between Cornelia Richter, whose dazzling salon is the most illustrious in Berlin, attracting on occasion Prince Eulenburg himself. The Kaiser, however, dislikes women who push themselves forward, and it's feared he might discount her report as "malicious nonsense." Wilhelm's military cabinet finally settles on the reluctant Crown Prince to break the news to his father. The Kaiser is at first disbelieving and dismissive, insisting that his dear Eulenburg has been defamed. But when told that the dignity of the Crown is at stake, Wilhelm reverses fields and lets it be known that Eulenburg must be "cleared or stoned." On May 4, 1907, the Kaiser instructs his Adjutant-General to send Eulenburg an ultimatum: "the All-Highest Person [*i.e.*, Wilhelm] expects to hear whether you have taken steps, and if so what steps, to start a legal action against certain suspicions expressed in ... recent articles in the 'Zukunft' ... His Majesty awaits an explanation as to whether you consider yourself beyond reproach with regard to these allusions ... Your report is to be sent direct to His Majesty."

Eulenburg immediately responds. "I declare to Yr. Majesty," he writes, "*that I consider myself beyond reproach*. I believe I may also assume that more than twenty years of life together and the extremely thorough knowledge of my nature and character which Your Majesty's perspicacious mind possesses cannot ever have allowed any doubt to arise on this score." In regard to bringing a law suit, Eulenburg hedges: "I have hitherto hesitated to react to the gibes of the *Zukunft* ... due *purely* to political considerations ... I saw it as my *duty* towards Yr. Majesty and Yr. Majesty's Government to overlook many a personal attack in order to *avoid* a lawsuit." To bring action against *Die Zukunft*, Eulenburg argues, would provide Harden with an opportunity to fan the flames still further. In an attempt to bolster the Kaiser's sympathy, Eulenburg adds that he's taken to his bed, "completely paralysed by neuritis in both feet and knees."

The Kaiser declines to call upon his (paltry) reserve of compassion. Having read the incriminating contents of Eulenburg's correspondence with von Moltke, as well as secret reports of the vice police in Vienna, Munich, and Berlin, Wilhelm orders Chancellor von Bülow—who seems to have needed no urging—to send Eulenburg a peremptory directive: the Prince must forthwith return his decoration, the

Order of the Black Eagle, and go abroad at once. Wilhelm has decided that the evidence against the Prince is so strong that it would be impossible for Eulenburg to exonerate himself in a court trial, and a verdict of guilty would have disastrous consequences for the prestige of the monarchy.

Eulenburg discovers within himself an untapped vein of iron. He lets von Bülow know that he considers flight abroad tantamount to admitting guilt, and reiterates—the product of denial mixed with a mistaken assumption of pedigreed immunity—his protestations of innocence. But he takes care to avoid any direct rejection of the Kaiser's "suggestion" that he leave Germany, announcing instead that a debilitating attack of gout has confined him to bed at his Liebenberg estate. Harden, for his part, lets it be known that he has in his possession enough additional, and "crushing," evidence to wreak considerably more damage if he chooses, though he's content for now to let matters lie. He has, after all, already achieved his essential objective—to destroy the influence of the Liebenberg Circle and the support it unflaggingly gave to the Kaiser's misguided sense of infallibility.

In the midst of this rapidfire cascade of demands and accommodations, no one seems to have given much thought to Kuno von Moltke—which has long been the story of this "likeable and decent" chap's innocuous life. Yet Moltke himself has not been idle. Sharing Eulenburg's misguided conviction that his noble pedigree will protect him, Moltke makes the disastrously bold decision to bring a civil suit against Harden for libel. Soon after, a hearing is convened in Moabit, at Berlin's monstrously eclectic central courthouse.

Harden's defense attorney, Max Bernstein, is a well-regarded figure in German juridical circles and an equally renowned hater of homosexuals. His known bias makes it all the more puzzling when he announces that the prominent sexologist Dr. Magnus Hirschfeld, himself openly homosexual, and a Jew, will appear as a medical expert. Is he being called by the prosecution or the defense? Has Bernstein himself suggested Hirschfeld's appearance or has it occurred over his objection? Will Hirschfeld's view that homosexuality is an inborn, benign natural

variant put him on the side of Moltke—or Harden? Confusing matters further, Hirschfeld is a known member of the Social Democratic
Party, dominated by anti-monarchists and defenders of socialism, and
a growing thorn in the Kaiser's side. The rumor mill leans to the view
that Hirschfeld will use his opportunity on the stand to exaggerate the
amount of homosexuality in Wilhelm's entourage; since he regards
homosexuality as no cause for apology, will the result of his testimony
be to discredit or to sanctify the Liebenberg Circle?

The more widely speculation spreads, the more expectations grow
that the pending Moltke case will rival in notoriety the scrumptious
scandal that surrounded the trial of Oscar Wilde in England a dozen
years earlier. That seems all the more likely when the *Berliner Morgen-
post* digs up and publishes a statement Hirschfeld made at the time of
Wilde's trial: "The married man who seduces the governess of his children remains free, but this genius of a writer has been put into prison."
Yes, the breathless public agrees, the prospects for the Harden trial are
in every sense ravishing.

Though still only 39, Hirschfeld has already made a considerable reputation for himself—even while simultaneously becoming, as an openly
homosexual man and a Jew, a figure of ridicule and disgust. He'd grown
up in a large, progressive family in the spa town of Kolberg in pres-
ent-day Poland and seems to have had a happy childhood. His father,
Hermann Hirschfeld, a secularized Jew and civic-minded physician,
became the leading figure in the small Jewish community in Kolberg,
and helped bring to the town both running water and a sewer system.
Among his acquaintances he'd counted August Bebel, one of the
founders of the Social Democratic Party—and an early proponent of
decriminalizing homosexual behavior.

Another of Hermann Hirschfeld's early acquaintances had been the
remarkable Rudolf Virchow under whom he completed his medical
studies at Berlin University. Virchow had been among the few medical experts who (unsuccessfully) advised *against* the adoption of the
anti-sodomy clause—the notorious Paragraph 175—in the German

constitution of 1871. He was also the first German scientist to challenge the then-standard view of Jews as an entirely separate racial group unchanged through time in physiognomy and temperament. As early as the 1880s Virchow had insisted that there was no such thing as "pure" races, that Jews, like other Germans, displayed a variety of character traits—that, for example (and tellingly), at least 10 percent of Jews were blond (as were only about 30 percent of other Germans).

Virchow's views found little favor in Wilhelmine Germany. The popular stereotype of the Jew was of a creature apart, biologically different from—and inferior to—Nordic Germans. Jews were believed to suffer a predisposition to insanity, hysteria, sexual perversion, and melancholia. Both the leading German psychiatric figures of the late 19th century, Emil Kraepelin and Richard von Krafft-Ebing, cited race—"hereditary degeneration"—as a leading cause (religious fervor was another) of the Jewish propensity to mental illness. And even the unconventional Karl Marx once commented, when characterizing his opponent, the Jewish socialist Ferdinand Lassalle, that Jews were "descended from the negroes who joined Moses in his flight from Egypt" and were "nigger-like"— which is to say, inferior to whites.

At the dawn of the 20th century, it's widely agreed that the presumed "physical disabilities" which set the Jews apart denote moral incapacities as well: Jewish men may no longer be thought to menstruate (as was believed in the Middle Ages), and a certain amount of social assimilation exists in Germany's cities, yet—to a greater extent than elsewhere in Europe—widespread antipathy to the Jews continues; they remain decidedly Other. In England, in contrast, Jews have become more comfortably assimilated and no notable racialist science has arisen to explain their "dangerously peculiar" attributes. Even in France—where vicious anti-Semitism periodically surfaces, as in the notorious Dreyfus affair—civil rights had been granted to Jews by the late 18th century.

In Germany endemic anti-Semitism exists side-by-side with an uneasy awareness that, although Jews make up only 1 percent of the population in 1900, they figure prominently in business and industry, account for more than 15 percent of the country's doctors, and turn out more than 6 percent of university graduates. Yet prestigious academic and government appointments remain largely closed to them; a German Disraeli is unthinkable. Some German Jews, paradoxically, regard themselves as more fully integrated into German culture, and more widely accepted as "good Germans," than in fact they are. Richard Wagner had in 1850 exemplified the deep-seated disparagement of Jews when he declared that "our whole European art and civilization ... have remained to the Jew a foreign tongue."

A bookish young man, Magnus Hirschfeld is physically unprepossessing—short and overweight, with stereotypically Jewish facial features, except for the bushy walrus moustache he grows (so his detractors whisper) to disguise them. As a young adult Hirschfeld acknowledges that his family's Judaism has to have had some formative influence on him, but only, he insists, in a vague, tangential way. When a university student filling out a standard matriculation form, Hirschfeld lists under "religious affiliation" not "Jewish," but "dissident"—consciously rejecting institutionalized religion in favor of scientific rationalism as his guiding principle in life. As someone who will be taunted and denounced as "a dirty Jew" throughout his life, Hirschfeld, ironically, never has more than incidental contact with Jewish life and institutions. During World War I he'll attend a Zionist conference, but will come away from it more convinced than ever that the mission of the Jews is not to establish a separate state but to assimilate into—and *change*—the various countries of their birth.

Similarly, when tens of thousands of Eastern European Jews migrate to Germany in the early decades of the 20th century, bringing with them a revival of interest in Hebrew and Yiddish culture, some German Jews welcome them as bearers of the "authentic" version of their own watered down and hollowed-out assimilationist Judaism. But Hirschfeld—like the majority of Germany's Jews—continues to give primacy instead to his national rather than religious identity. He does attend a performance of the Hebrew theater group Habimah, but, unlike Max Reinhardt and

Albert Einstein who, respectively, hail it as "thrilling" and "truly monumental," Hirschfeld rejects the revival of Hebrew as part of a regrettable tendency to emphasize Jewish "apartness"—instead of the preferred goal of creative assimilation.

From an early age Hirschfeld has been the predictable butt of jokesters and bullies, derided for being both a Jew and—in local parlance—a "sweetie," a soft sister. He manages to insulate himself somewhat by focusing on his strengths—a fine intelligence, a profound capacity for hard work, and a high tolerance for isolation. As a young man he's drawn to the arts, but eventually follows his father into medicine and opens a practice in the Charlottenburg area of Berlin. Initially specializing in hydrotherapy (the "water cure"), he begins, in 1896, to study human sexual behavior, with particular attention to homosexuality.

That same year, still only 28, Hirschfeld publishes under "Th. Ramien"—the first and last time he'll use a pseudonym—the pamphlet, *Sappho and Socrates, or What Explains the Love of Men and Women for Persons of Their Own Sex*. In it, he lays out many of the views that will underlie his attitude towards human sexuality throughout his life, though he'll constantly modify it around the edges. His bedrock principle is that same-sex erotic desire is biological—predetermined, fixed at birth, homosexuality can neither be acquired through experience nor changed through theological exhortation or medical intervention. Nor was homosexuality a pathology; it was simply one aspect of the "almost limitless" variety of erotic expression that characterized human sexuality—with no single form morally superior to any other. Only science—certainly not religion—could, in Hirschfeld's view, bring us to the liberating understanding that "love is as varied as people are." Religion, oppositely, with its emphasis on abstinence and procreation, propagated the *mis*-understanding that pleasure was sinful.

Quoting Nietzsche's purported dictum, "That which is natural cannot be immoral"—Hirschfeld further argues that laws against homosexuality have no effect other than to instill disabling self-hate—and the

suicidal destruction that often follows. It makes no more sense to persecute homosexuals, Hirschfeld insists, than it would to haul into court
people with blue eyes; in neither case is choice at issue, nor, therefore,
the legitimacy of punishment. Which is not to say, Hirschfeld contends,
that all homosexuals are alike; along with Edward Carpenter and Havelock Ellis in England, Hirschfeld argues that homosexuals are no less
diverse in personality, intelligence, aptitude and, yes, desire, than are
heterosexuals. To elucidate the latter point, he posits—50 years before
Alfred Kinsey—a scale ranging from 1–10 (Kinsey's would be 0–6) for
designating the object and strength of sexual desire.

The following year Hirschfeld establishes the Scientific Humanitarian
Committee—chiefly aimed at the repeal of the anti-homosexual Paragraph 175 of the German penal code, which makes intercourse among
men (not women) a punishable offense. One of the first to join the SHC
is Leopold von Meerscheidt-Hüllessem, Berlin's police commissioner.
Married with children, Hüllessem is aware of his own homosexual
inclinations—and also aware, in his official capacity, of the horrors
wrought by the legion of blackmailers who prey on Berlin's homosexuals. As early as 1885, Hüllessem establishes a police sub-division, the
"Department of Homosexuals"—a testimony both to his enlightenment
and to the flourishing nature of Berlin's homosexual subculture (which
Hüllessem's leniency helps expand still further).

Hüllessem lets it be known that henceforth homosexual bars and
clubs—but not the multiplicity of outdoor cruising spots, nor male prostitution—will be tolerated: no more police raids, plainclothes spies, paid
informants, or graft. Hüllessem goes so far as to arrange "tours" for *bona
fide* medical professionals and writers to the city's homosexual nightspots, including the occasional same-sex costume ball. No less a figure
than the sexologist Richard von Krafft-Ebing acknowledges Hüllessem's
assistance when he publishes the pioneering *Psychopathia sexualis*.
(Though one of the avant-garde members of *PAN*, August Strindberg,
who also participates in a tour, pronounces it "the most horrible thing
he has ever seen"). Involved in a cover-up to protect a well-placed friend
from charges of rape, Hüllessem commits suicide in 1900. His policy of

benign neglect of bars and clubs is continued by his successor, Hans von Tresckow.

Thanks to the Napoleonic Penal Code of 1810, homosexual acts between consenting adults were made legal in France, Holland, and Italy, but not in Germany, nor England. Under the combined influence of the Enlightenment and the French Revolution, there had been a period of forbearance in Germany regarding homosexuality at the beginning of the 19th century, particularly in Bavaria, where in 1813 all laws regarding sex had been liberalized, including those that punished homosexual acts. But by mid-century attitudes had again reversed; in 1851, Prussia had declared such acts "unnatural"—and punished those caught with prison terms. Then, in 1871, the newly united Germany passed a legal code that included the notorious Paragraph 175 which, using earlier Prussian law as a model, characterized male-male sexuality as "criminally indecent," with jail terms mandated for those apprehended.

The Scientific Humanitarian Committee's petition campaign to repeal Paragraph 175 gathers momentum over time; among those who sign it early on are Hermann Hesse, Franz Werfel, George Grosz, the socialist leader Eduard Bernstein, the theologian Martin Buber, Albert Einstein, Count Harry Kessler, Käthe Kollwitz, Thomas Mann, Stefan Zweig, Gerhart Hauptmann, Rainer Maria Rilke, Arthur Schnitzler, Émile Zola, and Leo Tolstoy—a veritable pantheon of celebrated figures. One of the earliest signatories is Hermann Hirschfeld's old friend, August Bebel, head of the Social Democratic Party, who in 1898 introduces as well an unsuccessful bill in the Reichstag to void the offending paragraph.

Following the formation of Hirschfeld's Scientific Humanitarian Committee, several other groups devoted to homosexual rights soon emerge, their views and agendas often at odds with his, leading to prolonged in-fighting and frequent character assassination. In 1902 Benedict Friedlaender and Adolf Brand organize the Community of the Special in opposition to Hirschfeld's theory that homosexuality is inborn and confined to a distinct minority of "intermediaries" (the so-called "third sex" model). In their long-lasting journal *Der Eigene*, Friedlaender and Brand focus their efforts on eradicating the association of homosexuality with effeminacy and on restoring the "glory that was Greece"— emphasizing traditional "masculine" behavior and the primacy of homoerotic relationships between older and younger men. A third organization, the League for Human Rights, follows in 1903; based on a broad concern with the rights of the individual, including homosexuals, it proves particularly attractive to politically conservative homosexuals, and by the 1920s will become the largest homosexual organization in Germany.

Several leading members of the Scientific Humanitarian Committee (SHC) try to talk Hirschfeld out of appearing—as has been announced in advance—as an expert witness in the upcoming von Moltke trial. Among the most outspoken is Max Spohr, the pioneering publisher of Hirschfeld's 1896 *Sappho and Socrates*—and three years later of his *Jahrbuch* (*Yearbook for Intermediate Sexes*), the scientific journal of sexology that sometimes runs to 1,000 pages and which is published annually for nearly 25 years. Nothing comparable is happening in English publishing: the pioneering figures—like Edward Carpenter and John Addington Symonds—either circularize their work privately or, in the case of Havelock Ellis's *Sexual Inversion*, see their work officially banned. England is somewhat in advance of Germany in the easing of hostility towards Jews, but behind it in accepting homosexuality. In France, the censorship of books relating to homosexuality is tame compared to England—but public discourse on the subject is negligible compared to Germany, where the SHC offers a variety of lectures over the years that draw sizeable audiences.

Max Spohr is a man to whom Hirschfeld owes much, whose sympathy he counts on, and whose opinion he values. When Spohr warns him, during one of their afternoon walks through the Tiergarten, that "serving as a witness in Harden's trial will run the risk of seeming to defend, whether meaning to or not, the journalist's equation in his articles of homosexuality with immorality," Hirschfeld takes the warning seriously.

"All that I will do," he uncertainly replies, "is to provide my opinion that—"

"—your *expert* opinion."

"—very well: my expert opinion, as to whether Count Moltke is homosexual or not. That is all."

"And how," Spohr asks, "do you propose to 'prove' that one way or the other? No man has come forward—certainly not Eulenburg—willing to testify that he's had sexual congress with Moltke. Nothing less than that can 'prove' a damn thing. Only detailed testimony from his sexual partners could be convincing."

"Not so, Max. It's possible, I believe, to identify constitutional homosexuality through non-sexual behavior. For instance: the extent to which a man exhibits feminine characteristics or shows a certain kind of temperamental disposition which distinguishes him as a member of the 'Third Sex.'"

Spohr snorts with derision. "The 'Third Sex'! You know perfectly well what Benedict Friedlaender and others think about *that*!"

"Friedlaender, Brand—my detractors are many—as I needn't tell *you*. Not to mention Albert Moll, still peddling the notion of homosexuality as a mental disturbance, though as a neurologist he should know better. I suppose," Hirschfeld sighs, "this disarray of conflicting views is to be expected in a new field like sexology. I do regret, though, that Friedlaender and Brand are such misogynists."

"In their hostility to Helene Stöcker and feminism they speak for many more male homosexuals than you do, with your support of her extremist views."

"That I cannot help. I will not join Friedlaender in confining women to the kitchen."

"The kitchen *and* motherhood!—he's very broad-minded." They both laugh.

"Yes, 'broad-minded,'" Hirschfeld says sarcastically, "*if* you agree with him that men are more important than women, homosexuals more virile than other men, Christians more moral than Jews, and Germans superior to all other nationalities! No thanks."

"He accuses *you* of an excessive interest in cross-dressers and prostitutes—of conflating them with homosexuals."

"He accuses me of many things. So be it. I've invited him to give a lecture to the SHC."

Spohr groans. "Oh Magnus . . . he'll contradict everything you stand for. I don't think he even believes homosexuality is inborn—let alone born with a female soul."

"I'll ask Helene to attend," Hirschfeld good-naturedly says. "She'll set him to rights."

Spohr laughs derisively. "She'll side with *him*. Helene *doesn't* know, nor do I, that there are *male* souls and *female* souls. There are *people*, people with infinite variations."

"About which we need infinitely more study."

"On that we can agree. But Friedlaender and his kind are more interested in propaganda than scholarship. Look at how they explain lesbians—women disappointed or mistreated by men! They want nothing to do with the 'inferior' female species. They pine for the rebirth of ancient Greece, where handsome warriors with decidedly male souls"— Spohr smiles broadly at his own cleverness—"lusted after post-pubescent boys! . . . But we've gotten off the subject—I tell you, Magnus, that if you appear as an 'expert' in the Moltke trial, Friedlaender and Brand will denounce you as a charlatan."

"They do anyway. I can't help that. My position is no different from Carpenter and Havelock Ellis, not to mention our own predecessors in Germany, Karl Ulrichs and Krafft-Ebing. I'm content to be in such company."

"Krafft-Ebing, no less! For Heaven's sake, Magnus, he thinks homosexuality results from a degeneration of the central nervous system— that it's a disease! Whereas you insist it's nothing more than a benign human variant. *Do* show more discrimination in your associations!" Spohr adds with some heat.

"Krafft-Ebing has made some real contributions . . ." Hirschfeld responds haltingly.

His indecisiveness further provokes Spohr. "Why in heaven's name, for example, have you let Baron von Teschenberg join the SHC—especially after circulating that bizarre picture of himself!—oh so stylishly dressed, and leaning ever so coyly over a basket of flowers! Friedlaender has sent it everywhere, chuckling at his good fortune—and he includes von Teschenberg's statement that the photo reveals his true nature—a poor womanly soul languishing away in a man's body."

"You shouldn't make fun of people who are different, Max. I'm surprised at you. Teschenberg sincerely means what he says."

Spohr stops walking and raises his voice. "Of course he *means* it! That's precisely the trouble."

"I don't see it that way," Hirschfeld calmly replies. "The mind takes precedence over the body."

"Oh I see," Spohr sputters. "If I think I'm a sea bass, then my ability to survive out of water is irrelevant?"

"You're making an absurd analogy."

They resume their walk. "I can understand the political advantage of insisting that erotic desire is *in*voluntary. 'What is inborn cannot be helped and should not be punished.' Yes, yes, I understand all that," Spohr impatiently goes on, "but one consequence of your biological explanation is that it confines same-sex desire to a small minority, the members of your precious Third Sex. You're categorizing homosexuals as a separate species—as entirely Other."

Hirschfeld looks unperturbed. "And your problem with that is . . . what?"

"Can't you see?!"

"Apparently not, my dear Spohr. Do enlighten me."

"In my view homosexual desire is much more common—even if not acted upon—than your theory allows."

Hirschfeld looks genuinely puzzled.

"But it isn't. It's the biological property of a small minority."

"There—there, you've said it! That's precisely what bothers me about this Third Sex business. If only a small minority finds members of the same gender erotic, then how do you explain ancient Greece?"

"I don't know enough about the ancient world to explain anything."

"Come, come Hirschfeld! You're an educated man, a polymath. You have all sorts of knowledge. Surely you know that in Periclean Athens *every* adult male citizen went down to watch the naked young men perform gymnastics, drooling over the curve of a calf, the musculature of the back, the—"

"—*every* male citizen?" Hirschfeld looks incredulous.

"Only the normal ones!" Spohr bursts out laughing at his own quick wit. "An adult male who did *not* lust after a comely teenager was considered *highly* peculiar!"

"I've lost your point . . ."

"How can you argue that today only a few third sexers find young men erotic when Athenian culture all but uniformly agreed they were?! You've backed yourself into a corner, Hirschfeld—unless you want to argue that it's only in this enlightened century that we've succeeded in shifting the appreciation of male beauty from a near-universal to a small group of biologically-driven inverts. Some progress!"

"Isn't it quite possible that Athenian culture over time—for reasons not yet understood—mandated an erotic attraction that ran counter to biology?"

"Possible—barely. But do you really want to characterize the fount of Western civilization as based on the *un*-natural?"

"Spohr, Spohr . . . you're playing with words . . . 'natural', 'unnatural', who can define such abstractions?"

"No one! That's my point! It's absurd to pretend to know, to start pronouncing, on what is inborn and what is not!"

"Please, Spohr, STOP! I don't 'pronounce', I inquire . . ."

Spohr is adamant. "You sometimes pronounce. And you're about to again."

Hirschfeld looks puzzled. "I don't follow you. I'm about to pronounce about—what?"

"The trial—the trial, for heaven's sake! You're about to testify, to state a point of view—isn't that 'pronouncing'? Isn't that where this whole discussion began?!"

"I can't shirk my responsibility to testify. After all, I'm widely considered an expert on—"

"—this trial is malignant!" Spohr nearly shouts. "Harden has brought the libel suit on himself! Who knows where the truth lies? If Eulenburg and Moltke *are* homosexual, let Harden prove it, though I don't see how he can. Nor do I see how you can enter the lists in any capacity without falling off the horse. I predict a disaster for you—and for the Committee."

Hirschfeld holds to an even tone: "I do not think so. But we will soon see, will we not?"

The *Moltke v. Harden* trial begins on October 23, 1907, in a courtroom so crowded with spectators that they spill out for several blocks outside the huge Criminal Court building located in the recently fashionable northwest Moabit section of Berlin, an area surrounded by elegant apartment houses, broad avenues, the Glass Palace, and Exhibition Park. The court building itself is a massive, anachronistic pile seemingly glued together from the leftovers of four centuries worth of architectural discards. Victorian church towers frame and collide with a 17th-century façade rumored to be a relic from the Wars of Religion. The building's interior is dark and dreary: wood carvings, stained-glass windows, and look-alike portraits of past dignitaries underscore the stale air and the bewildering maze of halls, courtrooms, passageways, holding cells, and law offices. The most that can be said for the building is that it stands at the convenient intersection of an omnibus line and a horse-drawn streetcar—the attendant ruckus outclamoring the bustle and pace characteristic of all of Berlin's rapidly expanding metropolis.

As his first witness, Harden's lawyer Max Bernstein calls to the stand Moltke's former wife, Lily von Elbe. Elegantly attired and strikingly attractive, von Elbe takes her seat in the witness box in an unhurried manner. Bernstein gives her a respectful nod, aware that her modish self-presentation will add conviction to her testimony.

Despite his reputation for brusque provocation, Bernstein begins politely: "I'm sure that I speak for the court, my dear Madame, in expressing our thanks for your willingness to provide testimony on matters of a most delicate nature. We are sensible of the fact that references will be made in these proceedings rarely heard in the public sphere, and never in the presence of a woman of refined disposition. We will do our utmost to limit the potential for embarrassment and will confine our questions as much as possible to generalities. Our highest priority, I assure you, is to avoid any needless offense to your sensibilities. We thank you in advance for your forbearance."

A caustic trace of amusement crosses Lily's face—no surprise to friends who know her tart temperament—but she quickly erases it, adjusting her features to that look of bland imperturbability considered appropriate to a woman of her station.

"Difficult as these circumstances are for me," Lily says in a muted voice, "I consider it my duty to testify truthfully, however painful the obligation."

"For which we are most grateful, Madame. I would like to begin, if I may, by asking you to characterize the conjugal relations that existed between you and your husband, Count Kuno von Moltke, during the two-year period of your marriage."

"Yes of course," Lily replies, a bare hint of mockery in her voice.

There's a brief pause.

"Whenever you feel comfortable," Bernstein says solicitously.

"In our two years of marriage we had conjugal relations on the first two nights."

Another pause.

"Yes?" Bernstein prods.

"Yes?" Lily responds, with the merest suggestion of impishness.

She's enjoying all this, Bernstein thinks. But the game will be played my way.

"I well understand how this inquiry offends your sense of propriety," Bernstein says, feigning courtly concern. "Alas, the nature of this case dictates a line of questioning we would all, in ordinary circumstances, prefer to avoid. Regrettably, I must ask you what the nature of your conjugal relations consisted of subsequent to the first two nights of your marriage."

"Nothing."

"Nothing?" Bernstein inadvertently sounds surprised.

"Nothing. After the first two nights we rarely shared a bed."

"And whose choice was that?"

"My husband's."

"Did he offer any explanation?"

"No." Lily *is* enjoying her recalcitrance.

"Did you *ever* share a bed subsequent to the first two nights?"

"Yes. But rarely. Only when paying an overnight visit to family or friends—our hosts assumed we wished to sleep together. On those occasions my husband placed a pan of water between us."

There are audible gasps in the audience. Deliberately pausing for maximum effect, Lily continues. "He did so, he said, in order to discourage advances between us. As if I would dream of such a thing," she haughtily adds. "By then I knew perfectly well that he preferred the company of men."

"Do you mean in bed?"

"Good heavens!—how would I know that?!"

Bernstein hurriedly retreats. "Of course, of course, I see what you mean."

"I cannot testify to what I never saw. If you recall, I wasn't invited into his bedroom." After a slight pause, Lily adds a *non sequitur*: "He said marriage was 'a filthy business,' that 'a woman was no more than a lavatory.'"

There's a collective grumble of astonishment from the audience.

Bernstein stumbles for words, sounding lost: " ...As for 'preferring the company of men ...'"

"What I *can* say," Lily slyly begins, "is that I once saw my ex-husband take a handkerchief Prince Eulenburg had left behind after a visit, press it to his lips, and murmur, 'My soul, my love!'"

This time, the stir in the courtroom is considerably louder and above the din one man audibly hisses, "A disgrace!"

The judge bangs his gavel and admonishes the spectators, threatening to clear the courtroom should there be further outbursts.

Bernstein proceeds. "May I ask what your reaction was to the incident with the handkerchief?"

"I considered it disgraceful!" Lily replies, deliberately echoing the anonymous shouter. "Revolting. At other times," she continues, "I heard him refer to Prince Eulenburg as 'my soulmate,' and once I even overheard him tell another man that Eulenburg was his 'one and only cuddly bear.' They often referred to Kaiser Wilhelm as their 'darling.'"

A growl of disapproval rises from the spectators. The judge again bangs his gavel, but doesn't make good on his threat to clear the courtroom.

"What was your reaction on hearing those terms of endearment?"

Ignoring the question, von Elbe says with unexpected vehemence, "Prince Eulenburg had opposed my marriage from the beginning, opposed it vehemently. He once said to me angrily, 'Set my friend free, give my friend back to me.' I never suspected the real reason for his—" She stops in mid-sentence.

For a moment, Bernstein lets her abrupt silence hang in the air, then coaxes her into finishing the thought.

"—Yes? What was it that you never suspected?"

Von Elbe again ignores his question. "Kuno—Count Moltke—spent more time with Eulenburg than with his own family, including on Christmas Eve. I told my husband that I wanted a divorce."

"How did he react?"

"With utter calmness. He said he would make no objection if I began proceedings. Indeed, he seemed relieved at the idea. We separated soon after. He said to me, 'I don't find you revolting as a human being, but rather as a woman.'"

"Good heavens!"—Bernstein's shock is calculated, and he quickly recovers. "I don't believe I have any further questions for the witness," he says, his tone now one of gratified complacency.

As Lily von Elbe steps down from the witness chair, the crowd vigorously applauds her. The judge makes no objection. Lily momentarily glances towards Harden. The two exchange a barely perceptible smile.

The next witness called is an attractive young man in his early twenties wearing the uniform of the Volunteer Rifle Corps, Lancer Squadron. Bernstein begins by asking him to state his full name and the regiment in which he serves.

"My name is Stefan Bollhardt. I enlisted in the Cuirassiers Rifle

Corps two years ago and currently hold the rank of Oberleutnant. Until recently, I was stationed in Potsdam."

"Thank you, Oberleutnant Bollhardt. Let me begin by asking whether the name Adolf Brand, or the publication *Der Eigene*, mean anything to you?"

"One of my fellow officers told me that he was a friend of that fellow Brand. I'm pretty sure that was the publication he showed me."

"*Der Eigene*?"

"Yes, I'm pretty sure."

"What did you make of it?"

"It talked about ancient Greece."

"Can you be more specific?"

"The lost heritage of Greece ..." Thinking Bollhardt is about to complete the sentence, Bernstein lets a moment pass, then somewhat irritably says, "Yes ... yes ... the 'lost heritage' of—*what*?"

"Oh—of male bonding, which, it said, was the highest kind of relationship ..."

"Spiritual or carnal bonding?" Bernstein abruptly asks.

Bollhardt looks stunned, as if someone had slapped him hard across the face. "I ... I ... don't know," he stumbles on. "I really just, uh, glanced ... at it, you know. I remember something about ... about—"

"—Yes?" Bernstein again interrupts, his voice snappish. "Surely, my dear Oberleutnant, you are able to recall *something* of—"

"—it was about male bonding ... the lost Greek tradition because of ... of—yes, lost because of 'the barbarous repression of Christianity,' it said."

A few angry murmurs erupt in the courtroom.

"Very good, Oberleutnant. Now, please tell the court more about your experiences when stationed in Potsdam."

"You mean what I told you about Johannes Count von Lynar?"

"Yes," Bernstein gruffly responds, annoyed at the exposed implication that Bollhardt has been rehearsed.

"Well, Count Lynar has a villa in Potsdam and he often throws parties ..."

"What sort of parties?"

"Parties for ... men ..." Bollhardt stops himself. Bernstein makes the instant, shrewd decision to throw Bollhardt a curve: "Tell the court, if you will, about the 'cuirassiers'' uniforms." A puzzled murmur spreads among the spectators. Bollhardt himself seems confused.

"Our uniforms?"

"If you would."

"Well ... as everyone knows, we wear white pants and knee-high boots ... Everyone knows that ... But now that's been forbidden. I mean in public."

"And why has it been forbidden?"

Bollhardt's face flushes. "It brought us unwanted attention."

"'Unwanted'? Please explain."

"Well, you see, our uniforms, the white pants, are ... tight and ... and that seems to appeal to ... to an element ... in the male population."

"A homosexual element, is that not correct?"

"Well, yes. But it's okay to wear the pants at private parties, like at Count Lynar's villa."

"At the Count's parties."

"Yes. Both officers and enlisted men."

Bernstein swirls around dramatically and points directly at Count Moltke, seated at the prosecution's table. "And was Count Moltke among those officers?"

"Yes sir. I saw him often at the parties. We would drink a lot of champagne."

"Were there women at these parties?"

"No, sir. After a lot of champagne, some of the men would, would ..."

"Would what, Officer Bollhardt?"

"Would ... well, I guess you could say, would ... get amorous."

A commotion erupts in the courtroom—sounds of laughter, punctuated by derisive hoots. This time, the judge does call the crowd to order.

Bernstein has remained stony-faced throughout. Clearing his throat loudly, he turns to the witness: "And did you yourself participate in these, er, activities, Officer Bollhardt?"

Bollhardt looks stricken, and blushes.

Bernstein repeats his question, this time reminding Bollhardt that he's testifying under oath.

Bollhardt swallows hard, then mumbles a few words: " . . . Well, participating? . . . I wouldn't call it that, I think . . . some caresses maybe . . . allowing myself to be caressed . . ."

"You say 'caressed,' Officer Bollhardt. Caressed by several people?"

"Yes sir." Bollhardt looks sheepish.

"And was one of those people Count Moltke, perhaps?"

"Oh, I couldn't say, sir," Bollhardt bursts out. "It was . . . it was *quite dark*, you know!"

The spectators erupt in laughter. Two young men in the middle of the crowd stand up and pantomime being blind men "accidentally" bumping into each other, feeling up each other's pant legs—to a sprinkling of applause, and high-spirited shouts of "Degenerates! Villains!"

The judge again bangs his gavel, but to no avail. Unable to silence the crowd, he shouts above the din that "Court is adjourned! . . . We reconvene . . . at ten tomorrow morning." He then pushes back his chair and strides from the platform. Officer Bollhardt beats a hasty retreat through a side door while Bernstein stands his ground, arms folded across his chest, a contented smile on his face.

The following morning the judge opens the court session with a brief but stern warning that, should there be any "outrageous breach of decorum" such as characterized the preceding day's testimony, he will bar all spectators for the remainder of the trial. "The dignity of the juridical system," he sonorously intones, "is no trifling matter." The crowd takes his no-nonsense tone seriously. Noise dies down to an intermittent whisper. A general stiffening of posture is perceptible.

The morning session opens with Harden's lawyer, Max Bernstein, calling Doctor Magnus Hirschfeld to the stand. Visually, Hirschfeld fits the physical stereotype of a Jew and his appearance elicits a low murmur of disapproval—which the judge chooses to ignore.

"The concluding witness for the Harden defense," Bernstein solemnly intones, "is Doctor Magnus Hirschfeld, the well-known expert on human sexuality. Would you be good enough, Dr. Hirschfeld, to begin by telling the court why it is that you qualify as an expert witness in these matters."

"I chair the Scientific Humanitarian Committee," Hirschfeld matter-of-factly states, "an organization devoted to the repeal of Paragraph 175 of the German penal code, the paragraph that calls for the punishment of homosexual behavior."

"You do not feel that punishment is befitting?"

"I do not. I consider homosexuality to be a natural variant found among some men and women. Certainly not a majority of men and women. Of course only a minority of human beings are left-handed, or have blue eyes. We do not send them to prison for having been born with uncommon features."

"When you use the term 'natural variant,' is that merely your opinion or is it established scientific fact?"

"The scientific study of homosexuality goes back no further than the middle of the last century. Yet we *have* amassed a considerable body of evidence on the subject. Specialists in the field, among whom I count myself, disagree on some matters but are nearly unanimous in the view that homosexuality is innate. One is born homosexual, one does not become homosexual."

"The court will no doubt be eager to learn"—Bernstein's tone is arch—"on which matters the experts in the field agree or disagree. But may I ask you, Doctor Hirschfeld, to begin what will no doubt be your edifying testimony by telling us whether you believe homosexuality to be a disability?"

"Yes, in some sense. Because our society—unlike Periclean Athens, say—tends to regard male-male sexuality as degenerate, sinful or criminal—often all three. This attitude, in turn, leads to self-doubt, blackmail, and sometimes suicide. I refer you to the recent well-known case involving Friedrich Alfred Krupp, the industrialist."

There's a stir in the audience at the mention of Krupp's name, but Hirschfeld continues imperturbably. "In the Middle Ages, the mentally disabled were thought to be possessed of the devil—and were often burned at the stake. Fortunately that view has become outmoded. Not so with homosexuality. One well-known journalist recently referred to it as 'dog morality.' That view will in time become equally outmoded."

"You referred to the Krupp case."

"Yes. I feel sure that most people recall it vividly. The German press made a scandal of it, hounding the poor man to his death. Nor is his an uncommon case. There have been numerous instances when both the press and individual blackmailers have led the persecuted victim to kill himself. There was the terrible death recently at the—"

Bernstein, exasperated, interrupts: "—without going into *too* much detail, Dr. Hirschfeld, about matters extraneous to this trial, I should like to call your attention to—"

"—'extraneous'? I hardly think so. Were it not for the terrible consequences in our society of being labeled a 'homosexual,' I cannot think Count Moltke would ever have brought a libel suit against Mr. Harden in order to clear—"

"—yes, yes, Dr. Hirschfeld, I do see your point."

"Then I may continue?"

Bernstein sighs deeply. "If you wish . . . though not *too* detailed, if you please . . ."

"My point is simply that when a prominent journalist like Mr. Harden calls someone 'homosexual,' it's taken to be a libelous accusation. Yet speaking scientifically, the designation is morally neutral. From what I've been able to learn, Mr. Harden has no particular prejudice against homosexuals and has even been a signatory to our petition to drop Paragraph 175 from the penal code. He appears to be less biased than is the case with most Berliners. I cannot pretend, of course, to know what was in his mind when he referred to Count Moltke as a 'homosexual.' Was the intent to pay him a compliment? I very much doubt it. Was he attempting to defame Count Moltke? It would seem so. Perhaps he was merely being descriptive, with no moral judgment whatever implied. Only Mr. Harden can tell us."

As all eyes turn towards Harden, seated at the defense table, he instantly wipes away what had been a smile of amusement.

Bernstein feels momentarily paralyzed, his head full of contradictory impulses about how to proceed. The landscape seems strewn with unexploded bombs.

"Am I correct in assuming," he tentatively begins, "that had you been in Count von Moltke's place, you would not have brought charges of libel against Mr. Harden for calling you homosexual?"

"I would not," Hirschfeld urbanely replies. "I have long been entirely open about being homosexual. There are no grounds for shame or guilt. Many of the world's greatest figures have been homosexual. Shall I name a few?" Hirschfeld throws Bernstein a mischievous smile.

"I take your point. Doubtless the list is long." He pauses, as if again uncertain about what question might yield testimony favorable to his client.

"Germany," Bernstein hears himself saying, as if portentously channeling the muse of history. "What can we say about Germany? Our traditions, our standards ... Are we not a singular people, with our own perspective on these matters?"

Hirschfeld smiles inwardly at so artless a question. He'd expected more subtlety from the well-known lawyer. "Goethe, Germany's greatest man of letters, might be a good place to begin. How, for example, are we to understand Goethe's lines, 'Happy are they who, without hatred, hide from the world, hold a friend in their heart, and enjoy life with that friend'? Is that not a very German form of expression? It speaks to the romance of friendship, the deeply held German conviction that male bonding has a profound spiritual dimension that transcends any relationship between a man and a woman."

A stunned silence greets Hirschfeld's invocation of the revered Goethe.

Bernstein finally ends it: "Perhaps some will feel," he suggests, "that artists and writers are a peculiar breed. Can you provide examples from other fields?"

"Yes of course. But let me first say that in this country, the glorification of male friendship has, unfortunately, been the handmaiden of female denigration. Misogyny, I would venture to say, is more pronounced in Germany than elsewhere in Europe—despite the best efforts of feminists like Helene Stöcker, with whom I feel a deeply sympathetic—"

"—really, Dr. Hirschfeld!" Bernstein's annoyance is more apparent than he intended. "I don't wish to be rude, and the court very much appreciates your remarkable erudition ... but I, I must ask you to share only that part of it which is directly responsive to the question."

Hirschfeld appears unruffled. "And that question was—?"

"Never mind, never mind ..."

"Oh—now I recall. You wanted some examples of distinguished Germans who were homosexual. You wanted non-artists, I believe, since artists are known to be peculiar." Hirschfeld intended a bit of comic relief and is pleased to hear some laughter from the audience.

"Will King Ludwig II of Bavaria do? Perhaps he's a bit obscure. A better choice might be Frederick the Great." Hirschfeld grins happily, a small pachyderm dancing among the daisies. "As you probably know, Frederick never cohabited with his wife. When a young man, he tried to run away with his dearest friend, Hans von Katte; after the King—King Frederick William I—apprehended the pair, he forced his son to witness von Katte's beheading. Yes, it's safe to say that Frederick the Great is among those who—shall we say, 'jumped the line'—that is, between spiritism and eroticism—as his correspondence with Fredersdorf makes abundantly clear, and which—"

"—forgive my interrupting again, Dr. Hirschfeld, but your use of the term 'spiritism' inevitably brings to mind the Kaiser's known interest in the subject, along with certain members of his entourage, including Prince Eulenburg. Do you mean to imply that—?"

"—I'm aware that your client, Mr. Harden, has attacked the Liebenberg Circle, and in particular Prince Eulenburg, as—and here I believe I'm quoting him directly—'a nest of spiritism.' By which he meant, apparently, people with a pronounced interest in mysticism and the occult. I am myself an admirer of the Kaiser's, but have had no contact with him or his intimate circle, and am therefore in no position to evaluate the accuracy of Mr. Harden's description."

Bernstein sits resignedly in a chair near the witness box—an acknowledgement of defeat in his attempt to stop a locomotive with his bare hands.

Hirschfeld continues smoothly on: "I can only say that I myself have never been drawn to the practices of clairvoyance or hypnotism.

Far from being interested in contacting through séance the world of spirits, I have no religious conviction of any kind, nor any belief in the miraculous."

"I thank you for your candor, Dr. Hirschfeld," Bernstein says mechanically. "But I would urge you to conclude your current train of thought."

"I believe I was speaking of Frederick the Great and had been about to mention as well his brother Heinrich, who actually dedicated a temple to one close male friend, inscribing on its portal, 'Testimony of a grateful heart.' But one could go on and on ... German history provides an ample supply of candidates who seem to have crossed back and forth over the line dividing spiritual friendship and carnal knowledge."

Bernstein suddenly sees an opening and rises from his chair. "And are we to assume that your view of these matters is widely held among your colleagues?"

"Widely, yes. But not unanimously. Not even within the Scientific Humanitarian Committee. In his recent book *Renaissance of Uranian Eros*, Benedict Friedlaender uses the porous borderline between nonsexual friendship and amorous sexuality to posit what he calls 'physiological friendship'—that point, often reached, when tenderness merges into eroticism. The erasure of that fine line is regarded by Friedlaender as an achievement of the highest order."

"And how do you regard it?"

"How one views the difference between loving friendship and erotic love hinges on the historical moment, on the national customs then prevailing. What is considered acceptable or desirable behavior shifts through time and across cultures. I agree with Friedlaender's defense of homosexual behavior, but I would not rank it—or heterosexual behavior, for that matter—as being of "the highest order." I do not believe in a hierarchy of erotic expression, one form being 'better' than others. I find sexual expression of various kinds equally acceptable—as long as no force is involved, nor any person under the age of sixteen."

Bernstein is determined to bring closure: "Which brings us, Doctor Hirschfeld, to the heart of the matter for this hearing. In *Die Zukunft*, as you know, Mr. Harden has described Count von Moltke and Prince

Eulenburg as 'homosexual.' My question for you is: 'How does one know? What scientific criteria do you employ when deciding whether an individual is or is not 'homosexual?'"

"A very difficult question. In my own work, I have been much influenced by the renowned evolutionary biologist Ernst Haeckel, and in particular by his view that the intricate interaction of internal secretions within individuals is principally responsible for outcomes relating both to gender and to sexual attraction."

Due to audible giggling in the audience, Hirschfeld pauses. When the commotion settles down, he continues: "That is what I meant earlier in referring to a continuum, a spectrum, different individuals landing on different sites along that spectrum. In a widely dispersed questionnaire, our Committee found that only 2 percent of the population is exclusively homosexual, but many more people fall along intermediate positions on the spectrum. Some people, for example, may be *psychically* homosexual, though they themselves are unaware of the fact and though they have never had a homosexual experience."

"Can you explain—*briefly*—what you mean by 'psychic' homosexuality?"

"Certainly. One must first ask, 'Is there a primary orientation towards members of one's own sex?' Does the individual man prefer the company of other men rather than women? Does he invest greater emotion in his friendships with men than he does with his female acquaintances, even with his wife? A further issue is that some *active* homosexual men show no outward signs of their nature—they give a thoroughly masculine impression; nothing in their manner, appearance, or behavior suggests sexual attraction to other men. Other homosexuals—no one has exact figures—betray their erotic natures in various ways: nervousness and oversensitivity, for example, squeamishness, a tendency to depression. Other manifestations might be the elegant decoration of one's home, the profusion of silks and satins, the excellence of the cooking, an interest in flowers and birds; and as well, oppositely, a *lack* of interest in typical male pursuits like politics or hunting."

"Perhaps I misunderstand you, Doctor Hirschfeld, but haven't you just described symptoms, qualities, and behaviors that we associate with the female sex, but not necessarily with male homosexuality?"

"You have understood me perfectly," Hirschfeld replies. "I have been describing a female soul. But a soul, in the case of a homosexual man, housed in a male body, and a body, incidentally, anatomically intact regarding the testes, prostate, penis, and—under the microscope—spermatozoa. This is precisely why I have referred to such men as a Third Sex: a female soul in a male body."

"Am I correct in assuming, then, that it is accurate to refer to an individual as homosexual even if he has never engaged in the crass acts of oral or anal copulation with a member of his own sex?"

"You would be correct. Not having engaged in such behavior, the individual you describe would be entirely sincere in denying that he is a homosexual, since he is defining that term—as do most people—in regard to his *behavior*, not his psyche."

"Allow me at this point, if I may, to underscore your point, Dr. Hirschfeld. In the articles Mr. Harden wrote for *Die Zukunft*, he never once accused Kuno von Moltke of engaging in homosexual acts. He confined his description *solely* to the Count's homosexual orientation."

"To the best of my knowledge, that is correct. Some men, I might add, including some decidedly virile ones, are quite unaware of the feminine features of their own psyches or, for that matter, their erotic attraction to other men. Such an individual could accurately insist that he is not homosexual. He is not lying, nor guilty of perjury. According to his understanding, he cannot legitimately be labeled homosexual because he has never had sexual congress with another man."

Hirschfeld adds—in testimony that would become much quoted—that "whether a person engages in homosexual behavior is irrelevant from a scientific perspective. Just as some heterosexuals live celibate lives, so too can homosexuals express their love in an idealized, platonic manner."

"Moreover"—as Hirschfeld signals that he's still not finished, Bernstein unintentionally lets out a sigh of resignation. Catching it, Hirschfeld laughs good-naturedly and calls over, "Do not despair, Counselor, I have very nearly completed my testimony."

Bernstein gives Hirschfeld a mock-courtly bow, as the audience breaks into laughter.

"To conclude," Hirschfeld goes on, "the phenomenon of bisexuality is quite real. Many men who engage in erotic behavior with other men, at various points in their lives also have quite satisfactory sexual congress with women. And the same, in reverse, is true of lesbians; many have had sex with men and many are married to men. Indeed, as we know from the study of embryology, the fetus up to a certain point is undifferentiated in regard to sex."

Hirschfeld catches a glimpse of Bernstein rolling his eyes upward, as if to say "When *will* he stop talking?!"

In reaction, Hirschfeld makes a quick adjustment: "I fear some of this is too technical—too scientific—to be readily understandable to non-professionals."

There's a collective groan of agreement from the audience. In response, Hirschfeld good-naturedly says, " . . . I will try to conclude in everyday language."

Bernstein smiles with relief: "That would be much appreciated, Dr. Hirschfeld. If I may, I would like to pose a direct question to you."

"By all means. I assure you that I wish to make this difficult subject as intelligible as possible."

"And what an *excellent* job you've made of it!" Bernstein's tone is transparently insincere. "I believe we've now arrived at the point where I can pose directly the central question at issue in this trial."

As Hirschfeld's mouth opens to reply, Bernstein hurries on: "Was Mr. Harden accurate in describing Count von Moltke as 'homosexual,' or, to put it another way, Is Mr. Harden guilty of libel, as Count von Moltke insists? With the background you've already given us, I now ask you to address that question directly." Bernstein gives Hirschfeld a sharp look. "And *only* that question."

"Certainly," Hirschfeld agreeably responds. "To do justice to the question, however, I must begin with—"

"—forgive me, Dr. Hirschfeld, but given the lateness of the hour, we do not wish, surely, to try the court's patience." Bernstein's exhaustion is now patent.

Hirschfeld "innocently" sails on: "I simply wish to make clear that I have no personal acquaintance with any of the parties to this legal suit. The conclusions I've offered are drawn not only from my scientific studies but from what I've observed in the course of this trial. I refer in particular to the testimony of Count von Moltke's wife. She has made it clear that he is strongly aversive to sexual contact with women. I would add that his visage appears unmanly, neurasthenic, lacking in strength and vigor. Conclusive as well, in my opinion, is the fullness with which he has expressed his romantically passionate devotion and intense love for, among other men, Prince Eulenburg and Kaiser Wilhelm II."

"The court duly notes, Dr. Hirschfeld"—Bernstein's tone drips with sarcasm—"that your admirable integrity propels you to situate your observations so carefully. Now then: *do* let us proceed."

"In conclusion, then, I believe that given the plaintiff's feminine side, which strongly deviates from the norm, he could accurately be described as an 'unconscious homosexual.'"

Hirschfeld's statement is so unexpectedly stark that it produces a considerable stir among the spectators.

The judge uses his gavel to quiet the courtroom, while Bernstein, nearly inaudible, profusely compliments Hirschfeld on having concluded his testimony.

As he rises to step down from the witness box, Hirschfeld again speaks, his voice carrying over the courtroom commotion: "I want it to be absolutely clear that I am not saying Count von Moltke ever progressed to actual sexual activity with other men. I've heard no evidence to that effect. The Count has not broken the law as defined by Paragraph 175 in the German penal code."

In the ensuing tumult the judge manages to adjourn the court until the following day.

On reconvening the next morning, von Moltke's lawyer begins calling witnesses for what turns out to be a brief and pedestrian response. He attempts no cross-examination of Hirschfeld's testimony, though it proves centrally important—and immediately controversial, with some of his fellow experts questioning the very existence of a "psychical" form of homosexuality ("Is a man's 'softness of skin,'" one asks, "also a sign of psychic homosexuality?").

In the upshot, the judge acquits Harden of the libel charge—which is tantamount to validating the assertion that von Moltke *is* homosexual—and the Count is forced to pay all court costs. In announcing his verdict, the judge declares that von Moltke clearly "has an aversion to the female sex and an attraction to the male sex." The judge adds, echoing Hirschfeld's testimony, that Moltke "has certain feminine features"—his passive temperament is cited—"characteristic of homosexuals." The judge then adopts Hirschfeld's distinction between homosexual acts and "abnormal sexual *feelings*" in order to conclude that, although no evidence of von Moltke *acting* on his attraction to men has been claimed or established, he *is* homosexual "and has not been able to disguise this orientation in the presence of others."

Von Moltke has lost his libel suit, but the situation is hardly concluded. A storm of outrage at the verdict sweeps the country. Press coverage of the trial has been extensive, with dozens of journalists from continental Europe as well as from Germany present throughout the proceedings. People everywhere begin to discuss the startling concept of a homosexual *identity* that's emerged during the trial. Many are not persuaded, and others (mostly from among the aristocracy) protest the "dangerous" precedent of trying a member of the ruling elite as a common criminal—and finding him guilty no less.

Those on the left, oppositely, consider the courtroom revelations proof of the "debauchery" of the Kaiser's entourage, and members of the Social Democratic Party enlarge that indictment to include the "idle, decadent" upper classes in general. The response of monarchists and conservatives is to denounce the trial as a dangerous farce. They ascribe Moltke's weak legal defense to a deliberate plot engineered—the means unspecified—by the Social Democrats, and further charge that Harden made his accusations not out of moral concern about homosexuality, but as a backdoor way of discrediting the Kaiser.

"Hirschfeld the Jew" is widely attacked in the press for having invented accusations against his "betters." That much Hirschfeld expected. But his composure is decidedly ruffled by the sharp criticism he sustains from within the ranks of his own Scientific Humanitarian Committee. A heterosexual ally in the petition drive to repeal Paragraph 175 tells Hirschfeld that one regrettable result of his testimony will be to conflate feelings of deep friendship between men with homosexual desire; as a correspondent of Hirschfeld's puts it, "I lived for three years as a student inseparable from my dear, old friend . . . We had not the slightest notion that any suspicion could stain such a relationship. I reject out of my own experience the assumption that such friendship must always carry a sexual connotation." A number of wealthy homosexual supporters resign from the SHC out of fear that Hirschfeld might someday prove willing to testify against *them*. Financial contributions fall from over 17,000 marks in 1907 to a little over 6,000 in 1909.

The scientific views Hirschfeld expressed during his testimony also come in for censure, even ridicule, from fellow sexologists. Adolf Brand, editor of *Der Eigene*, angrily denounces the equation Hirschfeld drew at the trial between effeminacy and homosexuality. Brand and others reject as well his insistence on the biological nature of homosexual eros. To these critics, homosexuality is culturally, not biologically, determined—as are definitions of "masculinity" and "femininity."

Moltke and Eulenburg—through letters, intermediaries (in particular their close mutual friend, Axel Varnbüler) and occasional clandestine meetings—consider their plight and review their options. During one secret meeting, Moltke, certain that his reputation has been irremediably damaged, is reduced to tears. "Harden," he weepily tells Eulenburg, "has put an absolutely devilish misinterpretation on our affectionate being."

"We must not view ourselves in terms invented by our enemies," Philipp responds, meaning to comfort his friend. "We were simply given different shells and differently coloured wings than most men. We have both been granted the magic gifts of artistic talent. Let us be gladdened, not downcast."

"I do not have your strength, Philipp. Not even your bearing."

"We are middle-aged men, Kuno. We are not fragile youths. You remain, after all, aide-de-camp to His Majesty. That is no small mark of distinction. So long as we serve him, we are required to present an effective image to the world."

"It is you he values. Poor Kuno serves only at your behest," Moltke says, with more than a touch of self-pity.

"The Emperor takes everything personally, as you know. In order to get and keep his approval, never forget to praise him. If you do not fail to express appreciation for his ideas and actions, he will not fail to sustain you. But if you—if we—fall into a hole, he will let us lie there."

"You speak as if in a trance! We *are* in a hole!" Moltke cries. "Are you telling me the Kaiser will do nothing to extricate us from it?"

"That is precisely what I am telling you. We must act on our own behalf. If we do, the Kaiser will continue to embrace us. Remember what happened to my poor brother, and let it be a lesson."

"Ah, poor Friedrich! His Majesty was not kind."

"His Majesty had little choice. When Friedrich's wife accused him of 'unnatural passions,' he should have resigned at once from his regiment and demanded an investigation to clear his name. Once the charges became public, His Majesty had no choice but to treat Friedrich with absolute hostility. He even demanded—this you may not know—that I break off all contact with my brother. But I refused."

"Only you could have gotten away with such a refusal."

"I survived because I pleaded illness—severe rheumatic pain—and retired to Liebenberg. After a time, I returned to court. But it has never been quite the same between us. I have seen for the first time how hard His Majesty can be, and how all-consuming his ego. Let us act accordingly this time around."

"I do not see, my dear Phili, how we are in any less of a hole than was your dear brother."

"Do you trust me, Kuno?"

"You know I do. Why, what are you planning?"

"On the assumption that I still have powerful friends—a shaky assumption, perhaps—my goal is to get the verdict in your trial reversed."

"What?" Kuno is suddenly animated. "Is that possible?!"

"I believe it can be voided on grounds of 'faulty procedures'—a mistrial, in other words. That would be the first goal. Then I will 'persuade' the state prosecutor to retry Harden—this time on grounds of criminal libel."

"I'm astonished. What a marvel you are!"

"I haven't done anything yet. My first step, I think, should be a consultation with Axel. He's more a master of intrigue than the two of us combined. He'll know how to prepare for all eventualities."

Axel Varnbüler himself has one primary goal: to avoid any suspicion of homosexuality falling on his own head. He lets it be known that he considers Phili's male friendships "highly idealized and often enraptured"—a formulation sufficiently abstract to avoid the charge that he's turning on an old friend. At the same time Axel goes to considerable lengths to spread rumors of his own extramarital affairs with women. When Kuno Moltke sends him a tempestuous letter lamenting the fact that their "beloved circle" is in jeopardy and urging that "we must hold on to each other doubly, more firmly," Axel decides not to reply. Ah poor Kuno, Axel thinks to himself. All suffering sensibility, and no sense.

Axel's attitude toward Philipp Eulenburg is quite different. Phili remains, at least for the time being, a powerful figure, perhaps not as close to the Kaiser as he'd once been, but far closer than Axel. He agrees to Phili's suggestion of a secret meeting at the estate of Count Emil Görtz, a close mutual friend whose sexual "abnormality" has also been rumored. Görtz, like many in the Liebenberg Circle, is drawn far more to the worlds of theater and art than to the administrative or military duties for which they've been groomed and at which they've often groaningly labored. When Axel and Philipp arrive—separately—at Görtz's estate, he leads each directly—avoiding even perfunctory contact with his family—to an inconspicuously small room off the library. Discreetly, he leaves the two alone.

Axel, with no intent at irony, begins by asking after Philipp's wife and children.

"I enjoy my family but little," Philipp says with impolitic candor. "Not because of our current situation. I love my family, but I go my own way ..."

"Yes—what I call 'the oppressive atmosphere of the 'normal,'" Axel replies with a smile. "We must take care to preserve the specialness of our innermost being."

"And take care as well," Philipp enigmatically responds, "to shroud our efforts at self-preservation."

"Which is something, I fear, that our beloved Kuno is not adept at." Axel lowers his lanky frame into a chair, and Philipp follows suit. "Lily's testimony at the trial," Axel continues, "in my view sealed the verdict against him."

"I warned Kuno before he married her that she was a jealous vixen. The more I got to know her, the less I liked her. Still, I believe she can be influenced; and if not, then discredited. Kuno's reputation can be cleared, though he doesn't make it easy. The first step, of course, is to ensure a second trial. I'm grateful for your help in that regard."

"I assure you that I am the grateful one. My appointment to the Federal Council is due entirely to your influence with His Majesty. Now I have an opportunity to repay my indebtedness."

Philipp smiles warmly. "You exaggerate the importance of my intervention, I assure you."

"I know better. But never mind. Your modesty, dear Philipp, has always been one of your most endearing qualities. That, and your reluctance ever to push your own advantage. I, on the other hand, am as thick-skinned as the rest of the hippopotami who surround His Majesty."

Philipp laughs. "That long black beard you're sporting is, I believe, the telltale sign of a plotter."

"A plotter who brings news that will please you. Von Bülow, well aware of the role you played in securing the Chancellorship for him, is willing to exert backstairs influence in securing a mistrial."

Philipp jumps up from his chair with excitement. "It's the Guiding Hand of Providence that lies behind this! I feel certain of it!"

"I don't share your mystical confidence, dear Phili. Especially since Bülow is carefully hedging his bets."

"I don't follow."

"Bülow has secured the secret reports of the vice police and sequestered them in the Foreign Office safes."

Philipp reacts with alarm, which Axel picks up on. "Yes, Phili, some of those reports do name both you and Kuno."

"Good heavens," Phili whispers.

"Bülow thinks the implications are serious. He asks me to convey to you his opinion that you should forego a second trial and go on 'sick leave' until this whole nasty business dies down."

"That old bully! He's been waiting for the chance to get me out of the picture. I put nothing past him."

"In Bülow's view, the secret files contain material that would not only damage you personally but would reflect badly on the Kaiser as your close friend."

"Bülow knows perfectly well that I would do nothing to undermine public confidence in the regime! He's trying to force me from the scene. So much for his gratitude about the Chancellorship!"

Axel hesitates before completing the picture, but decides he must. Lowering his voice, he quietly adds, "Bülow suggests you go abroad for a time."

"Admit my guilt by fleeing, eh?! Certainly not!" Philipp wheels around to face Axel: "If you can arrange for a second trial," he says firmly, "I give you my solemn promise to appear."

"Very well then. Consider it done."

Knowing all three principals—Moltke, Eulenburg, and Harden—Count Harry Kessler has followed the first trial closely, noting down his reactions in his voluminous diary. His interest is not impersonal, having himself, at age 40, recently taken up with a 17-year-old male lover, the bicycle racer and jockey, Gaston Colin. In the summer of 1907, on one of Kessler's frequent trips to Paris, he commissions Aristide Maillol—one of several artists his patronage helps to support—to do a nude sculpture of Colin. Yet in his diary Kessler never once directly references sexual desire or activity in relation to him; Colin is simply described as "a very nice, clever young fellow" whom he's decided to help out from time to time (and will continue to do so even after Colin marries).

Yet if circumspect, Kessler now and then does express views in the privacy of his diary about sexuality in general that are dangerously in advance of official morality (which he describes as "resting merely on social convention"). To Kessler, the moral of the Oscar Wilde case is that there "is no ugly sensuality. Everything that is truly sensual is beautiful . . . A beautiful boy's body and the great love that Plato establishes as the axis of the world are—like cause and effect—one." In his view, so-called "perversion" is best seen as representing the "penetration of the imagination into sexual desire"; he believes "there is no sexual act that some culture or drive has not promoted, and you never hear that those practicing it suffered somehow in their 'psyche.'" Kessler sees no reason, other than baseless prejudice, "why it should be more objectionable to amuse yourself with young lads rather than with young girls." "It is unnatural," he writes in one diary entry, "that Don Juan would be limited to the *female*." Generalizing further in another entry, he rhetorically asks, "Are there absolute truths?" His answer is an unqualified "No . . . They are not absolutely true but indeed absolutely compelling."

He is, however, temperamentally a noncombatant. He stands poised above the fray, every fray—the exact opposite of Harden, whose pugnacity and doggedness he finds mildly alarming. Politically, Kessler often agrees with Harden—agrees, above all, that the Kaiser's "personality is certainly damaging the prestige and position of Germany"—but he writes those sentiments in his diary, not in the pages of *Die Zukunft*, as Harden does. Kessler disapproves, however, of Harden's penchant for personal attacks, including his recent naming of Count Johannes Lynar as another member of what Kessler humorously refers to as the "black band of allied criminals"; yet at the same time he feels that "if you want to amuse yourself with boys, you should at least refrain," as Lynar has not, "from doing it with your orderlies."

On the few occasions when Kessler has run into Moltke and Eulenburg at Cornelia Richter's salon, where literature and music are discussed far more often than politics, he's found them both congenial; Moltke, in particular, has always been kind to him. While the first trial was still in progress, Moltke put in a surprise appearance at the Richter salon one evening, and Kessler went out of his way to express sympathy to him, praising "the dignity" he'd been maintaining throughout the ordeal. Knowing that Harden has little personal prejudice against homosexuals, Kessler wonders—as he writes in his diary—"How far are you justified in using a prejudice that you don't share to destroy a political opponent and, to be sure, not simply politically, but utterly and totally?"

Kessler decides that his dinner with Harden, however abrupt its close, has placed them on familiar enough terms to allow him to put the question to him directly. When he does, Harden points out that Moltke, not he, brought the libel suit, thus making a trial inevitable. Kessler can't get himself to condemn Harden completely, but he continues to feel that the journalist's intelligent, decent instincts are at war with his "passionate, extremely egoistic temperament"—and his divided soul makes him, in Kessler's view, a dangerous and unscrupulous foe.

The second trial opens on December 18, 1907. It lasts only two weeks, but within the first few days the conclusion is predictable. The proceedings open with "expert" medical witnesses attesting to the "fact" that Moltke's wife, Lily von Elbe, is "obviously" suffering from what they call "unstable hysteria." Given her state of mind, the learned doctors testify, the inflammatory account she gave of her marriage with Count von Moltke at the first trial should be considered utterly unsound, and discounted.

Next up on the stand are Count Moltke and Prince Eulenburg, each of whom in turn swears under oath that he has never transgressed in regard to the strictures of Paragraph 175 (which judicial opinion has earlier interpreted to mean anal intercourse, leaving activities ranging from hand-holding to mutual masturbation to oral sex between men non-actionable). While Eulenburg is on the stand, Bernstein, still Harden's advocate, presses him to state whether or not he's ever committed *any* homosexual act.

Eulenburg's evasive reply—that he has "never engaged in any 'depravity' whatsoever"—is allowed to pass, and the emboldened Prince then proceeds effectively to challenge the distinction Hirschfeld had drawn in the first trial between psychical homosexuality and actual homosexual contact. The former, Eulenburg heatedly insists, is nothing more or less than the kind of deeply spiritual male friendship that the German nation has long rightly prided itself on. "I have been an enthusiastic friend in my youth," he tells the court, "and am proud of having had such good friends! Had I known that twenty-five to thirty years later a man would come forward to claim that potential filth lurked in every such friendship, I would have truly forsaken the search for friends. The best that we Germans have is friendship, and friendship has always been honored!"

Magnus Hirschfeld is also put briefly back on the stand—just long enough to retract his earlier statement that Moltke was, psychically-speaking, homosexual. Hirschfeld claims that he based that conclusion primarily on Lily von Elbe's now "discredited" account of her marriage—though at the time he'd in fact given a number of additional reasons for concluding that Moltke was "psychically" homosexual. This is not Hirschfeld's finest hour; he'll later acknowledge that his initial testimony was the single worst professional error of his career.

The verdict in the second trial is handed down on January 4, 1908: Harden is convicted of libel and sentenced to a prison term of four months. In the commotion that follows, Axel Varnbüler rushes to the front of the courtroom to embrace his dear friends, Moltke and Eulenburg. Within days, the Kaiser—who'd been enraged at the results of the first trial and had (in Kessler's view) shown "ignoble haste" in "suddenly discarding his old friends without even hearing them"—lets it be known that he's delighted with the new verdict and looks forward to once again (metaphorically) clasping Moltke and Eulenburg to his bosom. In his view both men have been fully exonerated of the "perfidious" attempts at character assassination during the first trial—brought, the Kaiser insists, by the wretched enemies of his regime. The so-called Eulenburg Affair is over.

Or so it is widely thought. What few have taken into account is the bellicosity and resourcefulness of Maximilian Harden. He's convinced that Eulenburg has perjured himself in denying any participation in homosexual acts and is determined to find the evidence that will irrefutably prove it. Personally he rather admires Eulenburg as a decent man whose pacific temperament has long served as a brake on the Kaiser's combative dreams of an expansive German empire. But if Harden can restore his own good name only at Eulenburg's expense, then so be it.

Harden lays his plans carefully. He hires a private detective to scour the resort area around Lake Starnberg in southern Germany—where Eulenburg often took vacations in the 1880s, before his marriage—in search of potential witnesses. Through a series of bribes to local informants, the detective hits pay dirt. He's put in touch with two men, Jakob Ernst, a day laborer, and Georg Riedel, a fisherman whom Eulenburg had initially befriended and then hired as his valet. Both are reluctant to testify, but after being alternately threatened with imprisonment or reassured that the statute of limitations has run out and there's no risk of self-incrimination, they agree to appear as witnesses.

Harden sees one remaining problem: finding a sympathetic venue for the trial. He wants to avoid a Berlin courtroom, with its deferential attitude towards Prussian aristocrats, and devises a brilliant option: He persuades a journalistic friend, Anton Städele, a Bavarian editor, to publish an entirely bogus article claiming that Eulenburg paid Harden the enormous sum of a million marks to desist from further attacks. As agreed beforehand, Harden then brings suit against Städele for libel and arranges to have it heard on April 21, 1908 in a courtroom in Munich—a city known for its antagonism towards Prussian nobility. The libel suit hasn't been staged to disprove Harden's receipt of hush money—which never happened—but to provide him with an opportunity to put Ernst and Riedel on the stand. As pre-arranged, Städele "accuses" Harden in court of being unable to prove that Eulenburg ever engaged in homosexual relations, thus giving Harden the chance to present the new evidence that's been dug up in the interim.

On the stand, both men come across as entirely credible witnesses. Ernst claims to recall only a single instance of sexual contact with

Eulenburg, but Riedel confesses to a long-term arrangement. When he was 19, Riedel tells the court, Eulenburg seduced him, thus initiating a relationship that's continued until recently. His testimony is devastating:

"If I have to say it: What people say is true. What it's called I don't know. He taught it to me. Having fun. Fooling around. I don't know of no real name for it. When we went rowing we just did it in the boat. He started it. How would I have ever dared! And I didn't know anything about it. First he asked me if I had a girlfriend. Then it went on from there. I was willing to oblige a fine gentleman."

The trial causes a sensation—just as Harden has hoped and planned. To the German middle class, long convinced that "licentiousness" and moral rot are characteristic of the aristocracy, it now seems clear as day that princely prerogative has led an unworldly young fisherman into depravity.

Eulenburg's close friend, Axel Varnbüler, reads the court testimony in the newspaper and finds it "devastating." Deeply shaken, he no longer doubts that Eulenburg had earlier perjured himself and lied both to the court and to his friends. Varnbüler's primary concern is to avoid guilt by association. He considers Eulenburg "irretrievably lost" and is determined not to be brought down with him. He convinces himself that it's his duty as a friend to try and persuade Eulenburg to kill himself. Not wanting to risk being seen at Liebenberg, he sends an intermediary to convey the suggestion. He even manages to persuade himself that he's performing an act of great compassion. Unremarkably, Eulenburg doesn't see it that way. He takes to his bed, "severely unwell," continues to maintain his innocence, and claims that Harden bribed Riedel and Ernst to give false testimony.

But the damage is done. A mere two weeks after the sensational Munich trial, the state prosecutor indicts Eulenburg on charges of perjury. The police do a thoroughgoing search of his Liebenberg home and turn up a number of books relating to homosexuality issued by "Max Spohr Verlag"—Hirschfeld's own publisher and the man who had tried to persuade him not to appear as a witness at the first trial. The police also discover a letter Eulenburg sent Jakob Ernst in December 1907, imploring him to recant his testimony of events that happened "far too long ago"—which is tantamount to admitting that the "events" had indeed taken place.

Eulenburg's doctor claims that he's too ill to travel from his estate to Berlin in order to appear at the perjury trial. But the climate of opinion has decisively shifted: The court orders Eulenburg taken to a hospital in the capital to facilitate his availability. When the new trial opens on June 29, 1908, Eulenburg is carried into court on a stretcher. He again maintains his innocence, but does adjust his earlier testimony; what he now insists is that he has never engaged in any "*punishable* depravities" (judicial opinion has interpreted Paragraph 175 as criminalizing only anal copulation between men). But dozens of witnesses, one after another, take the stand to testify against him, including a working-class man from Munich who recounts looking through the keyhole of a hotel room and seeing Eulenburg having sex with another man. On July 13, Eulenburg collapses in court, and the doctors in attendance declare him "dangerously ill." In September, he is allowed to return to his Liebenberg estate. The trial is postponed until the defendant's health improves.

The outcome infuriates the Kaiser. He sends an indignant telegraph to Chancellor von Bülow saying he's been "very unpleasantly surprised" at the "sudden calamitous decision" of the court. Perhaps with Hirschfeld's testimony in mind, Wilhelm blames the destruction of his "close circle of friends" on "Jewish impudence, slander, and lies." But he also rages against the contradiction inherent in Eulenburg's apparent ability on the one hand to give a speech in his own defense, and the doctors on the other hand declaring him unfit to provide evidence. "How can these two things go together?" the Kaiser fulminates. "The trial should have continued, even if Eulenburg is consumed by the flames."

Harden sees matters quite differently. Though he's brought no public testimony against Moltke, he hints to a variety of prominent people that he's withheld a great deal of evidence implicating additional, highly-placed individuals. To those still pushing him explicitly to exonerate Moltke, Harden darkly implies that they will end up forcing him to "produce without scruple all evidence, letters, and witnesses and to give the matter a scope which for

years, at the greatest sacrifice" he has done his best to avoid. His own preference, Harden adds, is to let the matter lie dormant.

Unlike the Kaiser, Alex Varnbüler does come round. He soon changes
his mind about urging Eulenburg to commit suicide and gradually
renews—unlike the rest of Philipp's old friends—distant contact with
him. He no longer believes in Eulenburg's innocence, but he understands why his friend has had to insist upon it, given the climate of
opinion. After all, no less a figure than the famed psychiatrist Professor
Emil Kraepelin of Heidelberg University has spoken for most people in
classifying "contrary sexual proclivities" as a form of "lunacy"—along
with "cretinism" and "congenital feeblemindedness."

Yet another trial is convened in mid-1909, but Eulenburg again
faints in court and the proceedings are again postponed. For the next
decade—nearly up to the time of Eulenburg's death in 1921—he's subjected to periodic medical examinations with the aim of determining
whether he's fit to stand trial. He never is. Nor is he ever restored to
favor, which Harden himself comes to regret, given Eulenburg's tem-
perate influence on the Kaiser's saber-rattling tendencies—which will
soon enough escalate.

Hirschfeld, too, has reason to feel contrite. In declaring Moltke a "psychic" homosexual (and, by implication, Eulenburg as well), he's failed
to understand, or perhaps care, that the consequences for them, given
the hostility of public opinion, would be grave. And not only for them.
The prominence of the "culprits," and Harden's claim that he's withheld
a great deal of evidence about a still wider contamination, has left the
impression that the spread of homosexuality has reached epidemic pro-
portions in Germany. Support for the repeal of Paragraph 175 weakens
in tandem with a sharp rise in arrest rates under its aegis.

The "natural variant" views of Hirschfeld, and of Count Harry Kessler
as well, have little immediate impact at the turn of the century. Yet both
men are sanguine about the future. As Kessler writes in his diary, "Once
the 'outrage' has run its course—that is, in ten to twenty years—the movement will start once again with an intensity never achieved nor achiev-
able before." The result, he predicts, will be "a kind of sexual revolution

through which Germany will very quickly overtake the lead that France and England have had up to now in these things. Around 1920 we will hold the record . . . like Sparta in Greece, which is not the case today."

Kessler has uncannily predicted Weimar Germany of the 1920s.

~

PART II

COUNT HARRY KESSLER
AND WALTHER RATHENAU

"JUST LOOK AT that boy's buttocks!" Maillol cheerfully shouts. He and Harry Kessler are standing on the rail of their ship, having arrived in Naples that same morning. Maillol can hardly believe the beauty of the youngsters, one of whom has lost his bathing suit diving for the coins that passengers are tossing from the deck. Kessler is inwardly amused, along with feeling a trace of envy. With what ease, he thinks, does the sculptor—safely famous for his depictions of the female body—revel in the graceful athleticism of adolescent males. Whereas I, their true patron, must admire in silence.

Out loud he says, "Your praise is immodest, Aristide. After all, they're just ordinary boys."

"Modesty is a sentiment I do not recognize," Maillol replies, as they move down the rail towards the gangplank to disembark. "That's why I had my wife pose naked in front of my student, Claude, so he could get used to not thinking about it."

"Yet not even you can portray subjects *too* far beyond public acceptance."

"True. I'd like to sculpt men and women fornicating, but *Christians*"—he spits the word out—"would denounce such naturalness."

"Christianity, fortunately, is nearly dead," Harry replies with a laugh.

"Is Hofmannsthal joining us in Stromboli?" Maillol asks.

"No, he arrives the day after tomorrow. He'll meet us in Athens."

"I don't like poets and playwrights. Not that it matters."

"I don't care for him all the time myself. Nor his verse plays."

"Verse?—that's bad. Hurts the ears. I will not like this man. He's probably witty."

Kessler laughs. "Come, come Maillol. Give the fellow a chance. Mind you, he does have his faults."

"You see. I know."

"And can be *very agreeable*, too! Charming. You'll see."

With his father's death in 1905, Kessler has come into a considerable fortune, and, though he's already traveled widely, is eager to do more. When he suggests the 1908 trip to Greece to von Hofmannsthal and Maillol, Kessler doesn't know either man well, but he thinks the combination might prove interesting—he's become adept at putting together potentially creative partnerships.

Kessler first met Hofmannsthal through an old college friend from the University of Leipzig, and initially found him (as he wrote in his diary) "thoroughly nice and natural in manner." He soon developed a more nuanced view. While director of the Weimar Grand Ducal Museum, Kessler had invited any number of artists to come for extended stays—among them, André Gide, the playwright Gerhart Hauptmann, the theatrical innovator Gordon Craig and—on separate occasions—both Maillol and von Hofmannsthal. During Hofmannsthal's stay, his vanity soon became apparent, and Kessler considered it unwarranted, given the failure of his recent plays. He also developed doubts about Hofmannsthal's character, at one point acidly characterizing him as having "a sharp eye for the superficial depths of life." What also became obvious to Kessler over time was that Hofmannsthal took pride in his nervous sensitivity and his quicksilver change of moods. At the time of the trip to Greece in 1908, the Austrian poet was in his mid-30s, Kessler five years older, and Maillol six years older than that.

When at Weimar, Maillol had made a strong initial impression on Kessler, and he'd soon become the sculptor's foremost patron, a relationship that would last more than 30 years. He'd paid his first visit to Maillol in the summer of 1904 at his small house in the last French village on the coast before the Spanish border. When he knocked on the front door, Kessler was startled to see a woman appear on the balcony above, glance down at him, and then shout "Aristide! Aristide!" in the direction of the fruit orchard that surrounded the house. Maillol, in his early forties, soon appeared, his long, untrimmed black beard draped over the front of his blouse, a peasant's broad-brimmed hat on his head, luminescent blue eyes drawing attention away from his gaunt frame, and (as Kessler described it) "a long eagle's nose of a pronounced Spanish type." Maillol considered Catalonia, not France, his true homeland.

On that first visit, Maillol led Kessler to his studio, a small building in the middle of the orchard that, aside from the tools of his trade, contained nothing but a solid wooden table and two chairs. Maillol showed Kessler some recent sketches, as well as the model he'd made of a crouching woman. Kessler immediately bought the model for 800 francs, and, in looking over the sketches, was particularly struck by one of a squatting female figure. He proposed to Maillol that he sculpt it life-size in stone, and purchased it in advance.

Over the next few years, there had been many visits to Maillol. On one occasion Kessler asked him why he never did male figures. "Because, unlike Rodin," the sculptor replied, "I cannot afford models, and the young boys in town won't pose for me in the nude. For women figures I can use my wife; if you put your hand up her skirt," he chortled, "you will feel a block of marble. I would like to do a male figure. I find the body of the man much more beautiful than that of the woman." Kessler decided on the spot that he'd send his young lover, Gaston Colin, to pose in the nude for Maillol.

From the very beginning of the trip to Greece, Maillol, carrying the little he needs in a small sack, has seemed entirely at home. But when Hofmannsthal meets them in Athens on May 1, 1908, the mood changes. Hofmannsthal seems depressed. At dinner that first night, he confesses that, although he's traveled through Corinth on his way to meet them, nothing that he's seen so far interests him. What is it, he wants to know, that everyone adores so much about Greece?

"It's simple," Maillol responds, "It's the place in the world where every-thing I love was created. When I saw the figures of the Erechtheion," he tells Hofmannsthal, "I became so emotional I embraced one of them—until a guard pulled me away."

Greece, Kessler adds, represents a world view "in which all feelings and thoughts have their place; nothing has been banned or excluded."

Hofmannsthal shakes his head in disagreement. "No, no, I don't see it," he insists. "I don't grasp it. Perhaps that's why my plays, *Electra* and *Oedipus*, have failed. I cannot get a firm grip on this place." He seems far more upset, more deeply frustrated, than the situation warrants.

"My dear Hofmannsthal," Kessler says in an attempt at comfort, "you have only just arrived! Give yourself time. You've barely had a chance to look around."

As if not hearing Kessler, Hofmannsthal grows more, not less, agitated. "Venice! Venice is where I feel at home, not here! It is *my* misfortune, as I well know, *my* inadequacy, but nothing in this landscape crystallizes for me. Everything is in contradiction to everything else! *Barrenness*—the *barrenness* of the country oppresses me, jangles my nerves. I need woods, and rivers, and green fields—*these* are my life's blood, the source of my inspiration!"

He seems to the contained Kessler inordinately upset, nearly beside himself with wanton sadness. It's tragicomedy, Kessler thinks to himself, a form without appeal to me. He tries to soothe and reassure Hofmannsthal but he seems tempestuously, willfully, out of reach. Maillol lapses into complete silence, his disapproval manifest.

The next morning Hofmannsthal speaks more calmly, yet it's clear he remains unhappy. Maillol abhors the dandified, decides that Hofmannsthal embodies it, and proceeds to ignore him. Such detachment proves a red flag to a young poet who automatically assumes he should be the center of attention, and his anxiety heads towards petulance. Kessler has all his life learned to respond to turmoil with urbane poise, and he serenely announces that what they all need is to wend their way up to the Parthenon. Hofmannsthal replies testily that he prefers to read, and promptly retires to his hotel room.

Kessler and Maillol make their way to the Acropolis, Maillol stopping now and then to touch the marble columns lying haphazardly along the road. "It feels like the buttocks of a woman," he murmurs happily. "Here, feel them," he says, bringing Kessler's hand down on a column, "heated by the sun, it feels like flesh. You could sleep with these columns. You don't need women in this country—you have the columns." Maillol's eyes shine with happiness.

"It's the most beautiful day of my life," he tells Kessler.

Later that night, Hofmannsthal knocks on Kessler's hotel room door. Kessler opens it to find Hofmannsthal on the verge of tears. "I have never in my life wanted to leave a place so urgently!" he blurts out. "I wish I had never come. I feel I'm in prison, prison!"

Startled though he is, Kessler calmly invites Hofmannsthal into the room and pours him some cognac. "As I'm sure you know, my friend, you can leave whenever you wish. And our friendship will survive it, I promise you."

Hofmannsthal eases himself into a chair. A sip of the cognac seems to calm him. "I've tried to figure out what's wrong, but I cannot. I don't know why I feel so wretchedly out of sorts . . . I'm a mystery to myself . . ."

"My guess," Kessler offers, "is language."

"Language?"

"The fact that we've had to speak French the whole time, since Maillol knows no German. It's been a matter of politeness to use French. You're a *writer*, Hugo! The German language means everything to you! To strip you of it is like stripping off your skin!"

"You're right! By God, I do believe you're right!" The touch of hysteria in Hofmannsthal's voice doesn't reassure Kessler. Emotional exhibitionism, even the threat of it, always brings out his defensive reserve.

"Now, now," he says distantly. "I feel sure that tomorrow's excursion to Delphi will prove just the right tonic, will put you back into relationship with the Greece you once loved."

"How I wish that you and I, just you and I, could go by horseback through the Peloponnesus. How wonderful it would be to break camp at five in the morning and ride out into the beautiful mountain landscape."

Good heavens, Kessler thinks to himself. The dear boy really is over-doing his role as Romantic Poet.

"We cannot desert poor Maillol," Kessler finally says.

"And 'poor Maillol' does not ride, of course." There's more than a trace of rancor in Hofmannsthal's voice. "He refuses even to *mount* a horse. He says"—here Hofmannsthal adopts a coarse French accent—"it would break my ass."

"Mimicking one's friends isn't becoming, as you well know, Hugo." Kessler keeps his tone neutral. "Maillol is a decent fellow, though a little primitive for your—for our—taste. But do try and be kind to him. He is, as I say, a good man. *And* a great artist."

"Your specialty! It's all very well to *collect* us, but why insist that we socialize together?"

This is appalling, Kessler thinks. "Is it my turn, then, to be attacked?" he calmly asks. There's a pause, during which Hofmannsthal internally berates himself for being unfair. "I don't know how you put up with me, Harry," he says quietly.

As the needy little boy resurfaces; Kessler, a thoroughly agreeable man, feels his sympathy for Hofmannsthal returning: "That's not difficult," he replies, "you can be very loveable, Hugo. You're a person of many fine qualities. We all get to feeling down-and-out."

"Not Maillol."

Hofmannsthal does decide to stay. The next day, the three men board a ship at Piraeus and sail along the coast to Salamis. Once in the gulf, the waters grow rough, and both Hofmannsthal and Maillol become sea-sick; it's a bond of sorts. Kessler remains serenely alone on deck, glad for the respite from his two singular companions.

Hofmannsthal lasts another week, but not contentedly. On departing, he insists that overall he's had a splendid time. Everyone knows better. That same morning, on entering his own room, Kessler finds Hofmannsthal rummaging through his luggage, in the process actually opening a wrapped package—all on the pretext of looking for something to read. Kessler is horrified: "I felt," he writes in his diary, "like I was being slapped for letting someone, who was so far from a gentleman, come close to me." To Hofmannsthal he simply says, "I am astonished"—a rebuke from on high. That's enough to produce from Hofmannsthal a sobbing, overwrought apology hardly welcome to a man of Kessler's impeccably subdued manners. To forestall any extension of the uncongenial scene, he assures Hofmannsthal that he's already forgotten the matter. The friendship will survive. They will later even become collaborators on *Der Rosenkavalier*—though during that joint effort, Hofmannsthal will give Kessler additional grounds for remaining on his guard.

Left alone with Maillol, Kessler finds himself less taken with him. The vivid tales Maillol recounts over meals about his unhappy childhood, replete with sexually predatory priests, become less picturesque when accompanied by his habit of eating with his fingers and spitting out fish bones on the floor. Nor is Kessler pleased when it becomes clear that Maillol has a thousand tricks for disappearing when it comes time to pay for anything, even when just a few pennies are at issue. Not that the fastidious Kessler would dream of mentioning the matter, especially since he finds Maillol's cunning dodges somewhat comic. He's less amused at the impossibility of civilized conversation. Maillol has a habit of stating an opinion, often picturesque but usually narrow-minded and rigid, and then patronizing any contrary view as "stupid." A discussion, a conversation, is out of the question.

Kessler is relieved when the trip draws to a close. He's something of a genius at friendship and at introducing likely companions to each other. His experiment with Maillol and Hofmannsthal is among his rare failures.

To shake off his lingering disappointment, Kessler decides on a long tour through Normandy, partly by bicycle, with his young lover Gaston Colin. The trip is a kind of idyll, soothing compensation for the turbulence of the month in Greece. Gaston, a professional rider, is careful to adjust the pace to the older man's stamina—though Kessler himself is trim, and a bit vain about his appearance. The landscape south of Cherbourg enthralls him: "Large groves of trees," he writes in his diary, "green meadows, white chateaus, and on the lawns, apple trees, thick with red fruit and beautiful, fat cows, picturesquely spotted." It's a landscape, he feels, "only possible in Europe. Biking along the coast to Mont-Saint Michel, the scene becomes "unbelievably fairy-tale-like, the most mysterious, unfathomable landscape perhaps in the world . . . In this dream world with the castle rising sharply, the entire North, the entire northern Middle Ages, seems to be summed up, as the Parthenon, in its glowing, clearly defined seascape, does for the antique South."

The experience puts Kessler in a meditative mood about the role of art—his guiding passion—in the contemporary world. The times, he feels, are currently focused on politics, industry, science, and finance. Great art continues to be produced, but the sense that it's needed has diminished. Art has become a luxury, a plaything, a badge of prestige for the privileged. Few, to his despair, any longer feel that art is intrinsically necessary to daily life—in the sense that church architecture had been during the Middle Ages.

Being close to Gaston reminds Kessler of the curious contradiction in his own nature—his self-conscious restraint in regard to most matters, in contrast to his uninhibited enjoyment of sex.

He says as much to Gaston one day, who good-naturedly laughs; "I've noticed," he says.

"Don't you think it strange that most people equate sexual restraint with morality?"

"No, Harry," Gaston says with matter-of-fact maturity, "most people don't inhabit their bodies."

"True. And are therefore startled by the bodies of others. Whereas in Plato's world, no sensual feeling or activity is shameful or—"

"—no, no, Harry!" Gaston smiles indulgently, "no more lectures about the glories of ancient Greece!"

Kessler laughs. "I promise. That is, after I make one final, remarkably astute comment. Namely: The idea that sexual inhibition is somehow superior ethics is the besetting sin of Protestantism."

"Not bad. Fortunately, I'm Catholic!"

When the pair reach Le Mans-Auvours, they happen upon Wilbur

Wright, the pioneering American aviator. He shows them the "machine" he's been tinkering with and tells them that he's scheduled to actually fly it the following day at the Aero club—should it not be too windy. It isn't, and Harry and Gaston appear promptly on the field at 3:00 p.m. to watch the promised ascent. Wright actually manages three flights that day, and Kessler is enchanted with the plane's majestic and graceful arcs. Flying seems to him entirely safe—more so, he feels, than driving an automobile.

When they reach Paris, it's time for Gaston to take his leave; thanks to Harry providing the funds, he's off to participate in bike races in Spain, Africa, Italy, and the Tour de France. After parting, Gaston writes Harry devoted letters. "I am enormously bored without you," reads one. "Tell me what you are doing . . . All the time I think of you. I only live for you." Lest Harry take that last too literally, Gaston adds that he'd been "amusing himself nicely" with an English girl. That's fine with Harry: He recognizes bisexuality as a real phenomenon, not a strategy for evasion, and he recognizes, too, that any expectation of cross-generational monogamy is foolishness.

Indeed, within a few years Gaston will marry, and Harry will now and then send the couple money. The two men will continue to see each other occasionally, and as late as 1928 Gaston sends a note commemorating the 20th anniversary of their meeting: "I recall especially many days of happiness."

When Gaston departs for the races that day in 1908, Kessler consoles himself with visiting the numerous friends he's already made in Paris's artistic circles. By now he's added to his sumptuous list of friends and acquaintances Pierre Bonnard, Matisse, Degas, and Rodin—plus a host of others working in different media, like Richard Strauss and Rainer Maria Rilke.

Kessler has decided preferences among them but in general deplores the limited "breadth of spirit" he finds among Frenchmen, including most of those he ranks as artistic geniuses. He thinks them doctrinaire, insufficiently "connected," limited in their sympathies. When he first meets Degas, who looks—as he writes in his diary—like "an elegant grandfather," Kessler is astonished to learn that the painter *dislikes* fresh flowers. During one evening at the painter's house, when talk turns to the Bernheim family—the Belgian owners of a trend-setting Parisian art gallery—Degas bursts out, "How can you chat with people like that? With a Jewish Belgian who is a naturalized Frenchman! It's as if one wished to speak with a hyena, a boa. Such people do not belong to the same humanity as us."

The remark appalls Kessler (who isn't Jewish), but worse is to come. When talk later turns to a young painter named Chaplin, Degas and his other guests mock the man as a *tapette*—a homosexual. From there Degas flies into a rage against the popularization of art, the increase in exhibitions and artists; it's part and parcel, he says with disgust, of everyone being expected to have taste. From there Degas launches into a denunciation of the notion that everyone should be educated—"It's the Jews and the Protestants," he shouts, "who do that, who ruin races through education. Compulsory education is an infamy, voila!" Summing up the unpleasant evening, Kessler describes Degas as "a deranged and maniacal innocent."

Dining on another occasion at the home of the avant-garde dealer Ambroise Vollard, along with Bonnard, the publisher Louis Rouart, Odilon Redon, the Degas protégé Jean-Louis Forain, and others, Kessler finds the conversation mostly "malicious gossip"—though Redon, Kessler acidly notes, manages to maintain the silent, "ecstatic solemnity of one of his mystical and biblical lithographs." Forain, oppositely, gives free rein throughout to his caustic wit. When Bonnard brings up the subject of Max Harden (the first trial has just concluded) Kessler says that in his opinion "Moltke is certainly innocent but Harden"—Kessler had been impressed at his demeanor throughout the trial—"has acted in good faith."

Forain's immediate response is a question: "He's a Jew, Harden?"

"Yes," Kessler replies.

"And you believe that he has acted in good faith?" Forain smirks—"Go on, then! I hope that one will fleece him, your Harden. One doesn't calumniate people like that. After all, it's no one's business what Messieurs Moltke and Eulenburg do. One doesn't persecute a journalist. One despises him or buys him off."

Vollard manages to change the subject, telling the others that he's recently seen some paintings by the young artist Picasso: "He, like other young artists, is returning to Negro art—bigger than life-size heads, naïve in a Negro way, made of wide, square surfaces, almost like parquet pieces, brown, yellow, and black."

A look of disgust on his face, Bonnard turns to Kessler: "This will remain as a document of our artistic corruption. That a man like Picasso who has all the skill, all the range of colors, should feel the need to come back to this."

Kessler's reply is a diplomatic defense of sorts: "Clearly he believes that he's discovered power in such completely primitive things."

"Nonsense," Bonnard replies sharply. "Picasso has all the means of expression and nothing to express."

Louis Rouart shifts the subject sideways but not the tone of hidebound certainty. "What is absolutely essential," he announces, "is the need to preserve French culture from foreign influences—from the Negro certainly, but more important still, because more immediately threatening, from the flooding of the intellectual market by Jewish productions."

"I don't understand," Kessler replies, with calculated innocence. "Do you wish to bar their influence in science as well? Many of our leading scientific figures are Jews. I trust you've heard of Max Planck. Or perhaps Fritz Haber, or Einstein? They have opened up an entirely new way of understanding the universe."

"What they've opened up is maximizing the influence of the State," Rouart heatedly replies. "'The universe,' you say—the universe! The only counterweight to the leveling tyranny of the state and its elevation of the Jews is—*Catholicism!*"

Seeing that polemics, not mutual discussion, is the order of the day, Kessler tries to steer it into quieter waters. "I might agree that extreme nationalism poses a threat to all of Europe, but"—to his own surprise,

Kessler suddenly drops the ceremonial tone—"I fail to see that debate over the divinity of Christ is central to the matter."

An agitated Rouart jumps to his feet, in the process knocking over his chair. "The truth of Christianity is proven by the fact that it has been the chief source of French culture for nineteen centuries! This isn't a matter of debate!"

"Perhaps discussion, then," Kessler smoothly responds. "Is it not true that Buddhism has proven *its* truth even more forcefully, since it has been the chief source of Chinese culture for twenty-five centuries?"

Rouart loses his temper, goes red in the face: "To compare ... to compare French culture with, with Chinese culture is, is—well, the height of absurdity! If you cannot see that, then there is no point continuing this discussion!" Rouart curtly bows to the other guests, fails to thank his host—and abruptly leaves the room.

For Kessler, the two chief exceptions to his reservations about the human qualities of most French intellectuals and artists are Monet and Renoir. On his first visit to Monet's home in Giverny in 1903, Kessler finds a man of "simple and clear" speech and gestures, lacking any trace of bitterness towards those "who did him a bad turn" in the past—in all, "a beautiful, open character." With Renoir—already nearing 70 when Kessler meets him and suffering from rheumatism, his hands and fingers thickening with knob-like growths—he has but to speak, Kessler writes in his diary, and he becomes "a kind of 'Prince Charming,' enchantingly fresh and youthful: the spirit, tempo, voice of a twenty-year-old, and always—no matter what he says—the palpable proximity to women and love that colors and warms all of his utterances." Renoir's only complaint to Kessler is that the recent moralistic turn away from the nude figure "will soon make it impossible to find models." Kessler falls deeply and permanently under the spell of Renoir's personality.

In England, Kessler uses—just as he has in Paris—his initial contacts with gallery owners and art critics to gradually broaden his access to many of the leading figures in the world of English painting, theater, music, and dance. And because he's himself a splendid companion—knowledgeable, charming, and sensitive—access often leads to genuine friendship. Among the longest-lasting of his connections is his friendship with Gordon Craig, the path-breaking theater designer and director, whose 1903 production of Ibsen's *Vikings* Kessler thought remarkable.

The young painter Augustus John is another early acquaintance. Though rarely given to hyperbole, Kessler pronounces John "the most important painter of English art," worthy of comparison with the 18th-century French painter Chardin—one of his few overestimates. Somewhat diffident and modest himself, Kessler is drawn to John's compensating forcefulness (which others see as mere bluster). He even accompanies John to a boxing match in Whitechapel, though he saves some of his reactions to the event for his diary: "The boxers fought naked, or almost as good as naked, in swimming trunks and shoes. A few magnificently slender and thoroughbred young fellows among them."

Kessler keeps his personal tastes regarding sexual attraction mostly to himself, and rarely introduces his part-time lover, Gaston Colin, to anyone in his social set. Yet he has strong views on the subject. When Kessler meets the English writer Arthur Symons, who co-edits with Aubrey Beardsley the "decadent" journal *Savoy*, he finds him dry and gaunt—ascribing his appearance to repressed homosexuality.

As a younger man, Harry Kessler's political views are much less adventuresome than his taste in art—and not predictive of his later emergence as a socialist sympathizer. In his mid-20s, he's still conservative enough to question whether "the democratic impulse is the friend or enemy of high culture," and he expresses doubt in his diary as to whether the masses have sufficient patriotic "fanaticism" to sustain a functional government. The state, in his view, requires a large number of civil servants to function well, and Kessler doubts if the masses are morally and intellectually up to the job (not that the Kaiser is offering it to them). "The mistake of the democratic principle," Kessler writes, "is an overestimation of the sum of intellect and an underestimation of the sum of character that is necessary for the fulfillment of civic duties."

The youthful Harry Kessler shows little awareness that his wide range of opportunities places him among the fortunate few, nor does he demonstrate any marked sympathy for the vast multitude who lack his options. The aesthetic young man who, on a visit to Oxford, adores its "little Gothic windows" and "hundred-year-old roses," also describes "one of the chief pleasures" of a trip to the Derby at Epsom as "tossing a pin at a live Negro. He sticks his head through a hole and for a penny anyone who wishes can throw a ball at his skull; who hits the target gets a prize." Such off-handed racism is common in Europeans of the day— which doesn't prevent them from deploring the fact that in the United States black men are routinely lynched.

Harry's youthful loyalties are primarily directed to his prestigious (noblemen only) Third Guard Lancers of the Prussian army, and his sympathy for the starving multitude is confined largely to starving artists—a number of whom, including Edvard Munch, he does help to support. Harry as a young man places most of his confidence in the handful of aristocrats who stand at the apex of the governing class which bases its behavior—so young Harry chooses to believe—on familial traditions of honor; though Kessler wants them thoroughly monitored by a free press and public opinion.

Fortunately for his character, Harry is homosexual—the one vantage point available to him for understanding what it's like not to belong, to reside among the despised. And the glimmers of empathy he shows as a young man for the less fortunate will expand dramatically over the years—ultimately earning him the soubriquet of "The Red Count." Even when still in his teens, he deplores the fact that "it is very cheap fun to exult over people who are too weak to hurt you." And by age 21 he's ascribing the common view that "a straight nose is more beautiful than a hooked or even a flat one" to "certain prejudices of race and education." When in Japan in 1892 as part of the standard "finishing school" grand tour for young male aristocrats, he finds the image of Buddha, eyes half closed, "meditating in blessed calm," more worthy of emulation than the hysterics of Christianity's martyrs or the bloodthirsty zeal of its warring crusaders.

Nor does Kessler, even as an essentially apolitical young man, regard with any great awe the notion of a powerful leader, and certainly not the "All-High" Kaiser Wilhelm II. When presented at court in 1895, the glittering spectacle of brocaded gowns, muted candlelight, embroidered uniforms, satin-jacketed pages, and fearsomely rigid sentries, does dazzle Kessler—but does not persuade him of their worth. As for the Kaiser, gaudily gotten up to outshine all others, his two predominant moods, it seems to Kessler, are glazed discomfort and nervous excitability. The whole scene reeks to him of "affectation" which—even as a young man—he deplores in all its guises.

The Kaiser's third posture, tactless effusion, has recently been embodied in his decision to line the boulevard surrounding Tiergarten park, Berlin's largest, with a row of third-rate, kitschy statues depicting his Hohenzollern ancestors. The sight of them is so repellent to Kessler that to avoid seeing them he always makes a point when crossing the Tiergarten of taking an indirect, time-consuming path.

∾

Returning to Germany late in 1908 after some nine months of traveling abroad, Kessler, like most true cosmopolites, isn't particularly pleased to be back—though he has no wish to separate himself permanently from Berlin, or from Weimar (where he's retained a home). Both cities serve, as he puts it, as "a sort of mythical background, approximately like 'heaven' for Christians." Central to Kessler's sense of place is the superb apartment in Berlin that his friend Henry van de Velde—the pioneering Belgian designer and future founding member of the Bauhaus—has created for him at 28 Kothnerstrasse. Its uncluttered, understated elegance perfectly mirrors the personality of its owner—just as its walls, covered with Kessler's large and growing collection of Impressionist and post-Impressionist art, reflects his passionate involvement in contemporary culture.

His second home in Weimar is also a temple to art, its white book-cases filled to the brim, its walls and tabletops covered with small sculp-tures and large multicolored canvases—the whole somehow managing to combine a sense of restless intensity with absolute equilibrium. Kes-sler's celebrated "at homes" include delicately blended meals, musical performances of virtuoso excellence, and a Rilke or a Gerhardt Haupt-mann reading from one of their recent works while leaning against the fireplace or standing in front of the ancient bronze Chinese vessel that the artists of three nations have presented to Kessler in gratitude for his understanding and support. It's a setting of privileged perfection, in his case a reflection less of snobbery than of refinement of spirit.

If as a young man Kessler primarily isolated himself in the world of the aesthete, by the time he reaches his mid-30s he's become increas-ingly absorbed in political issues—not least because of his developing friendship with Walther Rathenau. When the two men first meet at Cornelia Richter's salon, Kessler is immediately struck by Rathenau's imposing physical presence—tall, with fierce, anguished eyes, measured movement, and a deep voice seemingly projected from a great distance, as if the speaker is covered by a wall of glass. His conversation is mes-merizing; he speaks with equal fluency and insight about the Kaiser ("His misfortune is that he came to the throne too young, before he had learned about the *resistance* of the world"), and the rivalry between Germany, England, and America ("England has all the preconditions for world domination ... Germany's trump card is its enormous effi-ciency and conscientiousness"). Kessler decides at once that Rathenau is "someone with whom it pays to come together." They soon start to see each other with increasing regularity.

Walther Rathenau's father, Emil, established the family fortune when he bought the European rights to Edison's patent, formed the Allge-meine Elektrizitätsgesellschaft (AEG), and over time became widely known as "the (Jewish) Bismarck of Germany's industrial empire." Emil was a hardworking, shrewd man—and a tough taskmaster to his son. Dismissive of Walther's philosophical bent and artistic gifts, he made him work for years in the company's trenches, from which he gradually ascended to the AEG hierarchy. On Emil's death in 1915, Walther will not only become head of the company, but will be simultaneously serving on the boards of no less than 86 German companies.

Rathenau, like Kessler, develops a large number of acquaintances in a wide variety of fields. Unlike Kessler, he has few real friends, prefers solitude, and can be overbearing and disdainful. The genial Kessler comes to regard Rathenau's imperious side as a shield against intimacy—with acute loneliness its end product. He isn't intimidated by Rathenau's hauteur, as are many others; he's seen worse, far worse and with far less reason, among the dullards of the aristocracy—none of whom, in Kessler's opinion, can match Rathenau's acute political instincts and conversational brilliance.

Within the strict guidelines that he imposes on closeness, Rathenau is drawn to Kessler's easy sociability, exquisite manners, and artistic sensibility—drawn precisely to those qualities he feels lacking in himself. The two soon become close enough to dine together with some frequency. For Kessler these occasions are true feasts—of the intellect. He regards Rathenau as a superb guide and mentor through the confusing thicket of current political intrigue, and their dinners together often go on for hours, with Kessler usually deferring to Rathenau's deeper knowledge of public affairs—and to his loftily authoritative intellect and spellbinding voice. But Kessler's intelligence is also keen, though oriented more toward people than politics, and he sometimes enjoys tweaking Rathenau with an arch insight or interjecting a witty aside to gently puncture one of his more Delphic pronouncements.

Invited to dine at Rathenau's one evening at his spacious home—a small palace, really—in the Freienwalde, along with Hugo von Hofmannsthal and the theater director Max Reinhardt, Kessler deliberately arrives a bit early; he wants the chance to get Rathenau's opinion on the shift in attitude he sensed on his recent trip to London.

The Freienwalde house had been built a hundred years earlier for Queen Louisa, the Princess of Prussia, and as a servant ushers Kessler into the salon, he's struck again at the beauty of its white and silver décor, as well as the adjoining room with its Chinese rice-paper paintings on the walls and embroidered yellow chairs. Kessler considers the house "a jewel of decorative art, light, alive, and feminine"—so curiously at odds with Rathenau's formidable exterior.

Rathenau appears almost at once and the two adjourn to his study, a rather overstuffed room (in Kessler's opinion) with bookshelves and uncomfortably large leather chairs—a more obvious reflection of its owner's personality than the entryway salons. After the usual pleasantries, Kessler surprises himself with the naïve-sounding way he formulates his quandary to Rathenau: "I don't think as well of the English as I once did. Am I wrong?"

Rathenau seems surprised at the question. "If you refer to our deteriorating relationship with England, I wholly blame the Kaiser."

"No, I meant the comment more generally."

"You'll have to explain. Aren't you, by the way, descended from Irish-English stock—on your mother's side, I believe?"

"I am. And as a youngster I spent two years at St. George's at Ascot. What's more, I've haunted English museums since my twenties and go back and forth to London frequently. I still go into raptures over the William Blakes at the South Kensington Museum."

"Then what *are* you referring to? I don't understand."

"I can't quite explain it, but I feel a decided decline in enthusiasm for all things English. Perhaps I'm maturing politically." Kessler smiles: "That sounds foolish, I suppose. If my politics *have* 'matured,' I hold you to blame."

"A charming indictment. I accept it willingly."

"It's the damned English ruling class. It's so brutally restrictive and closed-minded."

"Compared to what? The German Junkers are positively paranoid in their obsession with blood lines. Surely you know that King Edward, when still the Prince of Wales, introduced Jews into his own social set."

"You mean Lord Rothschild and Baron de Hirsch."

"Of course that's who I mean. And now that he's King, they're *still* his intimate friends. A cardinal sin in the Kaiser's eyes."

"But Bertie's his *uncle!*"

"We don't refer to the King any longer as 'Bertie,'" Rathenau says in an admonishing tone. "He's King Edward VII."

"You admire the King?"

"You don't?" Rathenau's raised eyebrows forecast a thunderclap.

"But all those dissolute years of womanizing and . . . and frivolity . . ."

"How would you like to wait around for six decades for the chance to rule?! And all the while, your mother is looking down her nose at you as if you're an incompetent fool. It's a wonder King Edward has turned out so well."

Kessler is genuinely surprised; he's never heard Rathenau speak favorably of anyone in power. "I see . . ." he says tentatively, with no idea of how to continue.

Rathenau helps him over the awkward spot. "When the King agreed to meet with the Kaiser at Kronberg to discuss the naval race, Wilhelm spent half their time together railing against the French as 'a female race, a bundle of nerves,' and the other half *utterly* declining to modify the pace of German shipbuilding to *any* extent. Is it any wonder that Edward made the decision then and there to build up the British navy still further?"

Kessler mumbles something about "how confusing the whole topic is for me . . . the naval race, I mean . . . I need to sort it out better."

"You're not alone in your confusion. Most of Germany is confused— thanks to the Kaiser's appalling inability to recognize that he might be at fault to any degree."

"I should add," Kessler says, recovering his aplomb somewhat, "that I do still admire the English political system. I wish the Reichstag had the same power as the House of Lords to place limits on the Emperor's wishes. On the other hand, I do think that the German working class is better off than the English—has more security, better living conditions."

"I agree with you," Rathenau responds—again surprising Kessler. "Though not nearly as well off as it should be, as it has a right to be."

"On my last trip to London, I found myself wandering around the docks and I was struck at the vast wasteland of tiny, bare, houses. They look like endless prison cells. And not only that: look at how the

English treated the Dutch during the Boer War—rounding them up into concentration camps with an appalling loss of life from disease and starvation."

"Oh I see." Rathenau's tone is mocking. "It's *imperialism* that bothers you so much about the English! My dear Kessler, every European country is racing to grab colonies; what sets the English apart is their overwhelming *success* at it! That's precisely what enrages the Kaiser—he wants a larger share of the pie!"

At that point, Rathenau's valet announces the arrival—precisely on time, to Kessler's mixed feelings of relief and regret—of both Hofmannsthal and Reinhardt. As he rises to greet them, Rathenau suggests to Kessler that they "pick up the topic again after dinner, when we have two more opinions on the subject." Kessler again feels ambushed: he's never known Rathenau to require more than one opinion—his own.

Over supper—an exquisitely prepared and served meal of saddle of venison, along with a superb Burgundy—the conversation is largely confined to a benign exchange of surface gossip—about Bernard Shaw's amusing run-in with Vienna's Burg Theater; about whether Elisabeth Förster-Nietzsche's claim that her life is as "heroic" as her brother's only demonstrates that she matches him in insanity; and so on. The conversation briefly takes a serious turn when Hofmannsthal praises Max Harden for refusing to back down in his attacks on Prince Eulenburg. The comment rouses Reinhardt to an uncharacteristically lengthy response (ordinarily he prefers to listen—listens with such keen intensity that someone once dubbed him "the master of the art of creative listening").

Not this time. Reinhardt has already heard enough and dissents vigorously from Hofmannsthal's view. "What I find often to be the case," he says, "is that within a small circle of intimate friends, social forms are developed that, seen from the outside, appear to permit all kinds of conclusions, but that mean nothing to the participants."

"In general I might agree," Hofmannsthal replies, "but in this instance the language employed is so effusive as to be unmistakable. I consider Kessler a close friend—though we quarrel often enough—but I'd never dream of referring to him as 'Beloved Soul', or some other extravagant expression that the Liebenberg Circle seems to trade in."

"Perhaps," Kessler suggests, "they're simply more emancipated than we are, more expansive in expressing their intimate feelings, their sense of connection."

Reinhardt laughs. "Well, my dear Kessler—*perhaps*! But even I—who find Harden so distasteful—have to admit that when I hear someone say 'Beloved Soul', I have the feeling *here*"—Reinhardt vigorously rubs his tummy—"that the other person is coming too near to me. Among us actors, if one uses a phrase like that, we call him 'sweet'—a 'sweet man.' I can't believe it's different among military men."

"Oh but it *is!*" Kessler interjects, with a bit more animation than he intended. "I can vouch for that from my own experience. During my days in the Garde du Corps, the officers would make a young cadet named Pfeil—a boy as pretty as a picture—drunk, and then demand that he strip off his clothes."

Rathenau pushes back his chair loudly from the table and announces that cognac awaits them in the study. He hasn't said a word during the discussion of Harden, but as soon as the four men reassemble in the study—and as if to guarantee no repetition of the subject—he steers them strongly on a different course.

"Before the two of you arrived, Kessler and I were discussing how serious the antagonism between England and Germany has become. In my view, the peculiarities of the Kaiser, his vanity and indiscretion, are in large part to blame. Whereas Kessler finds considerable fault with the English. Can we have your views on the subject?"

Both Hofmannsthal and Reinhardt are taken aback; neither man is particularly political and both know better than to cross swords with Rathenau, especially on a subject dear to his heart.

Hofmannsthal decides it's best to begin with a question, preferably an irrelevant one. He hears himself asking, "Wasn't the Kaiser's mother the eldest daughter of Queen Victoria?"

Kessler glimpses the impatience in Rathenau's eyes and jumps in to soothe the waters: "Indeed yes. It's widely believed that 'Vicki' was her mother's favorite. A tragic figure. Failed in her hopes for liberalizing Germany."

Hofmannsthal presses on: "And isn't the Kaiser somewhat justified in feeling that England consistently rebuffs his many gestures of friendship?"

Rathenau's patience has run out. "The Kaiser is unable to grasp the simple fact," Rathenau sternly announces, "that his accelerated shipbuilding has fed England's suspicion that he's intent on challenging her supremacy on the sea."

"Eulenburg," Kessler suggests, "did try to modulate the Kaiser's imperialist ambitions—but Prince Eulenburg, alas, is no longer at court."

"Even when he was," Rathenau adds, "he encouraged the 'All-Highest' to pursue a foreign policy of *personal* diplomacy. At which his talent is deplorable."

"Isn't that why he ousted Holstein?" Hofmannsthal asks. "It seems to me Holstein had an independent mind."

"Quite so," Rathenau says, "and his successor, von Bülow, doesn't have the spine to contradict a single word Wilhelm says. Every time the Kaiser has an impulsive thought, Bülow hurriedly elevates it into a *policy*! He gives groveling a whole new dimension." Rathenau's tone is angrily dismissive.

To lighten the mood, Reinhardt proceeds to offer his imitation of Bülow: "'It gives me the greatest joy, it is the focus of all my thoughts, all my cares, all my efforts, my dearest Majesty, to smooth the way for your fame, happiness, and well-being."

The others laugh and applaud. "You ought to put yourself on the stage, Reinhardt," Kessler says.

Reinhardt laughs. "I'm *always* on the stage! Don't you know theater people?!"

"There is *one* person Wilhelm listens to," Rathenau says. "An Englishman, in fact."

"His uncle, King Edward VII?" Hofmannsthal asks.

"Hardly!" Rathenau snorts. "Edward has made every effort at reconciliation, but Wilhelm seems bent on estrangement. No, the chosen one is Houston Stewart Chamberlain, son-in-law of Wagner and more than his match as an anti-Semite."

"Of course—that book of his. What was it called?" Kessler asks.

Rathenau spits out the title: "*The Foundations of the Nineteenth Century*. Modest, no?"

"I've heard of it," Reinhardt adds.

"Of course you have," Rathenau replies sternly. "It's been a runaway best-seller. It lists the Jews as one of the '*un*-German races.' The Kaiser devoured it. Quotes from it frequently."

"How do you know such things? Hofmannsthal asks.

"At AEG we hear most of the gossip. Some of it turns out to be true—including the Kaiser's admiration for Chamberlain. Did you know that Jesus wasn't a Jew, but rather a blond Aryan?"

Kessler cuts into the laughter: "It would be more amusing, it seems to me, if Wilhelm didn't actually believe such nonsense. I find the question of national character an interesting one, a valid topic for discussion. In my view national differences are real but unconnected to race. There's no such thing as a pure race; we're all mongrels of one sort or another. I myself would much prefer being seen as a good European than a good German."

"The Kaiser would strenuously disagree," Rathenau responds. "I'm told that in an attempt to flatter King Edward, Wilhelm recently characterized the 'male' races of Anglo-Saxons and Teutons as greatly superior to the 'female' French. When you combine Wilhelm's ineptness at diplomacy—the man gets into a rage if his terms aren't met instantly and in full—with his insistence on an ambitious policy of fleet-building, is it any wonder Germany scares her neighbors and finds herself in isolation?"

Hofmannsthal looks puzzled. "But the Kaiser claims his sole aim in building up the fleet is to protect German commerce."

"Of course he does," Rathenau shoots back. "When the English express skepticism, Wilhelm screams 'Nonsense! Balderdash!'" He gets *extremely* vexed—but never remorseful, oh never remorse! He's like the truant boy who gets caught with his hand in the cookie jar and screams, 'I'm not even hungry!'"

"I believe Holstein had it right," Reinhardt throws in. "Building more and more ships is popular with those in the armor-plating business—and with career naval officers. For the rest of Germany it's a disaster."

Kessler feels called upon to mention that "Holstein played an ugly role in the Eulenburg affair," but then agrees with the others that "the man did have common sense."

"I don't understand these matters very well," Hofmannsthal says. "but doesn't Germany already have a powerful fleet, an impressive number of battleships and cruisers?"

"What you don't understand, Hofmannsthal," Rathenau acidly responds, "is that our dear Kaiser's aspirations are as grandiose as his eccentricities."

"I blame the situation on Admiral Tirpitz and his bloody Plan," Reinhardt throws in.

"You're quite wrong," Rathenau instantly replies. "Tirpitz wants a strong navy, yes, but doesn't delude himself with thinking he can successfully challenge the British. If anything, it's the Kaiser who's pushing Tirpitz. It's the Kaiser who wants to throw down the gauntlet—even as he claims, in that wounded tone of his, that his overtures of friendship to England are unappreciated. You bet they are; the English understand the Kaiser's real intentions *very* clearly. They understand that nothing less than control of the seas and the European balance of power is at stake. Which is precisely what makes the situation so dangerous. Instead of modifying his shipbuilding program, the Kaiser insists on accelerating it."

The conversation ends with all four men agreeing that the serious deterioration in Anglo-German relations has become alarming. "I read that interview the Kaiser gave to the London *Daily Telegraph*," Kessler says. "Good grief! If that's his notion of a 'conciliatory' gesture, we're headed straight for war!"

That interview in the *Telegraph* has caused consternation in circles far wider than the confines of Rathenau's dinner party. Wilhelm's version of soothing the waters is to declare to the *Telegraph* reporter that "the prevailing sentiment among large sections of the middle and lower classes of my own people is not friendly to England." He follows up by expressing resentment that his support of England during the Boer War isn't sufficiently appreciated. Indeed, the Kaiser storms, "I have grown weary of having my overtures of friendship belittled: To be forever misjudged, to have my repeated offers of friendship weighed and scrutinized with zealous, mistrustful eyes, taxes my patience severely."

As for the Kaiser's refusal to slow German naval construction, the *Telegraph* interview quotes him as saying that the growing size of his fleet is in no sense designed to challenge British supremacy on the seas but is intended instead to help win the looming future struggle against the "Yellow Peril"—Japan and China—in the Pacific. For toppers, the Kaiser gratuitously, goofily, adds that the English are "mad, mad, mad as March hares" in their suspicions of him.

The interview has a disastrous international effect. Coming as it does only a few years after the Russian Revolution of 1905 has forced at least a partial constitution on the Tsar, Wilhelm's insistence on autocratic personal rule is widely seen as increasingly anachronistic. In Germany reaction to the *Telegraph* interview is, if anything, more tumultuous than even in England. Several high-ranking officials remember with a shudder that just two years previously, in response to a bomb attack against the King of Spain, the Kaiser had ranted against "those bastard anarchists" who he blamed for the attack, and had suggested that the best safeguard against future assassination attempts was to round up every known anarchist and have them beheaded on the spot.

During the uproar over the *Telegraph* interview, Max Harden publishes three articles in *Die Zukunft* that rage against the Kaiser's misrule, declare that "this monarch will *never* change," and actually propose a forced abdication. In the Reichstag, too, a two-day debate takes place during which views never before publicly uttered are given a remarkable airing, speaker after speaker from all five parties taking to the floor in a storm of protest and—risking arrest under the charge of *lèse-majesté*—freely venting their indignation at the Kaiser's autocratic rule, his gratuitous affront to English sensibilities, and his inept interference with the work of his own ministers. Germany has become "a laughing-stock" in the world, one Reichstag member declares; another demands "secure guarantees" to curtail the Kaiser's future power; a third insists that Wilhelm "submit to the criticism of the representatives of the people."

Wilhelm's response is to take to his bed and threaten abdication—though he soon enough allows his son, the Crown Prince, to talk him out of it. The Kaiser shows no recognition—just as Harden predicted—that he's erred in any way, learned anything from his mistakes, or might henceforth mend his ways.

$\sim$

Kessler's heightened interest in politics isn't at the expense of his long-standing devotion to the arts—and to its practitioners. Maillol, with his epic self-centeredness, makes more demands on his time than anyone else. He constantly complains to Kessler about his wife's extravagant jealousy, claiming that on the rare occasions when he risks hiring a female model, Mme. Maillol invariably stations herself behind the door to his studio, listening intently for any sign of "impropriety." Sensing her presence, Maillol claims, he's taken to angrily throwing open the door, toppling her from her perch. Screams and shouts follow, the ugly scenes usually ending with Mme. Maillol momentarily persuaded of her husband's innocence, or cowed by his insults, and swearing in future to curtail her suspicions. The vow rarely lasts beyond the next posing session.

"What can I do?" Maillol cheerily asks Kessler. "The woman is madly in love."

Kessler's response is cautiously tangential: "I, for one, have always preferred to live alone. But artists, I suppose, need someone to take care of them."

Kessler is patience itself with Maillol, but in truth the focus of his admiration and partisanship has shifted somewhat to the explosive developments taking place in the world of dance. Initially, he became intrigued with the careers of the astonishing trio of American women who were currently pioneering modern dance: Loie Fuller, Isadora

Duncan, and Ruth St. Denis. He'd first seen Loie Fuller dance as far back as 1897 in Paris; the "continual darkness" of the performance, the "arbitrary lighting" and "wild colors" had put him off. He never develops a taste for Fuller's work, and after seeing her dance the *Tragedy of Salomé* 10 years later (when she was 45), he casts her out with uncharacteristic severity, calling her "old, fat, and not flexible."

Initially, he's no less dismissive of Isadora Duncan. On his first exposure to her work in 1903, he sums her up as a sentimental amateur: she "has only one movement," he writes in his diary, "which she repeats until it's painful, dances without rhythm and without passion." He thinks her performance is so conventional that he likens it to academic art, his bête noire, and further decries what he calls her penchant for drawing attention to herself "through robes of a monstrous, Pre-Raphaelite style, confusing art and life."

Isadora learns of Kessler's negative opinion from the theater designer Gordon Craig, her lover at the time and one of Kessler's close friends. Realizing how widely regarded he is for impeccable *and* adventurous taste, Isadora becomes determined to change Kessler's mind. She invites him to her place at Neuilly, gives him a private demonstration of her technique—and manages to win his admiring applause. By temperament, to be sure, Kessler is a diplomat manqué, the soul of discretion, but his change of heart is genuine. Three years later, when he visits Duncan's school in Grunewald, he watches her students, varying in age between four and eight, move in their loose-limbed Liberty dresses with "great freshness and grace," following the lines of the music exactly.

In the years that follow, Kessler stays in occasional touch with Isadora, and, in 1913, when her two young children are killed in a monumentally tragic auto accident, Kessler attends the funeral. In his diary he describes the event as "the most moving ceremony I have ever been to" and admiringly recounts Isadora's behavior—"she is really heroic, encouraging the others, saying there is no death, really great in her terrible grief."

The third American, Ruth St. Denis, becomes Kessler's special favorite; he finds her dancing striking and contemporary. By 1906 he's met her personally, and the two start to see each other with some frequency. She confides to him that Max Reinhardt wants to present her in *Salomé* but she thinks the play too "literary." Kessler suggests that she meet instead with Hugo von Hofmannsthal as a possible collaborator, and promptly arranges a lunch to bring them together. (His role as artistic matchmaker goes some way toward muffling his disappointment at not having been blessed with special gifts himself; besides, he's good-willed). He offers St. Denis his services as a guide to the wonders of Berlin; given the depth of his knowledge and the range of his acquaintances, she pronounces him a learned and delightful companion.

A mere two years later, Ruth St. Denis and modern dance have disappeared from Kessler's horizon—swept away by the tsunami-like wave of acclaim that greets the debut in 1909 of Diaghilev's Ballets Russes. If the discovery of Ruth St. Denis had been the equivalent for Kessler of stumbling onto an unexpectedly good book, seeing Diaghilev's troupe is more like uncovering an entire, previously hidden library. The Paris premiere of *Sylphides*—Kessler invites the Maillols as his guests—is among the troupe's more memorable events. Even Maillol, miserly with compliments to other artists, finds the combination of Nijinsky and Pavlova the absolute embodiment, as he puts it, of Amor and Psyche, of "passion and refinement" united.

Kessler's interest focuses on Nijinsky—"handsome like a Greek god"— and he decides to invite Diaghilev and Nijinsky to lunch; given Kessler's reputation as an artistic entrepreneur, Diaghilev accepts for both of them. Kessler is aware that the two are lovers, but at lunch he's surprised at the way the pot-bellied impresario takes for granted his vassal's submission. The power of Nijinsky's physical presence astonishes Kessler—his "Mongolian" face and hesitant, modest manner remind Kessler of the Japanese. Nijinsky knows only a few words of French, and Diaghilev, ever on top, serves as interpreter. Kessler manages to get across his request that Nijinsky serve as the model for a statue of Apollo to be sculpted by Maillol and to grace the Nietzsche Memorial (which has become one of the more important of Kessler's current side projects, though it means constant meetings with Nietzsche's impossible sister, Elisabeth).

Maillol initially makes difficulties about Nijinsky posing for him. He wants to know if anyone has seen Nijinsky naked. Kessler, startled, and more than a little put out at Maillol's haughty hesitation, discreetly replies that Nijinsky is clothed perfection. Maillol claims the dancer looks a little "round" to him, and to Kessler's further annoyance insists that "the model must respond to the idea that the artist wishes to execute." Eventually Maillol deigns to accept the commission, but for Kessler it's been like trying to promote Cézanne to a devotee of Anton von Werner.

Diaghilev's favorite haunt in Paris is Larue's. There he gathers in his orbit a galaxy of admirers, each of whom rotates on their own axis: Rainer Maria Rilke, Misia Sert, Jean Cocteau, Max Reinhardt, Reynaldo Hahn, Stravinsky, Ravel—*tout la vie moderne*. Nijinsky, as always, conceals himself in a corner, pale and quietly smiling. Kessler notices that Reinhardt, perhaps with a pageant in mind, rarely takes his eyes off the dancer. When he does, it's to announce that the Russian "is the greatest miracle he has ever encountered ... still a schoolboy and yet a great genius." Diaghilev is only mildly put out.

Not everyone agrees about Nijinsky. When the Russians perform in London, several of England's great ladies express their deep concern to Kessler. Lady Speyer, for one, admits that Nijinsky's performance in *Afternoon of a Faun* has roused frightening "animalistic" feelings in her; she agrees that he's a genius of sorts—but also "a kind of monster." She confides to Kessler that Nijinsky has had an "emetic effect"—the polite term for vomiting—on her husband and "other very powerful, hard men" as well. Kessler believes that's all to the good, but doesn't say so. In the privacy of his diary he deplores the upper-class revulsion and hatred of all art that is "not yet sterilized and dead."

The renowned beauty Lady Ripon seems to Kessler an exception. She tells him that she has "great affection" for Nijinsky and feels like something of a protectress to Diaghilev. The feelings are not mutual. When Lady Ripon invites both men, along with Kessler and Léon Bakst, the Ballets Russes's extraordinary designer, to lunch at her estate at Coombe, Diaghilev soon makes it clear that he cares nothing for either her affection or protection. Lady Ripon makes the apparently grievous error of repeating to Diaghilev the current rumor that he's grown dissatisfied with famed dancer/choreographer Michel Fokine and will soon dismiss him from the company. She dares to suggest that Fokine's great popularity with the public might well be grounds for keeping him on. In response, Diaghilev turns on Lady Ripon—as Kessler sees it—"brutally."

"I don't give a damn about the public!" he shouts. "The public is there for one reason only—to be violated!" A startled Lady Ripon weakly apologizes.

On the trip back to London, Kessler remonstrates with Diaghilev, deplores his unnecessary rudeness to a gracious woman. Diaghilev sullenly replies that he's chosen precisely the right way to respond to such uninformed, pliable creatures. When the Ballets Russes returns to Coombe the following evening to perform in front of King Edward's wife, the beautiful, high-spirited Queen Alexandra, Diaghilev makes a point of snubbing Lady Ripon and an obedient Nijinsky fails even to greet her.

The next day she meets with Kessler in London and implores him to "put things right." He feels deeply for her "tragic-comic situation," goes directly to see Diaghilev and finds him "completely out of control." He refers to Lady Ripon as "that sow," swears he will never speak to her again, and declares that he's weighing the idea of challenging Lord Ripon to a duel. An appalled Kessler uses all of his considerable diplomatic skill to somehow arrange, during the intermission of another performance, for Diaghilev to meet Queen Alexandra, who bestows a few friendly words on him. "Beaming," Diaghilev wanders over to where Kessler and Lady Ripon are sitting and—"coldly but politely" (in Kessler's words)—kisses her hand. The poor lady stands up, takes a few steps, then falls down in a faint. Upon such monumental events, Kessler ironically muses, do empires rise and fall.

The circle that centers on Diaghilev and meets at Larue's café is often expanded to include various other contemporary eminences—among them, von Hofmannsthal (at Kessler's suggestion) and another flamboyant poet—and incipient fascist—Gabriele D'Annunzio (after meeting him Kessler remarks on his "cruelly indifferent eyes" and his old-fashioned views on women). Kessler attends the meetings at Larue's regularly. At one point the luncheon group becomes something of a war council. Gaston Calmette, editor of *Le Figaro*, publishes an attack on Nijinsky's performance in *Afternoon of a Faun*, declaring that "no decent public could ever accept such animal realism . . . such vile movements of erotic bestiality."

Calmette manages as well to denounce Auguste Rodin for having praised Nijinsky and for hanging "obscene" drawings in the chapel of Sacré-Coeur. Calmette demands that the state cease to subsidize the wealthy sculptor and that it at once evict him, though he's now an old man, from his home in the Hôtel Biron.

On reading Calmette's attack, Kessler drives at once to Diaghilev's to consult about a response. Cocteau has preceded him. Feeling himself in some way responsible, as a result of having introduced Rodin to the Ballets Russes as a guest of his, Kessler's first thought is to challenge Calmette to a duel. The suggestion astonishes Diaghilev and Cocteau. The anachronistic honor code, once the preserve of "true" gentlemen, has become illegal almost everywhere. Yet the gesture somehow fits, crazily, with the more incongruent elements in Kessler's personality: he's all at once an old-fashioned aristocrat of manners and an ardent champion of the avant-garde in art. Diaghilev and Cocteau remind Kessler that he's in Paris—meaning that all sides would consider him, as a foreigner, in the wrong. Kessler takes that with good grace, however much it contradicts his self-image as a cosmopolitan figure above the crude nationalistic fray.

Stravinsky, Hofmannsthal, and Nijinsky soon arrive at Diaghilev's, and the six of them together plot the next move. They decide to put themselves at Rodin's disposal, and Diaghilev and Kessler are sent off as emissaries to the Hôtel Biron. Rodin greets them looking, in Kessler's opinion, somewhat shaky and, his hair unbrushed, more disheveled than usual. Rodin tells them that he's decided to do nothing at all in regard to Calmette.

"I've been attacked all my life," he says. "I long ago decided that the best response is no response."

Kessler repeats his offer to challenge Calmette to a duel. Diaghilev looks askance at him, as if about to say, "I thought we'd put that nonsense behind us." But before he can speak, Rodin breaks in:

"I thank you for your solicitation," he tells Kessler (who records the conversation in his diary). "It does you honor, and I am honored by it. But my friend, if I had heeded the assorted calumnies that have come my way, I would have done nothing with my life but go back and forth to the dueling ground. I would never have become a sculptor. Yet it's been through my work that I've mounted the best possible rebuttal to those attacks."

There's no arguing with that. Diaghilev and Kessler help Rodin back to his bedroom and do their best to comfort the old man with a non-combative apéritif.

The next day they return again, this time with Nijinsky in tow. On entering, he immediately kisses Rodin's hands, as a child might—which makes the old man flush with embarrassment. Kessler moves the conversation forward. "How wonderful you look today!" he tells Rodin, who shyly touches his freshly waved hair and confesses that he's just emerged from a session with the curling tongs (which Kessler had already assumed from the pervasive smell of pomade). Rodin then smilingly shows the assembled trio the printed protest in *Gil Blas* that a number of leading writers and politicians have signed protesting the piece in *Le Figaro*. "Calmette is finished," Rodin says with satisfaction. Empires of every kind remain intact.

∼

Count Kessler enthusiastically urges Walther Rathenau to see Nijinsky perform. Enthusiasm isn't a trait Rathenau admires; it strikes him as unpleasantly akin to religious fervor. Yet he trusts Kessler's judgment—in the realm of art, at least—and eventually takes in a performance. He tells Kessler that he was "deeply impressed"—the equivalent for the austere Rathenau of banging a drum in the street. Rathenau immediately adds, "But there's altogether too much babbling about art—your own informed views excluded, of course."

"Shall we babble on about our favorite subject instead?" Kessler good-naturedly responds. "At least until dessert arrives." The two are dining together at the exclusive Carlton. The room is packed, but the conversation subdued—as if people were opening their mouths without any sound coming out. It's called behaving with the propriety due one's station.

"'Favorite subject'?" Rathenau is genuinely puzzled.

"The Kaiser, of course! People are openly laughing at his ineptitude. One acquaintance told me that Louis XVI didn't have nearly so much to answer for when they cut off his head, as Wilhelm does. As I see it—just between us—His Majesty seems more than a bit unbalanced."

"Let us say," Rathenau cautions, "that he's remarkably 'changeable'— fearful one day, and an assaultive bully the next."

"Isn't that one and the same?"

"You have a point," Rathenau concedes. "Wilhelm's disposition is essentially operatic. He never has 'a bad day'—he's always having 'a complete collapse.'"

"One view making the rounds is that the Kaiser, far from setting policy, is a mere figurehead, a toy vessel tossed around at will by his malignant ministers."

Rathenau stares at him in disbelief, his brow knit with anger.

Fortunately, the waiter arrives with a confection of macaroons, along with coffee. By the time he's poured it and again disappeared, Rathenau's temper has calmed a bit.

"The idea of the Kaiser as a figurehead is absurd," he finally says. "Am I to assume that you believe such nonsense?"

Kessler laughs at the insult; he's come to terms with Rathenau's rudeness—preferring to call it "candor."

"I might have believed it," he says with amusement, "had I not had the good sense to run it by you."

Rathenau isn't mollified. "Really, my dear Kessler, you must understand a few basic facts about the 'All-High.'"

Kessler smiles. "I gladly submit to your tutelage."

"To begin with, he *is* the supreme leader. Do not, like so many others, confuse his clownish personality with tractability. He, and he alone, sets policy for Germany. He'll let Admiral Tirpitz bill himself as the architect of the new German fleet, but it's Wilhelm who originated the Navy Bills that made it possible. He's not only his own Admiral but his own Reich Chancellor. Von Bülow holds the post, but strictly on sufferance. He'll be out of office the minute he opposes one of the Kaiser's pet projects. The whole court network of oligarchs, sportsmen, and aristocrats dance to Wilhelm's tune—no matter that they believe themselves the composer." Rathenau is flush with contempt.

"Surely Eulenburg in his day wielded real power?"

"More than anyone before or since. I'll give you that. But the Kaiser was an unformed young man when his friendship with Eulenburg began. And as you doubtless recall, once Eulenburg came under attack, the Emperor instantly spurned him. Wilhelm is a shallow man, incapable of loyalty. He still constantly refers to Eulenburg's 'betrayal.'"

Kessler laughs: "As if Eulenburg slept with a fisherman solely to embarrass him."

Rathenau's face appears carved from stone.

As if taking up an unspoken dare, Kessler continues along the same dangerous ground: "I suppose it's a sad situation for any man, never to let himself become close to others."

"You're being sentimental."

"Perhaps. Some might call it 'compassionate,'" Kessler says playfully.

"Call it whatever you like, but don't waste it on the Kaiser. Even Max Harden saw clearly that Wilhelm would instantly reject Eulenburg."

Aware that Rathenau has refused his invitation to become personal, Kessler lets him direct the conversation back to politics: "If Harden felt any pity for Eulenburg, he didn't let it stay his hand."

"Why should he have? Compassion isn't Harden's business. Becoming feared and powerful is. And that he's achieved."

"He's too sharp-tongued and aggressive for my taste. And not nearly special enough to be called 'eccentric.'"

"On that score, you're right. He follows the pack—and these days that means heading into the arms of the conservative nationalists."

"How the man does shift and wander!" Kessler adds, with an edge of impatience.

"Harden equates nationalism with patriotism. A common mistake." Rathenau pauses, then says, "Harden and I were quite friendly for a time."

"So I'd heard. The news surprised me. I've had lunch with him once or twice, which was quite enough."

"Harden and I had much in common—until he started braying about the philistinism of the masses, the threat that democracy poses to the historic values of the Fatherland. The bark is loud, but it issues from a mutt, not a thoroughbred. He's much like the Kaiser—two men who make a lot of noise but are basically timid."

"And trust no one," Kessler adds.

"For Wilhelm the distrust includes the Kaiserin and his own children. His confidence in anyone is wholly contingent on the extent to which they carry out his will. Mind you, in opening your eyes to the Kaiser's absolute power, I'm not suggesting for a moment that he's been using it well. Discontent is widespread, and growing, yet thus far impotent to assert itself."

"I often hear the Kaiser belittled, even mocked. Yet the grievances against him never seem to accumulate." Kessler sounds puzzled.

"I liken it to the situation of a bank that's been mismanaged for a number of years: some employees are quietly grumbling about it, but it's only when insolvency is suddenly declared that there's a great roar of disapproval. Just so with Germany. The disasters accumulate. Misrule could last for perhaps another twenty years. Then suddenly the consequences will show up everywhere. I predict we'll reach that point within *ten* years."

They sit silently for a moment. Finally Kessler says, "Should I believe everything you tell me, Rathenau?"

Rathenau smiles. "That would be the wisest course."

~

PART III

MAGNUS HIRSCHFELD
1908–1913

EVER SINCE HIS unfortunate testimony during the Eulen-
burg trial four years earlier, Hirschfeld's been insistently criticized for
the role he played. Even colleagues and friends continue to fault him—
above all for attesting to von Moltke's "psychic" homosexuality, and then
for reversing himself. Not only has the press vilified him, but membership enrollment in the Scientific Humanitarian Society has taken a
plunge as fear spreads that Hirschfeld might publicly reveal information about the private lives of other men. Hirschfeld himself considers
resigning the directorship, but settles instead on an opposite strategy—
accelerating his lecture schedule, traveling more widely than ever to
deliver speeches, and assiduously devoting his spare time to writing.

The publication in 1910 of his enormous book *Transvestites* is the first
major product of his onerous work schedule. It opens up a whole new
field of study, is widely reviewed—and, inevitably, becomes the subject
of considerable new controversy. Based on extensive and careful interviews, Hirschfeld's most original—and most offensive—contribution is
his conclusion that cross-dressing among males occurs at least as often
among heterosexuals as homosexuals (a conclusion later research will
confirm). The unexpected finding is for Hirschfeld himself a cautionary
lesson in the dangers of over-categorizing the many varieties of sensual
expression. As he recognizes, it's a tendency he himself has been prone
to in the past, though less so lately.

Instead, he's come increasingly to feel that, in regard both to gender and sexual orientation, it's more accurate to emphasize a subtle continuum rather than a rigid set of dualistic categories. He de-emphasizes his earlier notion of a "Third Sex," in favor of a fluid spectrum of preferences—prefiguring Alfred Kinsey's famous gradations in scale from zero to six (zero being "exclusively heterosexual" and six being "exclusively homosexual") with three designating an equal bisexual attraction to both genders, a valid orientation Hirschfeld never reduces to a "cop-out" or "cover."

In regard to gender, Hirschfeld posits another radical view—though he never pursues it with the same vigor that marks his investigations into sexual orientation. Every individual, he suggests, potentially contains all the qualities of temperament and intellect traditionally divided up as *either* "male" or "female." It's a view not widely heard again until the 1960s counter-cultural revolution, when "androgyny" is commonly cited as the ideal state of being.

One day an invitation arrives that represents something of an epiphany for Hirschfeld. It comes from the greatly respected Dr. Iwan Bloch, chairman of the newly formed Medical Society for Sexual Science and Eugenics, of which Hirschfeld is himself a member. Iwan Bloch's own book, *The Sexual Life of Our Time*, has achieved significant notoriety of late. At the time of its first appearance in 1907, the book was condemned in police court and taken off the shelves; after a successful appeal it was then reissued, though on condition that it be sold only to legal and medical professionals. Rapidly escaping those confines, *Sexual Life* had become a widely discussed and acclaimed work.

In the book, Bloch expresses agreement with Hirschfeld that homosexuality is a congenital, natural variant—though like Hirschfeld he acknowledges that certain environmental factors—experiences in school, say, or prison, or the military—can awaken a predisposition that might otherwise have remained dormant. Neither man includes among external factors what will later became the two favorite explanations of American psychiatry: that homosexual behavior is a normal stage in development that all individuals pass through during adolescence (that *must* be passed through); and the discordant notion that homosexuality occurs as the result of a particular (and pathological) family configuration: an absent or hostile father in combination with an overly solicitous or invasive mother. Both notions—and the tension between them—still linger in the culture.

Though Iwan Bloch in *The Sexual Life of Our Time* praises Hirschfeld as "the greatest, the most knowledgeable and experienced sexologist" of the day, that opinion isn't unanimously held among other specialists. Benedict Friedlaender and Adolf Brand are Hirschfeld's long-standing detractors; in their publication, *Der Eigene*, they regularly deplore "effeminacy" and excoriate Hirschfeld for failing to champion the ancient Greek pattern of cross-generational male-male sexuality. Another prominent opponent, Albert Moll, far from idealizing homosexuality, deplores it as pathological and denounces homosexuals as inherently mendacious and deceitful.

Sigmund Freud's position is equivocal; he shifts inconclusively in his attitude both toward homosexuality and Hirschfeld, its leading advocate. Initially Freud looks favorably on Hirschfeld's work, contributes articles to a journal he edits, and treats him as an honored guest at the 1911 meeting of the Psychoanalytical Association. Yet when Hirschfeld resigns from the Association, Freud says it's "no great loss," describing him as "a flabby, unappetizing fellow, incapable of learning anything."

Freud's writings on homosexuality are skimpy and irresolute—except for the decisive stands he takes against treating homosexuality as a disease or subjecting its adherents to punishment. He feels that homosexuality in adults *might* have a biological component, yet suggests that such behavior is no more pathological than the various perversions that characterize adult heterosexuals. Freud's bottom-line view seems to have been that homosexuality should only be seen as a neurotic "disturbance" when its practitioners prove unable or unwilling to meet cultural expectations of reproduction.

The Medical Society's invitation delights Hirschfeld. Here is a rare opportunity, he feels, to discuss with a friendly fellow specialist in front of a reasonably well-informed audience—one more likely to be well-disposed than most—some of the central questions currently emerging in the new field of sexology. On the evening of the debate, the auditorium quickly fills to capacity, with an overflow crowd lingering in the anteroom in the hope of gaining belated admission.

Both men are given laudatory introductions by Professor Eugen Steinach, the renowned Viennese biologist who has himself embarked on a well-publicized series of cross-gender animal transplants. The results have led Steinach and others to the view that a greater knowledge of glandular secretions is critical to an understanding of sexual behavior—a theory Hirschfeld himself has found intriguing.

After Steinach makes his formal introduction of the two speakers and suggests that Hirschfeld inaugurate the exchange, Hirschfeld, in turn, invites Steinach—"whose pioneering researches," he tells the audience, "have done so much to inform all specialists in sexology"—to become an integral part of a three-way discussion. When Steinach nods his agreement, Hirschfeld then turns to the audience:

"I recognize some of you," he cheerfully begins, "as fellow colleagues and researchers, and I assume others in this audience, if not themselves researchers, are nonetheless keenly interested in recent developments in sexology. Do let us also have your contributions—or complaints," he chuckles—"as this colloquy progresses. Let us convert the rather formal structure which typifies such events as this into an open forum where a wide variety of viewpoints can be heard. After all, this burgeoning field is still in its infancy and none of us has produced definitive answers."

From his chair on the stage, Steinach, smiling genially, calls out, "Quite wrong, Hirschfeld! I, for one, *have* reached definitive answers—which I shall be happy to share shortly." A jolly tut-tutting is heard from the audience, along with a few loud, seemingly derogatory whistles.

Wondering if he hasn't inadvertently turned a formal discussion into a raucous free-for-all, Hirschfeld rather nervously starts to address the audience:

"It's a great pleasure for me to share this platform with two such distinguished men of science as Iwan Bloch and Eugen Steinach,"

Hirschfeld begins. He then itemizes their extraordinary personal qualities, the seminal importance of their writings, and the large number of
awards each has already accumulated.

"And yet"—here Hirschfeld smiles deferentially—"though I am the
least accomplished of the three men who occupy this stage—that is, for
the time being"—a few polite guffaws from the audience—"there are
certain aspects of their work about which I have doubts, or perhaps I
should say questions. Let me begin with Dr. Bloch, whose remarkable
book, *The Sexual Life of Our Time*, I urge every person to read and study.

"You and I agree, Dr. Bloch—and please correct me if I misstate the
extent of that agreement—that homosexuality is not a choice—that
neither youthful experimentation nor, say, an extended stay in an all-
male environment, like on shipboard or in a prison, can alone provide a
satisfactory explanation for why some men and not others will engage
in sexual activities with other men. No, such behavior has its roots in
biology. It is the natural and benign predisposition of a minority of
people. And here, of course, I include—as few in our field do, I might
add in deserved chastisement—not only male homosexuals but also lesbians." Hirschfeld briefly turns his back to the audience in order to face
Iwan Bloch, seated behind him. "Am I accurately describing our shared
views, Dr. Bloch?"

"Yes, thus far," Bloch replies pleasantly. "Though when you use the
word 'natural' I find myself hesitating a bit."

"If I may explain that further—?" Hirschfeld asks.

"Certainly," Bloch responds.

"In using the word 'natural,' I want to draw attention to the fact that
homosexuality occurs worldwide and apparently through much of the
animal kingdom, thus proving that such behavior *is* an intrinsic feature
of nature. As an illustration of how common homosexuality is, need I
mention the recent rumors of 'homosexual orgies,' featuring Cardinal
Rafael Merry del Val, within the Vatican—that presumed bastion of celibacy and holiness. Homosexuality *is* everywhere!"

Someone from the audience calls out, "Spoken like the Jew you are!"
There's a shocked silence.

The mild-mannered Bloch instantly jumps up: "Spoken like the bigot *you* are!" A scattering of boos and applause arises in the audience. "I apologize for my vehemence," Bloch goes on, "but I cannot countenance blatant anti-Semitism. We are supposedly engaged in rational discourse. In the presence of subjective prejudice, scientific truth will always suffer."

Another man in the audience raises his hand. Hirschfeld acknowledges him, and the young man rises from his seat: "I'd like to join in apologizing to Dr. Hirschfeld for the inexcusable lack of civility to which he's just been subjected, and also to—"

"—that's very kind, thank you very much," Hirschfeld smilingly interjects.

"However," the man continues, "I rise for a second reason as well. I am currently a student in the new field of anthropology, which the eminent Dr. Franz Boas has done so much to foster. If you would be good enough to allow me just one minute—"

Steinach calls out from his seat: "Exactly one minute. I'll time it." He ostentatiously holds up his watch. "Ready? Go!"

Flustered, the young man clears his throat and starts: "Well, you see, I'm just at the beginning of my studies, of course, but the point I want to make is about biology. You claim sexual orientation is a biological phenomenon. That's not what we've learned in our anthropology studies. Homosexuality *is* found in many cultures, but not in the forms we're familiar with in the West. One tribe in—"

Steinach calls out: "—thirty seconds! Better hurry!"

"—Male-male sex around the world is almost always cross-generational, as it was in Periclean Athens—not between two adult men. In one tribal culture in New Guinea every young boy swallows the semen of an adult male on a regular basis; it's the prescribed route, the only route, to achieving adult manhood. The culture enforces that behavior, not biology. And it isn't a small minority of the boys, it's all of them. Besides, once those boys grow up, they marry women, have children—and never again have sex with other men. So contrary to what the panelists have been saying, homosexuality outside of the West is definitely a cultural, not a biological phenomenon. And it isn't confined to a small minority in a given culture. Our mores are quite parochial when compared to—"

Steinach shouts him down: "—that's it! You're done! Time's up! I gave you an extra thirty seconds. And wasted time it was! As far as I'm concerned, everything you've said is hogwash! When anthropology becomes a science, be sure to let us know!"

The audience breaks into laughter and applause. The young man nervously sits down.

Dr. Bloch speaks up. "Thank you, young man, for being brave enough to confront us with evidence that, if proven valid, will indeed cause us to rethink many of our assumptions and conclusions. As of now, it seems, such evidence from anthropology hasn't been replicated, nor stood the test of time—the very definitions of 'Science.' So we must reserve judgment. But I thank you for calling our attention to this new field. Now if Dr. Hirschfeld and I can return to—"

Hirschfeld breaks in: "—I would only add that I very much agree with Dr. Bloch and I will look further into these new studies."

Bloch continues: " . . . if we can return to our earlier discussion about what is or is not 'natural.' I would ask Dr. Hirschfeld if he continues to hold to the view that homosexual men constitute a 'third sex,' all of whose members exhibit traits—like effeminacy—traditionally associated with the female gender. In my opinion, if we limit the homosexual impulse to a small number of people, then how can Dr. Hirschfeld simultaneously claim that homosexuality is found everywhere?"

"If Hirschfeld believes that all homosexual men are effeminate," Steinach unexpectedly chimes in, "I can only conclude that he hasn't met many homosexual men."

There are sounds of laughter from the audience, and some applause, but "shushing" neighbors soon restore order.

Hirschfeld remains unruffled. "Both of you are right to criticize views I held more firmly at the start of my work than I do currently. In the beginning, as I now see, I was too much drawn to rigid categories, too bound up with the traditional view, for example, that profound and intrinsic differences separate men from women. Just so with 'heterosexual' and 'homosexual' individuals. I'm now more inclined to the idea of a continuum. Just as some women—I might mention Helene Stöcker—"

A loud "boo" echoes from the audience at the mention of Stöcker's name. Hirschfeld ignores it.

"—a woman like Helene Stöcker has an intellect and a gift for fundamental analysis, equal, if not superior, to any man I've ever known."

The "booing" grows louder. This time Hirschfeld addresses it directly. "My dear friends," he says, his voice calm and cordial, "almost every opinion we discuss today is subject to challenge. This is new territory. I urge us all tonight to discuss our legitimate differences with, if possible, the utmost civility. None of us pretends to have final answers."

"I do—as I said earlier!" Steinach interjects. "But"—here he smiles broadly, immensely pleased with himself—"I'll pretend, when the time comes, to hold those views with due humility."

There's scattered laughter from the audience. "And that time," Hirschfeld carefully responds, "will arrive shortly. I now realize—as Professor Steinach suggests—that the conventional equation of homosexuality with effeminacy fails to account for the many homosexual men who are indistinguishable from the manly demeanor of so-called 'normal' men. I might add that I've found the same with lesbians. To outward appearances, there is nothing at all 'mannish' about the many women I know who are erotically drawn to other women. Yet I continue to feel that what we might call 'psychic' homosexuality *is* common to those whose constitutional biology is—"

A voice booms out from the audience: "—as you wrongly claimed about Count von Moltke—ruining his life!"

Hirschfeld is startled—and mute. Iwan Bloch moves quickly to fill the silence: "If I may, Doctor Hirschfeld?"

"By all means, my dear Doctor . . ." Hirschfeld moves to the side of the podium to enable Bloch to have open access to the audience.

"I would offer one point of clarification. The proliferation of inquiries into homosexuality has had, in my view, one deleterious byproduct. And that is an increasing reluctance among heterosexual men openly to display the profound love they feel for their closest friends. It has become fashionable these days to mock as 'old-fashioned romanticism' what was once considered perfectly permissible, even exalted, expressions of love between two members of the same sex."

The audience vigorously applauds.

"Love and sex," Bloch continues, "are *not* the same phenomenon. A loving relationship does not inevitably lead to the development of sexual passion. Nor is sexual attraction necessarily a byproduct of affection. My main point is simply this: love between men ought to be possible without branding it 'homosexual.' What we are gaining in freedom of sexual expression is occurring in tandem with a growing unwillingness among heterosexual men to declare—even to feel—profound emotional attachment to certain members of their own gender. Not so long ago, in the circles that surrounded Goethe and Schiller, loving male friendship was widely hailed as among the crowning achievements of German culture."

Bloch resumes his seat to substantial applause, and Hirschfeld, himself applauding, resumes his place at the podium. "A point well taken, Dr. Bloch."

Professor Steinach now rises in his seat. "—If I may join the love fest..." He strides towards the front. "You, Hirschfeld, may be in full agreement with Bloch, but both of you have lost sight of the one critical dimension to any discussion of love and sex."

"I see I'm about to become the moderator rather than the inaugural speaker at this event," Hirschfeld good-naturedly says. "Before I yield the podium to you, Professor Steinach, let me quickly say that although my views and Dr. Bloch's *are* in essential agreement, I would want to add—and here he might *not* agree with me—that in some cases, a highly developed friendship does come to include an erotic dimension. Whether that attraction then leads to sexual acts is up to the two people involved." Hirschfeld, with a bow to Steinach, moves himself to the side of the podium.

"In adding *that*, Dr. Hirschfeld," Steinach replies, his voice dripping with sarcasm, "you make my rebuttal more imperative still. What neither you nor Bloch has addressed in this discussion is the one element *central* to the biology of homosexuality—namely, the role played by hormones!" Steinach's stentorian voice reverberates loudly. "It's like discussing Ibsen's *A Doll's House* without ever mentioning Nora!" he thunders.

"My experiments with hormonal and gonadal transplants is not yet complete," Steinach continues, "but I've already learned enough to become convinced that the solution to most disputes in the field of sexology lies in the endocrine glands. Allow me to allude briefly to some of my more telling work. When my laboratory in Vienna transplanted male testes into female rats and guinea pigs, and ovaries into males, the results were astonishing, confirming absolutely the biological origin both of gender and of sexual orientation."

Steinach pauses for maximum effect. From the sidelines Hirschfeld, aware of Steinach's experiments, and impressed by them, encourages him to go into more detail.

"Gladly," Steinach replies, having intended to proceed to specifics anyway. "There are glandular juices, male hormones and female hormones, that are—and this point I cannot over-emphasize—antagonistic to each other. When my laboratory transplanted ovaries into male rats, those rats promptly acted in ways intrinsic to females—they offered their non-existent teats to suckle babies and offered their rumps for mounting by adult males."

The audience noisily stirs. Steinach smiles with satisfaction. "Yes," he says, "I don't wonder that you find these results provocative. They will revolutionize our understanding! In my lab we are currently concluding negotiations for an adult heterosexual man to voluntarily provide one of his testicles for transplant into an effeminate, passive homosexual man. I fully expect that the homosexual man will be totally cured. I might add—"

Hirschfeld interrupts: "—'Cured'? But homosexuality is not a disease. We're afflicted not with faulty endocrine glands but with social hostility and the pain it induces in homosexuals."

"Yes, yes, so you say," Steinach replies, as if swatting away a fly. "What *I* say"—his eyes gleam triumphantly—"is that homosexuals have faulty biological equipment. And I will prove it! Homosexual men are the result either of excessive secretions from female glands, or insufficient secretion from male ones—and sometimes both. Moreover, I'm confident of our ability to cure impotence in *heterosexual* males! Testicular transplants between potent and impotent normal—that is, heterosexual—men will vitally rejuvenate the impotent man's sexual drive!"

"More likely these transplants of yours will cure the participants of *any* sexual desire!" a male voice shouts, then rises in his seat. "If I may add a word?"

Steinach, annoyed, gives a brisk half-nod: "You just have! Very well . . . but keep your comments brief."

"I only want to say that you use the words 'effeminate' and 'passive' as if they were synonyms. You're confusing two distinct behaviors, as any homosexual man—or heterosexual woman—would be quick to tell you!"

"Are you an expert in the field?" Steinach sniffily asks. "Do you have the credentials, sir, to challenge the findings of science?"

"I have the common sense!" the man shoots back. "Society tells women that they're incapable of understanding math and science, but that doesn't make it true—look at Marie Curie!"

The name produces scattered applause, and several shouts of "That's right!" and "Good for you!"

"And many men," Steinach's antagonist continues, "have *no* capacity for math and science."

"Individual variations," Steinach replies, flushing with anger, "do not negate group commonalities. May I inquire, sir, where you did your training in endocrinology?"

"I observe people in daily life," the man calls up to the stage.

"Splendid," Steinach acidly replies. "You come from that same so-called school of common sense that claims—absurdly claims—that women are in every way equal in capacity to men, and homosexuals to heterosexuals."

"Not 'equal,' not the same," the man shouts, "but *different*—marvelously different."

With the audience becoming more boisterous, Hirschfeld moves to Steinach's side and gestures for quiet. The crowd simmers down.

"Thank you," Hirschfeld says, "We very much appreciate your enthusiastic engagement with the topics under discussion, but in the name of reasoned debate we must insist on orderly procedures. I myself," Hirschfeld continues, "have been struck by the potential contribution which the new field of endocrinology can make to our understanding of gender and sexual behavior. Yet"—he smiles rather nervously in Steinach's direction—"I myself do not believe that we sufficiently understand the effects of internal secretions on external behavior to draw final conclusions. We do not even know, for instance, whether the testicular secretions of homosexual men differ either in quality or quantity from those of heterosexual men. Further study, I'd suggest, is necessary, though Professor Steinach's experiments unquestionably hold out great promise. I myself happen to believe that his work will be confirmed in future studies."

Suddenly Dr. Bloch speaks up from his seat. "If I may add a few words—?"

"Of course," Hirschfeld responds, ushering himself and a reluctant Steinach off to the side, freeing up the podium for Bloch. When he reaches it, he speaks quickly, as if in fear that Steinach will come thundering back to center stage.

"What I wish to add," Bloch says, "is simply this: Though all three of us agree that sexual behavior is rooted in biology, only Hirschfeld and I maintain that homosexuals are no less capable than heterosexuals of leading healthy, productive lives. Steinach apparently feels that homosexuality is aberrant, a biological mistake, and—convinced that there's no such thing as a contented, productive homosexual—envisions a time when corrective hormonal secretions can be introduced into homosexual bodies, thereby changing them into contented heterosexuals. I find that an objectionable—not to say, inhumane—goal and would deplore such an eventuality."

Bloch moves away from the podium, but before Steinach can reach it, scattered members of the audience are on their feet, some applauding

Bloch, some angrily shouting him down. When the pandemonium subsides, each of the three speakers proceeds to restate, sometimes in more nuanced form, their basic positions. By the end of the third summary, many members of the audience have left the auditorium, though those remaining continue both to compliment and to challenge the speakers. The discussion continues at a high pitch for an additional hour and a half.

～

Magnus Hirschfeld rarely goes out at night. Fear isn't the issue, though his short, squat physique makes him something of an obvious target for assailants of various kinds. There's also the danger, the more his public reputation grows as Berlin's foremost advocate for homosexual rights—and a Jew, no less—that he could be deliberately singled out for a roughing up. If Hirschfeld has many reasons to be wary, he never curtails his movements; like a doe in the tigers' lair, he moves skittishly through treacherous terrain. No, he stays home most evenings for the simple reason that his desk is always piled high with letters that need answering, articles that must be written, journals that have piled high, and minutes of meetings that require amendment.

On this particular evening, Dr. Georg Merzbach, a member of the Scientific Humanitarian Committee, has invited him to dinner at Café Kranzler on the corner of Unter den Linden and Friedrichstrasse. Merzbach has recently returned from a lecture tour in the United States on the subject of homosexuality and has coaxed Hirschfeld to the café with the promise of "exciting news, unexpected developments."

Kranzler's is a little too fashionable for Hirschfeld's simple tastes, but he's accepted the invitation out of curiosity. He knows Merzbach as a reliable observer, if given now and then to hyperbole. Hirschfeld himself hasn't been to America for some 15 years, not since traveling with a friend to the World's Columbian Exposition in 1893, where, as a young man of 25 who'd just completed his compulsory military service and hadn't yet settled on a career in medicine, he'd been dutifully awestruck.

Making his way through the city streets during the hustle and bustle of the dinner hour, a time when he's usually at home, Hirschfeld is astonished, even a little fearful, at what seems to him a sudden uptick in the pace of daily life. He isn't imagining it. The first decade of the 20th century has seen Berlin transformed. *Droschke* carriages and horse-drawn streetcars have mostly given way to elevated trains and electric buses. Hirschfeld's begun to grow accustomed to the radio and the tele-type machine, but not to the new craze for "shopping"—Berliners use the English word—that seems not only to have passionately seized the population but to have resulted in huge department stores like Tietz's or the still more expansive Wertheim's draping their ubiquitous advertise-ments over—so it appears—half the buildings in the city.

By the time he's seated at Kranzler's, Hirschfeld feels grateful for the comparative peace and quiet. But the dinner doesn't start well, with Merzbach complaining loudly about an uncomfortable boil on his neck, compounded by a "ghastly" hangover. Hirschfeld suggests lanolin for the boil, and a glass of bitters for the hangover. His sympathy—or the bitters—soon improves Merzbach's mood.

True to his promise, he does have much to report. After ordering from the menus, Merzbach launches into an energetic account of his visit with A.A. Brill, the highly regarded American psychoanalyst who studied with Freud in Vienna and currently heads the psychiatry clinic at Columbia University. Merzbach reports that he talked at length with Brill about his ongoing study of homosexual men, and tells Hirschfeld that Brill has become convinced a great injustice is being done, most of it deriving from the mistaken belief of his fellow psychiatrists that homosexual men are "degenerates."

"Good for him!" Hirschfeld says. "Most psychoanalysts—no, most *sci-entists*—don't know the difference between an anomaly and a pathology. Being in a minority isn't the same as being a degenerate. Darwin said it long ago—natural variations are essential to the entire evolutionary process."

"Brill is fully aware of our work on the Scientific Humanitarian Com-mittee," Merzbach tells Hirschfeld. "He's no less indignant than we are at the Committee's inability to win repeal of Paragraph 175. When I told him that we already have thousands of signatories to the petition, and mentioned that Einstein, Rainer Maria Rilke, Käthe Kollwitz, and Stefan Zweig are among them, Brill expressed astonishment at the Reichstag's failure to act."

"Surely Brill realizes," Hirschfeld cautions, "that the depth of prejudice in Germany is no less profound than in the United States."

"Brill speaks highly of you personally. He credits you with having inspired his development of what he calls 'adjustment therapy.'"

"I assume he means encouraging the patient to accept his or her sexuality as unproblematic."

"Except for the problems caused by society's prejudice."

"Yes—put the blame where it belongs."

"Though Brill studied under Freud he doesn't agree with his view that homosexuality results from early childhood experiences."

"Freud isn't that categorical. He leaves room for the possibility of biological factors."

The correction doesn't register; Merzbach is too consumed by his own news. "Brill wants his patients to understand that their homosexuality is a natural variant. To the extent they're uncomfortable with it, they need to understand that social disapproval is the cause, and not anything inherent to being homosexual." The further Merzbach gets into his report, the more enthusiastic he becomes—and the louder his voice grows.

"A sensible man. Would that there were more like him."

"Brill said that you and Edward Carpenter in England are leading the struggle to view homosexuality in a more accurate light."

"It's nice to be praised once in a while. We get so much of the opposite. Though I'm not sure Carpenter would be altogether pleased at being bracketed with me."

Their dinner having been served, Hirschfeld savors his first bite. "Ah—the sturgeon is superb. Say what you will about Kranzler's—their prices are steep but their food warrants it."

"I don't understand what you mean about Carpenter. He also believes homosexuality is biological."

"His position is more complicated. He feels closer—at least in some moods—to the views of Friedlaender and the Community of the Special."

"Friedlaender's views are absurd!" Merzbach nearly shouts. "He thinks we're some kind of chosen people!"

Hirschfeld reflexively bristles, aware that as a Jew "chosen people" is a double-edged sword. "Carpenter thinks so too. Though he does go back and forth. I hear Bernard Shaw has recently given him a tongue-lashing on the matter, enraged, apparently, at Carpenter's notion that 'intermediates' could possibly represent some sort of cultural vanguard. Well, perhaps we do . . ."

"Sounds like you're 'going back and forth' yourself. But really, Hirschfeld, the 'vanguard' view is quite mistaken. Homosexuals are just like everybody else—same hopes, needs, dreams . . ."

"Think of it this way, my dear Merzbach. Any group of people with a historical experience different from the norm will have a different—or at least somewhat different—set of values and perspectives. Being outside the mainstream, we're able to see that its values are *not* 'universal truths,' fixed for all time—like the notion, say, that the separate spheres men and women currently occupy are biologically determined. Contrary to Krafft-Ebing, the similarities between men and women are far greater than the dissimilarities. Genitalia aside, of course." (I wonder why I added that, Hirschfeld thinks to himself. I've seen so many variations, like undescended testes or vestigial penises, I'm sometimes not sure *what* finally counts in assigning infants to one category or another).

Merzbach wrinkles up his face in distaste: "I can't agree with you about Kranzler's. These marinated mushrooms taste more like pickles. But never mind . . . The point I wish to make, Hirschfeld, is that lots of heterosexuals grow up as outsiders, too."

"True, and a valuable caution. We need to talk less about group characteristics and more about individual ones. I don't want to embrace any theory that implies the innate superiority of one group of people over another. When we get down to the level of the individual, terms like 'male' and 'female' or 'heterosexual' and 'homosexual' are far too abstract to be descriptively useful ... We need to talk of continuums, not categories. But I'm rambling ..."

Merzbach is still mulling over Hirschfeld's earlier point. "When Friedlaender talks about individual complexity," Merzbach finally says, "he means *men* are complex. He equates women with oxen—interchangeable oxen!"

In his agitation, Merzbach has raised his voice to such a pitch that people at the two adjoining tables look over at them disapprovingly. Hirschfeld, amused, gives the enflamed patrons a courtly nod.

"Well," he says quietly, turning back to Merzbach, "cheerful tolerance is probably the most useful attitude. We're all stumbling around in the same pit of ignorance ... I speak more confidently in public about the 'Third Sex' than I sometimes feel. The theory isn't nuanced enough ..."

"It isn't a virtue to persuade people to a given view and then tell them you're not sure you believe it." Merzbach's tone is censorious.

"Tell me more about Brill."

"You have the gist of it. The rest might not please you as much."

"My dear Merzbach, do continue. I'm hardly a stranger to criticism!"

"Brill rejects the view—having worked with countless homosexual patients—that homosexuality is the result of a hereditary defect or a degenerative psyche. He's publicly stated that among his patients he hasn't found one who could reasonably be called a 'degenerate.'"

"Why wouldn't I like that? It's exactly what I believe."

"No, no, not that part. Brill also insists that most inverts are contented with their lives. They see no reason to consult a physician and no reason to join any public agitation over Paragraph 175. They simply want to be left alone."

"But will blackmailers and the law leave them alone? Surely Brill knows that the answer is no. If Prince Eulenburg and Count Moltke were forced to stand trial, what chance do men of lesser rank have?"

After a pause, Hirschfeld adds, "Now that some time has elapsed, I must tell you that I'm not comfortable with the role I played during Moltke's trial."

"I'm sure you've heard some of the grumbling about it."

"Of course. And I've come to more or less agree with it. I've gone over the matter many times in my mind. I'm no longer as sure as I sounded on the stand that certain features of an individual's psyche are sufficient to describe the person as homosexual. I now incline more to the view that behavior—actual sexual experience—*is* the critical indicator. I'm 'inclined,' though not yet convinced. After all, any number of men have come to me for counseling who don't hesitate to call themselves 'homosexual' even though they're too frightened to search for a partner or, on finding one, are too panicky to sustain an erection. We have so much more to learn before any of us can draw the kind of confident conclusions that I did at the trial."

"We all make mistakes. At least you acknowledge yours. May I return to Brill?" Merzbach asks grumpily.

Hirschfeld gives a little yelp of dismay. "I'm so sorry, my dear Merzbach. I'm being much too self-absorbed. Yes, of course, do tell me what else the great man had to say."

"He believes"—Merzbach lowers his voice to a confidential whisper and leans in toward Hirschfeld—"that physicians in Germany are more benign in their view of homosexuality than are those in England or the United States."

"Oh?" Hirschfeld sounds surprised. "On what grounds does Brill base his opinion?"

"Well, my dear Magnus, it seems that most physicians—especially in the States—show little or none of the compassion of someone like Krafft-Ebing, who claims we should be pitied, not punished."

"The Americans are great believers," Hirschfeld responds, "in *will power*. Anybody who wants to change their sexual pattern, they claim, *can* change it—they're too morally lazy to make the effort. America's unique confidence in the power of the individual is what makes them so intolerant—of poverty as well as homosexuality!"

"According to Brill, they've developed some pretty nasty 'cures' to deal with homosexuals who refuse to dedicate themselves to the hard work of becoming 'normal.' Including bladder washing and rectal massage!"

"The latter sounds rather enjoyable," Hirschfeld says playfully.

Finding no humor in the remark, Merzbach ignores it.

"And if those treatments fail," he continues—here his voice again rises—"the same physicians then strongly recommend CASTRATION!" From the adjoining tables heads once again turn.

"My dear Georg," Hirschfeld cautions, "they'll be tossing us out if you don't modulate your voice." Merzbach exhales and sits back.

"Since some physicians in Germany also recommend castration, Brill gives us too much credit."

"I know of no such case," Merzbach replies rather testily. He's still offended by Hirschfeld's off-handed impishness. Hoping to tease him out of it, Hirschfeld asks, brow furrowed with import, for more details on rectal massage, a technique, he says, previously unknown to him.

Still sounding wounded, Merzbach explains how American and English physicians massage the patient's prostate as a way of killing "homosexual cells, then to be replaced with heterosexual cells."

Hirschfeld can't help himself: "I don't know whether to laugh or cry," he says.

"Whichever tickles your fancy," Merzbach replies sternly.

"Has anyone ever seen a 'homosexual' cell under the microscope—or a 'heterosexual' one, for that matter?"

"I'm sure I don't know." Merzbach seems determined to hold on to his sense of injury. "You've cleared your plate, I see. Would that mine had been so tasty," he captiously adds. Tired of placation, Hirschfeld decides to change the subject entirely.

"I haven't told you, but I leave early in the morning for Italy. Regrettably, I must cut our pleasant visit short."

"Italy?!" Merzbach is taken off guard. "For heaven's sake, why?"

"I've gone often to Italy. The countryside is beautiful, the people equally so. I always find their easy-going warmth restorative. And frankly, I've been feeling worn out lately. The language that the Reichstag's Advisory Committee used this time around to reject action on Paragraph 175 has been troubling me. After all our work, they still refer to us as 'those sick people not worthy of our esteem or sympathy.' It's made me quite depressed. And here is Brill thinking we're so advanced . . ."

"We always knew it would be a long fight," Merzbach offers, without much conviction.

"On this trip I hope to fulfill a longstanding dream of mine—to go to Aquila and lay flowers on the grave of our great forebear, Karl Heinrich Ulrichs."

"Really?! How remarkable! I commend you, my dear Hirschfeld. It's a gesture worthy of your kind heart."

"Nonsense. It's a purely personal journey, benefiting no one but me."

∾

Traveling alone, Hirschfeld arrives at the hillside town of Aquila on April 18, 1909. Situated high in the Apennines, surrounded by snow-capped mountains, the picturesque town is a maze of narrow side streets that abruptly open out into large piazzas lined with small buildings and churches dating back to the Renaissance. So say the guidebooks—accurately enough. Though they make no mention of Karl Heinrich Ulrichs, Hirschfeld has long since become familiar with his story. Born into a pious, conservative family that included a long line of Lutheran pastors, Ulrichs distinguished himself at the University of Göttingen in theology and law, winning prizes for his Latin essays. After two years studying history at Berlin University he passed a rigorous set of exams for the civil service, and for a brief period served as legal adviser to the district court of the Kingdom of Hanover.

Ulrichs then took the momentous step—all but unique at the time—of openly declaring his homosexuality to family and friends; henceforth, he told them, he intended to devote himself entirely to studying the subject of same-sex male attraction. His family proved just as unique, supporting his determination to live honestly and to apply his gifts to the subject that most compelled his attention. The Hanoverian government proved far less tolerant than the Ulrichs family. When Karl Heinrich made the remarkable decision in 1867 to give a formal presentation on his chosen subject to the professional Association of Jurists—which represented lawyers, officials, and academics from the 39 principalities of the German Confederation (unified by Bismarck in 1871)—Ulrichs was greeted with horror, catcalls, and the threat of dismissal.

He resigned instead. Relying on a small inheritance, he began to publish a series of articles and pamphlets that challenged traditional views of male "Urnings"—the term Ulrichs invented and which was widely used for a time, giving way in the early 20th century to Karl Kertbeny's alternate designation, "homosexuals." In his articles Ulrichs contested the longstanding view of "sodomitical" behavior as resulting from decadent sexual excess or masturbation. He offered instead an alternative theory, the one Hirschfeld would later, with modifications, adopt: men attracted to other men constituted a "third sex," a predilection grounded in biology, not pathology; as the ancient Greeks had long ago assumed, the attraction was a natural phenomenon, *not*—as the dominant cultural view currently had it—the product of willful perversion.

The Uranian male, according to Ulrichs, was genitally intact but had an innately "feminine" nature. Sexual organs, in other words, did not determine sexual desire (or personality)—a view that would have profound implications for those who would later declare a transgender identity. Ulrichs subsequently modified his original thesis, acknowledging that some Urnings were entirely "masculine"—as traditionally defined—in their nature as well as their attractions; he also acknowledged, though he dwelt on neither matter, that the same was true for some women (*Urninden*), and that bisexuality (*Uranodionism*) constituted a genuine—that is, biological—reality.

That which is innate, Ulrichs argued, cannot be legitimately criminalized—no more than could other minority features like green eyes or red hair. All were natural variants, requiring no moral judgment. Nor, Ulrichs further contended, should male Urnings be stigmatized by citing passages from the Bible; what the Good Book denounced, he insisted—long before 20th-century "Biblical Criticism" adopted a comparable attitude—is male *prostitution*, not male love and lust.

At the time Ulrichs wrote, criminal laws varied widely in Europe. The French Revolution had produced a liberal code in 1791 that removed consensual sexual relations among adults entirely from state control.

Following France's lead, other European countries—pre-eminently the Netherlands, Spain, and many Italian states—rescinded their anti-sodomy statues. By the early 19th century all of Europe, including the German principalities, had disavowed the death penalty for sodomy; only Great Britain lagged behind, not dropping the death sentence until 1868.

Among the German states, Bavaria led the way in its legal tolerance of same sex relations. Those prescribing the most severe penalties included Austria (alone in criminalizing sex between women), Saxony, and Prussia. The conservative criminal code that Prussia adopted following German unification in 1871 proved widely influential. In 1868 the renowned Berlin physician, Rudolf Virchow—the same Virchow who'd been an acquaintance of Hirschfeld's father—had led a commission to study Prussia's anti-sodomy statute in preparation for a general revision of its legal code, and had concluded that it was "unable to offer reasons why sex between men should be punished by law when other forms of illicit relations," such as fornication or adultery, were not. But Prussian authorities rejected the Virchow report, and the principality retained its stringent anti-sodomy law.

What also remained common currency throughout much of the 19th century was the widespread notion that "sodomites" could be easily recognized by certain physical characteristics. A man who played the "passive" role in anal sex was said to have a funnel-shaped sphincter muscle and sagging buttocks. The "active" sodomite purportedly had an arrow-pointed penis (never to be confused with Cupid's arrow of love). Active and passive alike were thought peculiarly susceptible to a wide variety of ailments: their degenerate behavior led, as night followed day, to physical decay.

Ulrichs's writings were sometimes censored or banned outright (as in Prussia in 1864), but by then freedom of the press in Europe was sufficiently recognized to allow for word of his theories gradually to spread. The number of copies of his works in print was never substantial, but what was printed tended to fall into influential hands. Richard von Krafft-Ebing, the most notable of Hirschfeld's predecessors, cited Ulrichs's work in his best-selling and highly influential *Psychopathia Sexualis,* first published in 1886. Ulrichs's views also reached such pioneering sexologists as Havelock Ellis in England and Iwan Bloch in Germany. Even Karl Marx and Friedrich Engels commented on Ulrichs pamphlets, though negatively—setting the disparaging tone adopted ever after by the orthodox Old Left, which simultaneously champions revolutionary economic change and stand-pat sexual politics.

Italy, with its comparatively relaxed attitude towards "licentiousness," had for some time become a refuge for German and English homosexuals. And so it was with Ulrichs. After an extended tour of the country and three years residence in Naples (where "intemperance" related to murder, not sex), Ulrichs discovered the town of Aquila in the Abruzzo region and settled there in 1880. He sometimes talked of returning to Germany, but he remained in Aquila until his death in 1895.

Hirschfeld regarded Ulrichs as *the* pioneering figure, his theories the groundbreaking inspiration for his own work. He adopted many of Ulrichs's views—including his seminal insistence, not current since the Greeks, that male-male sexual attraction was an entirely natural, if not universal, phenomenon (Unlike Ulrichs, Hirschfeld developed a keen interest in female-female relations, and in feminism, as well). Over time Hirschfeld amends and supplements Ulrichs's views, but they continue to remain among his foundational assumptions.

Arriving in Aquila mid-day, Hirschfeld checks into a pensione close to the town's central cluster of markets and stalls—and to the cemetery where Ulrichs lies buried. He can feel his excitement building, but wants to husband it a while longer—much like the *gourmand* who delays entering a restaurant in order to savor the awareness that a churning stomach *will* be satisfied. Hirschfeld decides on a leisurely stroll through the market area.

One shop catches his eye. It's filled with pastries—an irresistible temptation for the diabetic Hirschfeld; the sight of a plate full of German linzer tortes in the shop's window instantly erases whatever resistance he might ordinarily have mustered. Vacation is no time, he tells himself, to be worrying about his waistline, expansive though it is. The small shop contains only two tables, and on entering Hirschfeld notices a rather elegantly dressed elderly man seated at one of them. When the man looks up, Hirschfeld nods pleasantly in his direction, which in turn produces an animated response.

"Do forgive my boldness, sir," the gentleman says, rising halfway out of his chair. "But may I inquire if you're a stranger to these parts?"

"I am indeed," Hirschfeld replies, torn between politeness and the pressing need to direct the proprietor's attention to the coveted platter of tortes. When he points to his choice, the proprietor picks up one of the tortes to wrap.

"No, no," Hirschfeld urgently signals—"two, please." Up to now all three parties have been speaking Italian—Hirschfeld hesitantly. He becomes uncomfortably aware that the elderly gentleman is now at his side.

"Allow me to introduce myself," the man says, holding out his hand. "I am the Marchese Doctor Persichetti. I don't wish to be rude, but am I correct in noting a German accent?"

"Yes, you are," Hirschfeld responds somewhat warily. "I'm afraid my Italian is decidedly sub-par." Persichetti? he thinks to himself. That sounds vaguely familiar. I wonder why?

"I ask," Persichetti says, switching at once to German, which he speaks fluently, "because a dear friend of mine, now alas deceased some dozen years, was German by birth, though he spent the last years of his life here in Aquila."

Good Lord! Hirschfeld realizes with a flash—Persichetti! Of course—Ulrichs's friend and benefactor. What an astonishing coincidence! To Persichetti, he blurts out, "Do you mean Karl Heinrich Ulrichs?"

It's Persichetti's turn to be astonished. "You *knew* him?!" he gasps.

"No, not personally. But his writings have long been inspirational for me. I doubt I'd be on my current path in life were it not for Ulrichs's pioneering work. My name is Magnus Hirschfeld. Is there any chance you may have heard of me?"

"Not only heard of you, my dear Hirschfeld, but read you!" Persichetti sits back down again, seemingly overcome with emotion. "I mean—good heavens!—you published Ulrichs's letters to his family!"

"No, not me—the Scientific Humanitarian Committee."

"Of which you are the head, are you not?"

"Of which I am the director, yes."

"This *is* too extraordinary!"

Hirschfeld takes Persichetti's hand and kisses it. "And for me, immense good fortune!" The two men then embrace, tears forming in Persichetti's eyes. "Almost no one in Aquila speaks of him now. They seem not to know or care that a great man once lived among them. I alone am left to bear testimony."

"Not so in the world at large. More and more people understand that Ulrichs is the great forerunner. My sole reason for coming to Aquila is to find my dear comrade's grave and mark it with some fitting tribute."

"I will lead you to it, it will be my great joy to do so. But first, will you not come to my home—it's quite nearby—and sit a while? I have so much to tell you . . ."

"With great pleasure, my dear Persichetti, great pleasure . . ."

The two end up talking together for many hours, with Persichetti doing most of it, delighting Hirschfeld with anecdote after anecdote, telling him much about Ulrichs's "very respectable but too modest" manner. Hirschfeld joyfully drinks in the abundance of new information, taking care to remember as many details as possible to repeat to his colleagues back in Berlin. At various points, Persichetti takes down one of Ulrichs's works from the bookshelves in order to find an apt quotation to illustrate some point. In general, Hirschfeld nods in agreement with his pronouncements, though now and then he feels the need gently to add a modifying comment to some passage Persichetti clearly regards as unvarnished Truth.

"Let us not forget Casper," Hirschfeld offers at one point, after Persichetti has fervently credited Ulrichs with single-handedly birthing the scientific study of *Urnings*.

The remark seems to startle Persichetti. "Casper? Who is Casper?"

"Johann Ludwig Casper—surely you know of him?" Hirschfeld instantly regrets the question.

"I most certainly do not," Persichetti indignantly replies. "Who is this 'Casper'? Why do you bring him up when we are discussing Ulrichs?"

Hirschfeld realizes that appeasement, not information, is the called-for response. "No direct connection, no, none at all. Casper edited a medical magazine in Berlin, wrote some pieces for it in the 1850s claiming that *Urnings* could *not* be identified by any external feature like effeminacy ... That's all ... though he agreed *Urnings* were a natural, biological phenomena ..."

"I assure you Karl Heinrich knew nothing of this Casper person," Persichetti huffs, failing to conceal his annoyance. "That name never once came up."

"No, no, of course not," Hirschfeld's reassurance is headlong. "Ulrichs's ideas originated with *him*, not with anyone else ..."

"Quite so."

The matter is gradually smoothed over, but later on a still more discomforting moment arrives when Hirschfeld suggests that Ulrichs's notion that male *Urnings* have "a woman's soul" may require some additional complication.

"What we are now beginning to understand," Hirschfeld says, aware that the remark might also antagonize the old man but feeling plagued by a sense of integrity, "is that what we call 'effeminacy' in men should not always be equated with having 'a woman's soul', nor for that matter with same gender sexual attraction." Failing to credit the scowl beginning to settle on Persichetti's brow, Hirschfeld unwisely continues: "We now have considerable evidence that some men with an over-abundance of traditional masculine qualities, such as muscular sport or military valor, are in fact sexually attracted only to other men, whereas some men who seem drawn only to so-called womanly pursuits are quite heterosexual in their—"

"—My dear Hirschfeld!" Persichetti interrupts, clearly upset. "I may not be abreast of the latest research being conducted in Germany's great cities and universities, but I do know my own experience, and from that I can affirm the absolute correctness of Ulrichs's observations on—"

"—I beg of you, dear Persichetti, do not excite yourself. I assure you that the theoretical modifications I mention remain at the level of speculation. The science of sexology is not well enough advanced to make categorical assertions of any kind."

"Ulrichs's assertions *were* categorical—and beyond dispute, no matter what today's pseudo-science might say." Persichetti is now as agitated as he is adamant. Hirschfeld prudently decides to shift the conversation back to a discussion of Ulrichs the man.

"I can assure you, my dear Marchese, no one admires Karl Ulrichs more than I. From what you've told me, he was as modest as he was brilliant. And like all true saints led a life of utmost simplicity."

"I let him have two upstairs rooms in a ramshackle old house I own—not this one. The only furniture in it was a bed and a table close to the window, where dear Ulrichs sat to do his writing." Perischetti's tone is tight-lipped, though he seems to have thawed somewhat. "Did you know that he wrote everything in Latin? He even edited a literary journal in Latin called *Alaudae*—The Lark. Its circulation was small, but its influence considerable.

"Some of his writings are only now being translated and published. I suspect more and more will be uncovered in the years to come. We still have much to learn from him."

Persichetti seems lost in his memories: "He cooked for himself, you know. I kept remonstrating with him about how little he ate. I'd invite him to dinner every Sunday to make sure he had at least one substantial meal. He was a remarkable conversationalist. Knew everything—astronomy, botany, theology, everything. Come!" Persichetti abruptly announces, "I will show you his rooms."

And he does. They're ramshackle to the point of barrenness. Hirschfeld finds it difficult to imagine how a gentleman scholar could have survived in such spartan circumstances. He knows that he could not.

"I wonder why he never considered moving to Berlin?"

"He had everything he needed right here," Persichetti tersely responds. "He wanted solitude, not frivolity."

Hirschfeld smiles. "I assure you, we are not very frivolous in Berlin. Well, at least I am not. Though opportunities do exist. Outdoor spots, like the Tiergarten or Unter den Linden, where men of—"

"—absurd!" Persichetti angrily interjects. "Such foolishness would never appeal to a man of Ulrichs's noble character!" The tour of Ulrichs's lodgings abruptly ends.

"I will give you instructions for locating Ulrichs's grave," Persichetti says sternly, avoiding eye contact with Hirschfeld. "I cannot join you after all. The walk is tiring, and I am quite exhausted from your visit. Let me warn you, though, that you will find the grave overgrown with weeds and debris. No one visits it. The people Karl Ulrichs fought for never come to see him."

"All that will change," Hirschfeld reassures the old man, knowing that another embrace will not accompany his departure. "The world will yet appreciate all that Ulrichs has done."

Persichetti shakes his head in disbelief, tears in his eyes. Then he quietly, but firmly, takes his leave. Hirschfeld does find the grave. It's no more than a flat metal plate, nearly obliterated with detritus. He carefully cleans it off, then places on the headstone the simple bouquet of flowers he's purchased in the town.

~

THE WAR
1911–1918
KESSLER, RATHENAU, HIRSCHFELD

KESSLER HAD enthusiastically praised Rathenau's renovation of the late-18th-century country house he purchased in 1910 in the town of Bad Freienwalde, and Rathenau had been pleased, though he never said so, at winning the approval of Kessler's discerning eye. When Rathenau completes work the following year on his villa in Berlin's fashionable Grunewald neighborhood, he invites Kessler to come and inspect it.

Kessler is appalled at what he finds: The décor is cold and formal—"the stiff bourgeois façade of dead 'culture.'" He puts that description in his diary, not in his comments to Rathenau. To preserve his integrity, he limits his reaction to a few bland, generalized words of praise—"How clever of you to have found a house on such a beautiful street," and so on. Still, Rathenau catches the drift, and by the time the two men settle down in Rathenau's study for an evening of cognac and talk, he's in a state of repressed irritability—as Kessler is well aware. He opts for a more innocuous topic for openers than he would have liked:

"Did I tell you—or have you heard elsewhere—about the letter-writing campaign William Rothenstein and I have inaugurated?"

"Who is William Rothenstein?" Rathenau's tone is disdainful; if he hasn't heard of someone, he assumes the person doesn't matter.

"The English critic. Now that Wilhelm's made clear his determination to continue building up the navy, I've noticed a decided shift in English public opinion against us. Rothenstein and I have organized an exchange of letters by prominent figures of both countries to affirm our friendship and to attest to our mutual cultural regard."

"An utter waste of time," Rathenau snorts in derision.

"Perhaps so. We've certainly had a number of rather bizarre responses."

"Bizarre enough to be interesting?"

The question seems to Kessler a bit outside Rathenau's usual range, and therefore intriguing, but he knows not to presume too much. "That depends on your interests. Take the poet Stefan George, for example. A boy lover—as you may have heard." Kessler deliberately avoids looking at Rathenau, who in any case registers no reaction.

"Stefan George," Kessler continues, "is among the substantial minority who refuse to sign; he insists, to quote him, that 'it would be no great tragedy if war *did* break out and Germany suffered a defeat.'"

"He sounds like a damned fool."

Kessler laughs. "Bernard Shaw is also among the naysayers; he calls the gesture 'a display of silly vanity.'"

"Quite right, too."

"He's reluctant to praise anyone for anything."

"A sensible rule of thumb."

"Anyway, we did get a weighty number of signatories, and perhaps have done some momentary good."

"Highly unlikely. Not unless you can change the Kaiser's personality along the way." Rathenau stands up. "More cognac?"

"Yes, thank you." Kessler extends his glass and Rathenau moves off to the sideboard where an array of liquor bottles sits on a glass tray. "It's unusually fine."

"It should be," Rathenau calls over. "It's two hundred years old."

"In keeping with the décor," Kessler says with a trace of archness. "Given your resources, after all, you could have built another monstrous pile like Krupp's Villa Hügel."

"That's not where my ambition lies. I've designed Grunewald in a respectably bourgeois style—in keeping with my aspirations."

Kessler laughs. "So you aspire to *descend* the social scale. An uncommon craving."

"All too true." Rathenau places the two drinks on the table between them and resumes his seat. "Unlike Krupp, AEG does not have colonies around the world. Nor wants them."

"Isn't that the Kaiser's doing? Ever since he married off Bertha Krupp to von Bohlen, doesn't Wilhelm more or less dictate the firm's policies?"

"He does. But how unlike you, Kessler," Rathenau says, with his muted version of a twinkle, "to know what's going on in the world of business."

"The race for colonies involves affairs of state, not just business."

"Quite right. The wretched Colonial Association reads like a telephone directory of prominent figures in the German business world—not just Krupp, but Stumm, Kirdorf, and Siemens as well. What none of them, including the Kaiser, seems to recognize, is that our colonial possessions make no significant contribution to German trade—unlike Britain and France. What drives the Kaiser, though he's the last to acknowledge it, is the "prestige" of owning faraway places like Samoa and New Guinea. It makes him one of the big boys. The 'All-High' can ascend no higher, though he continues to try."

"I would think Germany's astounding growth would satisfy even the insatiable Kaiser."

"It's an uneven growth," Rathenau sharply replies. "Yes, the boom in coal, iron, and steel production has produced a prosperous middle class—and also powerful cartels that have made the rich richer. For most workers, little has changed. Are you aware that on average a worker spends two-thirds of his salary on *food*?—on merely staying alive, in other words."

"Is that true of the workers in AEG's factories?"

"Of course it's true. How else could we stay competitive?" Rathenau's knotted brow foretells another outburst.

"You don't seem pleased about it."

"We live in a world apart, Kessler."

"I know we do. I've seen the English slums."

"It's slightly better in Germany—*slightly*. Oh yes, we now have some health clinics, a few more schools, lending libraries, campaigns against venereal disease, cycling clubs—and other similar rubbish. But *real* change—no, not a bit of it."

Rathenau's anger turns into a tirade: "Rural isolation is as profound as ever. And in the cities, increased mechanization has served mostly to increase the pace of work. Cranes, automatic lathes, pneumatic message tubes, sewing machines, typewriters— Wonderful! Marvelous! Meantime, the average worker still lives about thirty-five years—and spends them working twelve to fifteen hour days, hating their jobs, subject to lock-outs, living in rat holes, treated like—"

"—but Rathenau, wait—wait! Aren't you forgetting the substantial increase in trade unions, the rise of the Social Democratic Party, the—"

"—are you saying that a mine worker can buy a suit at Arnold Muller's? Take a vacation to the mountains? Treat his children to chocolate with whipped cream at Hillbrich's? Of course not."

"No, not yet."

"No, not ever—not so long as your precious trade unions continue to siphon off working class militancy—*buy* it off with a week salary raise of five marks! Really, Kessler—you're living in a dream world!" Rathenau abruptly gets up from his chair, leans over, and takes Kessler's glass. "We can both use another drink. Then let's try to change the subject, shall we? Return to some simple topic like the Kaiser."

Stunned into silence by Rathenau's vehemence, Kessler feels more than a little put upon. He resents the implication that he's unconcerned about the average German's lot—he's a sympathetic member of the Social Democratic Party and finds socialist doctrine increasingly appealing. Besides, it's all very well for Rathenau to go on about the workers' plight, but what is he *doing* about it? He himself admits that working conditions at AEG are no different than anywhere else among the large industrial firms.

Rathenau returns with the drinks. His brow is less furrowed, the tone of his voice more mellow. "Shall we turn our attention to beloved Wilhelm?"

"Have you become more of a fan?" Kessler asks, a trace of resentment still showing. "He's acting like a tinpot Caesar these days, so it seems to me."

"The Kaiser would rather march in a parade than govern a country. I know that. We all know that." Rathenau's tone is congenial. "But he shouldn't be underestimated. He's something more than a bombastic nitwit."

"Well! That's a more favorable assessment from you than usual. You must have seen him recently. Has he granted you another audience?" Kessler slyly asks.

"My views on public matters don't fluctuate on how often the Kaiser does or doesn't see me."

Rathenau is again sounding contentious, and Kessler wants to avoid another tirade.

"I only meant," Kessler quietly says, "that when face to face with an individual we're able to see qualities and nuances impossible to gather from a distance."

Rathenau, too, decides against another flare-up: "I've always regarded Wilhelm as incapable of consistency. He changes his opinion with every shift in the wind. But that's not the same as being a 'nitwit.'"

"All that I said was that when discussing the Kaiser you don't usually sound so generous—generosity, of course, is a quality I admire in anyone."

"Your mistake, Kessler, is that you think a few Great Men—rather than impersonal forces—control events." Rathenau's truculence has once more surfaced. "It so happens," Rathenau adds, "that I *have* been with His Majesty recently."

"And?" Kessler tries to sound neutral.

"And, Wilhelm isn't a pacifist and does make belligerent speeches, but he does not, I believe, want to incite war among the Great Powers."

"Though his belligerence might nonetheless cause it. England and France are drawing closer together."

"But not England and Germany. King Edward did his best to neutralize the Kaiser's pugnacity, but now Edward is gone and, with the untried King George on the throne, the Kaiser confidently sees himself as the most influential figure in Europe."

"Meaning peace on his terms, no? The way I hear it, Wilhelm does want a political détente with England, yet refuses to yield an inch on the one matter that stands in its way—German's continuing build-up of its naval power."

"That *is* the sticking point. The Kaiser continues to believe—mistakenly, in my view—that the ongoing competition in armaments actually helps to *maintain* the peace."

"Which his combative rhetoric does not."

"Then you've heard about his recent tirade at Prince Louis of Battenberg, who's about to take command of the British navy."

Kessler is taken by surprise. "What tirade?"

"Third parties to the conversation report the Kaiser as saying that in regard to the Continent he considers himself the *sole* arbiter of peace or war."

"Oh no."

"There's worse. He boasted that Germany has beaten France once and can easily do so again. And—here's the trump—England won't be able to do a damned thing about it. As the Kaiser so delicately put it, 'the English can't mount their Dreadnoughts on wheels and come to their dear friend's rescue.'"

"I tell you the man isn't quite sane."

"Which is precisely what they're saying in England. So you see, my dear Kessler, I'm not quite the 'fan' of our emperor that you think me. In my view Wilhelm will soon be back to predicting that 'perfidious Albion' is working everywhere behind the scenes to block Germany's 'destiny' to dominate all of Europe. Max Harden thinks so, too."

"Harden?! But he's been the Kaiser's strongest critic."

"*Was* the strongest critic. Harden's new enthusiasms are racism and imperialism. I expect he'll be hailing Wilhelm any day as the embodiment of Germanic virtue."

"I would think the Kaiser's anti-Semitism would alone stand in the way."

"Harden was born a Jew, but as you know, he has corrected that divine error by converting to Christianity. A deplorable action." Rathenau's anger goes up a notch. "Baptism is, quite simple, naked anti-Semitism. The goal of the Jewish people should be not capitulation, but assimilation—*as Jews*—in the name of producing a *general* cultural transformation. But for Harden to have retained his Judaism would have been to embrace suffering, and for that he has no talent—though he's masterful at inflicting it on others."

"He showed no scruples in ruining Eulenburg. But having destroyed the Kaiser's closest friend, can Harden now curry favor with Wilhelm simply by embracing imperialism?"

"Probably." Rathenau now sounds calmly detached. "The Kaiser and Harden, after all, have much in common—in particular, their combativeness. Harden *wants* war with England and France. And he wants it *right now*. He'll assure the Kaiser that the time will never be more propitious for Germany than it is in 1910."

"It's curious about Harden—I know for a fact that he couldn't care less about anyone's choice of a bed partner." In returning to a topic they've already moved beyond, Kessler knows that he's audaciously knocking on a door Rathenau has always declined to open. No matter, Kessler thinks, the conversation has been so peculiar that perhaps this is the evening we might dare mention carnality.

"You say you know it as a 'fact,'" Rathenau coldly replies. "That seems presumptuous."

Kessler spots the red flag and backs off. "And where are you in all this, my dear Rathenau?" he ambiguously asks.

"Where am I in connection to—what?"

"In connection to imperial politics."

"As a Jew—nowhere; I lack access to the higher echelons of the aristocracy, the military, and the academy. Yet as a Mighty Industrialist, as the head of AEG—the Kaiser needs to acknowledge me; I'm somewhere in the realm of 'necessary evils.' As a Social Democrat, of course, I'm unambiguously a confirmed enemy."

"Not legally. The 1871 Constitution granted equal citizenship to the Jewish people."

"I'm sure you're aware, my dear Kessler, traveling as you do in the highest social circles, that emancipation on paper is not the same as emancipation in practice. I *have* been allowed to accumulate considerable wealth, and the Kaiser even solicits my opinion now and then. But a Prince Eulenburg, even in his diminished state, would never invite me to dine—just as well, I might add." Rathenau allows himself the trace of a smile.

"You're a great puzzle, Rathenau. I risk saying it to you directly. You carry your Judaism before you like a sword, yet in some of your writings—yes, I make a point of reading you—you sometimes sound as if you agreed with the anti-Semites, as if the so-called blonde Aryan was somehow born superior to the dark, fearful Jew—as *you* have put it."

Kessler is surprised at his own daring. Having just retreated from one controversial topic, he's pushing another—something like the prisoner who engineers his escape and then reappears at dawn demanding readmittance. But Rathenau surprises him. Instead of flaring up, which he's prone to do under far less provocation, he grows silent and inward.

Finally he quietly says, "You do not understand Jews. And why should you, given your own impeccable pedigree? There are some Jews, of course, who do not understand Jews either. Take my cousin Max Liebermann, for one."

"—the painter Max Liebermann?!"

"Yes, of course. The painter—and anti-Semite. He's my mother's cousin."

"I've known Liebermann for years! He's been a mainstay of the Berlin Secession, and is in my view the most gifted of the German Impressionists. I'm stunned that you call him 'anti-Semitic.' In all the time I've known him, I've never—"

"—I use the term in a special sense. As a Jew speaking of another Jew. Liebermann is at bottom an academic painter spiritually connected to Dutch realism and its fascination with the petty bourgeois. He's never made German culture his own, never assimilated to it in order to transform it."

Rathenau stops abruptly, perhaps in response to the peculiar look on Kessler's face. A strained pause follows. Kessler, rarely discomforted, looks like a man trying to silence a steam kettle. He manages to force out a few words:

"I ... I find your characterization of Liebermann and ... and the attitude behind it ... most ... well, eccentric."

Rathenau allows himself a patronizing smile. "Of course you do, my dear friend."

"Liebermann *led* the Berlin 'Secession'—rejected the dominance of academic art!"

"And called as well for the absolute separation of art and politics—without having taken the measure of either."

Kessler sighs. "I won't contest the Liebermann matter further."

"I'm glad to hear it." Rathenau's tone is amiable.

"But this whole Jewish question, Rathenau—"

"—it's dangerous ground, my friend—"

"—there's something I simply *must* say. It would be remiss of me not to ... It's simply this, Rathenau: Speaking as a non-Jew, I'm indignant—if that's a strong enough word—that a man of your talent is denied access to the high office and public service his ability warrants. At least the Kaiser—unlike his witless nobility and brainless military—has the good sense to seek your counsel."

"I thank you for your concern. But I expect no change. The Kaiser, do you know, believes that the Jews killed Christ?"

Kessler silently gasps.

"During the Eulenburg scandal," Rathenau continues, "Wilhelm publicly denounced Harden—I remember his exact words—as 'a loathsome, dirty Jewish fiend, a poisonous toad.' Charming, no? For now his anti-Semitism is sporadic and guarded."

"Yet he consults with you."

"He consults with me *occasionally*. He has no real choice. He needs my cooperation in building up German armaments. The Kaiser can hardly *not* consult with me. Along with Hugo Stinnes, we dominate the field of German electrical power. I prefer cooperation with Stinnes to competition, but Stinnes is difficult to deal with."

"Stinnes *is* an out-and-out anti-Semite."

"Quite true."

"I don't know how you bear it."

"Stinnes and I must find a way to work together. For the good of Germany. He doesn't make it easy. I recently heard that he referred to me at a dinner party as having 'the soul of an alien race.' It's useful to know how he sees me."

"Your equanimity is remarkable."

Rathenau smiles. "I don't deceive myself. Not even about the fact that

I, too, harbor the sick notion, bred into my bones long since, that the Aryan race is somehow more 'courageous,' more 'valiant' than us poor fearful Jews." Rathenau's voice sinks to a near whisper. "This inner battle makes my struggle against the anti-Semites more difficult."

"I'm honored you share that with me. I know of no one whose path is more difficult than yours."

"Any member of the working class has a far more difficult time of it," Rathenau swiftly responds. "Their condition is deplorable—yes, within AEG's factories, too. The assumption that it's right and 'natural' for a large number of people, and their children's children, to continue slaving for the benefit of a tiny fraction of property owners, is a great crime. One in which I, too, participate, even while fully aware of the system's injustice."

"I'm sure you're the only German industrialist who thinks about his workers in any way but as cogs in the machine."

"Men like Stinnes prefer to tell themselves that any man who works hard enough can rise in the world and become an industrialist himself."

"A convenient assumption."

"And wholly false. For a worker to rise into the middle class requires not hard work, but a divine miracle. Over the years I've only *once* known of an AEG worker who rose into the *haute bourgeoisie. Once!* Some manage to become small shopkeepers, itself a marginal existence, but no higher."

"You sound like a trade union organizer, yet I know you oppose trade unions—though I've never understood why."

"As I said earlier, trade unions bargain for a bit more of the pie, but what's needed is a whole new recipe, right down to the pie crust. A worker can't become a man, can't awaken his *soul,* without a fundamental restructuring of society. What's needed is an organic state, in which the hereditary class structure is abolished, each citizen has a role to play, knows what that role is, and is content fulfilling it."

"Frankly, Rathenau, that makes me a little uncomfortable. 'Organic state' sounds like Marinetti and the Futurists. I have a concrete mind; abstractions confuse me, even frighten me a little. I wish you'd describe more fully the *practical* steps you feel we need to take."

Offended, but not prepared to admit it, Rathenau defiantly proceeds to still vaguer abstractions: "The whole tendency of the age is towards greater mechanization, even though we know that the increased production of material goods results not in happiness, but in heightening the desire for still more goods. Yet it's impossible to reverse mechanization. The challenge is to utilize it for different ends. Marx didn't go far enough. A redistribution of money and power cannot effect a change in cultural values."

"What can?" Kessler's voice is strangely muted.

"A deepening of spiritual experience."

"I don't know what that means."

"Nor do I—fully. The cultivation of inwardness ... of inner vitality ... fortitude ..."

Kessler looks puzzled. "I don't follow ... 'Cultivating inwardness' sounds like cultivating indifference—ignoring the suffering all around us. 'Inward' to—what? To religion and the promise of a joyful afterlife?"

"Not a bit of it!" Rathenau flushes with indignation. "You completely misunderstand me!"

"I don't wish to. I'm trying my best. Abstraction, as I said, is not my forte."

Rathenau clears his throat, prepared to try again. "*Every* dictated creed is the enemy of inwardness. Clericalism dominates the West, absolutism the East. And everywhere true patriotism—which is based on self-sacrifice—is confused with nationalism—which is based on self-interest."

Kessler sighs. "I'm afraid you've moved beyond my depth."

"Beyond mine as well, in a sense ... which is why I struggle for words. What I feel most keenly is that acquisitiveness and ostentation must be dethroned. The few enlightened people I meet share a way of life in which possessions and property play the smallest possible role and *passion* the largest—for craft, for science, for unselfish *solidarity*, for the soul ... Their whole being is absorbed in an endless struggle against their own imperfections ... But forgive me, I've turned this into a lecture. My apologies."

"Not at all," Kessler responds, his sincerity obvious.

"Very well then, you've brought it on yourself. The struggle, the search that I refer to is precisely what the proletariat has been robbed of ... It is among the Jews that the unimportance and deception of power has been known the longest."

Rathenau suddenly sits back, as if reluctant to continue. "It's difficult to find the appropriate words ..."

"I wish you'd try," Kessler says with conviction.

"I am in the grip," Rathenau finally says, "of forces, both good and bad, which control me, which determine the course of my life."

Kessler thinks the remark affected, the words of a man convinced he's the chosen receptacle for fighting a war of the worlds: God's elected, helpless vessel. But then he looks at Rathenau's tormented face and sees the authentic despair that consumes him. Kessler very much wants to offer comfort, though has no idea how. Is there a blanket big enough to throw over so huge and impenetrable a Sphinx?

"Dear Rathenau," he hesitantly begins, "few men in Germany are as highly respected as you ... Your writings alone, my dear fellow, your writings are widely influential ... Yet if you will allow me to say so, you drive yourself so zealously to purpose and duty that you leave no time for rest and succor. Yet you are, my dear friend, woefully in need of them."

"You're a good-hearted fellow, Kessler. I know you mean well, and I'm appreciative ... But as you should know by now," Rathenau says in quiet rebuke, "I do not discuss personal matters ..."

"I don't mean to intrude," Kessler replies. They sit in silence for a few moments.

Rathenau doesn't move. Finally, his voice distant, as if speaking in an echo chamber to no one in particular, he says, "I've been studying Hebrew for some time. Are you familiar with Martin Buber's work on the Hasidim?"

"I don't know the name," Kessler replies evenly, sensing that it's all-important at this juncture to sound neutral.

"No, why should you? Buber's first book, *The Tales of Rabbi Nachman*, was only published two–three years ago. I find it most remarkable. He's been much influenced by Fichte and Spinoza who—being German—I presume you do know."

"Only the names. I have no bent for philosophy."

"Of course not." Rathenau's tone is friendly, intimate. "You're drawn to the tactile, the visual. Something you can touch or draw close to. My own temperament climbs hazily toward the abstract. The speculative grounds me—ah, yet another contradiction!"

"If I may say so," Kessler riskily replies, "I think of you as someone eager to contradict himself before anyone else can." He hastens to give back the reins to Rathenau: "In any case, why," Kessler asks, his tone neutral, "do you bring up Martin Buber?"

"Buber contrasts the way German mysticism focuses on dissolving the individual soul with the very different Hasidic emphasis on the ecstatic *unfolding* of the soul, its spontaneous, transforming entry into God."

"I'm trying hard to follow . . ."

Rathenau seems not to have heard him. "Buber calls for the resurrection of the Jewish people from the partial life of secularization to the full life of resurrecting and reinventing Jewish literature and art."

Kessler perks up. "I would certainly agree that any group finds its purest expression in artistic creativity."

"Yes, I thought that would appeal to you," Rathenau replies, with a trace of irony. "Buber's analysis can be transposed to the role, still mostly a potential role, that Jews could play in German life, the possibility of their transforming entry into the mystical core of the German soul. Buber believes that every man—"

"—not every man and woman?" Kessler's voice trails off. He immediately realizes that in trying to play a more animated role in the conversation, he's risked side-tracking it. A look of Olympian disbelief crosses Rathenau's face, suggesting for a split second that he's been deeply offended—then shifts quickly back to an expression of unconcern.

" . . . Man is his own purpose, a unique end—a soul—unto himself. Most men become too engrossed in the daily pursuit of business or pleasure ever to develop their uniqueness. Yet even these men are quite capable of throwing off their bondage to greed and lust—to every limitation on their absolute freedom, including the imposed tyrannies of society and the state."

"Radical individualism."

"Not at all. A community, like an individual man"—Kessler thinks Rathenau's pronunciation of "man" is deliberately over-emphatic, but ignores it—"is able to express a collective soul, a soul that reveals itself in art, speech, mythology, and culture."

"And in war as well?" Kessler has relocated his courage.

"Surely you're in jest?"

"Why no—I thought I was following your—or Buber's—argument to its logical conclusion. Don't be offended—your views fascinate me even if a mere bumpkin like myself would never dare speak of—let alone possess—a 'soul.'"

The spell has been broken. Rathenau retreats to irony: "I apologize, dear friend, for having overtaxed you. I might add that you have about as much resemblance to a 'bumpkin' as an airplane does to a horsecart!"

Kessler thinks that in all probability Rathenau is patronizing him again. No matter. He feels sure that, despite his abrupt brutalities, Rathenau holds him in affectionate regard. They entered deeper water this evening than either intended and need to help each other reach a safer shore. Kessler feels it would be politic to take leave.

He rises from his chair, and then, before turning to go, he riskily takes Rathenau's hand in his, half-expecting him to repel such intimacy. He doesn't. Kessler quietly says, "Do not isolate yourself, my dear Rathenau. Your loneliness is palpable. What I fear most is that it's voluntary. You and I need never again return to tonight's agitating topics. But do let a few shallow types like myself take you to an extravagant lunch at Larue's now and then—perhaps even to a repeat performance of the carnal Russian ballet."

Touched and alarmed in equal measure, Rathenau almost reflexively bows from the waist. "A kind offer, my dear Kessler. I will certainly give it thought."

"You are someone," Kessler solemnly says, "whose company is a privilege. I cannot think of another person I would say that to." He turns towards the door.

"Thank you, my dear Kessler," Rathenau calls after him. "Thank you . . ."

~

In the summer of 1909, the Kaiser appoints Theobald von Beth-mann-Hollweg to succeed von Bülow as Reich Chancellor. It's almost a matter of indifference. Wilhelm thinks little of his minister's ability and isn't much taken with him personally; he once describes Bethmann as "an arrogant, pig-headed schoolmaster." But it hardly matters; *Wilhelm* initiates policy and makes the major decisions; he sees the new Chancellor, like von Bülow before him, as merely an instrument to execute his orders. And so it will turn out: Bethmann, like his predecessor, will prove a dutiful subordinate. Occasionally he'll try putting a brake on one of the Kaiser's headlong dashes, but when slapped down, he stays down.

Over the next few years, the underlying aim of Wilhelm's foreign policy will remain fixed: Germany must be recognized as a world power equal to Great Britain. Under the pressure of a given crisis, he'll veer this way and that, but the compass point never deviates for long: Germany's "destiny" is not to help maintain the balance of power in Europe, but rather to become its illustrious arbiter. Seeing himself essentially as a military figure—a warrior—Wilhelm will implacably challenge British supremacy on the seas (all the while denying that he's doing so), immune to the deterioration in Anglo-German relations, confident that the enervated English will never stand up to his Teutonic firmness, dismissive of potential consequences—except to claim that he's bent on peace, not war.

Thus in 1910, when Russia undertakes threatening military maneuvers, Wilhelm, in a brief spasm of goodwill, tries buttering up England. But when the English respond that a more cordial relationship hinges on the Kaiser's willingness to slow German naval construction, Wilhelm refuses to consider a cutback, and the status quo of distrust bounds back in place: "If a revolution were to endanger the throne in Russia," Wilhelm haughtily informs the English, "the Emperor of Austria and I would instantly march in shoulder to shoulder, to reinstate the Emperor Nicholas."

In the following year, 1911, during a heated international dispute over control of Morocco, the Kaiser publicly denounces the English government for having "blatantly insulted" the German nation. "They seem to have no interest in our friendship," Wilhelm tells Bethmann. "We are not yet strong enough. They are only impressed by force and power." The Kaiser follows up in 1912 with a new naval plan that calls not only for the construction of additional ships but for a near-doubling of naval personnel. He feels confident—though the logic is obscure—that this latest move will somehow sever the English-French alliance and guarantee British neutrality in any Franco-German war. Wilhelm's bluster produces exactly the opposite result: Britain provides France with additional guarantees that she will come to her ally's aid in case of a German attack. "Insolence and boundless effrontery!" Wilhelm rages.

Thereafter the scenario is pretty much fixed, give or take a few changes in personnel and temporary crises that briefly shift the focus of complaint; an ever-deepening fatalism sets in that an outbreak of open warfare is only a matter of time. Of all the major belligerents, Wilhelm is the least willing to adjust his policies "SIMPLY for the sake of peace," and the most willing to regard the basic nature of the conflict as a *racial* struggle between Teutons and Slavs.

Ever since his keen disappointment in Prince Eulenburg's "betrayal," Kaiser Wilhelm has made few friends; these days, he isn't consistently fond of anyone. One of the few exceptions is Archduke Franz Ferdinand, heir to the throne of the Austro-Hungarian Empire, German's ally. Most people view the Archduke as an unsmiling, cold man devoid of humor and lacking in natural charm—a narrow-minded martinet and devout Catholic who makes no effort to conceal his hostility to social democrats and Jews, usually conflating the two. What many regard as Franz Ferdinand's defects, Wilhelm sees as virtues.

Franz Ferdinand is the nephew, not son, of Emperor Franz Joseph, and he's become heir to the Austro-Hungarian throne only because his cousin

Crown Prince Rudolf killed himself and his mistress at Mayerling in 1889. Franz Joseph has never liked Franz Ferdinand and, after he insists on marrying Sophie Chotek—descended from mere aristocrats, not royalty—his outsider status becomes confirmed. The Emperor declares that the couple's children can never ascend to the Habsburg throne, and, taking his cue, the Austrian court proceeds to humiliate Sophie at every turn.

It's perhaps predictable that Wilhelm will embrace the Archduke. Their conservative political values are aligned, and the Kaiser, too, though hailed as the All-High, in his own mind has never fully "belonged," has continued to feel himself something of an outsider. Born with a withered arm, he's been unable to participate fully in the male activities he most admires: hunting animals and training for war. Despite the magnificent uniforms Wilhelm flaunts and the verbal bellicosity he cultivates, a man who cannot cut his own meat will never be entirely accepted as a warrior.

Wilhelm finds in Franz Ferdinand a comforting alter ego. When the Kaiser's entourage visits the Archduke's estate at Konopiště, the two men share some of their deepest convictions. "I dislike Hungarians," Franz Ferdinand confides to Wilhelm. "They are anti-dynastic, lying, unreliable fellows; and as for Slavs, they are simply 'pigs.'" Wilhelm agrees, adding that the British are still worse: "Only strength and brute power makes any impression across the Channel. Politeness is seen as weakness." He tells Franz Ferdinand that he's prepared to support Austria-Hungary "under all circumstances"—including an offensive war against Serbia. A grateful Franz Ferdinand congratulates the Kaiser on "the success of your policy," for which he has "the *greatest* admiration" and with which he "fully identifies."

Europe has known peace for 50 years and most of the great powers profess a determination to maintain it. Yet in the past decade military and commercial competition have accelerated and two opposing alliances have grown up; on one side stands the Triple Entente of England, France, and Russia, on the other the Triple Alliance of Germany, Austria-Hungary, and Italy. The privileged elites in each country cherish the view that the preceding years of the Belle Époque have been marked among the masses as a time of profound contentment and fulfillment—a myth more outsized than most.

The early years of the 20th century have in fact been a time of enormous change and upheaval. Horse carriages have given way to automobiles, candlelight to electricity, merry-go-rounds to movies. The demands of women—especially in Britain—for fundamental rights have been paralleled by the growing allegiance among the working class—especially in Germany—to militant socialism. The system of autocratic monarchy is decidedly on the wane as the democratic spirit continues to spread. The convulsive 1905 revolution in Russia, with its widespread strikes and uprisings, its spate of assassinations and civilian executions, has terrified the ruling class throughout Europe. The old order holds, and denial continues to reign, but it becomes *somewhat* more difficult to remain wholly oblivious to the multiplying perils to peace.

Walther Rathenau is among the few who dares to gaze steadily at the warning signs and try to read them. In 1912 he publishes a book, *Critique of the Times*, in which he states flat-out that Europe's current rulers are unequal to the tasks at hand. He predicts that the bourgeoisie, having proved themselves capable masters of industrialization, would—though resistant to art, science, community, and all intuitive, unconscious, transcendent values—employ an ever-heightened mechanization to successfully feed the masses and calm the waters. He flays the German ruling class for its indolence and its blindness—what he calls its "hereditary lack of talent." At the apex stands the Kaiser, whose world-view Rathenau argues—though he continues to have occasional audiences with Wilhelm—is based on superficial, inconsistent, and arbitrary assumptions.

The only way to guarantee peace in Europe, Rathenau insists, is to create an industrial customs union—a kind of supra-state agency. It could establish a fixed correlation between each nation's resources and its allowable expenditure for arms; as well, he argues, each country's population should be the basis for determining the permissible extent of its military. Disarmament is still plausible, he insists: if Europe's industries are fused into one, then the fusion of political interests will follow—a more advanced version of the European Union which would emerge many years later.

A rational system of quotas, however, is no match for irrational ambition and the emotional fervor of nationalism used to legitimize it. Rathenau's logical and tidy formulas for avoiding war have about as much appeal as soda pop to an alcoholic. The Austrian Habsburgs go right on planning for the abject submission (meaning dismemberment) of Serbia; the Kaiser goes right on pledging unconditional loyalty to Austria; Slavic Russia continues to promise undying support for Slavs everywhere (especially in Serbia); and France continues to pretend that its devotion to culture takes automatic precedence over vulgar pugnacity—meaning, it continues to harbor ferocious resentment for having lost the Franco-Prussian War of 1870. When Rathenau describes himself in a letter as "the loneliest man I know," his politics, as well as with his temperament, accounts for the accuracy of the description.

Rathenau is disappointed to discover that his friend Harry Kessler fails fully to share his sense of alarm. Kessler confidently predicts that, should war come, Germany would conquer France, and that the likely victory of the English fleet over the German one would prove a Pyrrhic victory since German privateers would prevent English vessels from procuring needed food imports. Russia, Kessler further believes, will offer Germany an easy peace, and possibly even an alliance, in exchange for parts of southern Persia. Kessler's forecasts will prove far off the mark, though, unlike Rathenau, he never pretends to be a gifted political prognosticator.

A true cosmopolitan, Kessler feels comfortable in a variety of milieus, and spends a good part of the period preceding the outbreak of war traveling on the continent. He thinks that Berlin suffers from comparison. The German national character, in his view, is the product of life in small towns, where the chief activities are spying on one's neighbors and begrudging their every advancement. On the positive side, he feels that the German nation, as a hodgepodge of petty principalities, contains a far greater abundance of social customs and idiosyncrasies than can be found in England or France.

Like so many who share his class pedigree, Kessler isn't convinced that war will actually come, and on his many excursions to London and Paris, he redoubles his socializing. He sometimes brings along his lover, Gaston Colin—though not to events involving high society. Instead, the two spend many an evening in the restaurants and bars that artists and their hangers-on frequent. One such occasion proves inadvertently memorable.

At the fashionable Château de Madrid, they're introduced to two women, one a painter—a blonde with closely-cropped hair and painted lips—and the other, "a little mannish brunette" (as Kessler describes her) about 40 years old. He notices that Colin blushes when introduced to the two women, suggesting to Kessler that he already knows them, or knows something about them that he considers embarrassing. When Colin has a chance, he whispers to Kessler that the blonde is a well-known procuress "who provides rich women with little girls," and that the brunette is a married woman; they're known in Montmartre as "Madame de Belbeuf" and "Colette Willy."

The latter of course is Colette; she's recently left her husband Willy, is now writing under her own name, and along with having female lovers is also having heterosexual affairs—including one with Gabriele D'Annunzio, the poet and incipient fascist. Annoyed at what he considers the two women's open sexual display, Kessler later writes in his diary that he found the evening "loathsome, loathsome." Comfortable with his own homosexuality, he disapproves of making a public issue of it—or even of allowing it to become visibly apparent.

Kessler also continues to make the rounds of galleries and museums and to see the host of luminaries he already knows. That often means lunch or dinner with Max Reinhardt; Bernard Shaw; Countess Élisabeth Greffulhe (the strikingly beautiful, patrician patron of the arts); Gordon Craig (who one evening brings along Aleister Crowley, the eccentric spiritualist who's mostly silent except for suggesting, as Kessler describes it, a late evening orgy "with a new kind of intoxicating drink that causes colorful visions"); and, in both London and Paris, Diaghilev and Nijinsky. Diaghilev continues to fascinate Kessler, but on closer acquaintance he dismisses Nijinsky as "a petty and spoiled child."

Politics is peripheral, though never absent. When in London in 1913, Kessler takes Bernard Shaw to lunch at the German Embassy to meet Prince Lichnowsky, the Kaiser's new ambassador to England. Kessler has known Lichnowsky for some time, enjoys his company, and tends to agree with his view that Germany's relationship with England is (as Lichnowsky puts it) "the linchpin of our entire foreign policy"; the Prince also feels certain that "the English will never declare war on us"—a view Kessler does not share.

At lunch Shaw, mixing as usual wit and insight, lays out for Lichnowsky his plan for ensuring peace. It's simple, he tells the Prince: Germany has to enter into a *new* Triple Alliance, this time with France and England. Other countries would then be notified that, should they be tempted to embark on aggression, the Alliance will land on them hard. Lichnowsky smiles benignly, as if humoring someone not quite in his right mind, and both he and Kessler point out to Shaw that in a modern war it's hard to tell *who* the aggressor is.

Ignoring the point, Shaw proceeds to disparage Sir Edward Grey, the English Foreign Secretary, while Lichnowsky—partial to all things English—is quick to defend him as a far-sighted statesman. Nonsense, Shaw replies, Grey's only distinctive feature is his big nose, and, since that's hereditary, he gets no credit even on that score. Besides, Shaw goes on, Grey speaks neither French nor Russian, and is in general so taciturn that "we're not sure he even speaks English." After the lunch Lichnowsky acknowledges to Kessler that Shaw is "exceptionally witty" but is "not to be taken seriously as a politician." Kessler isn't so sure; beneath Shaw's paradoxes, he tells the Prince, "there nevertheless mostly lies a truth."

What *is* distinctive about Grey is his deep abhorrence of war, which some blame for England's belated preparedness. Until the 11th hour Grey continues to hold out hope that Germany will use its influence with Austria to prevent the dangerous cross-currents in the Balkans from escalating into a general conflict—in the process further encouraging the Germans to believe that England might well remain neutral.

After meeting Grey socially, Kessler expresses admiration for his common-sense talk, but thinks he lacks any real sparkle or originality.

Now and then Kessler expresses concern in his diaries and letters over what he views as mounting chauvinism in France, but he lulls himself into believing—and Rathenau cannot convince him otherwise—that the Kaiser would *never* take Germany into war. If war should nonetheless come, Kessler feels confident that certain features of the German character—dutifulness, seriousness, stubbornness—guarantee a victorious outcome (a view Rathenau finds overly sanguine and naïve). In the meantime, Kessler continues to distract himself with art, friendship, and society, unabashedly enjoying his ever-widening entrée to select circles.

Invited to a garden party at the Asquiths, he brings along another Eminent Victorian, Lady Ottoline Morrell—a central figure in Bloomsbury—and during the evening also manages a nice chat with Lady Randolph Churchill. At a conspicuously grand dinner that the Lichnowskys throw at the German Embassy, the guests include none other than the King and Queen, Sir Edward Grey, and the Duchess of Marlborough. Kessler manages to feel sorry for the "poor, awkward" Queen, whom (as he writes in his diary) "you have to wind up like a clock" to keep the conversation going.

The higher Kessler moves in social circles, the more he seems to overlook their insular prejudice, even—to an extent he might have earlier protested—their anti-Semitism. He now seems casually indifferent to it, lamenting in his diary the "almost unfathomable lack of culture" that he finds in Jews and parvenus. He even decides that his friend Walther Rathenau is beginning to "parade" his Jewishness like a battering ram, that he's in fact "a great dandy, the dandy of Judaism"—much like Disraeli's behavior, he decides, in the ducal salons of London around 1840, "but without Disraeli's devilish spirit, and that makes a devilish difference." Still, Kessler considers himself a loyal friend of Rathenau's and freely describes him as "pure genius."

Ever since their ill-fated trip to Greece back in 1908, Kessler's relationship with Hugo von Hofmannsthal has been an on-again-off-again friendship, but, in these years immediately preceding the outbreak of war, it's mostly on the upswing. Yet he retains serious doubts about Hofmannsthal both as a writer and as a human being. He feels that the Austrian's recent output is no match for the miraculous poetry he wrote as a mere teenager. And he continues to have serious doubts about Hofmannsthal's character—"he never offers himself entirely to anything," Kessler writes in his diary. "He always remains on guard. In his gestures, his marriage, his passion for money, he is the most bourgeois person I have found among artists. That's why his appearance will always lack the magic of those who have risked something."

Yet Hofmannsthal becomes the instrument through which Kessler comes as close as he ever will to being an artist himself, rather than an appreciator of art. At Hofmannsthal's urging, Kessler has for some time been sending him ideas for poetry and plays. At one point he forwards to Hofmannsthal an erotic 18th-century novel; Hofmannsthal is taken with it, and the two friends decide to work together to convert it into an opera, with Richard Strauss composing the music. It premieres in Dresden early in 1911 as *Der Rosenkavalier*—and is a huge success.

Kessler has taken deep pleasure in the joint collaboration on the libretto, and he's profoundly shocked when Hofmannsthal dedicates the opera to his "hidden helper, Count Harry Kessler"—a patent under-representation of Kessler's contribution, the dedication infuriates him. When he protests, Hofmannsthal amends it to read "for Count Harry Kessler, to whose cooperation it owes so much," arguably an improvement over the first version, but still inaccurately relegating Kessler to a subordinate role.

Somehow—Kessler ascribes it to a mysterious sympathy between the two men which keeps surmounting their scrapes and quarrels—the friendship survives. But it's attenuated. Kessler never again feels that he can fully trust Hofmannsthal, though professionally he's willing to collaborate with him a second time. That joint effort becomes the ballet *The Legend of Joseph*, with Strauss again composing the music and Diaghilev serving as producer. The company goes into rehearsal in London, and it isn't long before Kessler sees what he calls "the Tartar" in Diaghilev—"a brutal but imperious temperament." He finds Strauss, on the other hand, kind and attentive.

The Legend of Joseph premieres two years later on May 14, 1914 at the Paris Opera, with Strauss conducting and with Léonide Massine in the title role. The ballet is well received and the production opens the following month at the Drury Lane in London with *tout le monde*—that is, with everyone who believes they make up the world—in attendance. The press is more mixed in London; a number of critics feel the piece is a decidedly lesser Strauss work. For the ballet's third performance on June 29th, royalty is due to attend. They do not: news reaches London the day before that Archduke and Duchess Franz and Sophie Ferdinand have been assassinated.

What is to be done? Is it possible that an actual war will occur? Few remain alive in 1914 who remember the horrors that war brings. It's instead recalled vaguely as a kind of stately pageantry peopled with virile men of courageous mien and courtly grace—a pageantry unstained with severed limbs, starving children, pillage, rape, and massacre. War is romance and adventure, ennobling to its participants, brief in duration, culturally energizing. Every capital in Europe reverberates with the dual sensations of excitement and alarm.

∽

Theobald von Bethmann-Hollweg has been Reich Chancellor since 1909 and Kessler has come to know him somewhat socially. At one dinner party, the two men, along with Prince Lichnowsky, the German ambassador to England, have a long talk together about foreign affairs. Kessler offers his opinion that England has her hands full with what amounts to the threat of civil war in Ireland, and Lichnowsky agrees that an accommodation with England should be a fairly easy matter. Bethmann, known for his indecisiveness, falls back on what he calls "the need to proceed from general principles"—though he fails to define them, other than to declare his view that it's up to England to initiate negotiations with Germany.

Rathenau has still closer ties with Bethmann. His country home in Freienwalde is near to the Chancellor's, and they dine with some frequency. Like Kessler, Rathenau urges an understanding with England, and when the English do put out a direct feeler to that end, he's dismayed that Bethmann gives an evasive reply. Beyond the shared assumption that England is crucial to maintaining peace, the divergence between Kessler and Rathenau's views has steadily widened. Kessler feels that his many contacts and long stays in England have made him a master of English psychology, and, at one of their periodic lunches at the fashionable Adlon, he decides, gingerly, to question Rathenau's assumption that he understands the English fully.

He sees a promising opening when Rathenau starts to expound his view that England, economically, is no longer competitive with Germany. "Do you realize?" he asks Kessler, "that thirty-five years ago, Britain produced twice as much steel as Germany, and that today the position is exactly reversed?! The same is true in regard to coal—we now produce a full quarter of the world's entire supply. What's more, we've taken over the leadership in exporting manufactured goods. Where once we were Britain's chief market, we're now her leading industrial competitor."

"Forgive me, my dear Rathenau, but you sound nearly as aggressive as the Kaiser."

Rathenau responds with calm authority. "For an old friend, you manage to misread me with remarkable regularity. In describing Germany's economic dynamism, I'm not advocating German *aggression*. Unlike the Kaiser, I do *not* believe that Germany has a "mission" to carry its values across the globe. As you should know, I've consistently and strongly opposed any imperialist expansion overseas; the argument that more colonies will all at once supply Germany with more raw materials and serve as a market for more German goods is utterly misguided."

Kessler is already feeling out of his depths. He manages, tentatively, to suggest that Rathenau may be overstating Germany's economic superiority. "What about the United States?" Kessler asks. "Isn't America a real threat, especially in the area of scientific research?—where I'm told Germany has begun to falter."

"There, I would agree. Not about our science 'faltering,' but about

America's all but unlimited potential—especially now that it's annexed the Philippines and began its own imperialist march across the globe."

"When you say that England—at least relative to Germany and the United States—is in decline, do you mean the parliamentary system too?"

Kessler's question isn't particularly germane to what Rathenau has just said. Thrown off stride, and not exactly pleased about it, he responds with a question of his own, "Are you asking what role a constitutional monarchy might play in England's future, or in Germany's?"

Without waiting for a response, Rathenau provides his own answer. "In some countries," he says with considerable relish, "it's the best brains that lead. In Germany, it's the insolent, vacuous offspring of a hare-brained nobility that holds the reins. The Kaiser and his entourage see every minor suggestion of democratic reform as the equivalent of revolutionary communism. He shackles himself to Austria's disintegrating Habsburg Empire and wonders why the English distrust his professions of friendship!"

Kessler tries to return the conversation to the situation in England, about which he feels more knowledgeable. "Don't the English have their hands full at the moment? The upheaval in Ireland, rising clamor for independence in India and elsewhere within their empire. At home, a militant suffragist movement, escalating strikes, a weak prime minister in Asquith."

"The English aren't likely to precipitate a general conflict. But nor are they likely to sit supinely by in the face of Germany's challenge to their supremacy on the seas. In my view the English *would* be open to negotiating some formula for quotas, say three English vessels built for every two German ones."

"I doubt if either the Kaiser or Admiral Tirpitz would ever agree to a quota system."

"Ah—now we come to the heart of it—the fundamental difficulty. The Kaiser's obsession with German naval power will, I predict, override all considerations of caution."

Seemingly out of nowhere, Kessler says, "I assume you've heard about Prince Heinrich of Prussia?"

"The Kaiser's brother?"

"Are there two Prince Heinrichs, God forbid?!"

"What in heaven's name does Prince Heinrich have to do with—"

"—I'm surprised you haven't heard," Kessler says, trying to conceal his satisfaction. "Heinrich told a British naval attaché that—quote—'the other large European maritime nations are not white men.'"

Rathenau lets out a sound somewhere between a growl and a groan. "I don't believe it! Not even of Prince Heinrich, whom everyone knows has a goose egg for a brain!"

"Last I heard, the Italians and French consider themselves 'white.'"

Rathenau's anger rapidly overcomes his dismay: "Heinrich is much like his brother; they declare undying admiration for England and then create a fleet big enough to unnerve her. Why can't Wilhelm see what's in front of his face?! England's a sea power, Germany's a land power! Our basic interests lie in continental Europe, whereas England's reside in its overseas empire."

"Is it possible the Reichstag can somehow restrain him? After all, the Social Democrats are now the leading party."

"The liberals also had considerable power in the Reichstag during the 1870s," Rathenau scornfully replies. "Elected, no less, by the universal franchise of all males over the age of twenty-five. You saw the results."

"No," Kessler laughs, "I was born in 1868."

"I was born in 1867. So what? I still know what happened. Bismarck, with his usual genius, isolated and manipulated the liberals, divided and conquered, passed severe anti-socialist legislation—and continued to rule undisturbed."

"The Kaiser isn't Bismarck."

"So you've noticed. I don't mean to be rude, my dear Kessler, but the Kaiser *doesn't have to be* Bismarck. He simply announces that the Reichstag is full of unpatriotic 'scoundrels' and lets his ministers strike enough deals and massage enough egos to continue to do pretty much what he wants to. 'Ach, that damned Reichstag!' he tells everybody, as if brushing away a noisome mosquito! Politics is a popular spectacle, but the system remains *sham* constitutionalism. The four major parties cancel each other out ideologically. You hear criticism of the Kaiser, but you don't hear criticism of the institution of the monarchy. Or not enough criticism, at any rate, to rattle the throne."

"Yet in theory the Reichstag does have the right to approve the federal budget."

"Quite so. *In theory*. In practice the Kaiser ignores them and implements his own policy."

"Do you believe the Kaiser has deliberately set out to antagonize the English?"

"The last time he deigned to ask my opinion, I told him that in return for a 'quota system' I believed England might stay neutral should war break out on the continent. But Tirpitz and the Kaiser outdo each other in obstinately rejecting any proposal for quotas."

"Then he *does* want war?"

"On the day I last saw him, he solemnly told me that 'a policy of adventure is far from our minds.' Which can only mean that his mind is playing tricks on him, since he continues to act on the international scene like a daredevil schoolboy."

"Yet I hear from many sources that Wilhelm *is* anxious to avoid war."

"So he says—often. He even means it in some moods. Yet his policies lead in the direction of war—though *that* he can't see."

"How often do you see the Kaiser?"

"Not often—even less than before." Rathenau is being accurate, not modest. "The last time he was in one of his moods."

"Depressed?"

"Yes—for ten minutes. Then bombastic. Then restless. Then infantile. Then petulant. Then—well, if you're in his presence for an hour you get to see most of the spectrum of human emotions. I even felt sorry for him—briefly."

"Sorry? How can you feel sympathy for a man who never shows any for others?"

"The private man is quite different from the public popinjay pretending to be masterly. In private you see much more of the fidgety little boy who can't be amused for five minutes without grabbing someone else's toy. It's sad, really. But if you dare express sympathy, he's likely to fly into a rage and walk out."

Now I see, Kessler thinks to himself. Of course Rathenau would feel *some* sympathy for a man so like him—a contradictory nature divided against itself, a determination to reject tenderness as inappropriate to "manliness." Not that the profoundly serious, disciplined Rathenau remotely resembles the Kaiser otherwise.

"What most perplexes me," Rathenau continues, "is why Wilhelm insists on binding Germany to Austria's collapsing fortunes. The Austro-Hungarian Empire consists of fifty million people and multiple nationalities rattling together like marbles in a teacup. Austria's new *chef de cabinet*, Count Hoyos, is filled with youthful ardor and has been recommending war—against almost anyone—as the likeliest way to reinvigorate the Empire. In fact, war will destroy it."

Kessler shifts uncomfortably in his seat. "I don't share your fear, you know, about the likelihood of war."

"Meaning you don't think it will happen? Or you don't think it will be awful? In either case, you're quite wrong."

"I think it might well happen. But not solely because the Kaiser refuses to entertain a compromise that might prevent it. French arrogance and English money-grubbing will play their role. As will Germany's weariness with constantly having its western boundary threatened, not to mention Russia's conviction that past concessions to Germany have only served to heighten our aggression and that Mother Russia has a historic—a *racial*—obligation to defend Slavs everywhere. Put all those factors together, and war seems to me something close to an inevitability. And not one necessarily to be shied away from."

Rathenau gives Kessler a piercing look of disbelief. "You astonish me," he says softly. "You simply astonish me. I thought we were as one about a war."

"I don't think we're far apart." Kessler looks uneasy, afraid that Rathenau is about to unleash one of his unstoppable tirades. "All that I'm saying," Kessler goes on, "is that I wouldn't give two marks for a world in which the possibility of war is abolished. War will transform our society as nothing else can, and cast it into a new form."

Kessler's little speech stuns Rathenau. This is no mere difference of opinion, he thinks to himself—it's an unbridgeable chasm. Rathenau can't restrain himself. "You speak of a 'new form'. A new form, indeed!" he hears himself shout. "It will produce desolation and death unknown since the Napoleonic Wars. Besides the millions who will die, there are the millions more who will be penniless, rootless, and desperate. Good luck with your 'transforming' war and your 'new form.' The *unfittest* will survive, and will swarm over each other like maggots!"

Rathenau is now on his feet, and without a further word storms out of the restaurant.

Kessler's views are far more typical of the day than Rathenau's. The upper classes especially—and not just in Germany—often sound as if war should be welcomed as a precious friend. It will dissolve, people claim, the petty, selfish concerns of individuals into a concord of unity that puts the needs of the nation above all else. "War," declares the Italian artist Filippo Marinetti, "is the sole hygiene of the world"—and, adds the German General Friedrich von Bernhardi, "War is a biological necessity . . . Without war, inferior or decaying races would easily choke the growth of healthy, budding elements, and a universal decadence would follow." In another variation on the same theme, Chancellor Bethmann, just as the war clouds darken, lectures the French ambassador to Germany about France having for 40 years pursued the "grandiose" policy of securing an immense empire for itself, and how it is now time for Germany to claim its own "place in the sun."

Kessler—and many others—believe that if war does break out, it will be a short one, and the last for many generations to come, if not forever. One widespread conviction is that the outbreak of hostilities will rapidly disrupt international trade and no government will be able to cope for long with rising food prices, the shrinkage in available credit, the confusion of re-routed rail travel, the irregularity of postal service, and the widespread disruptions attendant on massive troop movements. Mixed into such calculations is the German conviction of invincibility, based on the strong growth of its economy over the past two decades.

Opposition to the headlong march to war is found primarily in the international socialist and pacifist movements. As early as 1907, the

Second International Congress—founded to unite workers everywhere in a transnational bond—passes a resolution that characterizes the mounting crisis as a "rivalry for world markets" and attributes the rising tide of nationalism to the ruling class's deliberate effort to divert workers from their own class interests.

The Socialist cause gains considerable allegiance in Europe, and opposition to war is not negligible. By 1914, the British Labour Party has elected 42 members of Parliament, the French Socialists hold 103 seats, and the German Social Democratic Party, following the election of 1912, is the strongest of all—with 110 seats, making it the largest party in the Reichstag. In recent international crises involving Morocco and the Balkans, the SPD has demonstrated the ability to orchestrate huge demonstrations against armed conflict. Yet it remains to be seen whether the SPD's split personality of radical internationalists on the one hand and liberal reformers on the other will determine its attitude towards war.

If the working class can unite, it might still wield enough power to block the advancing discord. But the impediments to unity are substantial. Many workers, along with most of the privileged elite—and that includes Count Kessler—hope for and expect German domination of continental Europe as the end result of an armed contest. Besides, the divisions within socialism in every country are profound, the chief one being the split between orthodox Marxists advocating armed revolution as the most effective tool for bringing about social change, and "moderate" socialists insistent instead on the traditional means of the ballot box.

As socialist ranks swell, there's a parallel upswing throughout Europe against what's being called their "unpatriotic," even "treasonous," placing of class interests above national ones. On that issue, the Kaiser, predictably, leads the pack. Some years earlier, Wilhelm had instructed the German chancellor to "first cow the Socialists, behead them and make them harmless, with a bloodbath if necessary, and then make war abroad. But not before and not both together." The Kaiser's ferocious *diktat* periodically gives way—as every mood of the Kaiser's does—to gestures designed to be read as "peaceful," and even to his outright declaration that he opposes a general war. The German military and its aristocratic legion of right-wing conservatives, however, doesn't stoop to the pretense of ambiguity.

Mounting nationalist fervor even catches up with Magnus Hirschfeld, who previously counted himself a pacifist. He isn't alone among the Scientific Humanitarian Committee's membership, nearly half of whom express eagerness to volunteer for military service and, if need be, to die for the Fatherland. Some of the SHC's homosexual members who'd earlier fled Germany for fear of prosecution now return in order to join the army. Hirschfeld himself goes so far as to write a pamphlet—"Why Do Other Nations Hate Us?"—that reiterates many of the arguments currently being peddled by conservatives: France still festers with rage over its bitter loss to Germany in the war of 1870–71; Russia is fearful that Germany's superb fighting machine can vanquish the superior numbers in the Tsar's service; England has nothing but contempt for German culture. And so on. Hirschfeld even repeats the widespread contention in Germany that its industrial and economic advance has filled its enemies with jealousy; they "encircle" Germany and are eager to gobble it up.

Within a year, Hirschfeld—once he's experienced some of the reality of war as a physician for the Red Cross—will renounce his earlier views and declare warfare a form of delirium, a psychosis. Count Harry Kessler, too, will have an early change of heart—though later than Hirschfeld.

On June 28, 1914, one of Franz Ferdinand's Serbian "pigs," 19-year-old Gavrilo Princip, assassinates the Archduke and his wife at Sarajevo. The Kaiser mourns his friend's death more deeply than does the rest of Europe's ruling elite. The Habsburg court in Vienna settles for mere perfunctory ceremonials, yet it does see clearly that the Archduke's murder can be exploited for political ends.

What is the next step—and who will take it? In the days following the assassination, the drift towards war accelerates—though its outbreak is not predestined. In both Berlin and Vienna there *are* conciliatory voices, but at least as many are calling for a "preventive" war against Russia and France before those two countries can successfully mobilize their forces. A number of leading figures—notably Tsar Nicholas of Russia and Lord Grey in England—seem reluctant and changeable, fluttering like frightened birds at any rattling of their cages. Austria-Hungary gives them a thorough-going shake when it presents an ultimatum to Serbia on July 23rd.

Germany has for some time been urging Vienna to take a harsh line with the Serbs and has promised its full support. The Archduke's assassination, the Kaiser is convinced, provides the ideal moment for strong action, a Heaven-sent opportunity for pushing the Teutonic partners' expansionist goals. Others share Wilhelm's belief that an Austrian invasion of Serbia will prove little more than a local skirmish, not the inauguration of a world cataclysm—though it's generally accepted that Russia, however disinclined, will honor its earlier pledge to come to the aid of fellow Slavs. From the Kaiser's point of view, the sooner Austria strikes, the better.

But much to Wilhelm's furious chagrin, popular opinion in Germany seems seriously divided. Just two years before, the Social Democratic Party—the "Jewish" Party, in the Kaiser's view—polled 35 percent of the vote. Combined with the moderate Catholic Center Party's 23 percent, a clear majority seems to favor a conciliatory foreign policy; in the days following the Sarajevo assassinations, the SPD manages to put together an anti-war rally that draws some 100,000 people. But in the Prussian provinces, among conservative Christians and devoted monarchists, the Kaiser can still do no wrong.

The Kaiser certainly agrees. He treats his critics as upstarts and regards calls for moderation and compromise as the voice of weakness, if not treachery. To Wilhelm, these are but transient annoyances—bites of a gnat, easily brushed away—no cause for serious alarm, no legitimate threat to his autocratic domination. In the 25 years of his reign, Wilhelm points out, Germany has made enormous strides in trade and industry and has moved to the very center of European affairs. The so-called "democratic impulse" of the age is, from the Kaiser's perspective, a mirage; he announces that he rules "by grace of God," and will "go my way regardless of the views and opinions of the day."

The Kaiser's impulsive "way" in the summer of 1914 is to seize the occasion and settle forever the planetary conflict between Teutons and

Slavs. Wilhelm makes it clear to Austria that he regards the present moment "as more favorable than later," and he emphasizes "as *emphatically as possible* that Berlin is expecting the Monarchy to act against Serbia" and will not understand Austria allowing "the present opportunity to pass without striking a blow."

Austria dutifully proceeds to give Serbia a harsh ultimatum—and a mere 48 hours to reply. Its list of demands includes the right of Austria to participate directly in Serbian efforts to suppress and adjudicate "conspiratorial" plots. The ultimatum strikes some as designed to precipitate rather than to prevent war; Sir Edward Grey, the British Foreign Secretary, characterizes it as "the most formidable document I have ever seen addressed by one State to another," and his Russian counterpart, Sergei Sazonov, calls the terms "simply unacceptable."

With Russian support all but guaranteed, Serbia tells Austria that, although it bears no responsibility for the assassination of Franz Ferdinand, it will accept all the terms of the Austrian ultimatum *except* for the right of Austria to participate in Serbia's judicial inquiries. Wilhelm, for one, regards the Serbian response as conciliatory in tone and "a great moral victory for Vienna." He believes the need for war has been averted—if, that is, Austria finds the terms acceptable and if the Serbs follow words with deeds. By "deeds," it turns out, the Kaiser means that Austria can march unopposed into Serbia, even though both Russia and England have made it clear that they would regard such an invasion as deliberate provocation.

Austria is bent on *total* capitulation; it neither wants nor expects a peaceful outcome, is quick to denounce the Serbian reply as unacceptable—and promptly declares war. Three days later Russia, apparently in some confusion as to the Kaiser's intentions, announces the mobilization of its forces. A furious Wilhelm, in turn—in the muddled conviction that the Tsar has misled him—swiftly follows suit.

There's still some hope that the conflict can be localized, that France and England will choose neutrality rather than rush to aid their Russian ally. In England especially, there's a good deal of sentiment in the Asquith government against involvement; Sir Edward Grey twice suggests mediation between Austria and Russia, but Bethmann-Hollweg—

apparently determined that Russia should alone be saddled with blame for any war—sabotages both efforts. As late as August 1st the majority of ministers in the Asquith cabinet, led by Chancellor of the Exchequer Lloyd George, declare their opposition to intervention. In the opposite camp, the youthful, pugnacious Winston Churchill, First Lord of the Admiralty, writes his wife that "everything tends towards catastrophe & collapse. I am interested, geared-up & happy."

After Germany mobilizes on August 1, 1914, France decides to do so as well. The British make it clear that she will come at once to France's aid should that country be invaded; England will not tolerate German hegemony on the continent. Those still hoping for peace feebly tell themselves that mobilization isn't the equivalent of war, and they take some comfort in the refusal of the SPD deputies in the Reichstag to vote in favor of war credits. But when the Kaiser declares that "the sword has been forced into our hand," and announces that he sees "no more parties ... only Germans," patriotic pressure mounts and SPD opposition crumbles in tandem. When the SPD delegates gather on August 3rd to discuss what posture to adopt, a lopsided 78 members vote to support the government, with only 14 remaining in opposition. Among the latter is SPD co-chair Hugo Haase, who forlornly declares his hope that the horrors of war will at least have the secondary benefit of winning over millions to the cause of socialism and peace among nations.

An offensive war against France on Germany's part can only take place by marching through neutral Belgium—whose neutrality has long since been guaranteed by a European treaty dating back to 1839. Choosing to believe, contrary to considerable evidence, that England will decide not to intervene, the Kaiser proceeds to demand from Belgium unopposed access for his army. King Albert rejects Berlin's ultimatum, and on August 4th German troops invade. The Belgian people rally around their sovereign—as does foreign opinion. Germany has, apparently unwittingly, earned the undisputed laurel as *the* aggressor in destroying the peace of Europe. The Asquith government—though public opinion in England is still divided—promptly declares war against Germany, citing its "flagrant violation of international law."

In assuming the moral high ground, the Allies conveniently forget that "noble" Belgium has compiled, as a colonial power, a gruesome record of atrocities against the indigenous people of the Congo. Its cruel rule is matched only by Germany's record in its 1904–07 genocidal killings of the Herero and Namaqua peoples of Southwest Africa. Germany will now proceed to extend its reputation with the massacre of civilian populations in Belgium and France.

∿

As the Kaiser's triumphal motorcade moves down Unter den Linden, the streets fill to bursting with cheering crowds. Oblivious to the midday August heat, the Kaiser is decked out in the imposing full-dress uniform of the Garde du Corps—a bedazzlement of sashes, medals, encrusted helmet, and bejeweled sword. His waxed mustache pointed upwards at the corners and reaching his cheekbones, Wilhelm puffs out his chest with belligerent pride (no effeminate Frenchman, he), emanating satisfaction as the enthusiastic crowd surges up to his car and shouts its approval along the route of the processional.

A mere two days earlier, the scene had been very different. War not yet declared, but nerves raw with anticipation, work stoppages had occurred widely; people scurried to stock up on food; stores and cafés shuttered their doors; long lines formed in front of banks, with customers desperate to withdraw their funds; and everywhere in public squares solemn knots of people had gathered to exchange grim predictions of what was to come.

The sudden shift in mood, the displacement of panicky fears by ardent enthusiasm—and then back again—are commonplace these days. But not with Walther Rathenau. He's convinced that Germany has blundered its way into war, and has little confidence in the judgment and good sense of the Kaiser or his advisors; "We have no strategists and no statesmen," he tells Kessler (the two have resumed contact after Rathenau's stormy exit from the restaurant). Rathenau foresees—as do few of his contemporaries, including a man as attuned to nuance as Harry Kessler—that a lengthy and terrible bloodbath is on the horizon, producing devastation and demoralization that will afflict generations to come.

Despairing though he is—and prescient—Rathenau is determined to do what he can to mitigate the ineptitude he sees everywhere around him. During an audience with Chancellor Bethmann-Hollweg, Rathenau offers two proposals: first, the formation of a customs union to bind together the whole of Europe economically, thereby bringing a quick end to armed hostilities. The proposal finds no favor. Rathenau moves on to his second suggestion, prefacing it with a warning that in his estimate the country can rely on no more than a few months of stockpiled war materials; beyond that, Germany faces strangulation on both land and sea. Rathenau volunteers to put his vast experience in industry toward organizing Germany's raw materials for maximally efficient use. *That* proposal is taken up with enthusiasm. Rathenau makes the offer not out of ardor for the war, but from a grim sense of moral duty, what he calls, in one of his more grandiose moments, his "mission" *not* to act (as he sees it) "the fearful Jew" but rather the Aryan hero. The Chancellor appoints him on the spot to head the newly minted War Raw Materials Department.

From the Chancellor's Office, Rathenau goes directly to see his intimate friend, Lili Deutsch, the wife of a high official at AEG. The pending war, he tells Lili, will be a disaster. "What are we fighting for?" he plaintively asks, actually weeping with despair. "Do you know?—I don't and should be glad if you could tell me. What will come of it?" Rathenau and Lili have known each other for a number of years, but "deep affection" is as far as Rathenau can or will go in naming the bond between them. Indisputably a man of passion, Rathenau has no trouble revealing it in relation to public affairs, yet the expression of emotional intensity is under interdiction regarding personal relations. He can write Lili that she means "a great deal" to him, and at the same time confess to her that when the two are alone he feels tense and constrained.

There have been several other women in Rathenau's life, as well as several men whom he feels (briefly) close to, but none remain at the center of his life for long, and no relationship, apparently, ever becomes sexual. Speculation about the focus and nature of Rathenau's affections is widespread, but only Harry Kessler has, discreetly, ever broached the subject directly with him—and suffered an eruption of anger for his pains. Kessler confides to his lover Gaston Colin the belief that Rathenau is erotically attracted to men, though he feels sure he's never acted on those feelings, has never managed to scale the fortress walls that keep him in melancholy isolation.

No one is more surprised than Rathenau to find himself at the head of the War Raw Materials Department—that is, until he learns that the "department" consists of five people, has no clerical staff, and lacks jurisdiction over foodstuffs and liquid fuel. Initially he and his staff have to spend several hours a day licking stamps, which deeply offends Rathenau's sense of *amour propre*. Yet, before long, the list of materials defined as within his jurisdiction does lengthen, and his department is given the power to commandeer everything from metals and chemicals to wool, rubber, cotton, and leather. Subsequently, he's also given the right to requisition desired materials from neutral or occupied territory, and to set up manufacturing enterprises at home to produce supplies.

This accumulation of control ultimately amounts to a powerful mandate, and there's considerable grumbling among military bureaucrats about a civilian—a Jew, no less—being given so much authority. One morning Rathenau arrives in the War Office to find that a wooden partition has been set up around his department—suggestive, to a man of his acute sensibility, of a quarantine. Shrewdly, Rathenau chooses to ignore rather than protest the barrier; he refuses to dignify the insult by acting as if it bothers him. Instead he nullifies it through a prodigious amount of vital work.

Initially the most critical issue is the shortage of nitrate, the indispensable ingredient in explosives and one previously imported; for officers at the front in 1914, no issue is more urgent. Until steps can be implemented to manufacture nitrate within Germany itself, Rathenau comes up with the temporary solution of commandeering from farmers—over their furious objection—the small amounts of nitrate that they use in manure. After nine months of heading up the War Raw Materials Department, Rathenau is able to hand it on to a successor in superbly efficient shape.

Harry Kessler is amused at the "paradoxical" nature of Rathenau's success and points it out to him:

"You realize, my dear fellow—and I say this with the utmost esteem and admiration—that you've managed in short order to demonstrate the superior efficiency of state socialism over capitalist private enterprise!"

The notion gratifies Rathenau, though he denies its accuracy. "We're essentially functioning as a joint-stock company—the very embodiment of private enterprise."

Kessler will have none of it: "You're going to out-argue me by making technical distinctions that you know perfectly well I'm unable to decipher—let alone dispute. But my fundamental point, Rathenau, remains: you have the Materials Department—*in the public interest*—issuing neither dividends nor profits to its so-called stockholders. What you've produced is a blueprint for state control of industry—indeed of the entire economy—that no socialist to date has managed to duplicate."

Rathenau, in fact, thinks so too. He codifies his accomplishment in a book, *In Days To Come*. In it, he argues that powerful state organizations (the Allies, too, will gradually turn to centralized control of major industries) have demonstrated their superiority to traditional private enterprise. Rathenau insists that the new model of centralization will enable the dispossessed proletariat, long compelled to do joyless, routine work, to free up a significant portion of its time for pursuits aimed at providing pleasure and self-knowledge.

Military necessity, Rathenau maintains, has led to advances in technology that clearly demonstrate that the harsh conditions under which the proletariat works can no longer be justified as necessary to maintain viable production. To carry on the war, the state has taken over and even confiscated the resources of private wealth. In breaching the purported inviolability of private property, it has transformed the rote repetitions of labor into work of greater variety, responsibility, and freedom of choice. Placing the public interest above the sanctity of private property

has revealed—Rathenau claims—that the basis on which an idle aristocracy has long maintained its privileges is unsound.

Rathenau's policies and arguments go beyond the moderate socialist
vision of the current Social Democratic Party. In the name of abolishing
the traditional proletariat, he even urges the state to restrict the right of
inheritance. Custom alone, he maintains, has mandated the passing of
wealth from one generation to the next, but the practice has no basis in
morality. If continued, Rathenau argues, it will condemn the proletariat
"to perpetual servitude, and the rich man to perpetual enjoyment."

Additionally, he advocates reducing income disparity through taxation—especially on luxury goods, and under that rubric he includes
"extravagant" dwellings, horses, carriages and motor cars, costly furniture, and even "excessive" electrical expenditure. "Three hundred men,"
Rathenau declares, "control the economic destiny of the Continent," yet
the justification for that control is flimsy to the point of non-existence.
The wealth of the privileged derives not from labor, and only somewhat
from entrepreneurial activity; primarily it comes from the restriction of
competition, from artificially-enforced monopolies.

He includes the educational system in his overall indictment. Equal
access for all to education would be a start, he declares, but would not
in itself be sufficient to level the playing field. The children of the rich
arrive in a classroom having already been exposed to the cultural advantages of being brought up in cultivated circumstances. The children of
the poor quickly become aware of the chasm between themselves and
their more fortunate classmates and—taught to have little self-regard—
blame themselves for the disparity rather than the deprived conditions
of their upbringing—in the process becoming apathetic and hopeless.
That brings Rathenau back to his basic conviction: to create a more just
society, all private wealth must be progressively taxed out of existence.

Rathenau anticipates the obvious follow-up question: if private
property is abolished, what incentive will there be to work? His answer
is "joy in creation, love of work, and the feeling of solidarity." Nor, in
Rathenau's view, will shiftlessness reign and innovation disappear. Creative pioneers and risk-taking leaders have never, he argues, responded

primarily to the expectation of material reward, but rather to burning curiosity and to the satisfaction of traveling previously untrodden paths—like establishing a decent general standard of living for all.

Rathenau's remarkable argument isn't a call for reform; it's a demand for revolution. Not a Soviet-style revolution—Rathenau doesn't advocate sudden transformations of any kind, and certainly not through violence. In Rathenau's view, state confiscation is one of many preliminary stepping-stones needed to enthrone the "common good" above all else. Any attempt at overnight transfiguration, he feels, is doomed to fail simply because the psychological renovation of the citizenry has not preceded. The reorganization of industry and wealth can only take place *subsequent* to a gradual shift in consciousness and the cultivation of alternate sources of motivation, satisfaction, and responsibility. The New Citizen precedes the New Society.

As soon as hostilities begin, Harry Kessler, long a reserve officer in the Lancers, has a farewell weekend with Gaston Colin at Vichy; then, after purchasing boots, a coat, and a revolver, he joins his regiment in Potsdam. Age 46, Kessler is put in charge of an artillery munitions column—some 200 men and an equal number of horses. His soldiers haven't been coerced into serving; in a fit of intoxication, young German men flock eagerly to the colors—including some who've sworn they'd never take part in a war. What a joy to leave behind the boring pettiness of everyday life, the numbing routines, the sense that nothing would ever change! Besides, hasn't the Kaiser announced that "before the leaves fall, you will be back home"? In their excitement, the men decorate their wagons with oak leaves and pin flowers to their chests and carbines. It's all very festive—except Kessler soon hears that 11 "spies" have been shot in Kiel, four more in Spandau, and 40 "well poisoners" hanged in Alsace.

Still, he's pleased to find a "calm, cheerful confidence" within the regiment; everyone duly notes that setbacks are bound to occur, but Kessler, like most of his men, feels certain a German victory is inevitable. He thinks the onset of war (as he writes in his diary) has "brought forth something from unknown depths in our German people, which I can only compare with an earnest and cheerful spirituality. The whole population is as transformed—and cast into a new form."

Not quite. Kessler is speaking more for his class than for the German people as a whole. Rathenau's future New Citizen—he who places the public interest above mere personal needs—is exuberantly present in the cities, but far less so in the rural areas. The vast majority of German farmers in 1914 show no signs of transfiguration. When Rathenau's War Raw Materials Department commandeers their horses, oxen, and wagons, and without compensation, the rural areas explode in defiance. Germany's "destiny" may serve as a euphoric rallying cry for some, but not for a peasantry that still relies on their animals for livelihood and transport.

A transient protest, Kessler decides. His spirits cannot be dampened. When the young soldiers in his regiment burst into patriotic song, lustily singing stanza after stanza of "The Watch on the Rhine," Kessler thrills to "a new victorious life from out of the flames and smoke; forward over the graves!" "Whose graves?" becomes the question.

The answer quickly arrives: Belgian graves. Following King Albert of Belgium's rejection of the German ultimatum, on August 4, 1914 German troops invade. The decision is widely viewed—not in Germany, of course, nor by Kessler—as an outrage, an immoral attack on a small, neutral country. Unexpectedly, the Belgians resist the first German assault with both artillery and small-arms fire, forcing them back. Kessler's column is part of the massive German response that follows. Armed with powerful Krupp and Škoda howitzers, they ruthlessly destroy a number of small villages, following up with a rash of summary executions; in some instances, literally every building is burned to the ground, civilians strung up from roadside trees, women and children dragged from hiding places and indiscriminately killed. "German Beastliness" is emblazed in headlines around the world.

For most of August 1914, Kessler is in the thick of combat. He casually notes in his diary that his regiment had to kill the Belgian wounded "because they had sniped from behind at the troops while they were fighting." Between executions, he and his subordinate officers have lunch and chat. But this is not a case of an aesthete among the barbarians. When Kessler's regiment reaches the town of Seilles, already reduced to ashes, his troops make sure that no house is left with a roof or a window; 200 inhabitants are given *pro forma* court-martials and shot.

At one point five or six men, "hatless, stumbling, white as corpses" (in Kessler's description) are led into view. One of them holds his right hand aloft to signal that he has no weapon; the gesture fails to elicit mercy. After all, Kessler writes in his diary, the town's inhabitants killed 20 Germans when they were trying to build a bridge across the Maas River. In his mind that's sufficient justification for carrying out what he himself calls "such terrible executions," but the fault, he adds, "lies with the Belgian population."

Kessler does feel squeamish about one matter: the German troops continue to drink themselves into unconsciousness; that, and not the executions, causes him to worry that the war could "degenerate into an expedition of Huns." A week later, additional scruples begin to surface: "This kind of war," he writes in his diary, "suspends all ideas of what is right."

Attached to the Guards Reserve Corps, Kessler's regiment soon receives orders to move to East Prussia and reinforce the German army there; they're part of a vanguard that in late September 1914 crosses over the border of southern Poland. In Biała Błotna, Kessler, as the officer in charge, is put up in the gutted home of a Polish nobleman; the two drink the last bottles from a wine cellar that dates back to the 1870s. Kessler notes with apparent approval the "devotion" of the nobleman's peasants—how they run out from their houses to kiss his hands and even his knees.

The nobleman feels it necessary to explain to Kessler that his estate remains unrepaired "due to circumstances beyond my control"—which includes, he volunteers, the need to pay "to the Jews" a 12 percent interest rate on certain debts. Kessler is sympathetic. He's already noted what he takes to be the striking contrasts between the Catholics of Poland and its Jews; he sees the latter as "an alien minority" who "haggle, sneak around, offering everyone their services, filling the streets." In Kessler's view, the Jews, if allowed to, "will prevent any normal healthy development of a completely independent Polish state" following the war.

Having put on the uniform of a Prussian officer, Kessler—unpredictably, and to a far greater extent than during any other period of his life—has cloaked himself as well in the traditional snobbery and anti-Semitism of its officer corps. He shows no sense of contradiction with his longstanding and ongoing friendships with such notable Jewish figures as Rathenau, Hofmannsthal, and Max Reinhardt.

Early in the war, in the battle at Tannenberg in late August 1914, General Paul von Hindenburg and his chief of staff Erich von Ludendorff succeed in halting what has been an alarmingly rapid Russian advance. Both men become instant heroes in Germany, and Hindenburg is appointed commander-in-chief of the German forces in the East. Kessler makes the acquaintance of both men, and feels certain that the average German soldier admires their leadership. The string of victories that follows on the eastern front in 1914–15—the conquest of Poland, the ensnarement and slaughter of the Russian army—confirms for many Germans their initial trust and admiration for their military leaders. Kessler, like them, seems intoxicated; he extols the German officer corps as embodying "a kind of priesthood"; they are "delegates from a secret order serving the god of war," the incarnation of strength of will and organizational talent, cool, hard, unsentimental men.

Kessler's veneration of Germany's military leadership eclipses, in the early days of the war, his once finely tuned critical faculties, leading him placidly to accept the mounting piles of grotesquely maimed bodies. What does deeply impress him is "the naked matter-of-factness of the war, its lack of fake pathos and romanticism." His untroubled nonchalance is shaken at news that in the first two weeks following Austria's invasion of Serbia, 3,500 *civilians* have been forced to dig their own graves before being bayoneted to death—their gory executions photographed and widely published as a warning to "spies." The stupefying escalation in killing will shortly engulf all of Europe, and as it does, Kessler's detached attitude toward atrocities will disintegrate in tandem.

During the winter of 1914–15, Kessler becomes ordnance officer for Germany's 24th Corps, which participates in a massive attack on Russian positions in the Carpathian Mountains. The campaign is a disaster. German shells fail to explode in the bad weather, rendering its artillery useless. Its infantry soldiers, at times literally sunk up to their chests in snow, barely crawl forward, their silhouetted bodies easy targets for Russian sharpshooters. One army corps alone loses 40,000 men in a single week, and before the three-month campaign wholly collapses, an unimaginable 800,000 men have deserted, frozen to death, been wounded or killed. Throughout, Kessler himself—not through cowardice—is in a relatively protected area, and, to make matters easier still, he and a young staff aide embark on an intense love affair.

Yet he isn't any longer immune or indifferent to the hardships that everywhere surround him; his early, starry-eyed view of war's glory continues to disintegrate as he's increasingly confronted with war's reality. The German troops under his command become nearly numb with fatigue, and the fierce cold brings on any number of serious illnesses.

Sent on leave to Berlin to try and stir up newspaper coverage of German "victories," Kessler is astonished to find that the war has as yet had little impact on the home front; dining at the Richters' is different from a pre-war soirée only in the absence of decent bread; a performance at the Deutsches Theater is, as usual, sold out; and at a late supper with Max Reinhardt and others, Kessler eats—just as he did before the war—caviar, corn on the cob, and wild boar with truffles.

Angered at the normality of home front life and still a considerable enthusiast for the war, Kessler takes strenuous exception one day at the Adlon on hearing that Rainer Maria Rilke and Franz Werfel, among others, have become self-declared pacifists outraged at the conflict. Such a position, Kessler insists, is "incomprehensible; it weakens us for no reason." At lunch the very next day with Richard Strauss, Kessler vehemently takes issue with the composer's view that war is an anachronism, that whether or not a strip of land ends up in the hands of Germany or France is a matter of "complete indifference."

When Kessler visits Max Harden, he finds him tired and depressed.

He tells Kessler that he's inclined to conclude peace immediately on the basis of *status quo ante*—that is, according to national boundaries as they'd stood in July. Harden argues that Germany has already shown its power, and will in the future be secure from attack. Kessler tells Harden that he thinks his argument "catastrophic," which prompts Harden to say that his real position is that Germany should abandon Austria and seek peace unilaterally; the Austrian Habsburgs, he argues, are doomed in any case, so why prolong the inevitable? Kessler scornfully responds that such a suggestion is not worth discussing.

His friendship with Rathenau having weathered assorted storms, Kessler calls on him at his house in Grunewald. He finds Rathenau sunk in gloom and attributes it in part to the Grunewald home itself, which he's always detested, once describing its décor—with more than a hint at his view of Rathenau's sexual proclivities—as a mix of "petty sentimentality and stunted eroticism . . . as if a banker and a masturbating boy thought it up together."

But as Kessler well understands, Rathenau's depressed isolation is due to much more than the surrounding décor. When ushered into Rathenau's study, his host rather glumly offers him a seat but—as Kessler duly notes—neither food nor drink. Having resigned his post with the War Office, Rathenau hasn't moved on to another position. His sharp divergence from official opinion is partly responsible: Germans—as he now puts it to Kessler—have been "driven like a flock of sheep, understanding nothing, into the Unknown."

In the past Kessler would probably have deferred to Rathenau—whom he feels values him primarily as a kind of aesthete-at-large, not as someone centrally informed about the important questions of the day. Now, in uniform and straight from the front, Kessler's demeanor is more confident. "Driven?" he asks, a peremptory edge to his voice. "Driven by whom? I have the highest regard for both Hindenburg and Ludendorff."

Rathenau welcomes the new amplitude. "Come now! Everyone knows that it's Hindenburg who sits on the horse but Ludendorff who digs in the spurs."

"True. And a good thing, too. Ludendorff is a superb tactician."

"I met him at the beginning of the war. At first I thought he was a man who could lead us, if not to victory, then at least to an honorable peace, and I did everything in my power to smooth his path. It soon became clear to me that he's an advocate of German imperialism, specifically of gaining territory in Eastern Europe, which I strongly oppose. But he is an improvement over the Kaiser, I'll give you that. The Supreme War Lord seems to have only the vaguest notion of the realities of war— other than shouting abuse at the failure of our troops to have already overrun all of Europe. Fortunately, his commanders are rapidly learning to circumvent him entirely or to feed him misinformation."

"I've heard some talk," Kessler reluctantly admits, "of calling for his abdication. It will dissipate after a few more victories in the field. But even so, I think the Kaiser's autocratic rule has been irreparably damaged. In my view, a far more powerful Reichstag will emerge."

"Tell me, Kessler"—Rathenau's voice is heavy with irony—"as a man who's seen combat, do you still feel that Germany made the right decision in going to war?"

"Most assuredly. In saying that, I don't primarily mean the opportunity to expand our borders. No, I mean the expansion of the German spirit."

"Which is?" A lethargic Rathenau is still capable of being roused to debate.

"I would make a distinction between German *Kultur*, which is deep and mystical, and Western civilization, which is superficial, immature."

"And where does Austria-Hungary fit? Not that I mean to be contentious, but when the Kaiser gave Austria a blank check to invade Serbia, he based it on what he called our *shared* 'Nibelungen' heritage. The content of that heritage has, regrettably, never been revealed. Perhaps the Kaiser means our shared glorification of war."

"I think not," Kessler replies sternly.

"Or perhaps he means our shared distaste for Jews."

The remark is so unexpected that Kessler is taken aback.

"Surely, my dear Kessler, you aren't surprised at that suggestion? Only recently the remark of a certain army officer was passed on to me. When informed that I had done the state considerable service in the War Raw Materials Department, he replied, 'If this man Rathenau has helped us, then it is a scandal and a disgrace.'"

"I would assume the officer belongs to one of the conservative, nationalistic parties. Among such men anti-Semitism *is* profound."

"You don't find it so in the army?"

"Some of our leading officers are wayward on several counts," Kessler evasively replies. "They lack all stature. Not worthy of the men they lead."

"Your remark earlier about German *Kultur* . . ."

"Yes?"

"Some might regard the remark as racist."

"That would be a misconception."

"Would it?" Rathenau is feeling decidedly more energized. "Your assumption is that our *Kultur* is superior to that of France, England, and Russia. That was hardly your position when you took up the cause of French Impressionism and 'seceded' from Germany's philistine defense of academic art."

"One's attitudes change through time. Or should, to avoid stagnation."

Kessler's Olympian tone annoys Rathenau, though he's often adopted it himself. "How can the truth—or falsity—of your assumption that Germany's culture is more 'mature' than the rest of Europe possibly be measured? One need only start naming some of the giants of *non*-German culture to expose it for the nonsense it is—Tolstoy, perhaps? Dickens? Proust? Émile Zola? Do our German leaders think to justify war and its horrors as a means of spreading our purportedly superior culture to England—to *Shakespeare's* England, mind you? The proposition is imbecilic."

"You have never heard *me* endorse violence for such a purpose."

"I have heard you come close. I've heard you argue that the future existence of Germany depends on acquiring the Belgian coast. Peace, you've said, must not come without the guarantee of such an acquisition. I've had several reports of you arguing vehemently that the future security of Germany must be guaranteed—the Belgians and the Poles must first 'feel our fist'—isn't that the phrase you've used?—and then, and only then, should we allow them self-government."

"You do me a grave injustice, Rathenau." Kessler is seriously agitated—and embarrassed. "As you well know, or should know, I've devoted the greater part of my life to extolling the brilliance of French and English culture."

"I also know that you've repeatedly expressed the view that it's doubtful that Poland—even after 'feeling our fist'—will be able to maintain its independence as a state. And why not? Because, you've been quoted as saying, it has too large a Jewish population!"

"What I *said*, Rathenau, is that Catholic and Jewish Poles are two entirely separate elements, like a black and a white thread, which can never be seamlessly spun together."

"Which is perhaps true—but why not blame the Catholics rather than the Jews?"

"I don't blame either. We're old friends, Rathenau. I don't like this kind of quarreling between us."

"It might be healthy."

"If so, I'd point out—as I have before—your own ambivalence about the Jewish people."

It was Rathenau's turn to feel stung: "I have never been ambivalent about discrimination against Jews."

"And you yourself have suffered from it. Profoundly and unfairly. Yet you *do* sometimes sound like an anti-Semite."

Rathenau stiffens. "I have no idea what you're referring to."

"I doubt that. You take great care with your writing, and what you have written several times over is that there's a profound difference between non-Aryans—whom you call 'men of fear'—and Aryans—'men of courage.' You've also called the Aryan race 'a blond and marvelous people'—praise you withhold from darker-skinned people."

Rathenau turns away and starts to pace the room.

"You're misreading me." He sounds surprisingly neutral, not belligerent.

"I believe *you* misread your own divided feelings. You despise the arrogant, stupid Nordic warrior—as well you should—yet some part of you deeply envies and feels inferior to him. It's an inner division that tears at your soul, and keeps you in a state of self-imposed exile."

Kessler stops abruptly. He's said far more than he intended and more, he fears, that Rathenau can tolerate hearing. Yet Rathenau seems strangely becalmed, deflated and weary. He mumbles something about needing to complete a report for AEG and politely escorts Kessler to the door, holding it open until he reaches his car. Both men are relieved the evening is over—and both are deeply disquieted by it.

Kessler returns to the front lines in Poland and from there sees additional service in the struggle for Galicia, where the Russians inflicts huge losses on the Austrian army. Though never part of the now-repetitive slaughter taking place in the stalemated trench warfare in the western theater of war, Kessler sees his share of horrors—blackened corpses with their heads torn off, women and children scavenging the battlefield in search of bits of food, village after village reduced to rubble, a lone chimney left poking at the sky. He asks himself if even the devastation that accompanied the Thirty Years' War was comparable, and doubts it. "The longer war lasts," he writes in his diary, "the more the warlike spirit dies out."

He knows that compared with the foot soldiers and even most of the second-tier officers, he lives reasonably well; friends and family send him packages with cans of fruits and preserves through neutral Switzerland—even English turtle soup in violet tin buckets. By 1916, Kessler finally arrives at the conclusion—which had been Rathenau's starting point—that "war is a vile thing."

Soon after writing that line in his diary, he's able to leave the combat zone entirely. Assigned to Bern, Switzerland, Kessler is given the announced assignment of organizing pro-German cultural propaganda, and the unannounced one of secretly exploring the possibility of detaching France from the Allies and concluding a separate peace. Matching up artists with patrons has long been second nature to Kessler; but he now meets some of the younger generation of artists—George Grosz, for one—who will lay siege to his political boundaries. Establishing covert contact with anarchists and Bolsheviks will stretch them beyond recognition.

~

At the onset of war Magnus Hirschfeld's ardor closely parallels Harry Kessler's. Both men initially claim in 1914 that Germany is encircled by hostile neighbors intent on her destruction; that the English have rejected the Kaiser's attempts to avoid war; and that the Austrian invasion of Serbia has been appropriate and necessary. Hirschfeld's enthusiasm dissipates more quickly than Kessler's; and he concerns himself with one policy matter which Kessler keeps at arm's length: defending the right of homosexuals to serve openly in Germany's armed forces.

When Herr von Einem, the German Minister of War, announces the dismissal of known homosexual officers from the army, Hirschfeld protests the policy, insisting that they're no less willing than heterosexuals to die for their country—patriotism, he insists, trumps sexual orientation. To refute the "insult" that it does not, Hirschfeld points to the many homosexuals who, having fled Germany before the war to avoid discovery and persecution, have now returned to serve in the armed forces. Von Einem is unmoved, and the policy goes unchanged.

Hirschfeld shifts his tactics. He once more becomes an expert court witness. Ten years earlier, during the Eulenburg/von Moltke trials, he testified to the "psychic" attributes that would allow one to identify a hidden (or non-practicing) homosexual. Now he defends the high moral character of acknowledged homosexuals who've been dismissed from service. Where once he—misguidedly but not maliciously—helped to expose secret homosexuals, he now heaps praise on open ones for having all the requisite military skills: the ability to follow orders, endure hardship, devote oneself to the common good, and not to shrink from killing.

It's all a bit confusing. In his younger years, Hirschfeld, among others, simplistically argued that homosexual men are set apart by their "finer" natures, their refusal to obey the norms or follow the rules, their cultivated taste, their attraction to the arts, their abhorrence of violence. Now he's attempting to define them as no different from any other group of men—just as drawn to violence, morally obtuse, and emotionally anaesthetized. Ah well. In his case, as in every other effort to define *the* homosexual (or heterosexual), no rigidly-defined category can ever encompass the diverse group of human beings it purports to fit. Categories reflect the political purpose for which they're invented far more exactly than the individuals they claim to describe. By the second year of the war, Hirschfeld's enthusiasm for it greatly diminishes. By then he's actually experienced some of the reality of combat as a physician with the Red Cross, and he recognizes that war devalues all prior notions of human worth and dignity. Horrified at the spreading savagery, he now sees warfare as a collective psychosis rather than the cleansing catharsis he (like Kessler) once believed in.

In the last two years of the war, Hirschfeld, as a representative of the Red Cross, helps to negotiate the exchange of prisoners through the neutral auspices of Switzerland and Holland. In the course of his work, he comes to meet a number of the leading pacifists of the day, including Dr. Auguste Forel, René Schickele, editor of *Die Weissen Blätter*, and the writers Stefan Zweig, Annette Kolb, and Romain Rolland (who many have come to consider the great-hearted conscience of Europe).

Stefan Zweig will later write that pacifists were betrayed by their shared conviction that the statesmen of Europe would come to see the folly of war and back down at the last minute. When that failed to happen, many pacifists shifted their hopes to the working class and the Socialist International. As Zweig put it, "we thought railway workers would blow up the tracks rather than let their comrades be loaded into trains to be sent to the front as cannon fodder; we relied on women to refuse to see their children and husbands sacrificed to the idol Moloch; we were convinced that the intellectual and moral power of Europe would assert itself triumphantly at the critical last moment." None of that had come to pass. Nationalism proved stronger than class solidarity, and the thrill of "adventure" more beguiling than peaceful routine.

Harry Kessler, now stationed in Bern, is beginning to meet many of the same pacifists as Hirschfeld, and during the very same period—though he and Hirschfeld never cross paths. Hirschfeld is rapidly becoming a pacifist himself; in 1915–16 Kessler is only part-way there—he's still convinced that Hindenburg and Ludendorff are brilliant leaders who might yet bring the war to a victorious close for Germany.

In his double capacity as a Red Cross physician and head of the Scientific Humanitarian Committee, Hirschfeld learns a great deal about the experiences of homosexual men during wartime. He proudly reports that they'd greeted the outbreak of war with the same "tremendous rapture" that he himself had felt, and that they've acquitted themselves well in combat. Hirschfeld credits their zeal in part to simple patriotism, but in part, too, to the tragic hope that a bullet might redeem their "failed" lives. As one of them writes to Hirschfeld, "It is my greatest wish to get into the field as soon as possible and to meet an honorable death, for otherwise I will be compelled later on to make an end of my rotten life due to my homosexual tendencies..." Another, an officer, tells Hirschfeld that his "disregard of death is nothing more than disgust with life."

But the story of homosexual soldiers is not, at least as Hirschfeld tells it, solely a tale of gloom and sorrow. In a 1,200-page masterwork, *The Homosexuality of Men and Women*, Hirschfeld concludes—using "the numerous reports placed at my disposal"—that "from the highest ranks down to the youngest recruits," the German armed forces are "saturated with homogenic elements," with the number particularly high among army officers. And, he further concludes, they serve well. He quotes a fellow expert's conclusion that homosexual soldiers prove themselves "brave and loyal, and full of disciplined intelligence." That suspiciously generalized summary isn't made more persuasive by the comment Hirschfeld attaches to it—namely, that "bravery," etc., "does not at all contradict the feminine trait many of them possess." The "trait" goes undefined, but Hirschfeld apparently means—judging from the language he subsequently uses in describing homosexual officers— the great care they take to "encourage the ones who hesitate, teach the unskilled, restrain the wild ones, and support the weak." The stereotypic female becomes conflated with the patriotic homosexual officer.

Letters pour in to Hirschfeld from soldiers of varying sexual orientations asking for his advice on everything from prostitution to venereal disease. He knows the importance of heeding an individual's special circumstances, of not providing glib, generalized responses to highly particularized needs. He's quick to feel a client's pain, but not quick to provide instant balm.

One young man named Einar, rather than writing a letter, comes to see Hirschfeld in his office. He complains bitterly to Hirschfeld about his sheltered upbringing, explaining that his parents meant well in avoiding "difficult" subjects, like sex, but that their silence has had serious consequences for him. In the army, Einar goes on, he's come to enjoy soldierly comradeship, the way the men often look out for the safety and well-being of each other. Then one evening his friends bring him along to an "Institute of Massage" in Berlin; it turns out to be a brothel, which he only realizes when told to "make a choice" from the seven or eight girls standing about. Einar points to one of them, and she takes him down a small, windowless hall to a room which has only a bed and washbasin in it. "It was okay," Einar tells Hirschfeld. "I didn't really know what to do, thanks to my genteel parents. We got through it somehow."

"Brothels are safer, you know, than picking up a prostitute on the street," Hirschfeld tells Einar. "The girls are examined periodically in brothels. Poverty drives most women into the profession. They're to be pitied rather than punished."

"Does that go for male prostitutes as well?" Einar blurts out.

Hirschfeld takes a deep breath. "Did you become one, or did you patronize one?"

"Both. In reverse. First I picked up a soldier hanging around the Tiergarten waiting for a client. Then I started to wait around myself."

"Which do you do more often?"

"I don't like selling myself—the men are old and ugly. I only do it when I need extra money. I myself pick up soldiers more and more. Funny, I didn't know I was homosexual."

"Maybe you're not. Lots of people occasionally seek affection and release with someone of their own gender but basically prefer heterosexual activity. The variables are many. In any case, you can contract venereal disease from men as well as from women."

Einar laughs. "I sometimes think half my unit has it."

"You'll be pleased to know that your Wassermann test is negative. You do not have syphilis."

Einar reacts with a huge smile, and leans over Hirschfeld's desk to shake his hand. "Hooray!" he half-shouts.

"You've been lucky, Einar. But given your active sexual life, you need to take precautions."

Hirschfeld reaches over to a stack of pamphlets on his bookshelf and hands one to Einar. "Syphilis can be a serious affliction. This will tell you how best to protect yourself. No precaution is foolproof. Nor is any treatment a guaranteed cure. At one time, the most effective tool we had was mercury, but it has to be rubbed into the skin for many weeks, and gives off a noxious odor. Now we have condoms."

"And a good thing, too!" Einar enthusiastically adds.

"Not in everyone's opinion. Religious people believe that if we reduce the incidence of venereal infection, we encourage the spread of debauchery."

"No! Men like to fuck, always have, always will."

"Women too," Hirschfeld adds.

This time it's Einar who's surprised: "Oh yeah, a few whorish types maybe, but not a good girl, she has sex to make babies, that's all . . ."

"So we've been taught. But the teaching is false. I won't try to convince you."

Hirschfeld shifts in his chair, signaling a change of subject. "Before the war, the Scientific Humanitarian Committee wanted to provide all barracks with automatic machines from which, for a few pennies, condoms could be obtained."

"A great idea!"

Yielding to indiscretion, Hirschfeld confides that "the Kaiser's wife, Empress Augusta Victoria, denounced the proposal as immoral, and the Kaiser expressly forbid the machines. The Empress is very religious," Hirschfeld adds, a note of sarcasm in his voice. "She believes it's more important to ensure a rise in births—she has eight children, you know—than a decline in disease." Hirschfeld can't quite conceal a grim smile.

"Around the barracks, I hear men say that homeopathy—isn't that what they call it?—can cure syphilis."

"Yes, that's what they call it. But F-A-K-E-R-Y is how they should spell it. The homeopaths believe all medicines are poison and only their own dilutions are beneficial. There's not a drop of scientific evidence to back up the claim. You might as well go to the shrine at Lourdes."

"I'll stick with you, Doctor." Einar stands up to leave.

"I didn't cause your Wassermann to be negative. Luck is the real explanation. Remember that and maybe you'll also remember to read the pamphlet and to follow its precautions."

Einar gives Hirschfeld a big smile and vigorously shakes his hand goodbye.

∾

The Scientific Humanitarian Committee continues its work throughout the war and issues quarterly reports, often written by physicians in the field, about sexual behavior among the troops. German physicians are nearly uniform in their hymn of praise for the beneficial effects of enforced abstinence on the combatants. They consider the storing up of semen essential for preserving the body's physical and spiritual powers.

Hirschfeld is among the few skeptics to doubt the troops' obedience to the physicians' advice; he even claims, controversially, that evidence of a significant rise in homosexuality during the war is overwhelming. As for "storing up semen," Hirschfeld suggests that surely *some* semen is being discharged through masturbation—these are, after all, young lads in their teens and 20s. No, no, the medical fraternity responds, the evil of self-abuse might ordinarily have been expected to continue or even rise, given the need to reduce stress, but the difficult conditions of trench warfare have had the excellent side benefit of depriving soldiers of privacy.

The dense concentration, as one officer puts it to Hirschfeld, "never permits men to have time alone ... Various military chores at the post, sentry duty, the public nature of the latrines, the common mess, make privacy next to impossible, and hence it's extremely difficult to go through the motions of masturbation." The few soldiers who do somehow find a way, another doctor tells Hirschfeld, are likely to fall into "twilight states in which various crimes, like desertion, are committed." In the medical fraternity masturbation and desertion somehow become causally linked, leaving non-masturbating turncoats in an explanatory no man's land populated by disgraced pacifists and demented victims of shell shock—a land duplicative of trench warfare itself.

Those who, like Hirschfeld, doubt that abstinence is the rule among the troops can cite one of the best known soldier's quips during the war: "Formerly my wife was my right hand, now my right hand *is* my wife." That's part of the rebuttal. The other part has to do with the uncontested fact that the trade in pornographic photographs among the troops keeps rising exponentially. Are resulting erections left unattended? Do spontaneous—or nocturnal—emissions not count as masturbation? The rejoinder tends towards the Biblical: "So long as the hand toucheth not the penis, shell shock and desertion existeth not."

The fact that many soldiers get tattoos proves another source of earnest analysis. Italian psychiatrists, with considerable ingenuity, confidently trace tattooing to "sex hunger." Men denied the company of women for long, the theory goes, "turn back their libido fixation on themselves." Does that mean that ordinarily "libido fixation" accounts for male-female sexual attraction, and when thwarted turns naturally to alternate outlets?

Apparently, yes; and among those alternatives are, along with tattooing, a regression to "infantilism" (centrally defined as a lazy refusal to work), bestiality, and anal eroticism. Men, in short, become animals: "Placed in the primitive conditions at the front," as one prominent physician puts it, "men lose practically all the achievements of civilization and are sexually unsatisfied."

The reference is to literal bestiality. A leading military doctor connected to the Austro-Hungarian army publishes an article in a scientific journal that recounts how he "frequently" observes soldiers having sex with animals. This, the doctor finds, is particularly true of Hungarian hussars, including their officers, who "use the mares entrusted to their care" for sexual purposes. So commonplace is the practice, the doctor reports, that soldiers caught in the act are never brought before military courts—that would entail too much time and expense; instead the offending men are flogged on the spot. Another medical authority places the incidence of bestiality in his division at 10 percent. A figure that high, he reports, has previously been known only among idiots and morons who (as the authority puts it), "despised and mocked by every girl, retire to the quiet of the stable to seek and find consolation with a cow."

In referencing "anal eroticism" the learned doctors do not mean male-male anal sex—the same "lack of privacy" that purportedly inhibits masturbation would prevent as well—should so grotesque a notion arise—the still more exorbitant "flailings about" associated with partner sex. No, "anal eroticism," according to a number of doctors serving with the troops, means sitting on the can for long periods of time. Supposedly the cozy little boxes provided for defecation imprints on the soldier a pleasurable association—and makes lengthy sessions on the latrine seats a commonplace. According to medical testimony, the satisfaction gained from the excremental function makes it a powerful rival among the troops to eating and drinking as the favorite source of pleasure. The experts agree that this is particularly true for German soldiers—and show an admirable awareness that the finding is difficult to reconcile with the well-known Germanic obsession with cleanliness.

Diligent though military physicians are in reporting the various forms of sexual behavior among the soldiers, their relief jumps off the page when they feel able to conclude that, "among the men who are facing the enemy's fire directly, sexuality is almost completely obliterated," happily replaced by "all phases of impotence, from weakness of erections to that of complete absence of tumescence." You can almost hear the exhalation of relief.

∾

Rathenau's friends continuously urge him to return to an active political role. He prefers to remain a hermit, to feel unappreciated for the public service he's already rendered—though he does continue to work behind the scenes, away from the glare of publicity, to further impress his views—never tentative—on policy makers. He thinks of himself more than occasionally as a misunderstood prophet, a man ahead of his time—and has earned the right. But the sketchy, quixotic grandiosity of his scheme—nothing less than the ethical transformation of humanity—dooms him to misunderstanding, and temporal defeat.

As the head of AEG, Rathenau is irreducibly one of Germany's most powerful industrialists, though he's hardly a representative one. He insists that cooperation between employers and workers is the sole remaining hope for avoiding the Scylla and Charybdis of capitalistic monopoly on the one hand and Communist revolution on the other. Rathenau means it when he calls for the abolition of poverty and inheritance laws, an eight-hour work day, and a playing field of equal opportunity. Yet, as his left-wing critics point out, he refuses to attack the very basis of capitalism—the private ownership of the means of production and distribution—and rejects any form of socialism that calls for the confiscation or collectivist ownership of property.

Rathenau's stated goal is to free humanity from what he calls "the deadening weight of mechanization," to allow each individual "soul" to take flight. Yet he endows certain individuals—like the members of the Junker landed aristocracy that despises him—with superhuman power, thus dooming them to clay feet and himself to bitter disappointment. His special hero during the first two years of the war is General Erich von Ludendorff. Rathenau, an outsider who deeply wants to belong (and hates himself for it), initially sees in Ludendorff the personification of Germanic virtue. He writes to Ludendorff with some frequency and is occasionally received by him.

The General is notoriously irascible and a pronounced anti-Semite; when meeting face to face, he treats Rathenau with a kind of bland indifference that deeply insults him. No, Ludendorff tells Rathenau, he's not interested in any reform of the governing system that even vaguely smacks of parliamentarianism or democracy. No, he will not suspend submarine warfare in favor of a stepped-up land war. No, he will not disaffiliate from the Pan-Germanists who continue to launch schemes of annexation, especially in regard to Silesia and Courland.

By 1917 Rathenau's enthusiasm for the General has cooled considerably. No more reconciled to the war than at its outset, Rathenau feels that his countrymen's exaltation of the conflict as an ordeal which will ultimately prove "redemptive" is in fact "a dance of death," the overture to disaster. Looking to the future, he feels the difficulties of a possible peace process are "almost greater than those of the war." The chief task, in his view, is "to try to mitigate the hatred on all sides."

The Russian revolution in March 1917 evokes conflicting feelings in Rathenau. He tells Harry Kessler—they don't equate personal disagreement with disengagement, and continue to see each other—that he thinks Bolshevism is "an imposing system," and that "probably the future belongs to it." But at the same time he likens Russian Bolshevism to "an excellent play acted by some wretched company in a village barn"—and feels the same would be true of Germanic Bolshevism. He doesn't think either country has as yet developed the kind of human beings who could successfully maintain a theoretical system rooted in high idealism. As he puts it, "By night I am a Bolshevist; but when the morning comes and I enter the factory and see our workers and officials, then I am not—or at least not yet." He continues to believe that "moral and spiritual rejuvenation" has to precede a new social order.

The focus on "moral regeneration" is at the heart of Rathenau's cryptic vision. Visionaries do not specialize in coherent, systematic blueprints. Those, like Rathenau, who want to change "human nature" presume that such an entity exists—that is, beyond the rigidified accumulation of habits—and that childhood imprinting does not have the force of a biological imperative.

Like Rathenau, Harry Kessler regards the Russian Revolution as a "gigantic event," one of "incomparable world-historical importance"; intellectually, it rouses his strong interest and moves his political sympathies decidedly to the Left. Yet, unlike Rathenau, Kessler remains primarily a devotee of art, not politics; the rumor that the Bolsheviks have burned the entire unpublished correspondence between Tolstoy and his brother is alone sufficient to moderate his sympathies—though not to obliterate them.

When Germany forces a separate peace treaty on Russia, lopping off a great chunk of its western territory, the concern intensifies in England and France about Germany's expansionist aims. "If they saw the asses who sit in Berlin and guide the world empire and are supposed to administer it," Kessler writes in his diary, "they would be less anxious." He thinks a new world *is* coming into being, that the war has uprooted the old morality and much of the authority of its privileged elites, but he no longer has any expectation that the Ludendorffs and Hindenburgs will assist at its birth.

On a less outspoken, less activist basis, Magnus Hirschfeld also feels that the Russian Revolution is a hopeful augury for the future. He becomes part of a collaborative organization formed between German pacifists and their counterparts in Switzerland, Holland, and England, called the *Bund Neues Vaterland* (The League of the New Fatherland). The German *Bund* was originally formed in 1914 in an effort to foster Franco-German understanding and to prevent the outbreak of open warfare. It managed to produce some pamphlets and to draw the adherence of an impressive group of disparate left-wing intellectuals— including the militant feminist Helene Stöcker, Prince Lichnowsky (Germany's ambassador to England), Albert Einstein, Havelock Ellis, Edward Carpenter, Lowes Dickinson, and a significant number of prominent socialists of varying perspectives: Eduard Bernstein, Hugo Haase, Karl Kautsky, and Kurt Eisner among them. The prominent German historian Friedrich Meinecke would subsequently write appreciatively of those who joined the *Bund* as people "in whom the synthesis of classical liberalism was still working and in whom the classical idea of humanity and the feeling for the community of Western culture and for moderation in victory were still alive."

The Bundists are deeply resented and officially harassed. The chauvinists in every country who glorify war and detest the notion of a cultural community of West European nations denounce the *Bund* as a hothouse of traitorous defeatism. As late as the spring of 1918, Kaiser Wilhelm—more out of touch than ever—is still insisting that England and France are about to sue for peace, and that, when they do, they must formally acknowledge "the victory of monarchy over democracy." To his old friend, the racial panjandrum Houston Stewart Chamberlain, Wilhelm is still describing the war as a struggle between "Teutonic-German morality, right, loyalty and faith, genuine humanity, truth and real freedom, against the Anglo-Saxon worship of mammon, the power of money, pleasure, land-hunger, lies, betrayal and deceit." Far from viewing the war as a mistake, Wilhelm continues obstinately to characterize it as nothing less than a German "crusade against *evil*—Satan—in the world, prosecuted by us as *tools* of the Lord."

Harry Kessler is among those who beg to differ. Though once an enthusiastic defender of the war, he's long since become horrified at its mounting toll. "Blood is dumber than alcohol," he writes in his diary. "We have all lived like drunkards for four years." By 1918, some two million German men have been killed and more than four million wounded—10 percent of the entire male population. Shortages of food and coal have sent an army of women and children scouring railroad yards in hope of finding a chunk of either that might have fallen from a train.

The German troops are not much better off. Ordinary soldiers, given little more than barley soup and canned meat, are constantly hungry—and deeply resentful at the disparity between their plight and the more comfortable lives of their officers, who fatten themselves on pork, white bread, and butter, and who are known to feed sugar to their horses. The troops—sometimes driven to eating grass from the fields—are aware that officers can legally only receive as much food as those under their command; rage and bitterness deep enough to affect discipline and even to threaten revolution is growing among the rank and file.

Agitation within Germany for an end to the war has been gathering strength since 1917. "Europe's atmosphere becomes gradually that of a mortuary," Kessler writes in his diary. "We are becoming morally hollowed out by the long war." Towards the end of 1917 he meets for the first time Gustav Stresemann ("simple and good-natured"), a man who'd earlier been a strenuous annexationist and close to Ludendorff but who's been transformed by the war into a champion of democracy—and who will become the leading political figure in Germany during the 1920s.

Kessler and Stresemann begin to see each other with increasing frequency. When the number of militant workers' strikes on the home front begins to multiply early in 1918, both men come out against those in the government advocating "firmness" and the use of force, and instead support negotiations and concessions, especially in regard to abolishing Prussia's bizarre, longstanding "three-tier" system for limiting the suffrage. Above all else, they agree (in Kessler's words) that an end must be made to the ever-more widespread, "unendurable suffering."

Germany's last major offensive in March 1918 is marked by initial advances, but the subsequent attack on Reims is a disaster. Soon after, the British break through the German line at Amiens, and morale sinks to a new low. A large number of German troops surrender to the British, and the remaining men are so malnourished that they ignore their officers' command to advance in order to stuff themselves with provisions left behind by the Allies. By late summer, Germany loses what little ground it had earlier gained, and its troops are fleeing in panic before the advancing allied armies.

The Kaiser isn't getting the message. As late as September 1918 he visits the Krupp works at Essen, center of the armaments industry, and indulges in outmoded oratory about the godly-inspired struggle of Germanic virtue against Anglo-Saxon vice. The workers are having none of it. A few hecklers dare the unthinkable—they shout their complaints about hunger and exhaustion directly at the All-Highest. Things go no better a few days later when Wilhelm addresses some 400 officers; the Kaiser's antiquated remarks—"Our goal is in sight! Muskets at the ready! Defeatists up against the wall!"—are bizarrely inappropriate, and his reception is sullen.

But if the Kaiser remains enveloped in the fantasy that he leads "the warriors of God," his generals are facing the reality of "Satan's" victory. Following Germany's defeat on the Western Front in the summer of 1918, Hindenburg and Ludendorff approach Woodrow Wilson for an armistice (the US entered the war in 1917 in response to the unrestricted submarine warfare Rathenau had warned against). Rathenau, unpredictable as ever, speaks out *against* the bid for an armistice, calling it a peace of surrender (as indeed—of necessity—it decidedly is).

He argues instead—the visionary now giving way to the illusionist—for a *défense nationale*, for Germans voluntarily, mystically, to rise up and mobilize a million or so additional troops to carry on the struggle in order to ensure a "just" peace. To so bizarre a proposal, Ludendorff peremptorily turns his back. Even Max Harden, Rathenau's old friend (and sometime enemy), publicly deplores as chimerical the notion that an exhausted, demoralized German people can mobilize to assert its sovereign rights. Rathenau never forswears his conviction that, had Ludendorff stayed firm, Germany could have achieved a far more advantageous peace than it does.

Kessler, like Rathenau, thrashes about for some solution short of complete capitulation to the Allies—perhaps a new push eastward against Britain's colonies?—anything but what Kessler sees as the humiliation of groveling. Yes, peace is desirable, but not what he feels is a "premature" peace. Yet Kessler, unlike Rathenau, is resigned to the fact that in all probability the Allies *will* dictate peace terms and Germany can expect "absolutely nothing." Ludendorff, who for two years has run Germany more completely than the Kaiser, is finally forced to admit that the war is lost, that the army can't last 24 hours—and he's (falsely) rumored to have had a nervous collapse.

Kessler feels that if Germany is about to be decapitated, he prefers to put the workers' movement, now grown militant, in charge of the body. He becomes so overwrought—though showing few outward signs of it—that he refers to Woodrow Wilson as "the world's dictator." He even briefly endorses Rathenau's *levée en masse*—a moral offensive—against the looming American hegemony. Then, after taking a few deep breaths, Kessler decides that Wilson's proposed League of Nations, if set up "honestly," might eventuate after all in "a great and beautiful future for the German people"—meaning, as he elaborates in his diary, "in Europe itself we are and will remain the strongest ... This inalterable ratio of power will once again force its way through and blow up the illusory façade."

PART V

≈

THE PEACE

LATE IN 1918, EVENTS suddenly outstrip calculations. The Social Democrats, supported by the Center Party leader Matthias Erzberger, demand a peace without annexations and a swift move towards parliamentary control of the government. Peace and constitutional reform now become inseparably linked. The Kaiser, of course, resists. He will never, he announces, accept a "soft peace"; his returning troops, he predicts, will demand that he remain on the throne; his Prussian ancestors mandate the continuation of his imperial prerogatives.

But the war's terrible toll, the devastation and suffering marked by periodic protests and work stoppages over the past two years, overrule the Kaiser's tattered pretensions. At the insistence of civilian and military resisters alike, Wilhelm early in October 1918 appoints Prince Max von Baden as Chancellor of a new government, one that represents a significant departure from political tradition. Germany becomes a constitutional monarchy, with the government serving at the will of the Reichstag, not the Kaiser. Suffrage is also expanded, and Chancellor Baden's government requests an immediate end to hostilities based on Woodrow Wilson's previously enunciated "Fourteen Points."

Then, in late October 1918, an eruption of unpredictable magnitude occurs. When German sailors in the port of Kiel are ordered to put out to sea to try and break the British blockade, they denounce it as a pointless mission. Everyone knows that peace negotiations have begun. What is the German naval command thinking? Is it bent on some suicidal *Götterdämmerung*? On thousands of "heroic" deaths to glorify the eternal Reich?

The sailors are having none of it. On October 31st thousands mutiny. Initially their demands focus on the release of fellow sailors earlier arrested, but when naval authorities adamantly refuse concessions of any kind, the revolt quickly spreads. Within days, 6,000 people are demonstrating in the streets of Kiel for the sailors' release; some of the crowd break into army barracks, commandeer guns, and then free the sailors themselves. Emboldened by success, enraged when a naval patrol opens fire on them—killing seven and wounding dozens—and joined by a growing number of soldiers and workers, the revolt mushrooms.

Borrowing from the Bolshevik revolution, the rebels embrace the formation of political "councils," elected at mass meetings—a kind of grassroots form of pure democracy and, following the Russian precedent, people start addressing each other as "comrade Bolsheviks." In tandem, the rebels' demands escalate—they call for the abdication of Kaiser Wilhelm, the end of the Hohenzollern dynasty, universal suffrage for men *and* women, and an immediate peace that entails neither annexations nor indemnities.

From Kiel the movement spreads outward to factories, mines, and garrisons in other parts of Germany, first in the North and then moving south and inland across the country. In Bavaria, the left-wing intellectual and pacifist Kurt Eisner, who'd earlier been a member of the *Bund Neues Vaterland*, becomes head of the Independent Social Democratic Party (the USPD), a group which had broken away from the Social Democratic Party back in 1917 out of disgust with its refusal to oppose the war. The USPD in November 1918 proclaims the Socialist Republic of Bavaria, with Eisner serving as prime minister. For a brief, euphoric three months, revolutionary fervor reigns in Bavaria. "The new world has begun," the pacifist René Schickele writes ecstatically; "it is here: liberated mankind!"

Alas, no. Within weeks, civil war looms on the horizon. Radical socialists to the left of the USPD calling themselves the Spartacus League—named for the slave who (for a time) successfully rebelled against Rome—and led by Karl Liebknecht and Rosa Luxemburg, call for a Bolshevik-style revolution. But, as they soon learn, the majority of German workers and soldiers prefer a moderate, parliamentary form of social democracy to a Soviet-style "republic."

Simultaneous with the rise of a leftwing opposition, demands for the Kaiser's abdication increase daily; those close to him begin to fear that his life is in danger. The popular revolt, in combination with strong pressure from the Allies, in November 1918 finally produces Wilhelm's reluctant abdication—and swift removal, along with his family, to Holland. Harry Kessler can find no one who regrets the departure, least of all himself. "The monarchic idea," he writes in his diary, "was long before slowly done to death by the Emperor's utter personal failure, especially during the war, as well as by his flashy and disquieting incompetence." Kessler assigns much of the guilt for the war to Wilhelm's "false values" and his "pathologically excitable character."

He feels no sympathy for the Emperor's fall, but does feel a sense of complicity for having been part of a social order that should have been done away with long before. Not that Kessler is convinced it *has* been done away. He's sophisticated enough, and well-enough connected, to understand that the current upheaval may in the long run involve little more than a shift in the scenery; the traditional elite, and in particular the army, may currently be in disarray and may seem to have abdicated, but Kessler is uneasily aware that—to his own regret—it still waits confidently in the wings.

Wilhelm will live until 1941, and from his exile in Holland will grow, like an animal caged, ever more malignant, spewing forth venom against those odious enemies whom he sees as having long connived to bring down the Hohenzollern dynasty—pre-eminently, the Jews. He loudly declares that, since the turn of the century, Jews have been the chief figures behind the Socialist movement—"red apes," he calls them—working tirelessly to displace the monarchy with a republic. And it is Jewish treachery, he further insists, that prevented German victory in the war; Jews are "scum," "Satan's servants."

The plot against the monarchy began, Wilhelm now claims, with the charge of homosexuality Maximilian Harden—that "loathsome, dirty, Jewish fiend"—brought against Prince Eulenburg back in 1907. Conveniently forgetting that he'd leapt away from his dear friend Eulenburg as if stung by a wasp, never again uttering a word to him, Wilhelm now insists—Eulenburg having safely died in 1921—that the Prince had in fact been innocent all along. Twenty years later, when Hitler's Wehrmacht invades Holland, Wilhelm will send him a telegram congratulating him on his "powerful victory sent by God."

Fearing a Sparticist—a Bolshevist—revolution, Friedrich Ebert, head of the Social Democratic Party, decides to form an alliance with the more radical Independent Social Democratic Party (the USPD); together they form a caretaker government, and on November 9, 1918, Ebert proclaims Germany a republic. On the same day, from a nearby balcony of the royal palace, the Sparticist leader Karl Liebknecht—to the fury of Ebert and the SPD—declares Germany a *socialist* republic. Neither man can claim legitimate (electoral) authorization for their dissimilar pronouncements—and to conservatives, they are equally damnable.

In January 1919, elections for a National Assembly *are* held, but Eisner's USPD has already left the coalition in protest against the SPD's reluctance to carry out a thorough-going house-cleaning of conservative forces in the army, the bureaucracy, and the economic elite. In Berlin, the pacifist organization *Bund Neues Vaterland*, to which Magnus Hirschfeld belongs, calls for an outdoor meeting in front of Bismarck's statue on the Königsplatz. Between 4,000–5,000 people gather, and Hirschfeld is chosen to deliver the main address—marking his most prominent political appearance to date. He's hardly begun to speak when there's an exchange of gunfire between right-wing soldiers and the "Spartacists." The exchange—this time—is brief, and Hirschfeld, with considerable courage, tries again to speak to the reassembled crowd.

He praises the Kiel sailors who started the rebellion and claims that all Germans are indebted to them for "breaking the chains of militarism" ("denting" them would perhaps have been closer to the mark, as the Junker class will shortly make clear). Having initially, as an apolitical monarchist, hailed the war, Hirschfeld now salutes the radical goals of mutual aid and equality, a world parliament, and the triumph of internationalism over nationalism. He predicts that no monarch will ever again wield power in Germany (which is narrowly accurate, though Hitler will become a more powerful autocrat than Wilhelm II had ever been).

Neither Kessler nor Rathenau, with longer histories of political engagement, go as far as Hirschfeld in championing the goals of international socialism, but both press for substantive reforms sympathetic to socialists, and both remain more thoroughly engaged with a broader range of political questions than Hirschfeld. Rathenau plays an especially significant role, in the face of considerable opposition, in helping behind the scenes to push through legislation establishing an eight-hour work day. Focused as always more on ethical concerns than electoral ones, he also advocates for what he calls "the equalization of labor"—namely, manual and white-collar workers exchanging jobs for a period of time, based on the assumption that sharing of each other's experience will help foster working-class unity. He declares, further, that it's "the clear and definite task of the German mind to base the state and industry on justice and morality, and to make them an example for the commonwealth of nations."

As well, Rathenau issues an *Appeal* to the German people to unify behind the goals of ending "privileged classes," erasing distinctions between bourgeoisie and proletariat, creating equal opportunities for all, and abolishing "militarism, imperialism, feudalism, and bureaucracy." To convert those rounded phrases into practical policies, Rathenau turns to the newly established and progressive (but non-Marxist) German Democratic Party (DDP)—Kessler, too, becomes a member—and stands as its local candidate for the Reichstag's National Assembly. Strong opposition to Rathenau's candidacy, some of it based on anti-Semitism, leads to defeat; at the delegate convention he's even denied the right to speak on his own behalf. In bitterness, Rathenau once again turns away from any direct involvement in government. His disengagement will be short-lived.

Rathenau's high-theory speculations are finding their high-volume parallels in actions on the street. Germany, on November 11, 1918, signs an armistice at Compiègne with the Allied victors that formally ends hostilities. But an armistice isn't the same as a peace treaty. Those terms are yet to be dictated, and the period between Compiègne and the Versailles Treaty sees a further—and extended—internal upheaval within Germany itself.

Harry Kessler is on at least the periphery of much of it. For half a dozen years be becomes more of a political figure than he's ever been—or would be again. During the tumultuous winter of 1918–1919, his sympathies are decidedly left-wing, but of a kind close to those of the new Chancellor, Friedrich Ebert, whose impulses are democratic and who claims to envision for Germany an eventual conversion from capitalism to socialism, but whose immediate aim is to prevent Russian Bolshevism from planting deep roots in the country. Kessler stands a step or two to Ebert's left, since he doesn't share the Chancellor's belief that the maintenance of law and order requires winning the support of high-level army, civil service, and industrial hold-overs from the old regime. Kessler harbors more distrust than Ebert of the old guard (though in several senses he's been a part of it) and feels more, if incomplete, sympathy for the vibrant militancy of grassroots socialism as exemplified in the workers' council movement.

That movement puts Kessler politically and emotionally closer to several new friends he's made—George Grosz, the artist; the writer Wieland Herzfelde; and Fritz von Unruh, the playwright—than to Chancellor Ebert. During the war George Grosz suffered from what was then called "shell-shock" (and today "post-traumatic stress disorder"). Sent to a hospital and mental asylum, he was declared unfit to serve and released—thanks to the formal testimony of Doctor Magnus Hirschfeld.

Kessler's most pronounced attraction is to Herzfelde—the co-founder of a new journal, *Neue Jugend*. Herzfelde seems to have represented for Kessler something of an erotically-charged "manly" ideal: he writes admiringly—even lyrically—in his diary of Herzfelde's qualities: "The contempt for every self-importance, the realism without selfishness, the lovely self-confidence combined with modesty, the self-control, the will-ingness to sacrifice, the chastity regarding one's own holy goals: a youth that was overwhelmingly like this"—Kessler here approaches apothe-osis—"would renew the world, would make the spilled blood bloom." Young people like Herzfelde represent to Kessler what small consola-tion there is for the millions killed—and whatever hope there might be for a better world.

Other recent friends—the pacifists Annette Kolb and the journalist/editor René Schickele—see to it that Kessler has access to some of the radical socialists sporadically fighting it out on street corners against both Ebert's government troops and right-wing military diehards. Looking in one day on the chaotic upheaval at the Reichstag, Kessler is plunged into a scene of exhilarating chaos; various left-wing groups jam into the committee rooms to debate at top volume the issues of the day; cigarette butts and waste paper cover much of the chamber's carpeting; stacks of rifles are in every corner; energetic young radical sailors mingle with, and are in stark contrast to, the unkempt, war-weary remnants of the army; in the midst of the confusion, exhausted activists are sound asleep on the hard benches. Entering the Council Chamber, Kessler the aesthete reawakens: the ugly room seems to him a "ridiculous neo-Gothic crate."

There are compensations. One is an introduction to Hugo Haase, a leader of the USPD, whom he finds well-disposed and friendly, though he glimpses a profound stubbornness beneath the surface geniality. Kessler is also introduced to one of the sailors who leads the Red Guard and who's been actively involved since the uprising in Kiel; the sailor vehemently tells Kessler that his fellow radicals *do* support the new gov-ernment and do oppose any kind of violence. Kessler chooses to believe that the sailor's views echo the outlook of the vast majority of young left-wing revolutionaries.

Other friends procure a card for Kessler certifying that the "bearer of this credential" is authorized to help maintain order in the streets; Kessler has inadvertently (and dubiously) become "a policeman in the

Red Guard." He's given as well a Workers' and Soldiers' Council identity card declaring him "trustworthy and free to pass." Both cards carry the Reichstag stamp, though the legitimizing source for either credential is in fact unclear.

The crucial point for Kessler is whether the Bolshevik-inspired Spartacists or the more moderate socialists will—or should—win the day. He goes to see Hugo Haase in the Chancellery and they talk together about the importance of establishing contacts as soon as possible with French socialists; Haase asks Kessler and René Schickele to undertake the task and they agree to do so, though Kessler tells Haase that he'll gladly withdraw if the new government prefers someone else. But the following day Haase instead unexpectedly offers Kessler the appointment of "Minister at Warsaw," and he immediately accepts. The chief task he's assigned is to oversee the evacuation of German troops from Poland and the Ukraine.

Within days, Kessler arrives in Warsaw for what will be an intensely emotional, muddled mission lasting only a month. The fault isn't Kessler's but rather the general confusion of events and authorities. Germany's wartime occupation of Poland has entailed considerable brutality and left a legacy of intense distrust. Anti-German fury runs so high in the country that mobs of irate Poles several times attack the German Legation as well as Kessler's residence, forcing him to demand armed protection.

To further complicate his mission, the German High Command, still dominated by right-wing officers, issues periodic instructions that show little awareness of the realities facing Kessler on the ground. Meantime, reports arrive from home that German troops returning from the Western Front are being led by right-wing officers determined to destroy not only the Sparticist movement but Haase's USPD—the Independent Social Democratic Party—as well. By early December 1918 the situation has deteriorated into an open shooting-match on the streets of Berlin, the outcome uncertain.

Three weeks after Kessler's arrival in Warsaw, the Polish government breaks off diplomatic relations with Germany and "requests" that he leave the country immediately. Kessler blames the break on French pressure exerted on the Poles, fueled by what he views as a "demonic hatred" of Germany; the French, Kessler writes in his diary, "will continue to hate us and fight against us until they or we are exterminated." Arriving back in Berlin, he reports directly to Ebert; the Chancellor assures him that "nobody could have done more" and thanks him for his service.

Kessler finds Berlin far more enflamed than when he left a month earlier, and his marginal sympathy for the Spartacist radicals quickly evaporates. He decides that they're destabilizing the only sort of provisional government able to win even modest concessions from the triumphant Allies. Two days before Christmas, as Kessler walks down Unter den Linden, he runs into an armed, uniformed regiment—and discovers it's one of his own, the Third Battalion of Uhlan Guards. Ebert, it turns out, has sent for them, which makes Kessler queasily certain—accurately, it turns out—that civil and social upheaval are about to escalate further. "Not since the great days of the French Revolution," he muses, "has humanity depended so much on the outcome of street-fighting . . ."

The next six months are marked by a grim seesaw battle between constantly shifting ideological forces. The Sparticists are in a minority among left-wing elements contending for power and, when they officially change their name to the Communist Party of Germany early in 1919, they help to fuel the rise of right-wing paramilitary units—the so-called Freikorps—whose numbers thereafter rapidly increase and who are openly encouraged in their violence by the caretaker government's new defense minister, Gustav Noske. Yet early in 1919 a joint call from the Independent Social Democrats and the Communists is able to muster a huge demonstration, estimated at 700,000, on Berlin's streets, the crowd waving red flags and cheering on Bolshevik speakers. "The situation," Kessler notes in his diary, "is extremely unclear. The Government has not merely failed to achieve anything, but has been forced on the defensive and finds itself hard pushed."

The highly disciplined Freikorps strike back with ruthless force, methodically picking off nests of left-wing fighters and brutally murdering the Communists' two most prominent leaders, Karl Liebknecht and Rosa Luxemburg. Kessler, for one, is horrified at the murders; he credits both leaders with a "deep and genuine love for the poor and downtrodden" and honors "their spirit of self-sacrifice"; surely, he feels, they are "personalities preferable to careerists and trade union officials." As if spurred by their deaths, Kessler and his new friends Herzfelde and Grosz (whom Kessler has decided is "really a Bolshevist in the guise of a painter ... reactionary and revolutionary in one") decide to put out a new periodical broadly sympathetic to the idealism Liebknecht and Luxemburg represented. The principle aim of the new journal is, as Herzfelde puts it, "to sling mud at everything that Germans have so far held dear—'Great Man' sacrosanctity, and the stupidity as well as fustiness to be found among radicals."

Smack in the midst of the dangerously escalating civil conflict, the Ebert government calls for the election of a Constituent Assembly early in 1919. Germans go to the polls in record numbers—with women for the first time able to vote; the results, to no one's real surprise, show a profound division in public opinion. Soon after, the SPD and the Independent Social Democrats dissolve their coalition, and a month later right-wing soldiers murder the USPD's leader, Kurt Eisner; three other left-wing intellectuals take his place at the head of the Independent Social Democrats: the philosopher Gustav Landauer, the anarchist poet Erich Mühsam, and Ernst Toller, the radical pacifist ("I have always believed that socialists, despising force, should never employ it for their own ends").

Ebert, for his part, lurches to the Right and forms a new alliance with the German People's and Catholic Center Parties. Together, this "Weimar Coalition" organizes a new constitutional convention that aims at establishing democracy, safeguarding basic civil liberties, and electing by popular vote a president responsible to the Reichstag. The new constitution that emerges inevitably reflects current public divisions: it establishes a federal system that embraces 18 states, with the central government having the dominant power but with a significant governing role reserved for the divergent localities. The national assembly again selects Friedrich Ebert President of the Republic.

Kessler, now considerably to the left of Ebert, writes in his diary—

either indulging his occasional snobbery or parodying it—that "a master-saddler has been elected to the throne." He seems neither disappointed nor enthusiastic over the choice: Ebert, he believes, is "respectable, likeable, and efficient," though Kessler thinks it's questionable as to what extent he'll reinvigorate political life. "He will not cut any capers," Kessler writes, "and to that degree is an improvement on Wilhelm II, but he is no Cromwell either."

Kessler wants something more than a pragmatic caretaker—something more than "purely material changes and more equitable and better distribution and organization; the country needs something new of an idealist nature." After all the war's destruction and suffering, Kessler feels that more than a patchwork job is wanted; what is needed is some suggestion of "the birth-pangs of a new era." He believes the spur urging on the best among the Spartacists is precisely the desire he shares for a different and better world. He wonders if he isn't buoying himself up with "mirages of paradise." Whether his hope for a "new era" is a daydream will, he feels, determine in the long run whether the Spartacists are right or wrong.

Meantime, Defense Minister Gustav Noske has become a staunch supporter of the Freikorps militants who in mounting numbers are launching lethal assaults on regions of the country that have come under socialist control, particularly those cities—Bremen, Cuxhaven, Wilhelmshaven, and Hamburg—that have refused to accept the authority of the central government. In effect, the recently exhausted and humiliated German army has now morphed into the *Reichswehr*, and in May 1919 Noske is able to boast that he has 400,000 men under his command.

In tumultuous street-fighting, and using heavy weaponry that includes tanks, the Freikorps succeeds in systematically destroying the left-wing opposition—one operation alone leaves 15,000 dead and 12,000 wounded. The Independent Social Democrats hold out longest in Bavaria, where Ernst Toller leads a "Red Brigade" against the counter-revolutionary troops—simultaneously, touchingly, resisting force with force even as he dashes around trying to prevent captured

Freikorps soldiers from being executed. He's unsuccessful on all counts. The veteran shock troops decimate the Bavarian "Red Army" in the spring of 1919, murder Landauer, and imprison Toller and Mühsam. Only scattered mopping-up operations remain.

National attention shifts to a new sort of "enemy"—the pending Treaty of Versailles. Harry Kessler is friendly with the leader of the 180-person (all male) German delegation to Versailles, Ulrich, Count Brockdorff-Rantzau, a respected diplomat from an ancient land-holding family. Despite his monocle and stiff bearing, Kessler knows Brockdorff as a decent man (though an "intriguer" and an "old cocotte") and he places considerable hope in his ability to achieve at least a pacifist-oriented League of Nations. It's widely known that Brockdorff is homosexual—a matter of some concern to Kessler, who fears that prejudice against Brockdorff on those grounds will deepen hostility to the German delegation in general. Kessler knows that a dictated peace is inevitable but he hopes it won't be accompanied by gratuitous humiliation.

His hopes are disappointed. Even as the German delegation makes its way from Berlin to Paris, it's deliberately subjected to various taunts: the train carrying the delegates moves at a crawl in order to give the Germans a good look at the devastation they've wrought on the French countryside; in Paris they're harshly ordered onto buses to their hotel, where their luggage is dumped in a courtyard and they're told to carry their own bags. French animosity leaves Brockdorff feeling personally humiliated; he refuses to participate further and retreats from public life.

Despite the harsh terms of the Versailles Treaty, Germany has little choice but to sign it in June 1919. According to the terms of the Treaty, the German army is henceforth limited to 100,000 men, with no tanks, aircraft, or general staff permitted. The Treaty also mandates the withdrawal of all German troops to east of the Rhine, and the surrendering of its fleet—including all submarines—as well as a vast amount of military equipment. In addition, Germany is obligated to accept Article 231 of the Treaty, accepting "sole guilt" for the outbreak of hostilities, and agreeing to pay staggering financial reparations in compensation for the physical damage German troops wrought during the war.

A number of Freikorps generals balk at the terms and even grumble threateningly about the possibility of renewing the war. But the Allies hold firm—and, as an added humiliation, impose considerable loss of territory on Germany. Right-wing Germans never forget what they call the "shameful surrender" at Versailles, for which they primarily blame— who else?—"the Jews." It's a theory General von Ludendorff finds especially congenial; blaming Jewish "conspirators" for "stabbing Germany in the back," after all, helps divert attention from the simple fact that the German army was defeated on the battlefield. Most German Jews, in fact, are political centrists, not adherents of revolutionary socialism.

Throughout the tumultuous 1918–1919 period, both Rathenau and Kessler have been keen observers, and sometimes participants, in the rapidly-shifting turn of events. Many months have gone by since the two men have seen each other, but Kessler, eager to hear Rathenau's views on the muddled political situation and especially on the suggested League of Nations, seeks him out in late February 1919, while street fighting is still taking place.

There are brief pleasantries initially. Rathenau tells Kessler about his "many visitors of late, mostly from England and the United States. They come," he tells Kessler, "to extend condolences to me for belonging to the nation they regard with a tart mixture of loathing and contempt. They remind me of the attitude Christians adopt towards gifted Jews— they accept them, but with condolences for their bloodline connections to so many awful co-religionists. What my English friends don't seem to understand is that, as a result of our defeat, we have here in Germany— not in England, not in France, not in the United States—the chance at last to abolish the proletariat."

The oracular comment catches Kessler completely off guard. " ...abolish the—my dear Rathenau, thanks to Versailles, we have the power to do practically *nothing at all*! We're hardly masters in our own home."

"I'd put it somewhat differently: the landscape has been cleared, the inviolability of private property shaken to its roots. The State has intervened and expropriated at will. We can use that precedent to break down still further, through taxation, all resistance to equalization. No person should be allowed to acquire means beyond what is necessary for the ordinary amenities of life."

Kessler figuratively shakes his head in disbelief. Has Rathenau fallen so out of touch, he wonders, that he hasn't heard, or understood, that the right-wing forces of the Freikorps have utterly routed the radical Left? What Kessler says is far less offensive: "It sounds as if you've moved *beyond* the Socialists, beyond the . . . well, yes, beyond the Communists. Or are you simply playing with me?"

"I'm doing no more than pointing to a possibility," Rathenau replies, his tone solemn. "The wreckage of war makes possible not only a new economy—but a new citizen, one guided not by covetousness but by conscience and by creativity."

Kessler sighs. "Alas, Friedrich Ebert does not qualify on any count. We'll be lucky if he manages to neutralize—just neutralize—the Junkers' stubborn insistence on non-compliance. Material conditions have changed, but mental attitudes far less so."

"That change will be slow to take effect. Yet a *community* of production will emerge, with all members organically bound to one another— an organism, not a confederation." Rathenau speaks with the quiet glow of passionate prophecy.

"But the implementation, Rathenau—the *implementation*!"

"A functionally decentralized state," Rathenau calmly replies.

"As decreed by—? You sound like an English Guild Socialist . . . William Morris or G.D.H. Cole. Or closer still, the anarchists Fourier or Prince Kropotkin . . ."

"Better still, Nietzsche: 'We must aim to win freedom for renewed creation.' But first we must go through this—this dance of death everywhere around us. The difficulties of the peace are greater than those of the war. The hatred on all sides must be mitigated before any reconstruction is possible."

"As I see it," Kessler says, "three main forces are currently dividing nations—clericalism, capitalism (along with its offspring, militarism and imperialism), and communism, as represented, respectively, by the Pope, Woodrow Wilson, and Lenin, each with enormous power behind him. Their competition for Germany's soul will be the decisive site of the struggle." Kessler has been careful in his choice of words: "soul," he knows, can usually be counted on to animate Rathenau.

"Soul?!" he promptly echoes. "Capitalism has none. Clericalism claims a monopoly but peddles only hokum. Bolshevism alone embodies it. I'm strongly attracted to it. It's a splendid system and a century hence it will rule the globe. Not the Russian version."

Kessler rises to the bait. "If you mean Liebknecht and Luxemburg— then yes. If you mean Lenin—no, not remotely. Lenin is a master organizer—and opportunist: the autocrat disguised as a worker. About Woodrow Wilson we entirely agree: the high school principal, strap against palm, disguised as a democrat."

Rathenau actually laughs—an event in itself. "Wilson represents things as they are. I'm only concerned with the more distant future."

Kessler can feel his annoyance building at the way Rathenau enunciates every word as if delivering the secrets of an arcane wisdom. "What more should—or could—Wilson represent?" Kessler can hear the impatience in his voice, and regrets it.

If Rathenau hears it, he makes no effort to soften his pontification: "Wilson assumes that today's nation-states must remain the essential building blocks for international cooperation. That assumption dooms the League from the start. You cannot expect the selfish imperialism that characterizes the Great Powers to create any form of selfless cooperation."

"That's the crux of the matter. And you've expressed it better than anyone." Kessler is laying it on a bit thick, atoning for his earlier irritability. Besides, Rathenau tends to bring out the courtier in Kessler, the supplicant side which his alien sexuality further nurtures.

"Perhaps," Kessler continues, "the League should be based from the start on *international* bodies—like labor organizations, or Zionism, or trading federations that—"

"—*Zionism*?!" Rathenau is suddenly at full volume. "How did Zionism get in there?! Do you want to base the League on building a Jewish homeland in Palestine? Really, my dear Kessler—what in Heaven's name?!—"

"—it isn't only Jews who support the notion of—"

"—it isn't *even* Jews—not in Germany at least. Most Zionists are Russian or Polish, Jews unwilling or unable to assimilate in their native lands."

"Is it really very different here in Germany, even now with the Kaiser gone and a republic declared?" Kessler knows that he's on dangerous ground, edging close to one of Rathenau's most consequential inner conflicts.

"Surely you're aware that when war broke out in 1914," Rathenau says evenly, "self-declared German Zionists *already settled in Palestine* returned to defend the homeland."

"All of them? Surely not."

"I couldn't tell you. I wasn't there." Rathenau turns away in anger. Kessler lets a few seconds go by. Then, flattening his voice to resemble placation, he benignly proceeds:

"This is a matter I don't understand well. I've long been puzzled why ordinary Germans insistently sound the chord of 'Jewish domination,' though Jews—even now—are denied access to the highest offices in the government and the military."

"I cannot provide you with a primer of German Jewish history," Rathenau testily replies. Nothing in his countenance softens his rudeness.

Kessler swallows hard and continues to aim for a courteous tone: "Of course not. But perhaps you can explain why Martin Buber—whose books you once told me you greatly admired, and who is now so highly regarded—emphatically insists that the best among the Jews are those who have lost all national loyalty and who concentrate on cultivating the mystical, transnational essence of the Jewish spirit. Isn't Buber's view in direct conflict with the dominant tendency among Germany's Jews to become ever more successful and assimilated—ever more *nationalistic*?"

"Buber is a *cultural*, not a political, Zionist," Rathenau emphatically responds. "He wants to restore and maintain the organic Jewish folk community; the restoration of roots is what he cares about, not the creation of a political state. I've attended a number of Buber's 'Thursday Society' gatherings at his home in Zehlendorf."

"*Have* you?!" Kessler is genuinely surprised.

"There's no contradiction between Buber's teachings and the ongoing process of Jewish integration into all the institutions of German life."

Rathenau catches Kessler's skeptical look, but pushes ahead. "Nowhere else in the world are Jews more accepted than they are in Germany. Especially now, under the Republic. Of that you can be certain."

"More than in England?" Suddenly aware that he's raised his voice, Kessler retreats to a less agitated tone. "I have many Jewish friends in England . . . in different occupations . . . They uniformly tell me that they participate in all aspects of national life."

"Either they're deluded or you are." Rathenau's crude incivility brings Kessler up short. Before he can respond, Rathenau sails on, unheeding:

"Next thing you'll be telling me is how enlightened Russia is towards its Jews, that the pogroms are in actuality groups of Cossacks helping to clear—sorry, *till*—the land."

Offended, Kessler struggles to keep a measured tone. "It is you who speaks of Russia. My reference, as should be clear, was to England."

"You apparently forget that a mere twenty years ago, England imposed strict limitations on Jewish immigration. During those same years, Germany opened its borders to East European Jews attempting to escape the vile pogroms in Russia."

Kessler has regained his footing: "As did England. I know for a fact that tens of thousands of Russian Jews poured into London's East End. Yes, it led to a rise in anti-Semitism, but never to the kind of sustained campaign of hatred that we see in Germany."

Rathenau knows that Kessler's view is largely valid, but, rather than acknowledge the fact, he pridefully shifts ground:

"You also seem to forget that not long ago Captain Dreyfus, the only Jew on the French army's general staff, was railroaded by a well-placed cabal that included Paul Valéry and your precious Edgar Degas to a cell on Devil's Island in French Guiana. Is it any wonder that German Jews are confirmed patriots? Germany stands out as the country, more than any other, where social integration has taken firm root. Germanness and Jewishness are NOT incompatible!" Rathenau thunders.

"The Zionists don't agree with you. Their argument, I believe, is that anti-Semitism is so profound that there's no future for the Jewish people anywhere in Europe. They need a homeland of their own. Could it be one already exists—the United States?"

Rathenau smiles sardonically. "The United States!—Yes, if you can squeeze into Harvard under their strict quota system, or never try to stay at one of the better hotels—or for that matter try to become a full professor in one of their universities."

Kessler tries to move on: "As for the League of—"

"—I'll grant you this much, Kessler: One should never confuse the many honors Germany bestows on prominent Jewish artists and scientists—Einstein, Mahler, Ehrlich, and so on—with the condition of most German Jews. They are ordinary, hard-working Germans of no particular talent or influence. Yet they, too, thrive. Give or take the inevitable hooliganism now and then, they are left in peace."

Kessler gives up the contest: "If we could return to the League of Nations—"

"—to turn to international bodies is mistaken," Rathenau says with sonorous satisfaction, as if he's vanquished a foe. "Hatred of Germany is today so great that it infects every international organization—including the Socialist International."

"If we create a League with real power—with legal sanctions—to use against any state pursuing mere national interests, then perhaps—"

"—a League that would even-handedly administer Europe's colonies in Africa and Asia?" Rathenau scoffs. "Come now, my dear Kessler, who would vote to establish such a League? Your suggestion has abstract appeal, but no chance of practical implementation."

Kessler can't muster a persuasive comeback, having sometimes taken Rathenau's position in the argument. "What then do we do? Are we in any position to oppose Wilson?"

"We need a world economic organization that can regulate the equitable distribution of raw materials—and can set limits on expenditure for arms."

"And you accuse *me* of holding on to a pipe dream?!"

Rathenau acknowledges the hit: "The only hope is the new generation. Some of your friends, perhaps, like Wieland Herzfelde. Or Fritz von Unruh..."

"They're in a small minority. Most of today's youth despises political involvement. I predict that once the current crisis is passed, the young will wholly turn their backs on political life and devote energy entirely to the pursuit of pleasure. Take last night, for example: Friends insisted on carting me off to something called the Kleist Café. The one thing the patrons had in common, it seemed to me, was an absolute rejection of the kind of moral severity you advocate. The place was filled with noise, cigarette smoke, drunks, coquettes, pederasts, sailors—what have you— the patrons packed together on the dance floor performing movements I'd never imagined possible called the 'tango' and the 'foxtrot.'"

"It sounds repulsive."

"It was—but then again, I'm well into middle-age. Perhaps such 'decadence'—if that's the right word—is a necessary precursor to the 'new type of human being' you call for so fervently." Having expressed the possibility, Kessler finds himself suddenly taken with it. "Come to think of it, decadence might be the very path to such a new type. One thing is sure: A new style *is* emerging. And pleasure is central to it."

"When their 'style' includes a plank erasing all national borders, I'll be interested in hearing another report about them."

Kessler decides against an additional rebuttal.

Writing in his diary that night, Kessler gives free rein to his impatience with Rathenau. Yes, he had, as always, made some shrewd observations—but as always had delivered them with "self-assured loquacity" and "hollow condescension," his manner "a mixture of bitterness and conceit." Kessler decides that "there is something of a masculine old maid about Rathenau"—all that restricted stateliness. Spouting Bolshevism while "ensconced in a damask-covered chair...an ultra-modernist strumming an old lyre." The thought leads Kessler back to his experience at the Kleist Café. Perhaps next time, he thinks, "I should take Rathenau along."

~

Harry Kessler keeps hearing in his head some of the comments Rathenau made during their last conversation: Bolshevism as a system is theoretically superior to capitalism, but today's citizens have grown up in a society saturated with capitalistic values of consumerism, greed, and "each against all"—and are therefore incapable of bringing such a system into existence, or of inhabiting it should it somehow arrive. Kessler puzzles over priorities: Since the average citizen is (according to Rathenau) incapable of appreciating the superiority of Bolshevism, should it be established through force—as in Russia, and as championed by the Sparticists? Or should the focus instead be on introducing new values into the education of the young—above all, the transcendent importance of nonviolence as well as the doctrine of "each *for* all" to supplant the current apotheosis of "each against all"? And at how young an age should such education begin? Should it start with the working class? Yet how can it, since current factory conditions militate against the formation of effective communities? (In one of his spasms of class prejudice, Kessler tells himself at one point that, to the workers, "revolution" simply means the acquisition of cars and silk stockings.)

Perhaps, he thinks, education in new values should begin at the kindergarten level. But perhaps even that may be too late, the child's mind already confirmed in the primacy of self-aggrandizement. Should the development of new values be left to the newborn's parents?—but wouldn't they themselves, socialized for avarice, inculcate the very values that need uprooting? Conundrum upon conundrum, with the current social climate already delimiting the likely possibilities.

Kessler is still aristocrat enough to shy away from the notion of class struggle, even if it proceeds (somehow) without violence. Unlike his radical young friend Herzfelde, he can't believe that Bolshevism can possibly succeed in a country drenched in capitalist ideology, exhausted and ruined by a punishing war. Kessler fears that a counterrevolution from the Right is the more likely outcome. Nor can he get himself to swear allegiance to the currently-dominant Social Democratic Party either; when he and Ebert meet, Kessler finds himself in disagreement with Ebert's claim that the Russian experiment proves that communism is "impractical." Conditions there, he tells himself, simply aren't "ripe—no more than they are in Germany."

Buffeted as he feels—and as many left-leaning Germans feel—by contending ideological claims, Kessler decides to accept the leadership in Germany of the World Youth Movement, but only after insuring that the focus will be on *worker* youth and that socialism will be the guiding principle. He also joins, along with Rathenau, the recently-formed German Democratic Party, the most progressive of the three parties that constitute the governing Weimar Coalition (the SPD and the Catholic Center Party being the other two).

Back in 1918 Rathenau had attempted to form the Democratic Popular Union, devoted to a fundamental reshaping of the economic order along egalitarian lines; the Union had also attracted the support of, among others, Albert Einstein and Gerhart Hauptmann. But it failed—unsurprisingly—to appeal to most of Rathenau's fellow industrialists, without whose support no restructuring could happen, and the Union soon disbanded. It's at that point that Rathenau shifts allegiance to the German Democratic Party, which draws many middle-class professionals, including women, as well as many affluent Jewish members.

The German Democratic Party rejects both monopoly capitalism and the socialization of industry, but does call for the establishment of broad social welfare measures and the curtailment of gross economic inequalities. "Neither the played-out individualism of the West," Rathenau writes at the time, "nor the abstract and doctrinaire orthodoxy of Russia, will save us from the abyss." For both Rathenau and Kessler, joining the German Democratic Party is the equivalent of favoring the more cautious side of their natures and relinquishing, at least for a time, their more radical socialist leanings.

Until more people acquire the "new ethics" needed to successfully sustain state control of industry, Rathenau argues, it would be premature—indeed, a form of unintentional sabotage—to promote socialization of the economy. What most impedes the spread of the new ethics, in Rathenau's view, is the tedium inherent in the repetitive, mechanical labor of the assembly line. This, to him, is the central problem of socialism: the "weariness of soul" intrinsic to the specialized division of labor. The solution, he suggests, lies in his earlier suggestion to "equalize labor"—as part of every given day, workers would share in plant management and managers would share in mechanical labor. The practical obstacles to such a scheme are themselves a measure of how torn and pessimistic Rathenau has become.

∾

For a man rapidly becoming the world's most renowned sexologist, Magnus Hirschfeld isn't having a whole lot of sex. Short and pudgy, with a walrus moustache that droops down the sides of his mouth, he gives off few of the pheromones said to signal males in heat to come calling. What he does give off is a kindness, warmth, and sympathy that has less drawing power but does attract some emotionally—as opposed to erotically—needy admirers. Foremost among them is Karl Giese.

Giese comes into Hirschfeld's orbit in response to the plans he'd started formulating during the war for an Institute for Sexual Science. Until the cessation of hostilities, the Institute can exist only in Hirschfeld's head, not as a concrete entity with an actual address, staff, and membership. What he envisions is a broadly-inclusive Institute that will offer both basic research facilities and clinical services. It will be all at once a medical department and treatment facility; a library, archive, and museum for preserving historical material; and an information center that offers public lectures on topics ranging widely from marital problems to fetishistic sexual obsessions. The Institute will aim, in short, at establishing sexology for the first time as a legitimate subject for academic inquiry.

The celebration of Hirschfeld's 50th birthday on May 14, 1918 becomes the symbolic kick-off date for a successful fundraising drive that raises 30,000 marks—enough to provide an endowment for a non-profit foundation and for the purchase of a building spacious enough to accommodate Hirschfeld's expansive vision. Soon after the war ends, he's able to acquire the elegant mansion at No. 10 In den Zelten once owned by Count Hatzfeldt, the former ambassador to France (and before him, by the famed violinist Joseph Joachim). Two years later Hirschfeld adds the adjoining residential building—bringing the Institute's total number of rooms to 50.

The entire complex stands at the juncture where In den Zelten and Beethovenstrasse meet, and it is widely regarded as an architectural gem. The combined basements house the kitchen and various offices; the ground floor contains reception and consultation rooms (including one that has mementoes of Queen Louise and Napoleon—gifts from grateful patients); the second floor consists of Hirschfeld's living quarters, as well as laboratories. The adjoining building contains the Institute's museum, archives, and library—the largest collection of scientific literature on sexuality in the world, and one constantly being added to; additionally, it houses various clinics and a large lecture hall. The staff includes a librarian, four secretaries, and various assistants; and each department—pediatrics, neurology, physiology, endocrinology, and so on—is headed by established specialists, several of whom are heterosexual.

Fully operational by the end of 1919, the Institute in its inaugural year alone offers courses on sexual pathology, forensic sexology, and the physiology of sexual differences. Before long, a number of doctors and students from other countries flock to the Institute to attend courses, listen to lectures, and examine the archival collections. Additionally, the Institute handles 1,800 consultations in its first year alone—free of charge to the poor—the majority of them with sexually-variant patients. The consultations include a man who wants to marry but suffers from a lack of libido (he's referred to a sexual counselor); a man with a shoe fetish (referred for psychiatric treatment); a woman with her daughter who worries about a glandular condition (referred to the Department of Endocrinology); a transvestite seeking advice about cross-dressing (referred to a sexual counselor); a homosexual man with venereal disease who needs treatment (referred to the Medical Department); a woman who thinks her attraction to other women can be cured through heterosexual marriage (referred to a psychiatrist who tells her firmly that it will do no such thing)—and so on.

Matter-of-fact, commonsensical advice typifies the Institute's approach to the everyday issues that ordinary citizens bring to its consulting rooms. For a time, Hirschfeld co-authors a column with a feminist colleague that bases its advice on the down-to-earth assumption that sexual desire is a perfectly natural human phenomenon, and that variations on the norm are, more often than not, emancipatory. They defend a single woman's right to have sex—*and* to have children; give detailed instructions on the use of diaphragms; and brusquely chastise a husband complaining about his wife's lesbian affair by telling him that it's none of his business: "there is no property right to the body of another."

One of Hirschfeld's better-known colleagues at the Institute, Dr. Max Hodann, also writes a column, and it too routinely offers level-headed advice. When one anxious questioner wants to know if daily intercourse is advisable, Hodann replies, "If it feels good, why not?" To a worried husband who confesses that his wife "can only come when she's on top" and asks what he could do about it, Hodann sensibly responds that "if one position is more satisfying than another, there's absolutely no reason not to enjoy it." He discounts the common notion that masturbation is linked to insanity, and tells heterosexual couples that it's important to have sex *before* marriage. Hodann even asserts that "there is no such thing as a frigid woman, only incompetent men," and offers his opinion that "monogamy is a catastrophe" (while honorably adding that "the new path is still not clearly defined").

Hirschfeld understands far in advance of most specialists that counseling should include awakening the individual sufferer to the knowledge that he or she is not alone, that a potential community exists, and that becoming part of a social network can do wonders for depression and thoughts of suicide. Thanks to the enlightened attitudes of two successive police commissioners—Leopold von Meerscheidt-Hüllessem and Hans von Tresckow—who adopt a tolerant view of homosexual bars and gathering places (and a profound *in*tolerance for pimps and blackmailers), Berlin becomes in the 1920s the most wide-open city in Europe, the foremost place where sexual and gender nonconformists can meet publicly without fear of harassment and arrest. The police chiefs even organize official tours of homosexual nightspots to acquaint students of sexology with the social possibilities available, and Hirschfeld not only takes an occasional tour himself to keep up-to-date, but strongly urges clients to profit from the numerous social outlets.

The Institute provides a great deal besides counseling. It's devoted from the beginning to public education, and to that end becomes much in demand for advice on family planning, birth control, and contraception. The Institute also creates a "Museum of Sexuality," with banks of displays on everything from fetishism to sex toys to sadomasochism. And it does pioneering—though highly controversial—work in the fields of hormone treatment (Hirschfeld is much taken with the Austrian endocrinologist Eugen Steinach's current experiments), as well as what is now called "gender dysphoria." As early as 1921, surgeons at the Institute undertake one of the first sex-reassignment operations ever performed, a procedure that greatly influences the later work of the American transgender pioneer, Dr. Harry Benjamin—who first met Hirschfeld in 1907 and who visits the Institute frequently throughout the 1920s.

Imposing as the mansion is, Hirschfeld manages to create a friendly, inviting atmosphere—the feel of a private dwelling rather than an institution. Pictures (including several of cross-dressers) cover the walls, and the floors are carpeted; large windows look out on the Tiergarten; Biedermeier furnishings fill a number of rooms; collections of glassware and porcelain line many walls. There is no smell of disinfectant, no linoleum on the floors, no gray, empty walls, no forbidding signs warning "NO ENTRANCE." This is a welcoming refuge, a home. Hirschfeld himself occupies a bedroom on the first floor of the Institute, the floor that also houses some 30,000 books, plus massive collections of photographs and slides.

Karl Giese, nearly 30 years Hirschfeld's junior, heads up the Institute's archives. He's a good-looking young man, and, though lacking university degrees, has become a learned autodidact in the new field of sexology, knowledgeable enough to be entrusted with some of the public lectures that Hirschfeld considers an essential part of the Institute's commitment to general education. Giese has always been attracted to older men and Hirschfeld to younger, somewhat "effeminate" ones—he likes Giese calling him "Papa" (his friends call him "M.H." and his enemies "Auntie Magnesia")—and the two men make no secret of their love for each other. Giese has a strong, virile physique that belies his masochistic needs and his effeminate ways. Hirschfeld himself has no interest in sadomasochism but also no objection to Giese satisfying that need with other men; both believe that love tends towards monogamy but sexual attraction towards polygamy. Giese has his own cozy nest at the Institute and a circle of campy friends with whom he often goes to clubs of an evening to dance and drink.

Most of Hirschfeld's colleagues at the Institute—and they're of varied sexual persuasions—feel deep admiration and affection for him. One of them, Dr. Ludwig L. Lenz, himself heterosexual and head of the gynecology section of the Institute, regards Hirschfeld as a "benevolent man, whose scientific qualities are only equaled by his humane attributes." Hirschfeld is something of a polymath, conversant with current research in a wide variety of fields, including biology, sociology, and endocrinology. Lenz finds him a wise mentor and credits Hirschfeld with teaching him how to become "unprejudiced," how to reach the understanding that matters of "morality" and "perversion" are neither universal nor unchanging but instead reflect the cultural context of a given time and place—teaching him, in sum, that "morality" is little more than custom.

Hirschfeld begins work at 5:00 a.m. every day, sitting at his desk in front of the large French window that opens out into a splendid view of the Tiergarten. His days are packed with consultations, study, teaching, and meetings, but he lives simply. His only recreation is music; once a month an audience of eminent guests is invited to hear a particular trio or quartet perform. Hirschfeld's sole luxury is setting a good table—which is also his chief torture: as a diabetic with a sweet tooth, he's in constant battle—which Karl Giese carefully referees—over whether he dares to have yet another piece of cake.

Even in the pre-war years, Karl Giese and his circle of friends frequently patronized the lively Berlin cabaret scene. When the Weimar Republic comes into being there's a far more encompassing effort, some of it highly self-conscious, at casting off traditional culture and replacing it with new forms of expression—the Cubist and Surrealist movements; the atonal music of Arnold Schoenberg; the widespread popularity of African American jazz (and the stereotype of African Americans as "primitives"—one popular traveling carnival exhibits them in cages, like animals in the zoo); the preference for cocaine over liquor, the occult over the rational, short hair over long; the Bauhaus crusade to join "fine" art with utilitarian function; the vast expansion of radio programming; Brecht's "agit-prop" theater; the surge in anti-war literature, epitomized by Erich Maria Remarque's novel *All Quiet on the Western Front*; and the daring eroticism of dancehall revues and supper club entertainments.

Paralleling these liberatory developments, politics remains unstable, and the ruinous economy—at least until the runaway inflation is brought under some control after 1923—inflicts widespread misery on large segments of the population. Throughout the dozen years of the Republic, no political consensus is achieved—not even an underlying agreement that democracy is the preferred form of government. In the years 1919–1923 especially, authoritarian right-wing militias battle radical left-wing sympathizers in what literally becomes hand-to-hand combat, with assassinations and executions hallmarks of the era.

Before the war, the socialist vision, in all its varied manifestations, had widespread appeal in Germany; in the postwar period, the socialist call for the transformation of capitalism in the name of the well-being of all is consigned—even by the relatively strong Social Democratic Party—to some distant future. The major parties on the Right, meanwhile, assert the primacy of business interests, deplore concessions to workers, and warn against the dangers of "cosmopolitan"—*i.e.*, Jewish—elements.

The postwar German economy is even more precarious and volatile than its politics. High rates of unemployment and low rates of industrial production—in combination with runaway inflation through 1923—reduce living standards drastically; those lucky enough to find employment also find wages paid irregularly and the value of currency wildly unpredictable; infant mortality and disease rates rise significantly; bread lines multiply; city dwellers raid outlying farms to steal enough food to make it through the week. The German middle-class sinks to a level of "proletarianization" that succeeds—where socialism had failed—in producing a general leveling of living conditions. Only in 1924, when the German People's Party (which Rathenau and Kessler had joined at its inception) forms a coalition government, with Kessler's old friend Gustav Stresemann as Chancellor, does the tide finally begin to turn.

Karl Giese and his friends are well enough off, comparatively, to take advantage of the many new venues available in postwar Berlin that cater to same-sex sociability and entertainment—including drag bars, taverns known as hustler hangouts, supper clubs, and even costume balls. Some of the clubs are fly-by-night affairs that last only a few months, but others—thanks in part to a near-invasion of non-German homosexual tourists—become widely-known landmarks (one, the Mikado, open as far back as 1907, will last until the Nazis close it in 1933). The favorite hangout of the young English writer Christopher Isherwood is the Cosy Corner, with its abundance of prostitutes, mostly between the ages of 16 and 21; his friend W.H. Auden also frequents the place, though he's fond too of the Kleist Diele, as well as the numerous outdoor cruising spots. American patrons abound—including the painter Marsden Hartley and the architect Philip Johnson, who becomes fluent in German ("I learned it the best way, 'using the horizontal method.'")

The upscale Café Dorian Gray on Kleiststrasse is one of Karl Giese's preferred haunts. Certain evenings are reserved for women, others for men; there are also "theme" nights (including a festival of the Rhenish grape harvest), and dancing as well as stage shows. The performer whom Giese and his friends favor above all others is Claire Waldoff. She's risen to fame singing in Rudolf Nelson's Chat Noir, located on the corner of Friedrichstrasse and Unter den Linden. The club seats about 220 and caters to a wealthy clientele. The dominant style at Chat Noir is "urban glamour"—ragtime, the cakewalk, the fox trot—and the dominant theme is sex as the great social leveler. Before the war, censorship laws—rescinded with the advent of the Weimar Republic—had existed (though they were enforced irregularly when the patrons were of "a better class of people").

Claire Waldoff's enormous charisma doesn't derive from the standard cabaret model of the fetching soubrette. Round-faced, short, and stocky, the daughter of a miner, she comes from the Ruhr industrial basin and makes no effort to conceal it. If strikingly different from the stylish chanteuse then in vogue, Waldoff's emphasis on sexuality in her songs does mirror the current Weimar mode. But she avoids the typical focus on upper-class amorous peccadilloes, avoids flirtatious gestures, and eschews the fey double entendre. She stands stock still, her face deadpan, her powerful, guttural voice lustily recounting the tales of working-class sexual experience. And—especially endearing to Karl Giese and his friends—Waldoff never denies that in her private life she's lesbian.

After several unsuccessful tries—whenever invited, Hirschfeld claims to have urgent work that "*must* be completed tonight"—Giese finally persuades him to hear Waldoff perform. He's immediately enchanted—smitten, really. Her frank eroticism, her celebration of urban life and its sexual possibilities, seems to him the embodiment of the modern spirit. Even more, Waldoff helps him to see that the new media—be it cabaret, the huge Luna Park amusement site, or cinema—can be utilized to spread a liberatory message about alternate lifestyles and sexualities.

Her example helps Hirschfeld decide to go forward with a film project that's recently come his way. Richard Oswald, owner of a theater bearing his name, has approached Hirschfeld with an offer to produce a film about homosexuality. That such an offer can be made at all is illustrative of the new climate of openness and freedom of expression—

not that the old order of bourgeois morality and autocratic privilege abandons the field. Despite the disappearance of a multitude of ancient dynasties, the privileged elites of Wilhelmine Germany mostly retain their dominance. The army, the government bureaucracy, industry, the universities, and the legal profession all continue to be essentially controlled by those who were in power before the war. These entrenched elements harbor bitter resentment against a Social Democratic government that "bowed" to the humiliating terms of the Versailles Treaty— and are equally opposed to the new "frivolity" that threatens to unseat *Bildung*—high culture.

Nonetheless, a wave of spirited experimentation is decidedly in the air. Despite mounting hyperinflation that eats through savings and destroys livelihoods; despite the drastic plight of millions of widows, orphans, and war wounded; despite a still-powerful reactionary army and press; despite a continuing rash of political murders and armed bands of right-wing terrorists—despite all this, the revolutionary spirit that marked the workers' and soldiers' councils of 1918–19 evolves, during the years of Weimar, into an explosion of creativity in the arts. Germany remains torn by conflict, but is ripped open as well by a host of exploratory cultural developments.

Film is in the forefront of innovation, and Hirschfeld is aware of its potential to reach a far wider audience than the publications of the Institute ever can. He decides to place Oswald's offer to make a film about homosexuality before the Scientific Humanitarian Committee, and is pleased when the majority votes to sanction the project. Once given the green light, Oswald moves ahead with such speed that the film—*Anders als die Andern* ("*Different from the Others*") opens in the summer of 1919, at a time when the ink is barely dry on the Treaty of Versailles and when Harry Kessler's radical young friend, Wieland Herzfelde, is sadly concluding that the once-promising socialist revolution has come to a dead end.

Different from the Others—which survives today in truncated form— is arguably the first gay-themed film aimed at release to the general public. (During the 1920s Germany will be in the forefront of turning out films with gay and lesbian characters; *Different from the Others* is followed in 1924 by Carl Theodor Dreyer's *Michael* and in 1928 by what is probably the best of the three, William Dieterle's luridly titled but moving *Sex in Chains*.) *Different from the Others* tells the story of Paul Körner, a famous violinist—played as a younger man by Karl Giese, and as an established concert star by the gifted Conrad Veidt (who the following year will star in *The Cabinet of Dr. Caligari* and, later, in *Casablanca*). The cast also includes Anita Berber, famed for her nude dancing (though in *Different from the Others* she stays clothed).

In the film, Körner becomes romantically involved with an adult student of his, and the pair, arms entwined, is seen walking in the park by a melodramatically stereotypic "villain," a kind of professional hustlerblackmailer. He threatens Körner with exposure and (under the terms of the still-intact Paragraph 175) a possible five-year jail sentence—which initially persuades Körner to hand over hush money. He then goes to a hypnotist in an effort to "cure" his homosexuality, and, when that fails, seeks counsel from a "leading sexologist"—none other than Magnus Hirschfeld, of course (he also co-authored the script). Hirschfeld, impressively calm and seemingly relaxed in the film—tries to comfort Körner with well-worn aphorisms: "Nature is boundless in its creations ... Homosexuality is neither a crime nor a vice"—but is unable to wean Körner from self-hatred.

Yet he does summon up enough courage to resist further demands from the blackmailer. A double trial follows, each man accusing the other. The sympathetic judge sentences the blackmailer to three years in prison and Körner—whom the judge characterizes as "an honorable individual who has hurt no one"—to a token one week in jail, made necessary because Paragraph 175 is still the law of the land. But the public disgrace turns Körner into a social outcast. His concert tour is canceled, his agent departs, and his disgusted father suggests suicide as the only way out. Körner dutifully obliges. The film closes with Körner's distraught student-love collapsing in sobs on his mentor's deathbed and threatening suicide himself. Hirschfeld successfully talks him out of it, persuading the young man to devote himself instead to changing the law that has produced so much suffering and misery.

Different from the Others is shown throughout Germany—much less so in the Catholic Southwest—sometimes to sold-out houses, sometimes to instant closure by the local authorities. Enthusiastic applause and reviews greet some screenings, catcalls, walkouts, and even riots attend others. Those who for years have signed the SHC's petition to the Reichstag to void Paragraph 175 tend to praise the film, even if some discerning signatories privately groan a bit over its melodramatic, heavy-handed polemics. The right-wing press and its sympathizers predictably denounce *Different from the Others* as dangerous propaganda that will persuade impressionable youth to turn homosexual. In response to the negative criticism and closures, Hirschfeld and others connected to the SHC arrange a special invitational screening for members of the government and the civil service; most of them, purportedly, finds nothing objectionable in the film—either that, or they're too polite to say so in Hirschfeld's presence (which, if true, would itself mark an advance).

No such discretion stays the hand of street thugs. As Hirschfeld begins to lecture in various German cities as an accompaniment to the film, and as the right-wing press continues to denounce it as "a feast for degenerates," his personal safety becomes an issue. As both a Jew and a homosexual, Hirschfeld embodies the dual abomination on which right-wing revulsion converges and thrives.

That revulsion is ferociously displayed in March 1920 with the outbreak of what becomes known as the "Kapp Affair." Its origins go back to an order from the central government to demobilize some remaining 60,000 soldiers, many of them unreconciled to a republic and deeply embittered at their displaced status. The soldiers reject the government order to muster out and instead occupy a district of Berlin, declare their "putsch" a success, and appoint one of their own, Wolfgang Kapp, a sometime Prussian government official, as the new "Chancellor" of Germany.

The army chief of staff, General Hans von Seeckt, announces that "troops do not fire on troops" and refuses to take action against the Kapp forces; for his statesmanlike "neutrality," the anti-republican von Seeckt is soon rewarded with command of the army. General Walther von Lüttwitz, commander of all regular troops in and around Berlin, opts for a different course: he goes over to the defectors, along with the troops under his command. Harry Kessler—like most of those on the Left—denounce Lüttwitz's action as "traitorous," though Kessler considers the entire episode more farce than drama. That it will end as farce isn't immediately apparent. The central government's initial reaction to the rebellion is feeble and hesitant, and word quickly spreads that none other than General von Ludendorff—a mere two years earlier *the* most powerful figure in Germany—has sided with the Kapp forces. Kessler, who once admired Ludendorff, now views him as a "political imbecile."

The Kapp Putsch marks Rathenau's re-emergence as a political figure. Shrugging off his usual equivocations, he sides unambiguously with the republican government and offers his services as a possible mediator. The gesture wins him considerable respect, and will shortly lead to his appointment as adviser to the German delegation when it meets in July 1920 at the Belgian city of Spa to discuss the reparations question with representatives of the Allies. In an immediate sense Rathenau's offer to mediate becomes instantly obsolete: Having seized power, the Kapp forces manage to hold on to it for exactly four days. By the time right-wing elements in Munich mobilize their forces in support of the Kapp uprising, it's already disintegrated. Most of the civil service stays loyal to the Ebert government; Berlin's working class, bitterly hostile to the military, goes out on an effective general strike; and the Kapp forces dissolve into the night—some of them pursued and murdered.

Yet the struggle between right-wingers and radical leftists continues to produce insurgency and bloodshed in other parts of the country— in Munich especially, where seesaw battles between the "Schwabing Soviet" and the anti-Semitic nationalists of the Thule Society and the Schutz-und-Trutzbund rage throughout the 1919–1920 period. Bavarians have long resented the dominance of the Prussian central government in Berlin, and two of Munich's best-known haters, Dietrich Eckart and Julius Lehmann, both publishers, predict in their racist newspapers that the appearance of a "German savior" is bound to come, and soon. That same messianic anticipation characterizes Munich's beerhall orators—one of whom is the ex-corporal Adolf

Hitler, mustered out of the army a month before the attempted Kapp Putsch in 1920.

During the brief period when Kapp is in power, his forces marching toward Berlin and rabid with their expected triumph, Magnus Hirschfeld is scheduled to lecture in Hamburg on *Different from the Others*. Just before the event, his sponsors learn that the reactionary Schutz-und-Trutzbund is planning to disrupt it. The Bund's declaration of principles blames "the oppressive and corrosive influence of Judaism" for the moral collapse of the German people, and insists that the "removal" of Judaism is the precondition for "the rescue of German culture."

Even so, Hirschfeld refuses to cancel his appearance. He does accept police protection—and it's needed: Throughout his talk, Bund members shout ugly remarks—and even, at one point, set off firecrackers—constantly disrupting Hirschfeld's presentation. Most of the audience take his side and do their best to quell the hecklers. Hirschfeld himself later admits to having felt terrorized, but throughout the ordeal he gives no sign of it, calmly standing his ground.

The going gets even tougher in Munich. Hirschfeld arrives in the city soon after the Kapp Putsch has failed, but with local reactionary elements still largely in control. Despite warnings about threats to his safety—some Kapp supporters have openly declared that after seizing power they intend to "terminate Dr. Hirschfeld" for having "introduced Oriental mores into Germany"—Hirschfeld again refuses to cancel his talk. There are noisy interruptions throughout his lecture, but he does manage to finish it. Yet in the immediate aftermath, he has reason to feel alarm. In advance of his talk he'd asked for police protection—yet no officers had shown up. The event's organizers had assured him that following the speech a car would be at his service—but no car appears.

Knowing he's at risk—serious risk—Hirschfeld quickly leaves the building after his lecture, accompanied by two acquaintances. No sooner does he step away from the entrance than a barrage of rocks rain down on his head, knocking him to the ground unconscious. He groggily awakes in a surgical ward, bleeding badly from his head and back; he's told he has a concussion.

Hirschfeld later learns that a number of German newspapers report his death the next day, as well as the *New York Times*, which announces that "Dr. Magnus Hirschfeld, the well-known expert on sexual science, died in Munich today of injuries inflicted upon him by an anti-Jewish mob." Adolf Hitler, leader of the fledgling Nazi Party, deplores at a Munich beer hall that a "Jewish swine" like Hirschfeld had ever been allowed the freedom to spread his vile propaganda. The ferocity of the hatred against him is epitomized in a letter that arrives from a young nationalist expressing regret that the attempted assassination had failed—but promising to do better next time.

One newspaper editorial all but urges another attempt: "The well-known Dr. Magnus Hirschfeld had been hurt enough to be put on the death list. We hear now that he is in fact recovering from his wounds. We have no hesitation in saying that we regret that this shameless and horrible poisoner of our people has not found his well-deserved end." In its own newspaper, the germinal Nazi Party snickers that "it is not without charm to know that ... Hirschfeld was so beaten that his eloquent mouth could never again be kissed by one of his disciples." Hirschfeld later recalls that, as the rocks came raining down on him, one of his assailants shouted from the rooftop, "Hirschfeld brought Eulenburgish-ness to Germany!" The attack is on Hirschfeld the homosexual as well as Hirschfeld the Semite.

Friends console him—and urge him to stay out of the public eye for a time. He reluctantly agrees, and, while tending his wounds, devotes himself exclusively to the Institute and to his writing. When he finally does return to the lecture circuit he's initially encouraged by large, enthusiastic audiences in Vienna and Prague—only to have his equilibrium again shattered on a second trip to Vienna when right-wing thugs succeed in disrupting his talk. This time he rejects advice to "lie low" and insists on fulfilling all of his additional lecture engagements. He does so without further incident.

～

Kurt Tucholsky, a Jew and an intellectual, served without enthusiasm in the army during the war; instead of heightening his "patriotism," it sharpened his iconoclasm. In the postwar period, he starts to write for various journals, including *Die Freiheit* (the organ of the Independent Social Democrats) and, most frequently, *Die Weltbühne*, the most influential left-wing publication of the Weimar years, alongside such contributors as Erich Mühsam, Kurt Hiller, and Magnus Hirschfeld. Tucholsky's witty, trenchant articles call for "a nationwide epidemic of candor," a clean sweep "with an iron broom of all that is rotten in Germany." People begin to talk of him as "the new Max Harden," as a reincarnation of the older man's lively satiric voice and luminous intelligence. Tucholsky's attacks are aimed at the entrenched conservatism within the military, judiciary, and civil service branches of government, and at the orthodoxy that encourages the timidity of Weimar's leaders and prevents the republic from what it should be doing—making a clean break with the authoritarian past.

Unlike Harden, Tucholsky is a gentle, essentially kind soul; he has a humane sympathy for individual weaknesses, and is well aware of his own. But as regards institutional failings, Tucholsky is just as unsparing as Harden, and the reactionary judicial system arouses his special ire. In his view you can deduce the character of a country from its legal proceedings, and Tucholsky spends a great deal of time in court listening to trial testimony. During the years 1919–1922, when political murder is epidemic in Germany, he's horrified—though not really surprised—at the discriminatory distinctions that characterize the sentencing process. In the course of three years he sits in on 326 murder cases in which the perpetrator openly identifies with the political right wing; only one is convicted. In contrast, the 22 trials he attends of left-wing perpetrators yield no less than 17 convictions—and 10 executions.

One case above all others fires up Tucholsky's anger: the trial that results from a vicious assault in 1922 on Max Harden. From being initially a staunch supporter of the war and of German expansion, Harden has become by its end a disillusioned pacifist and socialist. He welcomes the harsh terms of the Versailles Treaty and advocates Germany's unilateral disarmament. For this "treachery" a group of right-wing young men attack him in broad daylight and nearly beat him to death with an iron pipe. One assailant, a nationalist clerk, is captured immediately, while another, a former army officer, escapes to Austria but is extradited. In the trial that follows, evidence emerges that the powerful right-wing "Organization Consul" is behind the attack, providing the money and introducing the miscreants to each other.

Severely injured, Harden is hospitalized and feared near death. Yet he rallies, and after the first week is allowed a few visitors. Harry Kessler had had lunch with Harden—now 60—only the week before and had found his conversation "witty, knowledgeable, sensible, and not in the least extreme." When he enters Harden's room at the hospital, he's surprised to find Kurt Tucholsky sitting at the bedside. The two have earlier met through their mutual friend, George Grosz, and think well of each other. Harden's head is wrapped in bandages and he can only speak in a whisper, but he tells his visitors that he's actually feeling quite lively and encourages them to stay a while and to "feel free to talk politics—it will help me recover faster." They take him at his word, but keep their voices subdued. Tucholsky tells Kessler what an outrage the trial has been so far:

"The judge treats the accused with astonishing respect—as if they're honored guests at a tea party. He makes it appear as if Harden is on trial."

"In the judge's mind he probably is," Kessler replies. Harden shakes his head in vigorous assent.

"It's a comedy, really," Tucholsky says—"though nothing to smile about. The defense is trying to prove that his clients are patriots—incited to act because of Harden's 'Bolshevik' writings."

With effort, Harden raises his head off the pillow. "He constantly refers," he hoarsely whispers, "to my Jewish origins ... playing to ... jury's anti-Semitism." Out of breath, Harden lets his head sink back down. "Once a Jew, always a Jew," he mutters.

"Try not to talk too much," Tucholsky coaxes. "No point letting a bunch of bigots upset you."

Tucholsky turns to Kessler. "Justice and fair play are apparently old-fashioned concepts."

"Since they're quoting from Max's writings, why not quote from the constant incitements in the right-wing press to attack 'Bolshevik Jews'? I read a piece just yesterday about Rathenau," Kessler indignantly adds, "insisting he should never have been allowed to publish his books in the first place! It's astonishing—we live in a republic!"

Harden, with difficulty, again raises his head. "Your friend Rathenau said I converted from Judaism for money . . . Said 'any spiritual measure like mine that leads to material advantages loses its purity'! . . . Or some such rot . . . Never liked the man!"

Weakened by the effort, Harden begins to cough; his face contorts with pain. It's a mistake, Kessler and Tucholsky realize, even to touch on politics. They ring for the nurse, smooth out Harden's bedding, and softly reassure him that he'll soon be his old self. After the nurse gives him a shot ("morphine," she whispers), they leave—though both return often during the weeks of recovery that lay ahead.

Throughout his comparative isolation during the past few years, Rathenau has remained a controversial figure. Though largely in retreat, he's deftly kept open his channels of communication with many of the prominent figures in German life, and has periodically published a number of provocative articles on questions of the day. His many admirers continue to find his writings penetrating and profound, while others have long since grown impatient with his enigmatic, sonorous style—and his sometimes contradictory pronouncements. In one article Rathenau states boldly that "it is peace we want, not war"—then manages to cast doubt on where he stands by adding that he doesn't mean "a peace of surrender." Similarly, he tells Kessler that he views Bolshevism as the wave of the future, yet then confides to a French journalist that the Russian Revolution is "the greatest danger of the day." That isn't an outright contradiction, since Rathenau's been clear that he doesn't believe Germany is yet ready for Bolshevism. But was autocratic Russia and its piously superstitious peasantry "ready"? What specific preconditions need to be filled before Germany can legitimately qualify? Has the short-lived Bavarian Soviet Republic somehow lived up to the mark, or is Rathenau giving way to the enthusiasm of the moment when he publicly expresses his approval of the Bavarian experiment? To some, he seems a creature of impulse, of ideological whimsy, toying with contrasting ideas rather than scrutinizing them.

Rathenau seems far more clear-headed and decisive when he comes down from the speculative clouds and deals with a concrete situation at hand. Thus he plays a substantial and crucial role in helping to put together a collaborative agreement late in 1918 between employers and trade unions—the Central Working Community—that succeeds in establishing collective bargaining and the eight-hour day, and without any cut in workers' wages. Similarly, during the attempted rightwing putsch, when Kapp declares that it's his "manifest duty" to defend the country against an imminent left-wing takeover, Rathenau, in a masterly matter-of-fact way, counters that a fair part of the area west of the Elbe—East Prussia, Pomerania, and Silesia—is on the side of the conservative army, not the levelers of socialism.

Unexpectedly, Rathenau is about to have more actual political power than—as a Jew and as a controversial polemicist—he ever imagined possible. It begins with a casual friendship that springs up between himself and Joseph Wirth, the new Minister of Finance, a man much younger than himself but who shares with him what Harry Kessler calls "moral earnestness"—and, as an unattached bachelor, shares as well a profound sense of loneliness. When the Allies in the spring of 1920 invite the German government to send delegates to the Belgian city of Spa for a discussion of questions arising from the terms of the Versailles Treaty, Wirth suggests adding Rathenau to the delegation.

Two of its most prominent members, General von Seeckt and Hugo Stinnes, strenuously resist the suggestion. Seeckt, never more than a reluctant supporter of the republic and devoted above all to guarding the prestige and privileges of the army, despises Rathenau as a Jew and as a "dangerous radical." Stinnes, a coal magnate of immense wealth and blunt, opaque arrogance, shares Seeckt's contempt for the Weimar government and feels free to announce publicly that he favors another war to "bring us out of our situation," predicting a German romp to victory over France. But Wirth is determined; he faces down the two right-wingers' objections and appoints Rathenau to the delegation.

Though both patriots, Stinnes and Rathenau are very nearly ideological opposites. Harry Kessler memorably captures their opposing styles and points of view: "On the one hand, Rathenau, the polished gentleman, who speaks as if from a pedestal, in wonderfully complicated periods and a highly ornamental style; and on the other, Stinnes, clad like a common workman and averse to fine phrases, who conceals visionary plans behind a thick veil of 'hard facts,' an impenetrable mask of misleading common sense."

Stinnes's opening words at the Spa gathering provide fair warning of what is to come: "I rise in order to be able to look the hostile delegates [the Allies] straight in the eyes," Stinnes begins—and ends by calling them "our insane conquerors." Though Rathenau also regards the Versailles Treaty as grotesquely unjust, he recognizes that a defeated Germany has to accommodate itself to its terms and discharge its obligations—what he calls the "Policy of Fulfillment"; his underlying assumption is that an honest attempt to meet Allied demands will demonstrate the impossibility of doing so. In Rathenau's view, Spa at the least represents the onset of negotiations, and once negotiations are begun anything becomes possible.

He specifically advocates—over Stinnes's fierce objection—that Germany pledge to deliver two million tons of coal monthly for a period of six months, after which a new conference could reconsider the entire question of reparations. Going still further, Rathenau hints, prophetically, at the future prospect of a European economic consortium in which cooperation will replace gratuitously wasteful competition.

Rathenau's performance at Spa is masterful throughout—so much so that, to the astonishment of the gathering, General von Seeckt, along with a majority of the German delegates, not only adopts Rathenau's coal formula but by implication his underlying Policy of Fulfillment. Stinnes, on the other hand, is furious in defeat; it's at Spa that he coins the phrase about Rathenau "having the soul of an alien race." Joseph Wirth, for his part, feels obligated and grateful to Rathenau for replacing the image of an unrepentant, still-aggressive Germany in the minds of the Allied nations with the image of a gracious Germany accepting responsibility for its role in precipitating war. To right-wing Germans, Rathenau's readiness to cooperate with the Allies is viewed as tantamount to treason.

The period immediately following the Spa conference hardly proves clear sailing. Premier Raymond Poincaré of France is less interested in a Policy of Fulfillment than in securing French influence in the Rhineland. Animosity towards Germany remains intense among France's conservative parties, and, by the early months of 1921, the Allies are again accusing Germany of breaching the Versailles Treaty; this time they impose sanctions that include the occupation of three German cities. Rathenau continues to urge the German government to make every effort to meet the harsh demands of reparations—hoping that such a demonstration will lead the Allies to better understand Germany's stark economic realities, and to renegotiate a settlement.

By then, Wirth has been elevated to the Chancellorship and, more impressed than ever with Rathenau, invites him to join the government as Minister of Reconstruction. Rathenau hesitates, knowing that any expansion of his visible power will come in tandem with an increase in vulnerability—will put him in real, not theoretical, danger. Yet he decides to accept Wirth's offer, resigns as president of AEG (and from his other directorships as well), and for the first time in his life becomes an official part of the ruling elite. He claims that the decision to enter the government is the most difficult he's ever made; he undoubtedly thinks so, and with reason; yet it's also the first time his subterranean hunger to *belong* is poised to become a reality. Rathenau is well aware that as a Jew, an outsider, his tenure could end abruptly.

There is no honeymoon period. Crisis continues to follow crisis—the size of the yearly reparations payments; the ongoing French threat to occupy the Ruhr; the rapidly rising inflation in Germany; the fluctuating diplomatic jockeying. Rathenau becomes more and more deeply involved as Wirth's unofficial envoy, going back and forth to London and Paris to attempt negotiations for modifying the reparations schedule.

He wins enormous respect, along with some concessions, from the Allied powers, and from Wirth enormous gratitude for his patient, skillful diplomacy.

As an inevitable byproduct of Rathenau's rising prominence and influence, personal attacks on him mount in the Reichstag, especially from the far-right German National People's Party. Anti-Semitic and nationalistic antagonism to him grows so great that, by 1922, when Chancellor Wirth makes the momentous decision to appoint him Minister of Foreign Affairs, he does so secretly at night. Albert Einstein, who's casually known and admired Rathenau for years, strongly advises him not to accept the new post; no Jew has ever held that high a position in the German government, and Einstein fears it will further fan the flames of anti-Semitism. Rathenau respectfully thanks him for the advice, but tells Einstein that he feels it's his duty to accept the post. When the appointment is announced, it immediately brings down an avalanche of denunciation from the Right—just as Einstein predicted.

When Harry Kessler visits his friend at the Foreign Affairs Office two months after his appointment, he finds Rathenau in a stew of exhaustion and resentment. He complains bitterly to Kessler about the unceasing demands on him, and the relentless calumnies against him. Knowing how hard Rathenau has always been on himself, and how relentlessly he insists on fulfilling obligations to the letter, Kessler is deeply sympathetic with his current situation. Aside from the insuperable tasks *anyone* holding the office of Minister of Foreign Affairs would face, Rathenau has to suffer the daily—literally, daily—affronts and abuse heaped on him by the Stinneses of the world, the threatening letters that arrive at his home and office, the police reports on right-wing terrorist groups plotting against his life.

Kessler thinks Rathenau has noticeably aged in the few months since their last meeting, and begs him to take the threats against his life seriously and to accept police protection. In response, Rathenau draws a Browning revolver from his desk and says, "I do take them seriously, as you can see. But police protection? No. It would be a public admission of weakness." At one point the police, acting without a request from

Rathenau for protection, station two men in civilian clothes outside his house in Grunewald. When an invited friend arrives for dinner, the plainclothesmen stop and question him. The friend produces identification papers and is allowed to pass. On entering the house, he tells Rathenau how pleased he is to see that he's finally accepted police protection. Furious, Rathenau hurries to the phone and categorically demands that the two guards be removed at once—he refuses to have his guests "molested."

A few weeks later, Kessler accepts Rathenau's invitation to meet Chancellor Wirth at dinner. The evening does nothing to diminish Kessler's concern. He's never met Wirth before and finds him alarmingly unimpressive—"moody, over-familiar, a drinker." And he's astonished at Rathenau's anomalous behavior towards Wirth; ordinarily aloof and impersonal, Rathenau acts like a mother hen with the Chancellor, cautioning him against having more to drink, praising his self-serving comments. Kessler has the fleeting thought that the two men might be lovers but—finding neither man physically appetizing—dismisses the possibility. He decides instead that the bond between them centers on their shared, half-embarrassed patriotism—and their wholly embarrassed, suppressed sexuality. His verdict on Wirth produces yet another of Kessler's occasional spasms of aristocratic disdain: he characterizes Wirth as "vulgar, impossible—a doorman as Chancellor." Within a short time, Kessler will radically revise his estimate.

Political assassination has become a routine event in Weimar Germany. As Tucholsky has noted, and carefully tracks, right-wing groups between 1918 and 1922 have murdered more than 300 people on the Left. After assuming office as Foreign Minister, Rathenau has been denounced almost daily in newspaper articles, Reichstag speeches, and public meetings; he's accused, as a result of his insistence on Germany attempting to fulfill its obligations under the Versailles Treaty, of having personally brought on a monumental inflation and ruining the middle class; of acquiescing in the spread of French influence in the Rhineland—and even of being in the pay of the French government. He is not, his antagonists endlessly repeat, a true German (translation: he's a Jew). Of Rathenau's many right-wing enemies, one stands out: Karl Helfferich, a banker and leading member of the right-wing National People's Party whom, ironically, Rathenau's parents had helped when he was a young man.

Hans Stubenrauch is a 17-year-old schoolboy, the son of a general, and already a member of the League of the Upright, a semi-secret right-wing organization. Precociously well-read, and vain about it, Stubenrauch comes across a pamphlet Rathenau wrote during the war, *The Kaiser*, that contains the line, "That day will never come on which the Kaiser will ride victorious through the Brandenburger Tor. On that day history would have lost all meaning." Stubenrauch interprets the rather vague prediction as definitive proof that Rathenau had hoped for Germany's defeat—that he is a traitor.

A mutual friend puts Stubenrauch in touch with another young man, Erwin Kern, who's also convinced that Rathenau is prominent among those enemies of Germany who have "stabbed her in the back" in the postwar period. Kern, 25 and an ex-naval officer, has the blue-eyed, blond-haired look of an Aryan archangel, as does his close friend Hermann Fischer; they personify the Aryan German that Rathenau idealizes—and hates himself for doing so.

Both young men are members of the notorious Organization Consul, a terrorist group that emerged in the aftermath of the failed Kapp Putsch, dedicated to destroying Germany's "enemies"—a dedication that includes the near-fatal beating of Max Harden. In October 1920 the group inaugurates a campaign of murder by strangling a young female servant for having reported to the Allied Disarmament Commission that her employer is, contrary to the terms of the Versailles Treaty, storing illegal arms. The assailants leave a sign on her body: "You lousy bitch; you have betrayed your Fatherland."

Erwin Kern gets in touch with the Berlin agent of the Organization Consul, 21-year-old Ernst Werner Techow, and enlists him in the developing plot—even though Kern finds Techow "decadent" and "rather effeminate." Still, Kern decides, he's someone who will follow orders and ask no questions. The handsome, charismatic Kern has emerged as the uncontested leader of the group—one of many semi-secret societies that form during these years, when the authority of a defeated older generation has been severely compromised. It's Harry Kessler's view that the friendships formed in such groups frequently reach a level of intimacy that perhaps are, or could be mistaken for, erotic attraction. The dashing Erwin Kern, in any case, becomes the undisputed lodestar of the now-completed coterie, the feared as well as sensual center of gravity; as Techow will later claim, "I *had* to do his bidding, or he would have shot me."

In mid-June 1922, the four young men start to fine-tune their plan to kill Rathenau. They know that he tends to leave his home in Grunewald for the Foreign Office in a chauffeur-driven open car at roughly the same time every morning. One of the group has a friend who owns a large six-seater that he says they can borrow. The plan is to lay in wait for Rathenau to leave his house, then to follow his car and, pulling up alongside of it, shoot him with an ordinary revolver. As a result of some target practice, doubts arise about the reliability of a revolver for their purposes and, after considerable debate, they decide on an automatic pistol instead—along with, to ensure success, a hand grenade.

On the evening of June 23, the four gather at the Ratskeller they frequent, down a large amount of beer and cognac, and, for a final time, review the reasons why—one of them has seemed a bit equivocal, even queasy—Rathenau deserves to die. The high-spirited Kern, liquor heightening his self-regard and his dreams of glory, holds forth authoritatively and without interruption on Rathenau's litany of crimes: He has expressed admiration for Bolshevism; he's a willing sell-out to the Allies; he's gotten his appointment as Foreign Minister by bribing the Chancellor; he's part of a covert Jewish conspiracy to bring Germany under Semite control.

More than liquor fuels their deliberations. That very afternoon in the Reichstag, Rathenau's longtime antagonist Karl Helfferich, a leader of the National People's Party, delivers a venomous attack on Rathenau, charging him with having ruined Germany economically and having conspired to bring the country under the permanent domination of France. Helfferich points in particular to Rathenau's response a few days previously in the Reichstag to a member's question about conditions in the Saar region of the country. Rathenau had described those conditions as "not pleasant," but had added that the population of the Saar "regard, as their most precious possession, their German nationality and culture."

"I know that God has given the diplomat the gift of speech," Helfferich tells the Reichstag, "in order to hide his thoughts. But there are moments when even a Foreign Minister should refrain from using this gift." From that suave opening, Helfferich quickly shifts to savagery: the state of affairs in the Saar, he thunders, "positively cries out to Heaven for redress"; the population in the region feels "both deserted and betrayed"—yet Rathenau has shown more regard for French "susceptibilities" than for the suffering of his own people. Summing up, Helfferich insists that Rathenau is personally responsible for having "brought poverty and misery on countless families," for having "driven countless people to suicide and despair," for having "sent abroad large and valuable portions of our national capital," and for having "shaken our industrial and social order to its very foundations!" The absurd exaggerations make one wag wonder if Helfferich is describing Rathenau—or the Roman emperor Caligula.

The following morning, June 24th, Rathenau—having been up till 4:00 a.m. arguing the reparations question with Hugo Stinnes over dinner at the American ambassador's house—leaves his Grunewald home a bit later than usual. The conspirators are waiting for him in their car at a spot where the Königsallee takes a double turn, causing vehicles to slow down. Techow is at the wheel, Kern is the designated shooter, and Fischer the assigned grenade thrower. Traffic is, as always on the Königsallee, crowded, yet several bricklayers working on a nearby building site, ordinarily indifferent to the cars whizzing by, are startled to see two young men seated in a high-powered touring car dressed in fashionable new leather coats with matching caps. The workers jeeringly dismiss them as wealthy good-for-nothings.

As Rathenau's car slowly drives into view, Kern and his cohort come up behind it, draw along the side, and then move half a length ahead. Startled at the proximity, Rathenau looks up from his seat in the back of the car. Just as he does, Kern leans forward, pulls out his long pistol and opens fire. The shots ring out in quick succession, Rathenau slumps into his seat, and Fischer jumps up and throws the grenade. As it explodes, the touring car jumps ahead and tears off down the road. Rathenau's chauffer survives, but Rathenau, hit five times, his jaw and spine smashed, succumbs soon after.

The distraught chauffeur drives the body back to Rathenau's house where servants carry him into the study. The body remains there for two days in an open coffin. Word of Rathenau's death spreads quickly. Hundreds of thousands of workers pour from the factories and begin marching through the streets, large numbers of ordinary citizens joining them; many of the marchers wear socialist red arm bands, others carry the black-red-gold banners of the republic. They move solemnly across Berlin's broad thoroughfares, their numbers mounting into a huge, disciplined processional.

Kessler learns the news shortly before noon. It stuns him, scrambles his brain; he bursts into tears. As the initial shock wears off, his first thought is that the Reichstag will surely be dissolved and Helfferich—"the real murderer," in Kessler's view—and his right-wing cohorts finally brought to account. Kessler heads out at once for the Reichstag, which he finds in a state of uproar, finally convening at 3:00 p.m. When Helfferich appears in the chamber, shouts of "Murderer! Murderer!" drive him out again. After the President of the Reichstag finally restores order, he says a few words of tribute to Rathenau and then turns the podium over to Chancellor Wirth.

Wirth rises slowly from his place on the government bench, next to the seat Rathenau had occupied—the seat now draped in crepe, with a bouquet of white roses placed on a table in front of it. Wirth solemnly makes his way to the platform. The entire chamber, including members of the right-wing parties, stand and remain standing throughout the Chancellor's speech. It's brief, mostly devoted to a grave promise that the government will take severe measures against cowardly terrorists who have for too long killed their enemies and gone unpunished. "Millions have been spent in pouring a deadly poison into the body of our people," Wirth quietly says, "and then people are surprised when mere deluded boys resort to murder." Wirth then announces that he is too overcome to speak at length, but will do so the following day at noon.

On the morning of June 25, the trade unions declare a 24-hour work stoppage in honor of Rathenau, and massive demonstrations wind their way through the streets of every city in Germany. Harry Kessler believes that "never before has a German citizen been so honored." He reads the general reaction as one of profound anger over the assassination and tells himself that the crowds show a sturdier dedication to the republic than ever existed towards the monarchy. At noon Kessler enters the Reichstag at Wirth's side and stands at the back of the government bench to hear the Chancellor's extemporaneous tribute to his Foreign Minister.

Wirth begins by denouncing the campaign of murder that has menaced the republic since its founding and then launches into a sharp indictment of the right-wing nationalist parties. Pointing to their nearly empty benches, he denounces Helfferich by name for the poison he's been pouring into the hearts and brains of Germany's youth, leading them to form dozens of secret nationalist, anti-Semitic, and monarchist societies. Then, dramatically gesturing towards the right-wing section of the Reichstag, Wirth declares that "we know where to seek the true enemies of our country—*The Enemy stands on the Right!*" The response is thunderous, with three-fifths of the packed assembly rising to their feet and staring directly at the right-wing benches. Writing in his diary that evening, Kessler gives Wirth his highest compliment: "I judged this man wrongly. He is someone, after all."

The Right fully deserves Wirth's opprobrium, yet there are those on the Left—understandably silent now in the face of Rathenau's murder— who through the years have also distrusted and even denounced him. Rathenau's own political statements (to say nothing of the enigmatic mask he chose to wear) can be held partly responsible for the puzzled suspicion in which many on the Left held him. Rathenau embodied contradiction: He could praise socialism in theory, yet deplore talk of socializing industry; he could attack the Prussian nobility, yet speak admiringly of its austere sense of duty; he could condemn German militarism, yet attempt to reignite a lost war by calling for a *levée en masse* which would have led to countless additional deaths; he could champion economic restructuring to end mechanical labor and free the "souls" of the working class, yet—having rejected socialization of the economy—offer no detailed, persuasive alternative for bringing about a greater egalitarianism. Rathenau once wrote that he was "the loneliest man I know," yet he never suggested—perhaps even to himself—that his isolation resulted not from his political views alone, but also from his entrenched fear of intimacy and the solace that might have come from embracing a tabooed sensuality.

That same afternoon of the 25th, Kessler goes out to Rathenau's home in Grunewald to take his farewell leave. His friend still lies in an open coffin in his study, a place where Rathenau and he had often talked about the issues of the day. Nearly alone in the room, Kessler leans over the coffin to look for a last time at Rathenau's ravaged, smashed face, emanating "immeasurable tragedy." "Like most great Jews," Kessler later writes in his diary, Rathenau had "something Messianic about him . . . a Moses who caught sight of the Promised Land but was not allowed to enter it . . . As a statesman, the legacy which he bequeaths is not a completed achievement but a pointer into the future, a hope whose realization depends on others."

Rathenau's funeral follows two days later in the Chamber of the Reichstag. The packed galleries are draped in crepe, and the lower floor, where his coffin rests under a large black canopy behind the speaker's rostrum, is filled with flowers, palm trees, and wreaths encircled with the republic's black-red-gold colors. Every seat in the Chamber is occupied, including those of the right-wing parties. Out of sight of the Chamber, an orchestra plays Beethoven's *Egmont* overture, followed by the Funeral March from *Götterdämmerung*. President Ebert speaks a few words over the coffin; they're partly inaudible, but when he says "this atrocious crime has struck not only at Rathenau the man but at the whole German people," the words ring out clearly. With many in the Chamber weeping, the coffin is then carried to the entryway, where it's greeted by a company of Reichswehr soldiers in their gray uniforms and steel helmets. The cortège sets off slowly in the rain, the coffin covered with a blanket of red roses, drum rolls resonating in the background.

Albert Einstein publishes his reaction to Rathenau's murder in the *Neue Rundschau*:

That hatred, delusion, and ingratitude could go so far—I still would not have thought it. But to those responsible for the ethical education of the German people for the last fifty years, I would want to call out: By their fruits you shall know them.

Weeks later, the assassins Kern and Fischer, while hiding out, die in a hail of police bullets. Eleven years after their deaths, in 1933, Heinrich Himmler, head of the Nazi SS, and Ernst Röhm, head of the SA, lead a large procession to the site of the Kern-Fischer graves. Himmler places floral wreaths and Ernst Röhm speaks in praise of the "martyrs":

"Your spirit, Kern and Fischer, is the spirit of the SS, Hitler's black soldiers."

PART VI

~

THE NEW ORDER

IN THE MONTHS FOLLOWING Rathenau's murder the instability of the German government, in combination with the mounting threat from organized squads of right-wing toughs, help persuade Harry Kessler to increase his involvement with the international pacifist movement. As honorary chairman of Germany's branch of the World Youth League and as a board member of the prominent German Peace Society (to which he gives a good deal of money), Kessler is widely called on to lecture, especially on the League of Nations and the issue of reparations. He believes, as had his friend Rathenau, not only in the "Policy of Fulfillment" but in Germany's moral obligation to aid in rebuilding areas in France heavily destroyed during the war.

The more often Kessler speaks publicly, the more in demand he becomes. His success is due as much to style as content; fluent in English and French, trim, elegant, impeccably dressed—his moustache discreetly waxed, his cravat flawlessly creased—able to conjure up anecdotes from his own longstanding contact with Europe's political and artistic elites, Kessler's manner on the platform is cosmopolitan, modest, subtle, and balanced—accurately reflecting the persona of an essentially decent, truth-telling man.

Though he sometimes has to deal with hecklers from both the Far Right and Left, and is several times warned that he's in personal danger, Kessler accepts speaking engagements from all over Germany, and occasionally elsewhere. Yet he hesitates when, in 1923, an invitation arrives from Munich University. In the same mail is a request for an interview following his speech from a young man named Hermann Esser, who describes himself as a freelance journalist in Munich. Kessler thinks it's "curious" that the young man doesn't identify himself as a student at the university, for how else would he know of the invitation to speak? Could the university have publicized it before he'd made up his mind about whether to accept? That seems unlikely.

Kessler's unease is heightened by ongoing events in the city. Munich over the past few years, as with Berlin, has seen a brutal, seesaw battle between the forces of the militant Left and Far Right, a battle symbolic of the political turmoil roiling all of Germany, and not yet resolved. Antipathy to the Berlin central government is more pronounced in Bavaria than elsewhere in Germany, further fed by the region's historic antipathy to Prussian domination. Violence and rioting have been wide-spread, Munich's famed beer halls resonating with enflamed oratory.

During the revolutionary upheavals of 1918 and 1919, it had been Munich, not Berlin, that for a time had seen the Left—led by Kurt Eisner, an unkempt, unprepossessing drama critic—gain triumphant control of the city. Socialists of various stripes had combined forces into a Council of Workers, Soldiers, and Peasants, and had elected Eisner its chairman. Two successive Soviet-style regimes had controlled city government, but Eisner, unlike Lenin, was a true egalitarian and lacked the Russian leader's ruthlessness in liquidating "enemies of the proletariat"—and lacked, too, his political skill in dealing with the widespread exhaustion and misery among the populace. Besides, Eisner was Jewish—not, for right-wingers, an appealing attribute; as one Munich newspaper put it, "This Jew should no longer stand at the head" of the city government.

That was a message Count Anton Arco auf Valley took to heart. Outspoken against the revolutionary Left, he'd confidently applied for admission to the paramilitary Thule Society, a semi-secret group aimed at overthrowing the left-wing Munich government; but Arco-Valley had been rejected for membership when it became known that his mother was Jewish. He thought he knew how to get the decision reversed. Stalking Eisner, he came up behind him on the street and shot him at point blank range in the head and back. Eisner died on the sidewalk, but one of his bodyguards managed to wound Arco-Valley as he fled from the scene. A leading German surgeon operated on him that same day and saved his life. The Thule Society sent a bouquet of roses to Arco-Valley's hospital room.

A new left-wing consortium, the Central Council, takes over the government and rejects rule by a Russian-style "soviet" in favor of a more centrist parliamentary system. Thousands of radical workers and soldiers threaten a general strike in the name of restoring a more militant administration, and subsequent weeks see a constantly shifting battle of manifestos, alliances, deliberations, rallies, threats, and takeovers that briefly includes the proclaiming of a soviet republic dedicated to the nonviolent overthrow of capitalism. That, in turn, is forcibly supplanted by a faction insisting *it* represents true communism—a proposition heartily endorsed by the swelling ranks of the right-wing Bavarian Freikorps dedicated to its destruction.

Authoritarian and racist, the well-trained Munich Freikorps is affiliated with the Thule Society and headed by Franz von Epp and his right-hand man, Ernst Röhm, the future head of Hitler's storm troopers. The communists are unable to mount effective resistance; the Freikorps quickly seizes control of Munich and goes on a savage killing spree. When it's over, the right-wing is in control, but below the surface Munich remains an embittered battleground.

Harry Kessler is well aware of Munich's recent history when he receives the invitation to speak at the university's Schwabing campus. Most of his friends advise against accepting. The poet Rainer Maria Rilke, who has himself recently fled Munich after learning that the Freikorps—having found some of his poetry in the apartment of a left-wing leader—is about to arrest him, warns Kessler that it would be foolhardy in the current climate for him to set foot in the city.

"But it's the Schwabing campus," Kessler protests uncertainly—"*Schwabing*, for heaven's sake—the artists' district."

"Yes," Rilke replies with a bleak twinkle. "But artists don't attend lectures on the League of Nations."

Kessler laughs, but remains unconvinced. "After all," he tells Rilke, "Munich's university has for centuries been a prestigious center of learning. Surely I can expect a respectful audience even if a portion of it disagrees with what I say."

Rilke tries another tack, reminding Kessler that, after the Bavarian government pardoned Arco-Valley, the great sociologist Max Weber was threatened by far-right students at Munich University for having protested the decision. No less a figure than Albert Einstein has recently canceled a scheduled lecture at the university following threats of an anti-Jewish demonstration. "If anything," Rilke adds, "the climate at the university is today *worse*."

Kessler hears variations of Rilke's warning from a wide assortment of friends, yet, to his own puzzlement, something inside him—he can't quite put his finger on it—resists their advice. He knows what it isn't. It isn't a sense of invulnerability. Yes, he escaped injury during the war, but he saw enough mutilated bodies to get the strong sense that he'd soon be among them if he stayed in a combat zone. Nor is it physical bravado. He's never had much of that. He prefers verbal dueling, at which he feels a gentleman's advantage. No, if he has to guess, he'd ascribe his decision to go to Munich to some kind of political itch. Yes, to politics of all things, to see with his own eyes what's going on, what this "right-wing threat" is all about—even though he can sense that, with Rathenau's death, he's already turning away from the public arena and returning to his earlier absorption in the arts.

Besides, he could take Max with him. What an excellent idea! Max *is* fearless, loves travel, and is always a lively companion. "Max" is Max Goertz, the young soldier Kessler had an idyllic affair with during the war and with whom he's unexpectedly renewed contact. They've recently been seeing a good deal of each other. They've gone to the theater a number of times, including the opening night of the Moscow Experimental Theater, and Kessler has also taken Max to see the Ballets Russes perform in Berlin, introducing him afterwards at supper to Diaghilev, Serge Lifar, and Boris Kochno.

Yes, Kessler enthusiastically decides, he'll take Max to Munich, show him Ludwig II's castle at Neuschwanstein, and perhaps the Nymphen-burg Palace where the ruling House of Wittelsbach had once idled away their summers. Or, a more leisurely idea, he thinks they might simply stroll the Marienplatz, Munich's central square since the 12th century. True, Max isn't especially drawn to architecture, or to history for that matter, but Kessler feels the exposure might awaken his interest.

And so it's decided. Kessler not only accepts the invitation to speak but also agrees to Hermann Esser's request for an interview, thinking he'll turn it into a two-way exchange that might contribute to his understanding of Munich's enflamed political scene. As for Max, he's delighted with the idea, never having been to Munich and further glam-orized by Kessler's insistence that they stay at the Vier Jahreszeiten, the city's finest hotel. With the lecture scheduled for late afternoon, with the Esser interview to follow, they arrive in Munich early enough to stroll the Marienplatz. Kessler does his best to make the bustling thorough-fare interesting to Max, recounting some of the highlights in the area's history, pointing out the varied shifts in architectural style over the centuries. Max dutifully grunts appreciation but is clearly bored. When they veer off into the narrow streets radiating from the central square, the dense congestion of cyclists and pedestrians noisily bumping into each other soon has Max pleading amiably for a break. Kessler decides a special treat is in order—sampling Munich's famed "white" sausages. Max gamely gives them a try—resulting in a hasty retreat to the hotel bathroom to cope with a case of the runs.

It's an inauspicious start. And Kessler's lecture that afternoon fails to improve matters. His announced topic, "Germany and the League of Nations," draws a disappointingly small crowd, no more than 50 people. Kessler's finely-wrought exposition of why the League should forswear the sovereign identity of nation-states in favor of self-governing eco-nomic corporations consisting of producers and consumers—a prop-osition Rathenau had raised much earlier—mostly produces yawns. It's only when he starts to talk about the necessary steps Germany must take in order to fulfill its treaty obligations and gain entry to the League, that the somnolent crowd becomes energized. When he daringly declares that "Germany bears the largest share of blame for armed hostilities breaking out in the first place," several people are immediately on their feet, shouting their displeasure. The furor catches Kessler off-guard; his famous poise briefly fractures. Turning to the friendly student who introduced him, now seated on the side of the stage, the expression on Kessler's face is a clear plea for help. The student immediately gets up and tries to quiet the ongoing ruckus, but, when the crowd ignores him, he points to one of the men in the audience who's stood up, calling him, his voice quavering, by name: "Professor Feder, do you have a question for our speaker, or a statement you wish to make?"

Those who hear the student say "Professor Feder" quickly quiet down. The sudden slackening in the noise level leads others to turn towards Feder, letting their agitated voices, without quite knowing why, subside as well. Feder, rather nondescript—a balding, portly, middle-aged man—remains standing, exuding authority as he waits for the noise to subside further, as he seems confident it will. Then he speaks, his voice solemn and detached:

"Allow me to introduce myself," he begins, staring directly at Kessler. "I am Professor Gottfried Feder of Munich University. As some members of this audience apparently know," Feder continues, his voice resonant with self-satisfaction, "I am both a professor of economic theory and a citizen active on behalf of the well-being of the German people."

By now Kessler's ingrained composure has resurfaced. "I'm pleased to make your acquaintance," he urbanely responds. "I apologize for not being familiar with your work or your political views," Kessler adds, deliberately lying, "but I'd be glad to hear which of my remarks you disagree with."

"I disagree with all of it," Feder replies, matching Kessler in suavity. "I can't be bothered to refute your absurd presentation point by point, since it's clear to me that truth is of no concern to you. I do, however, wish to note one bizarre feature of your speech: you made not a single reference to the Jews. I can only conclude that you are a Jew yourself." Feder sits down abruptly, to loud applause.

Kessler is nonplused, but his instincts quickly kick in. "As I am a

Count, my dear professor, you must be aware that I could not be Jewish. The ranks of the aristocracy have long been closed to people of the Jewish faith. Perhaps now, under the Weimar Republic, that discriminatory practice, of a piece with the barbaric hierarchy of privilege that has long dominated our society, will be permanently set aside." (Kessler has not forgotten his own casual if marginal anti-Semitism when younger, but he's not about to reference it in front of this crowd).

As an angry buzz sweeps through the auditorium, Feder again rises slowly to his feet. "You may not be a Jew, sir, but it is very clear to me that you are not a German."

"Not by your definition perhaps, which seems to center on irrational hatred." Kessler starts to move away from the podium, as if to signal that the session is at an end. But Feder has different plans.

"Have you ever heard, sir, of the National Socialist German Workers' Party—the 'NSDAP', as we call it?"

"No, I have not."

"It is rapidly becoming the largest political formation in Bavaria."

"Perhaps one day it will be important enough to reach Berlin," Kessler says with smooth condescension. "Thus far we know nothing of it."

"You Northern Germans haven't heard of much," Feder responds, as laughter erupts in the audience. "You *have* heard, I presume, of Benito Mussolini's recent March on Rome?"

"In 'Northern Germany' most of us regard Italian fascism as the first step in the counter-revolution. Mussolini rejects democracy and glorifies the autocratic rule of the Leader. It seems to me we've already had quite enough of that with Kaiser Wilhelm. Mussolini is a danger to Europe."

"He is a model for Europe," Feder replies. "What Mussolini has been able to do in Italy, we can do in Bavaria—in Germany as a whole. Yes, Mussolini is anti-democratic, and rightly so. He glorifies instead, as you correctly note, the principle of Leadership. That much you do seem to understand—which is rather surprising for a Berliner. Not to mention an *artistic* Berliner." The appreciative laughter from the audience puzzles Kessler. Is Feder implying something more than the fine arts?

"I do not make art," Kessler replies, "but yes—I do appreciate it. I hadn't realized that was a character failure."

"We gather that you especially appreciate art when packaged in a well-proportioned human form." The noise in the room grows louder. There's now no mistaking Feder's meaning, or rather double-meaning. Kessler catches sight of Max shifting uncomfortably in his chair in the back of the auditorium.

"What you do not appreciate," Feder continues, "is Germany's overwhelming need for a Leader made in Mussolini's mold." Feder's tone has turned steely. "Someone hard, ruthless, direct. A man who can purge Germany of traitors and cowards, of the Jews and Bolsheviks who now run it—and ruin it—a Leader who can restore the Fatherland to its former greatness." There's a sprinkling of applause in the room. "The time, I assure you, is not far distant . . ." As Feder sits back down, the applause increases. Kessler makes an instant decision to end the session. He hastily thanks the audience for having attended, and quickly leaves the stage, a chorus of boos greeting his exit.

～

Kessler and Max haven't been back in the hotel room more than a few minutes when the telephone rings. The desk clerk informs Kessler that a man named Hermann Esser has arrived. Is it alright to send him up? Yes, yes, Kessler says, and would the clerk please see to it that some hors d'oeuvres and perhaps a good brandy, be sent up as well? Hanging up the receiver, Kessler turns distractedly to Max.

"Good Lord—we've barely had a minute to collect ourselves. What an ordeal!"

"It wasn't pleasant." Max is given to understatement. "I mean—what a bunch of thugs."

"At least my wish has been granted—I've learned something about what passes for public opinion in Munich. Berlin will be a welcome relief."

"The sooner the better."

"I'm so sorry, Max. I thought this would be a pleasant excursion for you."

"It's not your fault. It's that bloody audience."

There's a brisk knock on the door. "Not *already*?! That's the fastest room service on record. Oh—perhaps it's the interviewer," Kessler says, adding with a smile: "Let's hope our Mister Esser is at least attractive."

When Kessler opens the door, his surprise is obvious. "Esser? Are you Mister Esser or . . . or . . . the bellboy?"

"Mister Esser, I assure you." The young man smiles broadly as Kessler gestures for him to enter the room.

"I'm so sorry, do come in," Kessler mumbles. "You see, we ordered some refreshment, and you . . . you—"

"—seem so young?" Esser completes the sentence. "Well yes—I am," Esser smiles ingratiatingly. "I look like a schoolboy, I know, but I assure you I'm all of twenty-two."

Kessler gestures for Esser to take a seat. "And already a freelance journalist? My, my, you must be very gifted."

"'Committed' would be more to the point," Esser replies, with a sudden flash of belligerence that he quickly covers over. "What a charming suite," he says, barely glancing around the room. "Very grand. Must cost a pretty penny."

Kessler ignores the overtone of hostility. "Do have a seat. What paper did you say you write for?"

"I didn't say." Esser smiles. There's an awkward pause. "Actually I write for several papers. The life of a free-lancer, you know—in these difficult times, we pick up what work we can get."

"Journalism has always seemed to me a most insecure profession." Kessler feels a twinge of uneasiness but can't pinpoint why. He knows that he wants to get this over with. "Well then," he says, "how can I help you? What is it you'd like to know?"

"I write mostly for the *Völkischer Beobachter*," Esser volunteers. "Occasionally for *Auf gut Deutsch* as well. Do you know them?"

"No, I don't know either one."

"You will, before long," Esser says with an ill-concealed smirk. "At the lecture, when Professor Feder mentioned the—"

"—you were at the lecture?"

"Yes indeed."

"How curious. I didn't notice you. Usually in a crowd that small nearly all the faces register."

"I was seated in the back."

"I see."

"As I started to say, when Professor Feder brought up the NSDAP, you said you hadn't heard of that either."

"The NSDAP? Sorry—could you refresh my memory?"

"The National Socialist German Workers' Party—the NSDAP."

Kessler brightens on hearing "Socialist." "No, it isn't familiar to me. But if its orientation is socialist, I assume it's affiliated with the Social Democratic Party, no?"

"No." Esser can't conceal the trace of a malicious grin. "It's not that kind of 'socialism.'"

"Socialism does take many forms," Kessler genially responds. "I call myself a socialist, but I'm not a traditional Marxist. What I favor is a structure of self-governing industrial cooperatives."

"In other words, the New Economy as worked out by your friend, Walther Rathenau."

A startled Kessler is slow to reply. "Well ... yes ... my views owe a great deal to Rathenau. How did you know we were friends?"

"Is it supposed to be a secret?" Esser leaves the question hanging. A considerable silence ensues, which Kessler finds somehow ominous. "Why in heaven's name would our friendship be a secret?" he finally asks. What he wants to say, but doesn't, is "I think I know what you're driving at, young man. And in regard to Rathenau, it may not even be true."

Esser picks up on Kessler's unease, and decides to press further. "Rathenau had a destructive influence on German politics. You and he apparently shared views—and even, shall we say, had a certain commonality in regard to your personal lives."

"Did you ever meet Rathenau?"

"I was denied that honor," Esser replies sarcastically. "Apparently he had a bloated sense of self-importance, was full of fuzzy abstractions. You, on the other hand, present yourself as direct and modest. Yet"—he gestures around the room—"you luxuriate in the unearned privileges of your class."

Kessler inadvertently gasps in astonishment. Esser, unflappable, smiles ingratiatingly, "What *are* you to make of me?" He flashes an impish, gamin-like smile.

"I have no wish to make anything of you!" Kessler sounds in equal parts startled and angry.

"Oh come now, Count Kessler, that's not what I heard . . ." Esser's tone is coquettish. "But to spare you further embarrassment, I suggest we—"

"—'embarrassment'? You flatter yourself, young man!"

"I often do, it's true. But to return to the NSDAP . . ." Esser doesn't wait for Kessler's response. "In the NSDAP," Esser continues, "we define socialism, unlike you and Rathenau, to include a strong devotion to the interests of industrial capitalism, the economic backbone of the state. 'National Socialism' also means the subordination of economics to the service of politics—to the struggle for a new world order."

"Which includes, I presume, extending Germany's borders."

"Of course. In the NSDAP we speak of a 'Greater Germany,' one that will reunite the Teutonic tribes of old."

"You make the boundary lines sound far more distinct than historians do."

In response, Esser merely smiles. There's another considerable silence. Why in heaven's name, Kessler asks himself, didn't I make inquiries about this offensive young man before agreeing to be interviewed? The point now is to get rid of him quickly without being overtly rude.

"To extend Germany's borders," Kessler offers, "would necessitate further wars. Wars of conquest. Such a scenario is in no one's best interest."

"All in due time." Esser continues to exude confidence and ease. It unnerves—and angers—Kessler.

"Few Germans," he says, "share your bellicose views."

Esser laughs derisively. "Not the sissies in petticoats! Our *German people* ridicule pacifism—as they do a League of—"

"—precisely who is 'our'?"

"Those who understand that *our* first priority must be regaining control of Germany from the international cabal of finance capitalists who now control it."

"A moment ago you were applauding capitalism," Kessler replies.

"I defended *industrial* capitalism. You aren't listening."

The uncivil remark incenses Kessler. He wants to tell this outlandish fellow that the interview is over, but Esser continues without pause: "Finance capitalism, not industrial capitalism, is our enemy."

"The distinction is false. Central to capitalism of every kind is the exploitation of workers."

"Behind finance capitalism stands—"

Kessler completes Esser's sentence "—yes I know: the international force of a Jewish world conspiracy. I've heard it all before. And don't need to hear it again." He stands up abruptly, signaling that the interview is over. Esser stands as well. Max had been sitting well off to the side, but, suddenly realizing that Esser might try to injure Kessler, rises quickly.

"Now, now," Esser says in a placating tone. "There's no need to be uncivil. I'm only trying to elicit your opinions."

"You seem to have a good many of your own," Kessler icily replies.

"Should I have kept them to myself? I thought that would be dishonest."

"Or polite." He thinks Esser does have a point, but is using it to prevaricate. "You haven't, after all, probed *my* views very deeply."

"May I have one final chance?" Esser disarmingly says, sounding for all the world like a sweet-natured supplicant. It throws Kessler off-guard, despite his better judgment.

"A chance for what?" he asks, trying to resist his own temptation to say yes.

"To get your opinion on another issue of great concern these days." Kessler and Max exchange anxious glances.

"Namely?" Kessler asks.

"The troubling question of women's role in the political world."

Kessler's taken aback—the question seems to come from out of the blue. All three men are still standing.

"Very well. In brief—and this interview is then over—women are fully capable of participating in all aspects of public and professional life that are currently the exclusive domain of men. There—we are finished." He moves towards the door. Esser remains stock still.

"You sound exactly like Doctor Magnus Hirschfeld," Esser says. "I presume you are—how shall I put it?—a co-religionist?"

"Doctor—who? Did you say Hirschfield?" Kessler knows perfectly well who Hirschfeld is, but is determined not to follow Esser down that particular garden path.

"Magnus Hirschfeld. The founder of the Institute for Sexual Science."

"Oh yes—I've heard of it."

"And what of the name Ernst Röhm? Have you heard of him as well?" The swift verbal punches are making it difficult for Kessler to follow the drift, let alone to give a considered reply.

"I believe so . . ." Kessler says, aiming for a tone of bored indifference, but falling short of the mark.

"Ernst Röhm is a prominent figure in our party. Second only to our undisputed leader, Adolf Hitler. Röhm heads the 'Storm Division', our paramilitary wing. They both believe—and I share the view, though I am nothing compared to them—that women belong in the home. In public life only the soldierly male virtues can rescue Germany. The virtues of loyalty, physical violence—and hatred."

Esser suddenly moves to the door, before Kessler can speak or move. Opening it, Esser turns back into the room: "And that is the world we band of brothers are giving birth to."

Kessler insists on the last word. "Should that birth come to pass," he shouts at Esser's receding back, "we will be headed into the darkest chapter in German history."

∾

The year 1923 opens with the French marching into the industrial Ruhr district in response to Germany falling behind on its reparations payment. The move sets off a profound crisis. When thousands of German workers walk out of the Ruhr factories, the government in Berlin announces its support for a campaign of "passive resistance," promising to cover lost wages. To meet that pledge, it sets 2,000 presses to work producing paper currency, heightening an inflationary spiral already wildly out of control. As the price of a single egg rises towards 10 billion marks, the currency loses all value. Misery and malnutrition are widespread. Only those with access to foreign currency or gold—dentures accepted—can avoid destitution.

The NSDAP—the National Socialist German Workers' Party—in Munich announces a "Reich Party Rally" featuring its gifted orator and emerging leader, Adolf Hitler, to take place at the end of January 1923. Hitler is not among the starving. His growing legion of supporters include a number of well-placed, well-fed luminaries: Putzi Hanfstaengl, descended from wealthy German-American stock (Putzi is a Harvard graduate); Helene and Edwin Bechstein (of piano fame); Elsa and Hugo Bruckmann, publisher of Houston Stewart Chamberlain, whose racist theories endeared him to the Kaiser; and Winifred and Siegfried Wagner (son of Richard, whom Hitler greatly admires). These well-placed friends do more than feed Hitler—they housebreak him, make him suitable for presentation in their high society circles. Elsa Bruckmann teaches him how to eat artichokes and lobster—and how to kiss a "lady's" hand. The more practical-minded Helene Bechstein presents him with what becomes his steady companion, a leather dog whip.

In his speech at the Reich Party Rally, Hitler—dressed in his trademark gangsterish trench coat and, yes, carrying his dog whip—releases a torrent of abuse at the "real enemy," the "treacherous Jewish-Marxist regime in Berlin," for its weakness in allowing French troops to invade Germany's Ruhr district at will. "France thinks less of Germany," Hitler rages, "than she does of a nigger state." Over the next few days, at a series of feverish rallies, large crowds cheer Hitler as their "savior," echoing the longstanding conviction among right-wing nationalists—Hermann Esser, the young man who interviewed and outraged Harry Kessler, is one—that only a strong man can rescue and restore Germany's prestige.

Simultaneously, Ernst Röhm, Hitler's closest associate, forms a

"Working Community" of right-wing paramilitary groups, a "warrior" elite that includes his own storm troopers, the SA. Röhm shows immense ingenuity in secretly building up an arsenal of small arms—including rubber truncheons, bombs, and grenades—in direct contravention of the strict armament limits set by the Treaty of Versailles. As an ex-Army officer, Röhm keeps Generals von Seeckt and Ludendorff informed of the NSDAP's growing prominence.

The impatient, agitated Hitler starts mulling over the prospect of direct action, an armed assault on—here the focus blurs—the French? the Bavarian government? the Socialists? the SPD in Berlin?—"the enemy." Out of a gigantic rally in late spring 1923 emerges—thanks to Ernst Röhm—the new German Combat League (the *Kampfbund*), with Hitler at its head. Hermann Esser is high in its ranks. Among the Kampfbund members, swastika armbands and gray ski caps are widely sported, along with flags declaring "Germany Awaken!" Hitler declares that "no member of that race which is our foe and which has led us into this most abject misery, no Jew, shall ever touch this flag."

∼

The title of the anonymous pamphlet Magnus Hirschfeld finds in his mail immediately catches his eye: "The Insane Asylum or the Gallows? The Truth about the Mass Murderer Haarmann of Hanover." The case of Fritz Haarmann, the homosexual serial killer, petty crook, and police informant, has been all over the newspapers for weeks, and Hirschfeld, like almost everyone else, has been inundated with the ghastly details of how Haarmann lured stray young men to his apartment and often killed them by biting them in the neck, sucking their blood, and then dismembering their bodies. (According to one rumor that sweeps the country, Haarmann cuts the flesh from his victims' bodies, puts it through a grinder, and sells it in expertly-wrapped packages as horsemeat). As hysteria mounts, a chilling rhyme makes the rounds:

Wait with patience, little mouse,

Fritz will soon come to your house,

With his axe so sharp and neat,
He'll make you into red chopped meat.

Hirschfeld rapidly concludes that Haarmann is simply deranged, a nightmarish freak of nature. What more is there to say? These days, he supposes, when a mountain is made of every molehill, some tiresome pedant will conjure up an international conspiracy of one sort or another, though in Haarmann's case it would take some doing. He puts the pamphlet to the side, thinking he'll glance at it at some idle point in the day, should that ever arrive.

That same afternoon, Hirschfeld is deeply absorbed in reading over a draft of his short book on birth control methods, when Karl Giese comes bursting into the room, already talking at the top of his voice.

"—an outrage, dear Papa, it's nothing less than an outrage! It has to be the work of Moll! Who but Albert Moll could employ such detestable language against you! Who but Moll could—"

"—calm down, dear Karl, do be calm, please ... Can't you see that I'm at work, that I'm deep into—"

"—you mean you haven't *seen* it?!" Karl, near tears, collapses into an armchair. "Oh, my poor Papa ..."

"Karl, my dear, you must collect yourself. I don't know what it is I should have seen, but I'll never know if you don't—"

"—the pamphlet on Haarmann! Every staff member at the Institute has received it in the—"

"—ah, now I see. That pamphlet ... yes ... Where did I put it?" Hirschfeld starts rummaging around his desk and quickly puts his hands on it. He reads the title aloud: "'The Insane Asylum, or the—"

"—yes, yes, that's it! Do you mean to say you haven't *read* it?!" Karl stands up and reaches for the pamphlet.

"Give it here. I know which page it's on ..." Karl quickly finds the passage and hands the pamphlet back to Hirschfeld. "Read it aloud, read it aloud ..." Karl begins to pace the room.

"'Magnus Hirschfeld and his allies, with the conscious backing of the Jewish press, are unleashing a contagious plague. By promoting deviant sexuality—'" Hirschfeld, aghast, stops and looks up. "Good heavens, Karl! Is the author blaming *me* for the crimes of Fritz Haarmann? That's too far-fetched even for a confirmed anti-Semite!"

"Not if you're convinced that Jews are literal vampires who suck the life blood out of the German body politic. Haarmann, you remember, bit his victims—his pure Aryans—in the throat, sucking—"

"—oh my ... yes, yes, I see ... I see."

"And for years, it now comes out, Haarmann has been on the police payroll as an informant. In other words, this 'homosexual Jewish beast' is directly connected to the state, to the Weimar Republic that all right-wingers despise. Jews, homosexuals, the Republic—all mashed together as if one."

"Which helps to explain why Haarmann's trial was so short," Hirschfeld pensively adds, "and his execution immediate—the same swift treatment that the Munich NSDAP recommends for dealing with the enemies of the German people."

"Now, Papa." Karl's tone verges on condescension. "You're doing it again. Worrying about all kinds of issues that divert you from your life's real mission—the acceptance of homosexuals."

"Should I forget that I'm also a Jew?"

"Of course not. How could you? But the Jewish people, compared to homosexuals, are not suppressed. They're everywhere, even including the government. Do you think Walther Rathenau could have become Foreign Minister if he'd been homosexual?"

Hirschfeld's smile carries a touch of secrecy. "My dear Karl ... surely the regular rumors about Rathenau must have reached even your pretty ears?"

"What rumors? Are you telling me that the esteemed Rathenau— handsome devil, except for that pot belly—was one of *us*?"

"That's not for me to say. Let us return to your earlier point about 'all kinds of issues.'"

"You can't do everything at once. Fight every battle, take on every cause. You need to be *less* cosmopolitan! To make headway in *our* struggle you need to concentrate on *our* issue. And I don't mean feminism, good as I am with occasional eye shadow."

Hirschfeld attempts an indulgent smile, but a frown supersedes it. "We've been over this before, Karl," he says softly. "Think about this, if you will: The press portrays Fritz Haarmann as a homosexual vampire. Adolf Hitler talks to ever larger crowds about how the *Jewish* vampire is sucking the life blood out of the German people. He links the evil Jew to the diseased homosexual and the 'liberated' woman as the tripartite plague of poisons that threaten the racially pure German people. Hitler promises to cleanse Germany of all such elements *at the same time.*"

"Are you about to defend Haarmann?!"

"Now you're being silly. Of course not. Most serial killers are heterosexual men. Haarmann was deranged. Homosexuality is not. *All* the linkages Hitler has invented must be revealed for the fictions they are. Those of us sewn onto Hitler's tapestry of evil must hold all the threads together. If you defend only this patch or that, the entire tapestry unravels. I ask you to think further about all this, Karl."

"I've heard it a thousand times," Karl responds, his tone a mixture of boredom and petulance.

Hirschfeld sounds resigned: "Very well, then. Let me get back to my manuscript. I have only two days left to correct it."

Karl moves towards the door, an irritable expression on his face. "You *are* going to print a response to the pamphlet, aren't you?"

"No. It would only give the anonymous author a second chance to denounce me."

"I think you're making a mistake."

"It won't be for the first time," Hirschfeld gently responds.

~

Hirschfeld stares at the letterhead in disbelief. "DOCTOR KARL-GÜN-THER HEIMSOTH." What can he possibly want? Hirschfeld wonders. It's years since I've seen the man, and the last run-in—when he said he regards me as an "enemy"—was hardly pleasant.

The letter is brief, pointed, and surprising. "I write to you," it begins, "fully cognizant of the wide divergence in our views about homosexuality and about politics in general. Despite this, I hope you will meet my request for a private interview. The matter I wish to discuss is of the utmost importance and confidentiality. I will be glad to come to the Institute on any afternoon you choose."

Glad indeed! Hirschfeld thinks. Up to now Heimsoth's been adamant in refusing to step foot in here. What can possibly have induced an about-face? Something extraordinary must have happened, or is about to happen. I'll see him of course. From curiosity alone.

Four days later the two men sit opposite each other in Hirschfeld's study. Their initial greetings have been stiff, not to say glacial. But Hirschfeld, warm and welcoming by nature, can't maintain the icy charade for long. He knows that he should wait for Heimsoth to bring up the reason for his visit, but his own amiability wins out over his unpleasant memories of the man.

"It might be well to begin, Heimsoth, with some attempt to air the past grievances which necessarily color this occasion."

"I wouldn't call them 'grievances,'" Heimsoth coldly replies, "but rather differences of opinion."

"Perhaps that's because *I* was the aggrieved party, not you." The remark sounds blunter than Hirschfeld intended and he softens it with a quick smile. "I was thinking back to your article in the *Völkischer Beobachter* denouncing what you call my 'bizarre, unscientific' views on homosexuality."

"I'm surprised to hear that you read the *Beobachter*. I didn't know," he says with amusement, "that you'd joined the Nazi Party."

"A colleague sent me the article. Along with a note warning me, as he put it, that 'although Heimsoth is himself homosexual, he does not share our views or goals.'"

Heimsoth's starchy expression remains unchanged. "None of that could have surprised you."

"Quite so," Hirschfeld says quietly. There's an awkward pause.

"My views are unchanged," Heimsoth begins. "Those of us who belong to the League for Human Rights—which has a far larger membership, I might add, than the Scientific Humanitarian Committee—do not believe, as you do, that homosexuality is a biological phenomenon."

"The number of members an organization has is not a reliable gauge of its importance." For the first time there's an edge to Hirschfeld's voice. "The Scientific Humanitarian Committee has for many years been in the forefront of the fight to remove Paragraph 175."

"Yes it has—and with remarkably little success." Heimsoth's bearing remains taut, his expression wooden.

"Perhaps because," Hirschfeld responds, "so many homosexuals refuse to fight on their own behalf."

"I believe it would be more accurate to say that they refuse to fight in the manner and according to the ideology that you prefer. The many homosexuals who read *Der Eigene* or belong to the League for Human Rights stress above all the *spiritual* dimensions of male friendship—its superiority to what can ever pass between a man and a woman."

Heimsoth and Hirschfeld can't resist lecturing each other, though each knows what the other will say.

"And does the spiritual never evolve into the erotic?" Hirschfeld pointedly asks.

"The passionate bonds of male friendship represent the highest possible emotional connection, whether the men involved are homosexual or heterosexual."

"You haven't answered my question."

"Your question is pointless. Intimate friendships between adult men take many different forms. When you link sexual acts to passionate friendship, you bring friendship into disrepute. Our greatest heroes—Goethe, Schiller—spoke openly about their love for other men, embraced and kissed their friends, and did so in terms of profound endearment."

Hirschfeld smiles distractedly. "You take me back many years... to the Eulenburg trials. He and von Moltke used the same words you do in describing their 'friendships.' And then Max Harden tracked down that fisherman Riedel and it turned out that 'friendship' can be irreducibly carnal."

"Are you saying that profound male friendships *must* include the carnal? I find that preposterous!"

"It is—the way you put. It is you who insist that sexual acts between men somehow brings friendship into 'disrepute'—to use your word."

"I was attempting to rescue the possibility of deep male bonding that does *not* include sex. It's precisely your inability to understand that distinction that makes you un-German."

"Really, my dear Heimsoth, your penchant for insult is remarkable. I should perhaps warn you that it doesn't predispose me to do you any favors. Which is why you've come, I presume." Hirschfeld smiles. "Surely, as a psychiatrist, you must know that aggressive behavior doesn't provoke a warmhearted response. Unless, of course, one is a masochist. Which I am not."

There is a pause.

"Perhaps I shouldn't have come. I very nearly didn't."

"But you have." Hirschfeld's tone isn't adversarial. "Having set aside this time to see you, it would be unintelligent not to use it."

"Yes, I agree." There's a hint of relief in Heimsoth's tone, though he zealously guards against letting it suggest gratitude. "Does the name Ernst Röhm mean anything to you?"

"Of course. He and Hitler head up the NSDAP—the Nazi Party, with its swastika armbands."

"No, that's not quite right. *Hitler* heads the party. Röhm is his chief of staff and closest friend. Röhm is also a close friend of mine." Hirschfeld thinks he detects a suggestive overtone of sexual partnership, but decides not to ask for clarification.

"So you are here on behalf of Ernst Röhm?"

"In a sense."

"In what sense? You must be more explicit. I don't know much about Röhm—other than the role he played in the failed Munich Putsch—the 'beer hall putsch,' isn't that what they're calling it?—but what little I do know doesn't predispose me in the man's favor."

"Röhm is much misunderstood. He served nobly in the war and has a disfiguring facial scar to prove it. He is a highly capable officer, immensely popular with his men."

"If he is as capable as you say, why then did the Munich Putsch fail?"

"It's a fair question. The answer is complicated. Hitler can perhaps be faulted for forcing the event precipitously. It turned out that the Bavarian police, as well as the Reichswehr, had an agenda significantly different from Hitler's. They feared that if Hitler succeeded in Munich, his paramilitary force would then march on Berlin—which the police opposed. But throughout, Röhm and his associates behaved in an exemplary manner—and for his pains he served jail time. He bears not a drop of blame for the failure, as Hitler well understands."

"The quality of their friendship is of no concern to me. I can only hope that the wretched business in Munich puts an end to their benighted careers."

Heimsoth visibly stiffens. "On that point we will never agree."

"How is it possible that you, a man openly homosexual, can sympathize with a party hostile to your very being?"

"On this matter you are not well informed. I myself am acquainted with a considerable number of homosexual men whose sympathies are with the Nazi Party."

"I believe you, much as I regret the fact. We have had several homosexual Nazi Party members come to us at the Institute for counseling. Theirs is a sad plight. It's well-established that a certain number of people will react to oppression by identifying with their oppressor."

"They are German nationalists first, and homosexuals second. Many German nationalists—including many Nazis—glorify the beauty of the male body; the well-proportioned, powerfully-built warrior is on a pedestal."

"You know how it is with pedestals—they cannot touch one another." Hirschfeld is clearly amused at his own remark. Heimsoth remains stony-faced.

"Smirk if you will," Heimsoth says angrily. "The glorification of male military bearing is erotically charged for many homosexuals who will have nothing to do with your feminized Scientific Humanitarian Committee. Your appeal is to Helene Stöcker, not Hermann Esser."

"Who is Hermann Esser? I've never heard of him. Why do you bring his name up?"

"He's an emerging young leader. Not homosexual. Though many homosexuals find him very attractive."

"I thought we were discussing Ernst Röhm. More particularly, the party's reaction to his homosexuality."

Heimsoth looks alarmed. "I don't know what you're referring to."

"Röhm is hardly circumspect."

"The Aryan view is that sexuality is for procreation. Those who do not procreate are not useful to the state."

"Does that mean that all single people who do not produce babies are anathema? Or merely second-class citizens?" Hirschfeld is having a fine time. "Can you be a storm trooper if you're not also a father?" Hirschfeld chuckles merrily. "Goodness, is Hitler a father? I've forgotten."

"We were speaking of homosexuality."

"What more is there to say?"

"The *official* party view is that homosexuality is not a biological phenomenon, as you would have it, but the product of decadence. It's dangerous because infectious, capable of spreading even among the most masculine natures."

"The notion of 'infectious' has always puzzled me. It seems to imply that heterosexuality is so fragile that it's easily overpowered—even by adolescent experimentation. I find it similar to the way the Nazis describe women—that they must be kept sequestered from public life lest they effeminize German men. Manhood sounds as fragile as heterosexuality. It makes the German 'warrior' seem rather delicate, don't you think?—a vulnerable reed."

"I don't find this line of inquiry productive."

Hirschfeld looks amused. "I dare say not. These contradictions must be bothersome."

"I see no contradictions. I see word games. And I don't appreciate them." Heimsoth reminds himself that he's come to ask a favor, and tries to contain his anger. "I would prefer to turn to the reason for my visit."

"Quite so. As interesting as these other matters are to me, I mustn't take advantage of your good nature and pursue them too rigorously."

There's a pause, during which Heimsoth gets the distinct feeling that Hirschfeld is mocking him.

Hirschfeld breaks the silence. "Now then, you've come to me, I deduce, to discuss some matter relating to Ernst Röhm. That much is correct, is it not?"

"It is."

"Frankly, my own political views are so contrary to Captain Röhm's that it's difficult to see how I—"

"—did you know that Röhm is a member of our League for Human Rights? What's more, he's let it be known that he favors the repeal of Paragraph 175."

"How strange that in all these years I've never heard his name mentioned once in regard to the movement for repeal."

"Ernst Röhm is a discreet man."

"Really? I've heard quite the opposite—that he's a roustabout."

"He likes his food and drink, if that's what you mean."

"That, and perhaps, too, his carousing—is that the right word? I'm told he's especially fond of the bathhouses."

"He might occasionally have been seen in the Marien Kasino or the Eldorado . . . Yes, in fact he told me frankly that he derives a good deal of contentment from the bathhouses."

"'Contentment?'" Hirschfeld barely suppresses the urge to laugh.

"Captain Röhm doesn't conceal his sexual inclinations from his friends, sometimes not even from casual contacts. But he is above all loyal to Hitler. And Hitler to him. Are you aware that Röhm is the only member of the Nazi leadership who addresses Hitler with the familiar '*Du*'?"

"No, I'm not aware. How would I be?" Hirschfeld asks, with just the trace of a smile.

"That should give you some measure of the esteem with which Röhm is held."

"By Hitler, you mean."

"Yes, Hitler. Of course. Who else?"

"Does that mean Hitler approves of Röhm's, er, activities?"

"He's tolerant of them."

"How surprising—given official Nazi *disapproval* of homosexuality."

"Tolerance is not approval. Hitler believes that a man's private life is nobody else's business. He scoffs at what he calls 'the League of Virtue.' He's a man-of-the-world. And loyal to his friends."

"I have it on good authority that both Himmler and Goebbels despise Röhm. And have *no* tolerance for homosexuality. In tolerating Röhm, isn't Hitler being disloyal to Himmler and Goebbels?"

"You're playing with me again, Hirschfeld. I don't appreciate it."

Hirschfeld acts surprised, wounded even. "I'm sorry you feel that way. I'm sincerely interested in these matters."

There is another pause. Heimsoth quiets down.

"May I come—at long last—to the point of my visit today?"

"By all means." Hirschfeld's tone is conciliatory.

"It is well known that you give expert legal testimony in court cases."

"Many times."

"Captain Röhm wishes to talk with you about a legal matter in which he is involved."

"What is its nature?"

"I'm not at liberty to discuss details with you. I've been delegated to arrange a meeting at which no one will be present other than Captain Röhm and yourself. Are those terms agreeable?"

"I see people all day long, of various genders and all sexual persuasions. No one is ever turned away."

"Then the answer is 'yes'?"

"Yes."

It is three days later. Röhm and Hirschfeld are in conversation. Röhm is dressed in full uniform, complete with several rows of medals and a black-white-red cockade on his cap. He is a fleshy man of medium height, with green eyes, dark hair, and a pronounced scar that runs from his cheek across his broken nose. His manner is hyper-masculine and direct. Hirschfeld is in mid-sentence:

" . . . and I believe you spent some time in prison when the putsch failed. Isn't that so?"

"I'm a military man. Prison is run along military lines, orderly and prescribed. If one wants an item not part of standard issue, one has to apply in writing for it. I refused. I do not make requests. I respond to them. I do not take orders, I give them."

"That must have made your life in prison difficult."

Röhm laughs. "Not at all. Most of the wardens are old soldiers who gladly bent the rules for me. My cell was always scrupulously clean. The wardens prided themselves on scrubbing it daily. During the brief time I spent in jail I never heard a disrespectful word."

"You were fortunate. The people I know who've been in prison tell horrifying tales of mistreatment."

"Perhaps they were scum."

Hirschfeld isn't sure he's heard right. "What did you say?"

"The guards do not respect *some* prisoners. We were in a special category. The wardens knew we'd been imprisoned for political reasons— that we are patriots attempting to restore the vitality of the German nation."

"As you define it."

"Of course. What else? But let me be clear: I am no defender of the prison system. Most of the men have been locked up for crimes against property—the result of misery, *need*. Many Germans are starving. They have no work, they cannot feed their families. Their so-called 'crimes' are minor. The real crooks, the big crooks, are the bourgeoisie who rule Germany. They never go to jail. Not yet anyway. But we have plans for them." Röhm's smile is closer to a sneer.

"You seem to see yourself as an outlaw. Mind you, I'm often treated as one myself." Hirschfeld chuckles over his own clever linkage.

"Official—bourgeois—morality is a lie. I take it as a point of pride not to be 'morally upright.' I'm no goody-goody, and don't much care for those who are. They're usually lying. What matters to me as a soldier is whether a man can be depended on—not how much he drinks or whores."

"I'm inclined to agree with you," Hirschfeld says, somewhat to his own surprise. "I know nothing about soldiers, of course. What I agree with is the notion that state enforcement of middle-class morality is doomed to fail. It too often goes against individual instinct, punishing creative non-conformers, stifling dissent."

"Well said, Doctor Hirschfeld. It is a battle against hypocrisy. The mask must be torn away."

"I must say, Captain Röhm, you sound very much like a man of the Left."

Röhm smiles enigmatically. "The Left and the Right do not disagree about everything. But do not mistake me: I don't champion all outcasts. I pick and choose. While in jail I met many political prisoners. The Communists impressed me most—their loyalty and devotion to their principles. They, too, hate appeasement. They are like our German nationalists—pledged to a cause, ardent in their commitment."

"I believe the Social Democrats are equally devoted to a cause—the cause of democracy."

Röhm looks affronted. "The SPD is impotent. It cannot manage its own party, let alone the government. But I'm not here to offend you, Dr. Hirschfeld. After all, I've come to ask for your help. But I cannot pretend to agree with anything you say. Salvation for Germany can only come through a strong leader."

"Adolf Hitler?"

"Precisely. Adolf Hitler and his fervent love for the Fatherland."

"Or for certain segments of it. Those who believe in democracy also passionately love Germany—all of it."

Both men seem suddenly on the verge of boiling over—and both pull back.

"Perhaps," Hirschfeld offers, "you should tell me straightaway why you're here. An argument over politics isn't likely to advance your mission, whatever it may be."

"Very well then. The story is this: As Heimsoth has made clear, and as I have never denied, my inclinations are homosexual. I've slept with women, many times in fact—and have had three cases of gonorrhea to prove it. But my basic nature is homosexual."

"As is mine. There—we have found a second thing in common."

"I would add a third: We both have a rebel's temperament. Mine is less pious, perhaps." He catches himself: "But let us not get sidetracked again . . ." Röhm clears his throat. "It comes to this . . . in the course of my wanderings, I met a young man in one of Berlin's bars. I—"

"—which bar?"

"What difference does it make?"

"I try to keep an up-to-date list."

Röhm burst out laughing. "So the busy doctor likes a bit of fun too, eh?"

"The police commissioner and I confer from time to time, so we can warn our members to stay away from the places that cater to hustlers—and blackmail. The worst, I hear, is a tobacco shop—a backroom brothel, not a bar at all."

"You wouldn't know the one I speak of. It's working class, north of the Museumsinsel."

"Of course I know it. It's on Kleine Hamburger Strasse, owned by fat Franz. 'Rita,' the piano player, likes to wear drag. The place is notorious. You should stay away."

"No doubt you'd recommend some respectable place like the Mikado, where I'm told you 'homosexual rights' types hang out. I hear they took the bathroom door off its hinges to prevent 'indecent' activity. No thanks. Boring."

"And the young man you were telling me about . . . *not* boring, I presume . . ."

"A ex-soldier. My sort of man. I invited him to return with me to my hotel room. When I was in the bathroom, he stole a luggage check out of my pants pocket and ran off. Went straightaway to the baggage terminal and retrieved my suitcase. I suppose he thought I'd never go to the police and have him arrested for fear he'd divulge our sex together. But I *did* go to the police. No guttersnipe will prevent Ernst Röhm from seeking his rights."

Röhm pauses, as if expecting to be patted on the back.

Hirschfeld finally speaks: "I fail to see how any of this relates to me."

"That should be obvious. Heimsoth says you've given expert testimony many times in cases of blackmail."

"Many times. And often with the result that the blackmailer receives severe punishment."

Röhm's eyes sparkle with relief. "Heimsoth was right! You *are* the man for me."

"Perhaps. But you should know that in nearly every instance my testimony has been on behalf of a man terrified of having his homosexuality revealed, of being socially and financially ruined. That doesn't seem the case with you. You've already *given away* the information that the blackmailer feels he holds over you. Often a homosexual victim will commit suicide rather than have the truth of his sexuality publicly revealed." Hirschfeld smiles: "One might say that yours is the only known case of a man volunteering to commit suicide—and living to tell the tale. Thus far, anyway."

Röhm stares at him blankly, as if not grasping the point. "The courts," he finally says, "what is the disposition of the courts? Are they, too, in the hands of the Jews? From that swindling bunch, I don't expect any sympathy."

The boldness of the insult startles Hirschfeld. "You do know, Captain Röhm, do you not, that I am a Jew?"

"Of course I know. All I had to do was look at you. Not exactly an Aryan Adonis, eh? No matter. There are Jews and there are Jews. I am not obsessed by the matter."

Hirschfeld shakes his head from side to side in disbelief.

"You dumbfound me," he says quietly.

"I speak my mind directly, as I said. Why should the truth 'dumbfound' you?"

Hirschfeld inhales deeply. "I can tell you how I would advise your young blackmailer to testify. Perhaps that will be enlightening. I would have him throw himself on the mercy of the court, declare that he'd gone with you only because he hadn't eaten in three days; or because his mother was dying and couldn't afford a doctor; or because he couldn't buy his beloved child a toy. Any defense along those lines would be persuasive. A merciful court would almost certainly set the poor lad free."

Röhm's eyes narrow. "Are you poking fun, Dr. Hirschfeld? That isn't something I tolerate well."

"I was picking up on the eloquent plea you made earlier. Remember? You spoke with great sympathy for all those prisoners you met who've been locked up for 'crimes against property'—those who stole out of desperate need. Perhaps your young blackmailer genuinely falls within that category. Would you not be forced—as a matter of principle—to let him off the hook?"

"You *are* toying with me, Hirschfeld."

"I am merely quoting you."

"I did say that millions of Germans are going hungry, yes; and that they deserve our sympathy. But one must then ask why they go hungry, why they suffer. It isn't because of Ernst Röhm or the Nazi Party. They live in misery because the Jewish stock exchange has artificially manipulated the money supply, throwing millions out of work. This cannot be allowed to continue."

"A few Jews are wealthy. A few even belong to the stock exchange. But the vast majority of the Jewish people are part of the suffering masses you describe. I'm not a particularly political person, but if I had to start apportioning blame for the plight of Germany's poor, I'd begin by singling out a capitalist economic system controlled by a small number of right-wing, *Christian* industrialists."

"You're wise to stay out of politics. I mean, given your ignorance."

Hirschfeld is taken aback. "Perhaps it's a match for your own."

Röhm can't help but smile at Hirschfeld's bravado. He could thrash him then and there, he thinks, but feels a kind of pungent amusement at listening to the man's freakish audacity.

"You know nothing of the working class," Röhm says. "Here you live"—he gestures around him—"in the lap of luxury, in this *villa*"—he spits the word out—"while the Social Democratic government treats workers like step-children."

"I'm not part of the government, but I know this much: Hitler's no defender of the working class, no socialist. He vows to protect private property *from* what he calls 'radical working-class scum'—*and* promises to disband all trade unions."

"*Race* is what is central to our mission, not class."

"Now that I *do* believe."

"It's the Jews who stabbed Germany in the back—handed us over to the Jewish bankers, the Rothschilds! That game is *over*—the Jews will pay for their treason! A new Germany is rising and it will make sure that—"

Hirschfeld stands up abruptly from his chair: "—I cannot, will not, listen a minute longer to your disgusting, your—your words stink of the barnyard! This interview, Captain Röhm, is over—"

Röhm jumps up from his chair, his face flushed. "Words, words!" he shouts. "It's actions you should worry about!—actions to stop Jewish racketeers once and for all from sucking the German people dry! Then you'll know what it's like to be afraid. You will *long* for the return of Ernst Röhm!"

He turns towards the door. "I should have known better than to seek you out."

"I told your emissary, Dr. Heimsoth, that at the Institute we have never turned away a single person seeking our help." Hirschfeld enunciates every word: "It gives me great pleasure to break that rule today for the first time."

"Many more rules will soon be broken." Röhm stalks from the room.

∼

Röhm's well-placed friends see to it that his blackmailer is found guilty and sent to prison. "I didn't need that damned Jew's help after all," he tells himself, gratified. The trial does, however, produce some unwanted publicity—as well as additional details to confirm rumors about Röhm's proclivities. In his own deposition to the Munich police he tells them that he's "bisexually oriented"—a legitimate-enough claim if his early history of affairs with women can be credited.

Röhm also tells the police that he's masturbated with other men but has never had "intercourse" with any of them—a claim conceivably true, though a sexual life rigidly confined to mutual masturbation would be highly atypical. Besides, constraint isn't one of Röhm's defining characteristics. In making the distinctions he does to the police, Röhm is shrewdly tailoring his behavior to fall within permissible legal limits. Paragraph 175 of the German penal code makes "activities resembling sexual intercourse" between two men punishable—but *not* mutual masturbation.

What the law technically finds innocuous, German public opinion does not. When Hirschfeld's Scientific Humanitarian Committee conducts a survey in the late 1920s of political parties' attitudes towards Paragraph 175, it concludes that "the sole party which has represented the SHC's standpoint without any reservations ... is the Communist Party," the KPD. In point of fact, the small league of German anarchists also shares that view. Its leading figures, Senna Hoy and the literary Bohemian and revolutionary Erich Mühsam, argue against *any* legal limitations on the sexual behavior of consenting adults. Mühsam denounces the persecution of homosexuals as based on "medieval delusion"; when the Nazis come to power, they declare Mühsam an enemy of the Reich and consign his printed work to a bonfire.

Neither anarchism nor communism, however, has anywhere near the political clout in Germany that the various forms of socialism do—and, in particular, the Social Democratic Party brand. At the turn of the century the SPD's foremost spokesmen, Eduard Bernstein and August Bebel, had been among the earliest signers of the petition to repeal Paragraph 175, Bernstein stoutly rejecting any attempt to categorize homosexuality as "unnatural" or "corrupt."

In the succeeding three decades the SPD (with Magnus Hirschfeld now affiliated) continues to lend official support for repeal, but does so with increasing ambivalence. The onset of the Great Depression and the deepening of economic misery leads to a vigorous revival of scapegoating, typified by one SPD member's reference to homosexuality during a Reichstag debate as a "constitutional disorder," a degenerate deviation from the norm. In tandem, there's a mounting emphasis within the SPD on the traditionalist assumption that heterosexual marriage, procreation, and the family are the necessary cornerstones of "civilized" life. This retreat to orthodoxy leads the Scientific Humanitarian Committee to request a statement from the SPD reiterating its support for the repeal of Paragraph 175.

The SPD replies that, at the moment, a public statement of support might have an adverse affect on the Party's current campaign to denounce the Nazi Party as a hothouse of homosexuality: The leading SPD daily, *Vorwärts*, has been excoriating the Nazis as a haven for "lustful perverts and their appalling harlotry," while the largest SPD daily in Bavaria, the *Münchener Post*—which earlier helped to destroy Prince Eulenburg—has been publishing a series of articles on what it calls "the 175ers" in the Nazi Party, focusing on Röhm and his SA storm troopers. With friends like the SPD, Hirschfeld muses, who needs enemies?

In pushing its campaign to link homosexuality and Nazism, the SPD is knowingly overstating the extent of homosexuality within SA ranks, as well as ignoring the abundant denunciations in the Nazi press of "this sickness." The leading Nazi paper, the *Völkischer Beobachter*, defines homosexuality as an "aberration" and lists it among the "evil propensities of the Jewish soul." And so the double campaign proceeds: the Nazis are zealously linking homosexuality to Judaism, while the Social Democratic Party, alternately, is actively coupling it with Nazism.

As early as 1925, Harry Kessler has become increasingly aware on the streets of Berlin of "swastika-carrying youths, with heavy cudgels, blonde and stupid as young bulls." The death of President Ebert from a ruptured appendix in February of that year has thrown open the office of President to an election—thanks to a provision in the 1919 Weimar Constitution—by popular vote. Kessler predicts that *the* marker of impending disaster for the country would be the election of Field Marshal Hindenburg—that exemplar of militaristic conservatism—to replace Ebert. Such an event, in Kessler's view, would inaugurate "a return to philistinism" and a farewell to the vision of a more just society.

Gustav Stresemann, the Foreign Minister and Kessler's old friend, shares his apprehension. At lunch one day in April 1925, he tells Kessler that Hindenburg, who's getting on in years, isn't at all keen to run for the office. But Stresemann fears that he'll be persuaded (in the upshot, he is)—and if so, Stresemann feels "in despair" over the catastrophic prospect. Kessler urges him to speak out forcefully against

Hindenburg's candidacy, but Stresemann feels it would prove counter-productive.

It's a serious miscalculation. Given Weimar's political fragmentation, the right-wing parties are able to unite behind Hindenburg—and he wins the Presidency by a clear majority. "The sequel," Kessler writes despairingly in his diary, "is likely to prove one of the darkest chapters in German history." On May 12, Kessler attends Hindenburg's swearing-in at the Reichstag. Wearing a frockcoat, Hindenburg looks for all the world like the throwback to an earlier day that he is. The Communist delegates in the hall shout out "Long live the Soviet Union!"—and march out in a body. "Farewell progress," Kessler writes in his diary, "farewell vision of a new world which was to be humanity's conscience money for the criminal war."

Over the next four years—years that see the flowering of Weimar culture and the (superficial) sense that democracy is taking firm root—the army, the civil service, and the economic elite remain as reactionary as ever, and increasingly powerful. The parties on the Left seem stuck in a prewar mindset that assumes the eventual overthrow of capitalism has been mandated in heaven and they need merely await the day's inevitable arrival. Yet the inevitable rarely arrives on schedule, and the Left is in no condition to hasten it. Following the violent upheavals of 1919–1922, the Independent Socialist Party has fallen apart; the Centre Party is deploying most of its energy on defending Catholic interests and fighting "pornography"; and the middle-class and industrial workers who constitute the backbone of the Social Democratic Party are gradually, perhaps inexorably, deserting the fold.

Harry Kessler clearly sees the warning signs: "Power lies in the hands," he writes in his diary, "of precisely the same set as before and during the war." The death of Paul Cassirer, the pioneering art gallery owner, early in 1926, deeply upsets him; it seems an omen, somehow, of the end of modernism, the foreboding onset of a reactionary spirit. When he visits Elisabeth Förster-Nietszche a month later, she's "bursting with the news of her Mussolini friendship"—and isn't pleased when Kessler tells her that he considers Mussolini "a danger to Europe."

He continues to give and attend elegant dinner parties that often include celebrated and influential figures like Albert Einstein ("his eyes still sparkle with almost childlike radiance and twinkling mischief"), Josephine Baker (who dances a solo for the other guests "with brilliant artistic mimicry and purity of style"), Max Harden, Max Reinhardt, Richard Strauss, George Grosz, Erwin Piscator, Jacques Maritain—and assorted other prominences from a variety of glamorous worlds. For much of 1927, Kessler travels with Max to Spain, to Italy, to Capri, to Zürich (where they celebrate his 59th birthday). They go to opera and the ballet, frequent the theater, are guests at any number of lively gatherings and dinner parties.

Yet Kessler's heart is no longer quite in it; the *joie de vivre* that in the past always accompanied his socializing now has an element of strained obligation. By mid-1927, he's reached the conclusion that "an increasing proportion of the nation regards the republic for the time being as an incontestable fact, whereas the great majority of the 'captains of industry,' the powerful financiers, the civil service, the Reichswehr, the bench, the large and medium-sized landowners (*Junkers*), and university professors and students are hostile to the republic." If Kessler is mildly depressed over conditions, the multitudes of those less fortunate than he are closer to desperation. The sharp reduction in economic productivity in combination with the burden of reparations produces a hyperinflation so grotesque that, in the years immediately following the war, salaries have to be carried home in wheelbarrows—that is, until banknotes lose their meaning entirely. In the early 1920s, literal starvation looms as an imminent threat—90 percent of an average family's budget goes to food—and even salaried middle-class Germans have to sell possessions (and in some cases loot stores or scavenge crops in the countryside).

In mid-1923, an international committee under the chairmanship of the American economist Charles Dawes re-negotiates the reparations schedule, and provides a large loan to Germany, allowing its central bank to issue a new currency based on the gold standard. The tide finally begins to turn. But for a significant number of middle-class creditors, the reconstruction entails ruinous losses, and support for the Social Democratic government declines in tandem. Not that industrialists and financiers are immune from economic troubles; the sharp deflation which ensues after the 1923 readjustment leads to widespread bankruptcies among those firms that had used borrowed money to over-invest in heavy machinery; Hugo Stinnes's financial empire is among those negatively affected.

Following the failed Beer Hall Putsch in 1923, the Nazi Party goes through a period of division and declining fortunes. In Bavaria, Ernst Röhm manages to unite the wild assortment of paramilitary organizations, but, as late as the Reichstag elections in May 1928, the party is still split into squabbling factions and polls a mere 2.5 percent of the vote—and in Berlin a meager 1.4 percent. Hitler continues to rant about Jews being a pestilence "worse than the Black Death" and, sounding another favorite theme, about the need of the German people for "living space"—for expansion to the East. Yet the Nazis are aware that they must broaden their electoral appeal if they're to come to power, and they put new emphasis on unifying the ultra-nationalist Right and on regional organizing.

They meet with some success, yet, at the end of 1927, the party still has only 75,000 members and has managed to elect only seven deputies to the Reichstag. Shrewdly—and here the organizing skills of Hitler's associate, Paul Joseph Goebbels, become of critical importance—the Nazis latch on to the urban economic plight of prolonged unemployment and reduced salaries among the lower middle-class, and in the countryside of peasants and small farmers the simultaneous suffering from a decline in agricultural prices and a rise in government taxation. By identifying the party with such sizeable pockets of discontent, the Nazis steadily grow in strength, particularly in rural areas like Schleswig-Holstein. By October 1928, party membership has doubled to 150,000, and, in June 1929, the party in Coburg wins control of a municipality for the first time.

The racial aspects of Nazi ideology are also strengthened and stressed. The German people—the *Volk*—must be protected, the Nazis angrily declare, from those who would infect the Fatherland with degenerate ideas and practices; the purity of the Aryan race must be preserved from Communist criminality and Jewish perversion—from "maggots in the decomposing body of Germany." The message takes hold: in the Reichstag election of 1928, the Nazis receive 800,000 votes. Two years later their vote soars to 6.4 million, and 107 Nazi candidates are elected to the Reichstag—thereby becoming the country's second-largest party.

The results, Harry Kessler writes in his diary, are "a black day for Germany, a national crisis." He sees the Nazi insurgency as "lunacy and infamy, a delirium of the German lower-middle class—shopkeepers, farmers, small businessmen, and the like"—and he lucidly foresees that the "poison of its disease may . . . bring down ruin on Germany and Europe for decades ahead . . . The former epoch is dead and done with."

One evening that fall Kessler and his lover Max Goertz board a train in Berlin to take them to Kessler's house in Weimar. In the station, they find themselves in the midst of a crowd of carousing young SA recruits. The "snotty-nosed brats," as Kessler calls them, are everywhere—on the platform, down the stairs, in the waiting rooms—drunkenly singing "patriotic" songs, abusing other passengers, clearly spoiling for a fight. Ten days later, Kessler runs into a much larger contingent of Nazis in Berlin's Leipziger Strasse, zestfully smashing windows in the Jewish-owned department store Wertheim, shouting "Germany Awake!!" and "Death to Judah!!" This time Kessler becomes enraged: "The vomit rises," he writes in his diary, "at so much pigheaded stupidity and spite."

As Nazi ranks swell and street brawls escalate, some of Kessler's friends confidently predict that—as one of them puts it—"the Hitler movement has passed its peak and is already on the way down." Even as late as 1932, his radical friend Fritz von Unruh assures Kessler that, should Hitler come to power, he will be unable to fulfill his many promises, and in short order the Communists will take over. In any case, Fritz tells him, a revolutionary state of mind prevails in Germany and the tepid Weimar Republic is doomed; Kessler at least agrees that the country "is coming apart." Unruh helps to found the anti-Nazi Iron Front, and Kessler, attending one of its rallies in the Lustgarten, is gratified at the size of the crowd, which he estimates at no less than 100,000.

By 1932, with unemployment rampant due to the depression, membership in the Communist Party (the KPD) does rapidly grow, tripling in number from 1929, with three-quarters of the jobless new recruits deeply antagonistic not only to the Nazis but to the dithering, irresolute Social Democrats as well, whom they see as having betrayed their own party's earlier egalitarian promise. At the same time, support for the Nazis—with Hitler claiming that "our fight against Marxism will be relentless"—grows among middle-class professionals as well as among the older generation of conservative nationalists who despise the Republic and fear a Bolshevik takeover.

Some of Kessler's long-standing aristocratic friends have begun openly to side with Hitler. When he attends, as so often in the past, an evening at Helene and Alfred von Nostitz—friends of some 30 years—he finds the atmosphere "reeks of Nazism." He dares to raise objections—and a cold, embarrassed silence ensues. Six weeks later, as the guest of the American Guggenheim family at Hiller's restaurant, he's seated next to Wanda Prittwitz, the daughter of old friends. She tells him excitedly that all her relatives are now Nazis, and isn't it splendid that so many young people have joined the movement?—"They share such a wonderful spirit of camaraderie." She shamefacedly confesses that she's not yet joined the Nazi Party but instantly adds—as if to salvage her reputation—that she is of course an anti-Semite. She assumes that he is too. "No," Kessler replies, "If I was I wouldn't be here tonight—the guest of a Jew." To his astonishment, she misses his stiletto thrust and goes gushingly on.

At the same dinner party, the Baroness Rebay, whose father was a general in World War I, tells Kessler that she, too, has strong Nazi leanings, though as a painter herself she scolds the party on one count: it should not have closed down the Bauhaus at Dessau. Never mind, she goes on, the wonderful thing about the Nazis is that they're teaching ordinary people that they, too, must make sacrifices—"whereas during the war it was only 'our sort' who sacrificed." Kessler's impeccable manners crack: "Several million ordinary folk," he tells the Baroness, "were killed in the war and several hundred thousand starved to death; none of *our* acquaintances died of hunger."

In the July 1932 Reichstag election, the Nazis more than double their vote—from 6.4 million to 13.1 million—making them, with 230 seats, the country's largest party. The centrist coalitions largely disappear, but the Social Democrats still retain 133 seats and the Communists 89. In yet another election a few months later, the Nazis lose some ground but still remain the largest party. The Left and the Right are faced off against each other more starkly than ever before. Some among the Nazi leaders, especially Goebbels, grow impatient; it is time, they argue, to employ "extralegal" methods.

Violence now becomes a daily occurrence. The Nazis conveniently lump the Social Democrats and Communists together as dangerous "Marxists" and unleash a harsh campaign of terror against them. SA and SS troopers rampage through the streets, brutally beating and often killing anyone who even *seems* like an opponent, destroying presses, interrupting meetings, occupying and smashing offices—including those of Fritz von Unruh's Iron Front, which dissolves. Hitler rejects any suggestion that he signal his willingness to accept a cabinet seat; he insists on nothing less than the Chancellorship.

In late January 1933, Hindenburg capitulates and invites Hitler to become Reich Chancellor.

PART VII

~

ENDINGS

KESSLER IS HARD AT WORK on what will be a brilliant biography of Walther Rathenau when Max barges into his study with the news of Hitler's appointment; Kessler is "astounded"—he hasn't anticipated that the climactic event would happen so soon. To his annoyance, the Nazi concierge downstairs hosts an exuberant celebration, and all of Berlin seems to join in as Goebbels—brilliant organizer that he is—coordinates jubilant revels throughout the country. A torchlit parade of thousands of SS and SA troopers marches boisterously through the streets, as festive crowds shout encouragement. Three days later the Reichstag is dissolved and new elections are called for March.

The transformation long prefigured now sweeps rapidly over Germany. The torching of the Reichstag late in February 1933 by a young Dutchman who'd belonged to a Communist Party organization in his youth provides the perfect excuse for launching one of Hitler's declared goals: the destruction of the powerful KPD, the German Communist Party. Wild press statements and phony police "discoveries" deliberately spread fear that the Bolsheviks are on the verge of carrying out a violent overthrow of the government. SA and SS legions escalate their reign of terror, rounding up, savagely beating, torturing, and murdering not only KPD officials and sympathizers but Social Democrats, trade unionists, Jews, and left-wing intellectuals as well. Opposition presses are silenced. The trade unions are dissolved. Kessler acidly comments that the struggle against "Marxism" turns out to mean "the struggle against the worker's right to self-determination."

In the March election Kessler—like Magnus Hirschfeld—votes for the Social Democratic Party. This time around, the Nazis win 288 seats; in combination with the Nationalists, they now *constitutionally* control the government. Kessler's left-wing friend Wieland Herzfelde tells him that he's heard from reliable sources that the Nazis are planning to fake an attempt on Hitler's life in order to settle some old scores. Another friend tells Kessler that he's on a list of those being rounded up and urges him to leave the country, at least until matters settle down. His manservant Friedrich resigns, on the grounds that his Nazi father insists there will be "unpleasantness" in the Kessler household soon and he doesn't want his son harmed. Kessler tells Friedrich that he has no desire to imperil him, and wishes him well. It's not the last he will hear of Friedrich.

Kessler realizes that the time has come to leave Berlin, at least until matters regarding his personal safety clarify. With the Nazis in undisputed control of the country, he concludes that Germany "is to become a snug stable where all obedient domestic animals will feel happy and, as necessity requires, allow themselves to be tamely led to slaughter. I cannot think of any idea which would seem to me more degrading and revolting."

In early March 1933, Kessler leaves for Paris.

A week later, Magnus Hirschfeld's Institute for Sexual Science is visited by a posse of Nazi troopers; they've come, they tell the receptionist, to look through the questionnaires that they've learned people have filled out over the years for various purposes, including surveys and applications for counseling. The receptionist politely tells them that the material is confidential and that researchers, unless affiliated with the Institute, have to formally request access in advance. The leader of the group is carrying what appears to be a stick or a whip in his right hand and he silently begins to tap it against the glove of his other hand. Unnerved, the receptionist politely asks what the nature of their research interest might be.

"You could say," the trooper spits out, "to learn about members of our party who might be in need of further 'counseling.'" The others in his group laugh appreciatively. The receptionist nervously replies that "the Archivist is currently out of the country, but if you'd like to come back in, say, a month's time, I'm sure he'll be glad to help you."

"Oh he'll help us awright." More laughter as the group noisily leaves.

Karl Giese is indeed out of the country—aware of the Institute's vulnerability under the new government, he's been going back and forth to Paris with as many of the Institute's files as he can manage to cart away for safekeeping. Two days later, the Institute's librarian arrives for work with a swastika on his lapel. He announces to the staff that he and two other administrators have sent a letter to Göring testifying to their loyalty, and advises them to do the same. No one else does.

Hirschfeld himself has long been on extended leave, traveling the world to lecture, to meet distant colleagues, and to satisfy his own expanding awareness of the fallacy of equating "sexual science" with European mores. He started his travels in the late 1920s partly out of exhaustion from his own productivity and from the ongoing internal tensions within the Institute. But he's primarily propelled out of his familiar—overly-familiar, he recognizes—comfort zone by a growing conviction that sexual behavior cannot be understood solely by studying the bourgeois-bound West; its norms must be evaluated through comparison with those of other cultures.

Over the years Hirschfeld—like Kessler and, until his death, Rathenau—has moved further and further to the Left. An admirer of the Soviet Union and a passionate opponent of Western imperialism, Hirschfeld increasingly questions Europe's smugly-grounded confidence that its own mores and institutions represent the *summum bonum* of human achievement. His absorption in the Institute for Sexual Science—revolutionary at its inception—has by the late 1920s opened out into the creation of a new organization, the World League for Sexual Reform, that better represents his own expanded horizons.

Yet during his extended wanderings of these years, begun in 1928 at age 60, Hirschfeld always, always, intends to return to Germany.

~

The SPD's Bavarian daily, the *Münchener Post*, runs a series of articles on the mounting scandal surrounding Ernst Röhm's indiscriminate run-ins with hustlers and payoffs to blackmailers. The *Post* also refers to him as "the passionate proclaimer of the Third 'Röhman' Reich"—hinting at his excessive ambition. Röhm threatens to sue the *Post* but then says he doesn't give a damn what lies about him the sick socialists make up. As the press attacks continue, they're paralleled by a rising tide of anger within the Nazi Party at the damage Röhm—since 1931 the SA's chief of staff—is doing to the "cause." The joke spreads that Hitler Youths are warning each other, "Arse to the wall, Röhm's on roll call."

In an effort to curtail the damage, Röhm does somewhat rein in his activity. He stops going to the baths—his favorite haunt till then—and uses a go-between to pick up young men, having sex with them in the apartments of various friends. Röhm's chief enemies within the party, Himmler and Goebbels, are bringing increasing pressure on Hitler to rein him in; Röhm, they warn, has become a liability; the man must be gotten rid of or—at the least—demoted. Himmler detests Röhm and is jealous of his power; he thinks homosexuality is a "contagious disease," a vice that, if allowed to spread, "will spell the end of Germany."

Hitler also despises homosexuality, but thus far has dealt with the accusations against Röhm through a combination of denial and distant "toleration." Early in 1931, he even issues a circular letter to high party functionaries which—though never mentioning homosexuality—declares the private lives of Nazi leaders off-limits and, in what many take as a reference to Röhm's SA, applauds the party's "rough and ready fighters." That leads the SPD's *Münchener Post* to attack Hitler for side-stepping Röhm's "carryings-on"; oppositely, some leaders of the homosexual rights movement applaud Hitler for his "sound judgment."

Röhm might have been expected to take what was essentially a public vote of confidence from Hitler with becoming modesty. Instead, he loudly boasts that "the German Revolution has been won not by philistines, bigots, and sermonizers, but by revolutionary fighters ... It is the

SA's task not to keep watch on the attire, complexion, and chastity of others, but to haul Germany to its feet by dint of their free and revolutionary fighting spirit."

By this point, neither affection nor tolerance is primarily guiding Hitler's attitude towards Röhm. What continues to stay his hand for a while longer is a shrewd awareness that the SA has been undergoing a period of immense growth, that its legions remain intensely loyal to Röhm, and that Röhm, despite his public assertion of loyalty to Hitler, has never fully subsumed his paramilitary organization to the political needs of the Nazi Party. Prominent figures in the Reichswehr (the regular army), are watching the increasing strength of the SA—membership has risen from 300,000 to half a million—with growing alarm. Hitler knows that Röhm's ultimate ambition is for the SA to replace the Reichswehr, that several of the army's leading officers are furious at his presumption, and that the growing conflict between the two could conceivably turn the Reichswehr against the Nazi Party. As early as 1929, Hitler had established the SS "blackshirts" under the leadership of Heinrich Himmler as a counterweight to the SA, but it has remained comparatively small.

As Hitler's earlier trust and affection for Röhm gradually converts into a decision to abandon him, one hears a ghostly echo of the earlier, parallel relationship between Kaiser Wilhelm II and Prince Eulenburg.

We enter the critical year of 1933.

SA violence explodes on the streets. The brownshirts unleash their brutal attacks without warning against a host of perceived and real enemies—against Communists, Socialists, and, above all, against Jews. Using rubber truncheons and iron bars, the storm troopers grab their selected victims unawares, beat them badly, then cart them off to their own makeshift prisons. Entering one of them, even the SS Gestapo chief Rudolf Diels is appalled at the scenes of depraved torture, at seeing "living skeletons with festering wounds" lying motionless on rotting straw. Even General Erich von Ludendorff—himself a right-wing specialist in violence—reports to Hindenburg that the SA's "unbelievable" attacks, still "mounting up in horrifying fashion," mark "the blackest time in German history." Complaints against Röhm and the SA pour in, but Hitler still bides his time. The torture of Jews and Communists leaves him unmoved.

Then Röhm makes a major misstep: He lets loose with a rip-roaring broadside that Hitler cannot ignore. Calling for "a second revolution," Röhm declares in a Nazi publication that the SA "will not allow the German Revolution to fall asleep or be betrayed halfway there by the non-fighters ... Whether they like it or not, we will carry on our struggle. If they finally grasp what it is about, *with* them! If they are not willing, *without* them! And if it has to be: *against* them!"

In advocating a "second revolution" Röhm is sounding a theme familiar from Trotsky's advocacy of a "permanent revolution"—and risks suffering Trotsky's fate. Röhm is vague about the specifics of his "second revolution" but he's known to sympathize with the view that the estates of the old aristocracy should be confiscated and worker control of certain major industries extended—notions that put him directly at odds with most of Hitler's supporters among the German elite. Hitler is finally on full alert. He announces that the Nazi revolution has never been designed as a permanent revolution; it must be channeled into "the secure bed of evolution." Göring, Goebbels, and other Nazi leaders take to the hustings to reinforce Hitler's message.

Röhm chooses not to hear it. As the leader of an organization with nearly half a million members ready and eager to do his bidding, he demands a more central decision-making role in Nazi councils; should he be denied, he hints at the possibility of the SA defecting— and not to establish another neutral Switzerland. Hitler comes up with what he views as a conciliatory gesture: henceforth Röhm will sit in the cabinet as Reich Minister without Portfolio. Röhm accepts the post, telling himself that it will lead in short order to his becoming head of the Defense Ministry—a clear case of pipe-dreaming, given the Reichswehr's unyielding opposition to his ambition. It doesn't help that Röhm's gregarious, boozy personal style is distinctly at odds with the Prussian emphasis on proper decorum—just as his belief in promoting officers on the basis of ability, not birth or connections, stands

in direct opposition to the Reichswehr's historic insistence on aristocratic bloodlines.

The ball is now back in Hitler's court. Remarkably, he again hesitates.
He knows that Röhm remains a brilliant organizer and manager of men,
as well as a kind of genius in securing and hiding extensive weaponry
in violation of the Versailles Treaty; Hitler continues to feel—though
uncertainly—that he still needs Röhm on his side. He tells himself that
the animosity between the SA leader and the Reichswehr will gradually
dissolve. What Röhm tells himself is quite different: that the unswerving
loyalty of his SA legions might swerve if rank-and-file brownshirts don't
soon see some of the financial rewards long promised but still withheld.
He's aware that his own luxurious Munich villa, replete with paintings
and antique furniture—Röhm isn't the one-dimensional loud-mouth
vulgarian his enemies claim, or not solely that at any rate—has created
grumbling among some SA troops, though his men believe that Röhm's
talk of a "second revolution" will finally put them on top of the heap.

General Blomberg, head of the Reichswehr, angrily informs Hitler
about Röhm's latest provocation—his reckless notification that henceforth the SA, not the army, will control decisions relating to national
defense. Blomberg may have made up the story to force Hitler to take
decisive action; whether he did or not, it works. Hitler has an agreement drawn up between Blomberg and Röhm, putting the Reichswehr
firmly in charge of defense and assigning border protection and military training to the SA. Both Röhm and Blomberg sign the agreement; champagne flows. But the geniality is fake. Röhm is later heard to
remark, "what the ridiculous corporal"—*i.e.*, Hitler—"declares doesn't
apply to us. Hitler has no loyalty and has at least to be sent on leave. If
not with, then we'll manage the thing without Hitler."

Röhm's remarks are passed on to Hitler. The die is finally cast. On
June 21, 1934, Reich President Hindenburg, nearing the end of his life,
grants Hitler an audience. Hindenburg makes it clear that he stands
behind the Reichswehr and tells Hitler "to bring the revolutionary trou-
ble-makers"—the SA—to heel. Hitler, for his own reasons, decides to
interpret that as a license to kill.

Within days, he announces that a meeting of all SA leaders will take place on June 30 at Bad Wiessee. That morning at 6:30 a.m. Hitler and his entourage—which includes 25 of Himmler's SS men—arrive at the Hotel Hanselbauer. Röhm and his SA lieutenants are still asleep. Hitler bursts into Röhm's room, shouting that he is a traitor and is under arrest. Röhm attempts to protest, but Hitler peremptorily orders him to get dressed, then leaves Röhm under the guard of two SS men. They accompany Röhm down to a foyer, where he sits silently by the fireplace.

Hitler drinks coffee while his cohorts, including Goebbels, rouse other SA leaders in their rooms; Edmund Heines (the notoriously violent head of the SA in Silesia) and his chauffeur-lover are found lying naked in bed—the mere sight, Goebbels later reports, made him want to vomit. The prisoners are locked up in the hotel's cellar. Hitler tells his entourage—falsely—that Röhm has planned a putsch; he calls the plot "the worst treachery in world history." His assembled loyalists express their horror at the revelation and demand that Hitler have all the prisoners shot.

Shown a list of those being held, Hitler marks an X next to six names. Röhm's is not among them. The six are shot in the hotel courtyard, loaded onto a lorry, and cremated the same day. By pre-arrangement, Goebbels telephones Göring and whispers "Kolibri" ("Hummingbird"), the agreed-upon signal to proceed to the next stage of the "cleansing process"—the revenge killings of more than 100 additional people in repayment for Hitler's old grudges. The victims include Dr. Karl-Günther Heimsoth, who'd played intermediary for Röhm with Hirschfeld; Kurt von Schleicher, the previous Chancellor of the Weimar Republic; Gregor Strasser, a close associate of Hitler's during the failed 1923 Beer Hall Putsch, whose pro-trade union sympathies have put him out of favor; and August Schneidhuber, member of the Reichstag and head of the police in Munich. Gustav von Kahr, the Prime Minister of Bavaria in the early 1920s who repudiated the Beer Hall Putsch, is hacked to death near the new Dachau concentration camp.

When the massacre—later named "The Night of the Long Knives"—is over, Ernst Röhm is still alive. In a moment of weakness Hitler mumbles something about "sparing him because of his services." But under pressure from Göring and Himmler, Hitler "comes to his senses" and agrees that Röhm must be liquidated. Hitler decides that Röhm will be allowed to kill himself—a residual gesture for his many years of loyalty. Röhm, however, refuses to oblige. Two SS men leave a pistol in his cell at Stadelheim Prison and tell him he has 10 minutes to act. They wait outside the cell. No shot is heard. Re-entering the cell they see the pistol is still on the table where they left it. Röhm stands bare-chested in the center of his room, and starts to say something. The SS men draw their guns, take careful aim, and shoot. One bullet strikes Röhm in the chest, another in the neck. He's pronounced dead.

Röhm's ashes are sent to his devoted mother. Hitler offers her a pension, but she angrily refuses what she calls "blood-money." Her son, she insists, was not a traitor, and not a homosexual.

Adorning himself with the mantle of morality, Hitler issues a new directive:

" . . . I should like every mother to be able to allow her son to join the SA, Nazi Party, and Hitler Youth without fear that he may become morally corrupted in their ranks. I therefore require all SA commanders to take the utmost pains to ensure that offenses under Paragraph 175 are met by immediate expulsion of the culprit from the SA and the Party. I want to see men as SA commanders, not ludicrous monkeys."

∾

Harry Kessler has no illusions about what the execution of Röhm and the clear ascendancy of Hitler means for Germany, and for himself personally. Even this late in the political game, many are continuing to predict that "the little corporal" has scant chance of retaining the Chancellorship for long. Kessler isn't among them.

He's barely gotten settled in Paris when Max Goertz, using a diplomatic courier to avoid prying eyes, writes to warn him that "something is afoot" that spells danger to his person should he reappear in Berlin. (Max is now married, but he and his wife Uschi remain close to Kessler).

An old friend in the Foreign Office confirms Max's warning: it is absolutely necessary, the friend writes, that Kessler prolong his stay in Paris; should he return to Germany, the government might well imprison him under the pretext of "protecting" him from "possible violence from irresponsible young men."

The German émigré community in Paris is growing, and includes a number of Kessler's old acquaintances, among them the banker Hugo Simon, his pacifist friends Ludwig Quidde and Annette Kolb, the journalist George Bernard, and the philosopher Hermann Keyserling. An embittered Bernard tells Kessler that he no longer regards himself as a German and never wants to return. Quidde confides his belief that only an army putsch can free Germany from "the brownshirt plague"—a curious suggestion, he acknowledges, coming from an old pacifist. The verbose, energetic Keyserling is among the more pessimistic: the regime, he tells Kessler, "has come to stay"—in his estimate, a full 70 percent of the German people "is delighted with what is happening."

Rudolf Hilferding, the brilliant SPD finance minister who will himself die at the hands of the Nazis, describes to Kessler the fate of their mutual friend, Wilhelm Sollmann, an SPD Reichstag deputy and a leading figure in the party in Cologne: attacked and beaten up in his own home by the SS, Sollmann was then taken to local Nazi headquarters and tortured for two hours before being hospitalized. "A clear case of sadism" is Kessler's reaction—"the pathology of power." Where once the "sick soul of the sexual murderer" was confined to an occasional Jack the Ripper or a Fritz Haarmann, it is now, in Kessler's opinion, "suddenly active among hundreds of thousands."

When he hears reports of the mounting number of round-ups and murders of Jews, Kessler feels sickened at (as he writes in his diary) this "criminal piece of lunacy." Not knowing what else to do, he carries on his daily round, revises his book on Rathenau, socializes with both his French and German émigré friends—and often feels as if he's sleepwalking, "going through an evil dream from which I shall suddenly awaken ... All the time I am aware of a muffled pain throbbing like a double-bass."

Then comes news from Max that Kessler's manservant Friedrich—who, at his father's insistence, had "regrettably" resigned—has been stealing him blind in Weimar; for an encore, Friedrich has told the Nazis where to find Kessler's safe and filled them with exaggerated tales of his employer's "traitorous" activities. Max also reports that the grounds of the house in Weimar remain indescribably lovely, the roses in magnificent flower, the magnolias "weighed down with blooms." To Kessler, it sounds like a combination nightmare and fairy-tale, a painful reminder of the garden of Eden from which he's been forcefully evicted.

His anxiety is compounded—for the first time in his life—by financial problems. They'd begun much earlier, as a result of his large outlay of money in the 1920s when he started—in line with his longstanding fascination with fine printing—the opulent Cranach Press. Kessler had spared no expense, hiring the finest artisans and using the costliest materials. His sister Wilma—whom he's seen infrequently through the years—has helped to support the Cranach Press, and it publishes two magnificent books, *Hamlet* (Gordon Craig's heralded version) and Virgil's *Ecologues*. The onset of the Great Depression, however, has destroyed any hope that the enterprise can continue, let alone earn back Kessler's investment. Wilma's resources, once plentiful, notably shrink, and the Press has to close its doors. Kessler continues to hope, forlornly, that he can someday restart it.

The Cranach closing proves the tip of the iceberg. The more the Nazis solidify their power and the longer Kessler is forced to live abroad, the more his assets dwindle. He has always spent extravagantly, confident—like most people born into wealth—that the coffers will magically refill. As early as the mid-1920s, faced with a temporary financial crunch, Kessler sold off Seurat's *Les Poseuses* for a tiny fraction of what it would later bring.

Using his substantial remaining collection as collateral, Kessler starts to take out more and more loans, especially from his sister, but also from the art dealer Eduard von der Heydt. Kessler tries desperately to hold on to the rest of his fabled collection; it has never been primarily a status symbol for him but simply a source of pleasure. Yet the day inexorably arrives when von der Heydt threatens a lawsuit unless Kessler makes an immediate payment on his longstanding debt. There's nothing to do but sell off a van Gogh—for $25,000—which does cut his indebtedness to von der Heydt in half, giving Kessler some temporary breathing room. He accepts a publisher's offer of an advance for his memoirs, and begins work on them, without any real confidence that potential sales will bring in large enough royalties to pay off his creditors.

Perhaps, he thinks, he should sell the house in Weimar, along with its elegant furnishings—or what remains, after Friedrich's predations. Or perhaps, he thinks, the solution to his financial troubles might be a lecture tour—to the United States possibly. He's heard that the sexologist Magnus Hirschfeld—whom he's never met—has been making his way around the world profitably lecturing on topics like "The Sexual Needs of Our Time." (Why, Kessler wonders, has sex become a subject for academic study rather than simply a pleasurable activity? *Discussing* sex has always struck him as absurd).

Should he attempt a tour in the States? He's done a good bit of lecturing in his day, and has been to the United States on four separate occasions. He gives the prospect real consideration, sifting through his mostly unpleasant memories of the place and wondering if he could bear another prolonged stay there. He recalls that when he docked in New York on his first trip, when only 23, he'd found the city full of "nervous haste and unrest. People don't walk, they run, most while reading a newspaper." He did admire the bold way American women freely led conversation, but found the American male appalling: "The older ones are often vulgar, the younger for the most part boring, loud, and suffering from ulcers."

On later trips, after his political consciousness had been awakened, he'd been horrified at the bitter poverty that surrounded the gilded upper crust: "The poor hungry creatures who you see are really suffering, beg quite softly so that your heart breaks." He also found the endemic nativism and racism deplorable, and thought the country's promise, such as it was, lay with its outsiders, its *non*-European elements—in particular, with the Indians in New Mexico and their "aesthetic relation to the world," and also with the rich culture of American blacks. No, Kessler finally decides, a return to the States is out of the question; "The more I mull over the idea, the less it appeals to me."

But what to do, where to go? Paris is expensive, and his resources are dwindling. A return to Germany is out of the question. With each dispatch from Berlin the prospects worsen. Rearmament has quickened, civil liberties are suspended, the Reichstag dissolved, violence endemic—a reign of terror has been unleashed against all "enemies of the state," Jews in particular.

Kessler seizes on someone's suggestion that he try Palma, on the Spanish island of Mallorca; it's described as all at once inexpensive and cosmopolitan. He succeeds in finding a small house for rent—pleasantly furnished and situated on a hill overlooking the sea—and he decides to take it. He invites Max and his wife Uschi to come with him. Both feel deeply loyal to Kessler—also, he's been encouraging about Max's prospects as a writer—and the young couple agrees to join him. On arriving, they soon discover that many other Germans have made the same move; Kessler is wary, though, of fraternizing with them until he can learn more about their politics. Max and Uschi begin to put the house in order. Kessler settles in to write his memoirs.

∾

As part of his own world tour, Magnus Hirschfeld spends many months in the United States and, unlike Kessler, finds quite a bit to admire. He sees the country, of course, under different auspices and with different eyes. His sponsor, Harry Benjamin—a longtime associate of the Institute who will become famous in the 1950s as a pioneering advocate of transgender people—sees to it that Hirschfeld gives a lecture at the American Society of Medical History in New York and that a dinner is held in his honor. Hirschfeld has always had a flair for publicity and he's pleased at the way his talk is introduced: "Sexology as a rational science belongs almost wholly to the twentieth century, and in this field there is no name more honorably conspicuous than that of Magnus Hirschfeld."

The introduction and the speech are both reprinted in the New York press. Hirschfeld's tour is off to a flying start.

He travels widely and lectures often. In his early 60s, and suffering from diabetes, his energy seems somehow unimpaired: in three and a half months he lectures 60 times and does some 40 interviews. He's a more natural orator than Kessler, more straightforward and passionate, though also less nuanced. It helps his popularity that he lectures on topics like "The Natural Laws of Love"—whereas poor Kessler had stuck to the non-gonadal subjects of "Austro-Serbian Relations in 1914" and "Towards a Franco-German Coal and Iron Trust." Besides, Hirschfeld shows slides—particularly to illustrate his talks on "Sexual Intermediaries."

Hirschfeld reciprocates his audiences' enthusiasm. He comes away from his tour convinced that the United States is now the world's leading power; Kessler thinks that might well happen in the near future, but rather hopes not. What the two men centrally share—and what sets them light years apart from the vast majority of their contemporaries—is their emphasis on the positive contribution that outsiders, both domestic renegades and foreign immigrants, have had and are still having on America's innovative spirit.

Hirschfeld travels alone. He and Karl Giese remain deeply bonded emotionally but are no longer sexual partners. Both men feel it's less important for Karl to accompany Hirschfeld abroad than it is for him—a non-Jew who can travel back and forth to Germany with relative ease—to devote his time to transporting to Paris as many of the Institute's treasures as possible in case the morally hidebound brownshirts should suddenly descend.

When Hirschfeld reaches China midway on his world tour, a 23-year-old named Tao Li (Li Shiu Tong) attends his first lecture and asks Hirschfeld if he may accompany him as interpreter and guide for the rest of his trip. A graduate in philosophy and medicine from Hong Kong University, Tao (as he is called by everyone) comes from a large, ennobled family. The two men quickly become attached, at least emotionally, perhaps sexually. Tao's father gives his warm consent; he expressly approves the relationship between Hirschfeld and his son, though may not be aware of all its dimensions.

Hirschfeld's insatiable curiosity hasn't diminished with age, and Tao helps him explore some uncommon byways in the cultures of Asia, including a visit to the miniature golf links in Tientsin to watch women dressed in men's clothes court each other; a trip to the matriarchal highlands of Java, where husbands take their wives' names and live outside the home—except when summoned for sexual intercourse; and several nights spent as the guests of various wealthy Jewish families in Baghdad—including one at the spectacular Marble Hall mansion of the well-known magnate Elly Kadoorie. Throughout, Hirschfeld remains keenly aware—and is outspoken against—Western imperialism and its devastating impact on local culture.

Everywhere he and Tao go, Hirschfeld's reputation precedes him. In Calcutta he's invited to meet the great poet Rabindranath Tagore, whom Hirschfeld describes as "a painting in white and silver." Also in India he renews acquaintance with Nehru, whom he'd met briefly years before in Germany, and again finds him brilliant and charming—departing from the Nehru family at the train station, Hirschfeld waves the flag of Indian Independence. In Egypt he meets with Nahas Pasha, a former president who currently leads the opposition to English occupation. Hirschfeld's pleasure on these occasions is diluted by the oppression of women that he sees everywhere, and, when in Egypt, he goes out of his way to greet representatives of the country's Women's Movement.

His travels further convince Hirschfeld of his long-held view that "no 'pure' race exists on this earth. The belief in a pure racial type," he writes, "leads to the arrogant idea of a master race—to Nazism." Visiting the Jewish settlement of Beth Alpha in the Emek Valley, Hirschfeld is impressed with the experiment in collective living, and is appreciative of those who long for a Jewish homeland. Still, Zionist talk of creating a permanent state in Palestine seems to him misguided: the Arabs, he predicts, will never agree to it and, without the goodwill of their neighbors, Palestine will settle into protracted warfare. One young member of Beth Alpha argues the issue with him: "This land is ours, and no worldly power will ever take it away from us." "Establishing a Jewish state," Hirschfeld replies, "is not our historic mission. We are meant," he says—as if channeling Walther Rathenau's spirit—"to live in many different countries, and through that diaspora invigorate many cultures— even as we intermarry with local people and adapt to many of their customs." Hirschfeld is describing and defending what many German Jews long believed was their historic role in their own country, a belief now rapidly unraveling.

~

Three weeks after arriving in Mallorca, Harry Kessler is sitting in front of the fireplace reading a newspaper when he's suddenly aware of feeling unwell. Minutes later blood starts to ooze from his mouth. He calls out feebly to Max and Uschi, who are on the terrace planting geraniums. Rushing to Kessler's side, Max phones the local doctor while Uschi tries to comfort Kessler and clean the blood off his face. But it continues to stream forth, and he loses consciousness. Minutes later, the doctor arrives and gives Kessler an injection that revives him and stops the flow of blood. He tells Kessler that it's from the right lobe of his lungs, but offers no specific diagnosis. He's lost more than a liter of blood; his clothes are soaked, the floor and nearby furniture bespattered. The fastidious Kessler deplores the "disgusting" sight. The doctor, somewhat gratuitously, advises "rest."

And for several months rest is nearly all that Kessler can manage. Rest, and omnipresent worry about the increasingly perilous state of his finances. He's gotten an advance on his memoirs, and small additional sums have come in for translations he undertakes into French and English. But the news from Weimar is bleak. In his haste to depart Germany Kessler forgot to pay his local taxes, along with other bills that were outstanding. Since he's now widely known in conservative circles by the disreputable moniker "The Red Count," the authorities feel entitled to let his creditors cart away whatever items from his home they deem "equivalent" to what he owes them. In July 1935 word reaches Kessler that the remainder of his furnishings—his sister Wilma has saved some items—are being auctioned off. He's heartbroken at the loss of his home, yet faces the fact that his failing health, in combination with Hitler's now-solidified power, means that his chances of ever returning to Germany are slight.

The Nazis are entrenched and powerful, not—as so many had predicted—a transient phenomenon. Hitler is now more and more sounding the theme of *Lebensraum*—room to live. "Pure-blooded" Germans, it seems—this has long been a central feature of the Far Right's doctrine of *Pan Germanium*—are wretchedly cramped for space. They cannot breathe. The superior Aryan race is being smothered by aggressive Jews in cahoots with Bolshevists. Hitler has come up with a double-barreled solution: destruction of the Jews within Germany's "overpopulated" internal borders, in tandem with an expansionist war against "Bolshevism" in Russia and elsewhere. This will take time, but a good start has been made: the completion of the first concentration camp at Dachau.

At the end of his marathon world tour, Magnus Hirschfeld, like Kessler, hungers for home. After nearly two years away, his boat finally arrives in Athens and Karl Giese is waiting dockside. He and Hirschfeld have an emotional reunion, and Karl greets Tao cordially, having learned all about him from Hirschfeld's letters.

Karl brings chilling news. The Institute hasn't fared well in Hirschfeld's absence. After their first appearance, the Nazis have returned frequently; all Jewish and non-Aryan personnel have been fired, and some arrested. Kurt Hiller, the courageous lawyer and poet who's headed the Institute during Hirschfeld's absence, has been carted off to the Oranienburg concentration camp and repeatedly tortured. Three staff members with Nazi affiliations had briefly been put in charge to oversee what little activity remained, but before long the Nazis had descended in force, ransacked the premises, taken away the card index listing all members of the World League for Sexual Reform, burnt most of the Institute's books in an *auto-da-fé* held in the courtyard—tossing in for good measure a bronze bust of Hirschfeld that had been presented to him on his 60th birthday—and locked the Institute's doors.

Karl also tries to make it clear to Hirschfeld that, as a Jew and a homosexual, he cannot hope to return to Germany within the foreseeable future. Hirschfeld isn't immediately convinced; having survived denunciation and physical attack in the past, he wonders if his luck might not hold out a bit longer—long enough, say, to get the Institute back on its feet.

Karl tries to let him down gently: "Please, Papa, you must accept the fact that you've been out of touch with what is going on in Germany. You can hardly imagine how bad things are."

"I do know, and not just from what you've been telling me. I've kept up with the newspapers here and there. Besides, we've long understood what the Nazis would be capable of should they come to power."

"They're *in* power. And it's much worse than we anticipated."

"We came so close in 1929," Hirschfeld says quietly.

"What do you mean?"

"When the parliamentary committee finally brought in a bill to strike down Paragraph 175."

"Oh—that!" Karl has trouble concealing his impatience. "For heaven's sake, Papa, that bill failed—and under the Nazis there's certainly no hope of resurrecting it!"

"I know," Hirschfeld says sadly. "How clever of the Nazis to have conjoined anti-Semitism and anti-homosexuality."

"Just today, Papa, just today ... Here, here on the front page!" Karl draws a newspaper out of his pocket and slaps his hand against it angrily. "Wilhelm Frick speaking in the Reichstag." He reads from the newspaper: "'Men practicing unnatural lechery between men must be persecuted with utmost severity. Such vices will lead to the disintegration of the German people. Anyone who thinks of homosexual love is our enemy.'"

"Terrible ... terrible," Hirschfeld mutters.

"There's no hope for us in Germany, not any longer. They're rounding up so-called 'sexual vagrants' and putting us in camps. Gruesome stories have been leaking out. It's mostly Jews in the camps. And Communists. Homosexuals are a minority, but all kinds of homosexuals are being mixed together—exceptional people along with hustlers and black-mailers."

"Who are also exceptional people," Hirschfeld says in rebuke. "Exceptionally unlucky. I'm surprised at you, Karl. We do not look down on anyone. Social outcasts are *us*. You know that."

"I'm sorry, Papa ... that came out wrong ... but you do see, I hope, that there is no chance whatsoever of you returning to Germany. Not for a *long* time."

" ... It breaks my heart."

After considering their options, the trio decide to go to Switzerland. Within a short time of their arrival, they discover that many pro-Nazis, especially in the German cantons, form a kind of fifth column, consti-tuting a threat to Hirschfeld's safety. They quickly leave Switzerland and seek refuge in Paris.

Harry Kessler is already there, having left Mallorca. His ongoing loss of weight has left him gaunt and fragile, yet still determined to make progress on his memoirs. Max and Uschi are deeply concerned about the state of his health and finally persuade him to consult a specialist in Paris. Old friends express shock at his appearance. Gordon Craig runs into him at the Café de la Paix and is dismayed to find Kessler—"the only man who never failed me"—"so altered as to be almost unrecogniz-able, his life has been disintegrating around him." The composer Nicolas Nabokov similarly describes Kessler as a ghost of his former self, a man despondent over the loss of his home, gloomily predicting that Hitler's rule "will be long" and that he would not live to see the end of it.

Kessler manages to make the trip outside of Paris to Marly in order to see Maillol again, and he's impressed when the sculptor shows him the large statue he's at work on, commissioned for the upcoming World Exhi-bition. But his pleasure at again seeing an old friend gives way to melan-choly: Maillol's "house, the garden, and the studio," Kessler writes, "put me in a pretty sadly reminiscent frame of mind." Returning to Paris, he visits another old friend, André Gide, just returned from the Soviet Union and "aghast" at Stalin's "show trials." "Freedom of intellect," Gide tells Kessler, is "undergoing an even more horrible suppression in Russia than in Germany." To Kessler, it's the devil and the deep blue sea. All that he knows for certain is that his hopes for social democracy in Germany and for the empowerment of the working class in Russia have alike proven illusory. The signposts of life as he knew it, and dreamed it, are sundered.

Hirschfeld, with the help of the archival material Karl earlier managed to spirit across the border, attempts to set up a version of the Institute in Paris. But the enterprise is lifeless from the beginning. The French seem disinterested in combining sex and science, and fail to share the German passion for categorizing pleasure. By this time Karl has decided to pursue academic credentials in medicine; initially he thinks of attending university in London, but ultimately settles on Vienna. Hirschfeld is sad to see him go, yet understanding; he helps pay for Karl's tuition. Tao remains at Hirschfeld's side and is a great comfort to him.

Hirschfeld soon decides formally to dissolve the moribund French Institute and to move to the warmer climate of Nice for his health. In March 1935, accompanied by Tao, he rents an apartment and begins to make what seems a good adjustment to his new surroundings. It helps that visitors keep arriving to seek counsel and pay respects, and that he's acquainted with a number of other Germans who have settled in Nice— two in his own apartment building. Hirschfeld again starts thinking about restarting the Institute. As spring arrives on the Riviera, he's overcome with the beauty of his surroundings and decides that he can make a good new life in Nice.

On May 14, 1935—the day of his 65th birthday—Hirschfeld celebrates modestly with a few friends at a café. Leaving them, he turns the corner leading to his apartment house—and suddenly falls to the sidewalk with a fatal stroke. He never regains consciousness, and dies that same day. Karl Giese returns from Vienna for the funeral, and in his oration aptly describes Hirschfeld as "a gentle fanatic." Tao returns to China. Three years later, when Nazi troops occupy Austria, Giese commits suicide.

~

For Harry Kessler, life has come down to discomfort and defeat. Walther Rathenau's hopes for the fundamental reshaping of the economic order along egalitarian lines no longer captures much attention. Political reality is now focused on the military uprising in Spain in July 1936, led by General Franco and his fascist minions. It means, among much else, that Kessler cannot return to Mallorca, as he'd planned. He gets word from friends on the island that the Spanish fascists are conducting roundups, even executions. He's left behind on the island all the source material he needs for his memoirs, and it is now beyond reach. What to do? Where to go?

He asks his sister Wilma—not easy for a proud man—if he can come to her home at Fournel in the Midi-Pyrénées region of France. He would be no bother, he assures her; he'd require only a few warm vests, a thick sweater, snow boots, and a woolen scarf. Wilma suggests that instead she arrange for him to live in a boarding house she owns in the town of Pontanevaux, near Lyon. Having no other option, he accepts her offer and moves alone into the boarding house. He's soon referring to it as "a spiritual desert." By 1937 Wilma's own financial problems become critical and she is forced to sell the boarding house.

Kessler returns to Paris, moving from one inexpensive hotel to another. Not only are his funds low but he again hemorrhages from the nose, nearly choking on his own blood. His heart has also begun to give out: "I cannot go up stairs," he writes Wilma, "cannot walk more than a few steps, cannot hold any long conversations with anybody." He refuses to give in to invalidism, continues to fight against its claims. He visits Misia Sert, whose salon he once regularly attended; takes tea with his old pacifist friend Annette Kolb; has lunch with Gordon Craig, recently returned from Moscow and full of the dispiriting news that spies "dogged his every step"; visits with the young lawyer and post-Nazi Foreign Minister of Germany, Heinrich von Brentano, widely rumored to be homosexual, whose comfortable study gives Kessler the strange, sad feeling of finding himself "once more in a proper, well-furnished" room.

Early in March 1937, Kessler awakens with a fever. Three days later he's taken to a nursing home with borderline pneumonia and an intestinal hemorrhage. After repeated transfusions, he's operated on—a gruesome ordeal, since he cannot be properly anaesthetized due to his heart condition. Yet he survives, and two and half months later is able, shakily, to leave the nursing home. He soldiers on for a few more months. At one point he has to go to the town of Marvejols for a special X-ray; the little village, "old-fashioned and picturesque," reminds him of his beloved Weimar. The resemblance is afflicting; he aches with the memory. Two months later, he's dead of a heart attack.

∽

Legacies? We mostly ignore and deny them, certain that the ground we traverse is unique, that there are no antecedents—none worth recalling, at any rate.

Perhaps a catchphrase or two will be allowed to substitute for a didactic moral, each representing the man at high ground rather than during the inevitable fallings-off of daily life.

For Eulenburg, a prime example of how personal loyalty can resemble an art form, yet an example, too, of how geniality and deference may assure arrival but are insufficient to sustain it—especially when social mores enforce a double life that allows for secret pleasures, but ultimately extracts its punishment.

For Rathenau, the insistence that being born into privilege should carry with it the obligation to work for the abolition of privilege; that economic ease and comfort are a trust, not an entitlement. And also, how standing constant guard against the risk of emotional invasion, never lowering the guarded gate, can dry up all the water in the moat.

For Kessler, the unself-conscious refusal of categories: a modernist in art co-habiting with a traditionalist in manners—and a renegade in sexual behavior; a man of humane values who can nonetheless give way, if briefly, to combative "patriotism." An aesthete, moreover, insistent on engaging in a political life aimed at winning some victories for humanity. And a tale, too, of how a trail of privilege can unwind under the blows of circumstance.

For Hirschfeld, the belief that tabooed subjects are those most in need of airing; that "normalcy" is a socially agreed-upon fiction of transient currency; that outsiders, homosexuals, say, or Jews, are often the catalysts for cultural renewal.

∼

I could simply call this a historical novel, and be done with it. But it isn't quite. Nor is it a traditional work of history. It forges a path somewhere between the two, and thus requires some explanation.

I started out wanting to learn more about the crucial period at the end of the 19th and the beginning of the 20th centuries when a critical mass of research, theory, and debate over issues relating to gender and sexual orientation first arose—issues constantly reformulated since, and still vitally contested today.

I began my research with the pioneering figure of Magnus Hirschfeld—Jewish, openly homosexual, and German—the pre-eminent sexologist of his day. Until recently Hirschfeld has not been well-served by historians. Thanks to the emergence of LGBTQ studies, the enormity of his impact on our understanding of sexuality has begun to be appreciated, along with an acknowledgement of the limitations, in some regards, of his theoretical views (his notion, for example, that homosexuals constitute a "third sex").

Along with Hirschfeld, I soon became intrigued with the personalities and perspectives of three of his contemporaries—Count Harry Kessler, Walther Rathenau, and Prince Philipp of Eulenburg—along with a host of other contemporary figures, including Kaiser Wilhelm II; the munitions king, Fritz Krupp; the journalist Maximilian Harden; and the head of Hitler's SA, Ernst Röhm. Taken together, they present a kaleidoscope of sexual—and political—scenarios available in the first three decades of the 20th century—one that illuminates, and perhaps challenges, our

contemporary range of declared identities. *Jews Queers Germans* attempts
to weave a tapestry of interlocking personalities and events that "queers"
standard histories of the period. The aim is to open up a reconfigured
landscape that questions traditional fictions of "normalcy" and highlights
the fact that innovation often moves from margin to center.

"Historia," we might remember, means "inquiry" in Greek. And inquiry,
in turn, implies imagination—an adjunct of objectivity, not its enemy.
Traditional definitions of "evidence" ignore the incontestable fact that
professional historians base their versions of the past on whatever acci-
dental (and therefore distorted) fragments—remnants of what actually happened—have come down to us. The reconstructions we create
from residual evidence pay little heed to the fluky ambushes of chance
that actually mold events or, from the inside, the subjective world of
fantasies and feelings that lay behind external behavior. Add to all this
the idiosyncratic values (often unconsciously held) which the historian
brings to bear on whatever evidence remains, and the result is necessarily a skewed, subjective product that at best approximates "objectivity" but can never achieve it. As Maya Jasanoff has recently put it,
"If postmodernism taught historians anything, it's that subjectivity can't
ever be avoided . . . [Yet] historians writing for a general audience still
more or less follow the forms set by the Victorians."*

In my view there remains room in historical writing for *informed*
speculation that moves beyond traditional constrictions. In *Jews Queers
Germans* I've let my historical research point me to presumptively
"likely" feelings and opinions for the personalities involved, though the
actual historical record won't definitively say so. I've also occasionally
blurred a date in order to maintain a dramatic narrative line, and have
let my own interests—particularly in regard to sexuality and anti-Semitism—thematically dominate, rather than doing some traditional worry
dance about "inclusiveness." Additionally, to heighten immediacy, I've
used the present tense throughout.

---

* *New York Review of Books*, October 13, 2016.

In a recent interview about her "process," Hilary Mantel comments, "For me, it is about using everything that is there and using the gaps in the record, figuring out why the gaps might be there. . . . I try to make it up based on what is on the record. So even my wildest speculations will have a root somewhere."

Exactly. *Jews Queers Germans* is reliably based on "the latest word" in historical scholarship—though I'd also like to believe that it profitably moves through and beyond it. As someone once said, "History cannot teach us, but historians might."

ACKNOWLEDGEMENTS

Along with my reliance on the assorted writings of three of the four main characters in this book—Magnus Hirschfeld, Count Harry Kessler, and Walter Rathenau—I want to single out and acknowledge my indebtedness to those historians, among the many I've read, whose work has been of special importance to me. I have starred the names of those whose work has been of central significance: Tony Atcherley and Mark Carey, *Robert Beachy, David Blackbourn, Michael Brenner, Lamar Cecil, H. G. Cocks, Istvan Deak, Edward Ross Dickinson, Ralf Dose, *Laird M. Easton, John M. Efron, Richard J. Evans, *Eleanor Hancock, *Max Hastings, *Gert Hekma, Benjamin Carter Hett, *Isabel V. Hull, James Joll, Peter Jelavich, Charles Kessler, Ian Kershaw, *Hubert Kennedy, Thomas A. Kohut, David Clay Lange, Rudiger Lautman, *Margaret Macmillan, Elena Mancini, *Laurie Marhoefer, Anthony McElligott, Annika Mombauer and Wilhelm Deist, George L. Mosse, *Harry Oosterhuis, Peter Paret, Richard Plant, Harold L. Poor, Jane Ridley, *John C. G. Rohl, Cynthia Saltzman, *James D. Steakley, *Fritz Stern, Pogge von Strandmann, Maria Tatar, Jennifer Terry, Shulamit Volkov, Bernard Wasserstein, and *Charlotte Wolff.

I'm also grateful to the staff at Seven Stories Press for their multiple skills and assists. Lauren Hooker responded to my endless queries with graceful patience; Jon Gilbert and Stewart Cauley came up with brilliant designs, respectively, for the book and its jacket; Michael Tencer did a splendid job of copy-editing; and Ruth Weiner again proved her resourceful mastery of the art of spreading the word. Above all I'm grateful to Dan Simon, Seven Stories' guiding spirit, for his uncommon openness to the unconventional.